ABOUT THE AUTHOR

I am a seasoned novelist from London, accredited by *Teen Ink* – a magazine read by over one million and on par with *The New Yorker* – for various fantasy, realistic and poetic articles. I was highly commended by distinguished writer Cathy Cassidy twice as a teenager. Literature is my first love and consequently I achieved an A* in my A-Level and outstanding grades in my related subjects. I have recently switched to a vegan diet and am a life-long feminist. My book celebrates multi-faceted characters from all classes, genders, ethnicities and personalities.

Enjoy – it's going to be a topsy-turvy ride!

23

E.S. GLASS

23

Vanguard Press

VANGUARD PAPERBACK

© Copyright 2021
E.S. Glass

The right of E.S. Glass to be identified as author of
this work has been asserted by her in accordance with the
Copyright, Designs and Patents Act 1988.

A CIP catalogue record for this title is
available from the British Library.

ISBN 978 1 78465 722 2

*Vanguard Press is an imprint of
Pegasus Elliot MacKenzie Publishers Ltd.*

www.pegasuspublishers.com

First Published in 2021

**Vanguard Press
Sheraton House Castle Park
Cambridge England**

Printed & Bound in Great Britain

Dedication

For my mum,
Who encouraged, praised and endlessly debated with me about the
finer points of the book.
We are both devotees of stories, and I trust that this entry will
endear you to the series.

Chapter One: Robots' Laboratory

I was never alone. Voices radioed like volts, murmuring in my veins, rapid as fruit flies. Nadia rasped: "Good morning, Ivy. Report to Wolves Firm ASAP. We promoted you to the Time Traveller Scheme. You're contracted at eight. Shrewd transport includes Shuttlebus 21, foot-rockets, legs or time machines. My compliments… may fortune strike the missions ahead. Winning players earn a silver ticket through time and space."

The tinny automaton snapped the signal. Rocking on the rugged mat, questions flared regarding my rivals. It sped me like a hard-drive, a rotating record; a film fast-forwarded, a link expired. More machine than human, my lobes no longer detected Aero's snores.

His granite gaze crystallised my taps. We tottered on speech, wheezing.

"The rent?"

Silence fractured - a nutshell.

"We owe again."

The wind whooshed my airways. "The rent?"

"Did someone say rent?"

Scotch-tinted saucers materialised from plaster hollows. Shimmering in the slit, flaxen curls hanging, stood sodden Cessie in a rainbow parasol. Vanilla and rhubarb wafted as she rolled her tongue:

"I paid an advance of £3,000 credits."

"Reception says we're running debts of £9,000 – plus interest." Aero scuffed his threadbare sandals, tendons wiring his olive-hued arm.

"How long 'til we're evicted?" Cessie adjusted her microchip setting, shuddering at the *zap*.

"A month," he answered gravely.

An emphatic cough issued from my stomach. "Did you get the message?"

"What message?" Their words melded together, akin to bluebirds rushing.

"Open your inbox." My lids slanted. "We need to get going."

They were breathless, consuming the airwaves. He turned puce; she stilled.

"Us?" Aero fingered the tear in his shirt. "This a sick hoax?"

"I was only ten when I told you Astrid Spike was in my living room," I said feebly. "It's real, I swear."

"He cried for weeks after that," Cessie said softly. "Are we really going to be Time Travellers? We're only interns —"

"We'll have to crush a few souls first," I said, coffee waves moulded in a bun. "We need to vacate."

"Just a minute – EVANGELINE!" Cessie summoned her – *it*.

A draft smacked the ajar door. Goose pimples shot my backbone.

She slithered like a dream, steel parts fused in a burnished head, wiry frame lit with lemon, lilac and candy buttons; mouthpiece stitched in a beam, voltage sizzling the air. With metallic bonds, she clothed her owner in bronze lace. Her reflex hummed: "Salutations, Ms Belle. How are you this dawn?"

Cessie parroted: "Sunny."

The Robot's visage lightened. "I am glad."

Clang! Neck muscles clicked as I hurried to the source.

My sister Pearl shuffled Cessie's first edition of *Sense and Sensibility* on the spiralled sill I'd fashioned, palming the dust. The shelf strained *The Bedroom* wallpaper, pausing at Aero's glass workroom, where snake plants and lilies soiled in their pots.

"I will assist." Evangeline wheeled in a blink, trained on the girl, sanitising the books. While we watched, she rummaged for utensils, mending the rip.

"I'm s-sorry," Pearl said. "It was the rat."

I gaped at the whiskered vermin on the mat. It was the twentieth to scuttle through the vents since summer. Evangeline's nostrils creased, and she deposited the twitching creature via the flap. It zoomed to the shrubberies, raced by a cherry-spotted lizard, whose tongue whipped.

I ironed my cobalt denim. "We've had news. I've to go into work early because I'm competing for the Time Traveller's Programme. It's our fantasy… I'll be an astronaut soon."

Pearl's pleats seesawed; animation lit at once. "You mean it? You're going to be a Time Traveller?"

"*If* I win," I said sternly.

She fiddled her watch. "But you've to take me to school."

"Can't Dad?"

The shook head jarred me. "He's archiving in the library."

"Mum?"

She gnawed her nails. "Still abroad. She hasn't found it."

My heart faltered. Inhaling was yoga, wax flames sizzling in frost.

Cessie flitted to the window in foot-jets, crested with the family name: Belle. She prised the handle, bathing in the breeze.

"The early hen misses the axe." There was a whistle, similar to a withered hearth.

The rest of our party congregated on the lawn to await Bus 21. My friend stroked the fleshy stems, turning the umber insides. "It's dying."

Tiny pools whirled in the bricked street.

"What do you expect – it's British shores." My chestnut stare mottled.

Pearl disengaged our grip.

A flutter escaped her, patent shoes pointed at the rectangular, billowing apartment, a clay cone embroidering the umbrella, the sign reading: "Open". I couldn't smell the leeched grass, but seagull excretion, sweltering rays, the crunch of conchs whitened with peach, and urchins sparkling. The budget allowed one ice cream a year, black chipped, Cornish vanilla, sauced in raspberry syrup. Venturing from the British Isles was as ominous as red wires.

"No pudding," I said sharply. "It costs three credits."

Her dimples engorged. "The bus!"

Colossal, it hovered, defaced with indelible ink, bulk staggering, brushed with charcoal. The Conductor hailed us – there were no seats left.

I often sported the mists… today's wisps were layered cupcakes, and Pearl daydreamed of fudge-brownie dessert, vaporising the window, until a shriek drew me up.

Androids patrolled on bladed balls by jagged fences layering the hills. Machine guns stabbed the spines of numbered prisoners, sweated and pallid.

"Don't stare." I yanked the chintz curtain. Pensioners howled abuse.

The fog dispersed: unveiling a classic car, Snow White red, drifting in clunks and roars that reverberated and clinched my attention. Yet that did not square my fists, but the driver miming: "Blasted robots!"

The glass shattered.

The Conductor monopolised the wheel to avoid the Ford, so shards flew, denting elderly holdalls. Airborne, we were fragile jars, splitting the countertop. Would jam mutate to leaking innards?

My hand clutched Pearl's before I knew what was happening.

Screams pierced the coach.

The winged motorist hammered the brakes… he inched, ignition firing, more pale than a tortoise, mahogany mane lionising him.

"Magnus." Aero's jaw hardened. "Must've bribed for his avian licence."

Pearl burrowed in my shoulder.

"We're okay," Aero said coaxingly. "It's a collision."

Aurora, Magnus' passenger, dipped her pristine, coal locks, dripping words. His contortion cleared, and he steered it higher in the clouds, unwinding to converse with our Conductor.

"Sorry about that," he was saying conciliatorily. "First time."

The bus worker huffed, shrugging. "The bloody flying motorway. Makes apes of us all."

"He nearly killed us." The words formed unconsciously. "He isn't fit for the skies."

Magnus shifted, in earshot.

For a minute slower than dust motes on a clock, we froze, in film-frames. It was not telepathy, but memories whistled… we had been nine, at the Science Fair. He had dismantled my self-invented steam train, weeks of toil unwritten. It had honoured Pearl's birth, the sacred second sister, never meant to be born. The sole time I had cried in class.

He was a Rubik cube, an insoluble riddle. We glowered from polar contraptions.

The gales swept us to the foot of the giant dome building: pinned by spider arches, beige tinted with raven, extending to the hothouse labs, hospital and library. The motto fixed you: *Timetravellers walk immortal.* A craggy wolf stoned the sign, daubed in beaver and must by sky-rising probation workers.

The exit juddered and we dashed into Headquarters, eggy scent luring us to the canteen, where Aero embraced his ebony-skinned, white-capped mother. The queue lined the corner, and my microchip steered me towards an iron-rich dish. Aero's mother Lydia Smith heaped a container of granola, berries, honey and cream.

"No credits," she said. "On the house."

"You don't have to," I said, but she wouldn't take it.

It was a bit of a school situation, when you don't know where to sit, and my feet led me towards Cessie. She resided with co-colleagues Alexandrina and Fire, the former a nectarine-haired, snarling individual; the second a squared man with a bulbous nose.

Digesting a lump, I whipped to see Aero jilt the line, requesting beans-and-sausages on toast. The wan woman behind sighed, mousy and sinewy as a kingfisher. I vaguely knew her from the labs – Aero's domain.

"Aero!" It was louder than intended. "She was first."

My best friend understood at once, retreating to allow – was it Bo – to place her order. The mechanic worker rustled its cooker, whirring and blending soya oats. She refused maple syrup, and no, she did not want apples.

"Saving the world, one soy porridge at a time?"

Magnus appeared, ruffled from the crash, fringed by associates – co-engineers, as we worked in that department. I wasn't exactly the most popular, and I was about to slide further down the ladder.

"Slaughtering people, one car drive at a time?" My brows thickened in serpent vines.

"Ivory, my favourite employee." He blazed like spears.

Our fellows tittered menacingly. I charred at friends witnessing the nickname – usually reserved for work. It was tempting, working with steel, to 'slip' and entail an accident... but I was a better person than that.

"Call me that again —"

"No —" Bo clutched my sleeve. "His parents will strike you off."

When your enemy is the offspring of the Head of Wolves and a Professor, you remain silent, even if ire congeals.

My back crooked, resembling a hardback. Aero quivered, mouthing to be careful. That smarted. I was always careful. I didn't trot in the woods to visit Grandma, I didn't operate Robots and I didn't stalk the streets at night, where spectral men and women waited with daggers.

While Magnus swaggered to Cessie's table with salmon, quail eggs, spinach, cheddar and sourdough, Ms Smith handed me smoking tea.

"What was that about killing people?" She furrowed.

I winced.

Aero intervened. "Common air accident, that's all. We've got bigger problems – the rent, for a start. We can't afford a sacking."

Flushes streaked me.

"I earn from the café, perhaps I can contribute." Her tone was careful.

"We're not charity cases," he said.

Lydia bustled to transmit another order.

In the hubbub, Cessie's table smoked cocoa, Robots whisked breakfasts, Pearl glugged a sugar-loaded banana milkshake, and transactions rung.

A knock shook my beverage, heat dampening my playsuit. To the side, a Dutch accent implored Aero's Mum.

"I have no money," he said. "Please. I need —" he gripped the stall, ashen.

"This is a business, not a soup kitchen," Lydia said coolly.

Robot staff jostled him, reading his rights on arrest. He was guilty of attempted theft; the hub fell silent. The thief acted immediately. He drew a spray from his large pocket, shooting at the Robots. Lydia trembled, pinafore unthreading.

My sole struck him; the crook landed on the clean polish. Before he tasted lemon zest, the workforce pressed him so he couldn't move, white gloves clinching with shackles.

"You!" the man said. "You damn machine, take your fists off me, or I'll —"

The end of the threat didn't occur. His torso curved mid-expletive, undertone waxen, chest rapid with oars of life and death. A mint card rolled from his blouse, and cataracts glazed his vision – he was immobilised.

"Help!" Bo shrieked at spectators. "A Doctor – someone fetch a Doctor!"

She buzzed a knob by the sprig texturing her uniform. As if a vampire, Magnus' father slid in, coasted on tidal waves, rimmed spectacles riving his nasal bridge. Professor Stone crumpled his faded, gingham blazer, glasses glinting, stirring the man's chest with electronics. The thief moaned in limbo, levitated by the treatment.

"Prognosis: viral infection. Will likely expire in six minutes if we do not tend to him. Mr Smith." He clicked, and Aero stuttered.

Cessie's popcorn strands nudged him: "Go."

She spoke gently, transfixed by the shallowing gasps of the robber.

He trod towards Professor Stone, who administered slaps to the man's chest.

"Breath into him," he said.

Aero leant, tearing his black coils, breathing air into the patient. He did it again. Again. No response.

Stone thumped his chest several times. The teashop was hushed as he faced the theatre.

"Dead," he said without a flicker of emotion. He adjusted a steel wristwatch, mapping the exact hour: "Life expired at seven a.m. on 11/10/2218."

Pasty-faced Bo joined the cream-coated pathology team, who trolleyed him to the morgue, deserting a shaken Aero. While Magnus led his father to the 'shock teas' aisle, I seized the dropped card, muttering to the amateur scientist: "You couldn't have saved him."

"I've never seen a person expire," he said mutedly.

"Get used to it," I said. "There'll be plenty more… ah… expirations if you qualify."

"Why didn't I study history with Cess, or engineering with you?" he said to himself. "I'm not ready to see people die."

"Even rotten eggs?" I said.

"Nobody warrants that," he said smartly. "Trust me."

Trust – I had yet to pencil it on the checklist. It bobbed, elusive, bottle heads anchoring the sky.

A name badge floated beside us. "Junior Bo Marsh" had returned, bob stringy as if hacked with Pearl's clippers.

"You checked he's dead?" Aero said chokingly.

"Dead as a dormouse," Bo responded grimly. "I performed a 3D scan, and nothing. We followed procedure, but sometimes people don't live. You were a lot better than most trainees. I've never seen the Professor call an intern to resuscitate. You must have scored really well."

Her lithe frame dipped and ducked away in a flash.

The crowd dispersed and Stone reappeared, specs askew, shirt fresh, ruddy-cheeked. "A private word," he said to my friend. "The Gardens should be unmonitored. We need to discuss the scene this morning."

They absented themselves as suddenly as Bo.

I slid the card out, slipping beside Pearl.

"Quarantined" was stamped in bloodied ink, a hospital logo emblemizing the cover. The dead man had been #324. My eyebrows threaded as the information sunk my belly. Had he been seeking medical asylum? How had he entered the country, since Britain had fenced itself against foreigners? What had he wanted with the Wolves Corporation? Why had he pilfered the café? I bent the slip and zipped it before Pearl inquired. However, she'd seen, primed for mysteries even at twelve. My abdomen clenched.

She dipped her straw for trickling syrup. "Mum might've heard something abroad, or Dad might know. His library's under the Government branch, isn't it?"

"Yes," I said grudgingly. "Don't bother Mum, P. She's studying cures, not people. Leave her alone."

"We haven't seen her in six months," she said empathetically. "I've grown two inches."

"Mum will get a lovely surprise when she returns," I said listlessly. "Soon."

"Why are dormice deader than other beings?" she said tersely.

"You'll find out in biology," I said, brushing myself and retrieving the magnetic bag that hummed and purred when clasped.

Upon sensing an intruder, it blew them to the ground. An eleventh birthday present knitted by Dad and booby-trapped by me. Cessie always reminisced about when gravity had forced an imposter from my locker, where they'd tried to peer at my maths answers. They'd gotten detention for ten weeks, and an educator had invited me to engineering classes. The thought made me smirk.

"Let's see Dad," Pearl pleaded. "If we keep it, Stone's associates will find us."

Slinking to the Central Library, we met Dad, dark fuzz grizzling his jawbone. Pearl gabbled the incident, explaining the commotion.

"Ivy found this." She slid the card in his possession. "Belonged to the dead guy. Put it in your safe, please, with the other artefacts? We think he was sick and came ashore. They can't be treated well where he comes from."

"Facts are sacred," Dad said sternly.

"Why else would he travel in his condition?" I said. "He was half-dead even as he thieved." I blushed, recalling tripping him. "He seemed to be a petty crook, but he changed."

"I'm not promising to believe you," Dad said stoically, "but I will lock this away."

There was a *clink*.

"Nadia's expecting you," Dad said, alarmed. "You won't compete, let alone qualify, if you don't run upstairs."

"How did you know?"

He tapped his temple. "Nowadays, there's more than one means of communication."

A blush dusted my roots. When Pearl was born, he told me a stork flew her from the edge of the world to London. In my naivety, the Earth was flat and you could trace the bed.

"Don't tell Mum until I know for sure."

He winked. "I swear on this third edition *Historie of the World*."

The gate unlocked, and we were departing when Dad halted us.

"One more thing," he said mistily. "Don't go looking for skeletons in the closet. There are things here that would ice stone. Working here was never the dream. You'll gamble your only chance of doing what I was too foolish to. You know how they feel about second children." A groan enumerated. "You don't want to end up like me, dusting book covers of greater heroes. You don't —" He stopped as though gagged.

Pearl towed my forearm. "We understand, Dad. See you later."

"Dad," I said. My voice spluttered. "What happens if you leave the Library?"

"I'll never work again," was the answer.

The shaft took an eon to descend. The stairs sung to me, but resistance was an art. Finally a chute voyaged, pillared with grey machinery, and we jabbed for the highest floor. At the penultimate it unbolted, although neither of us had indicated that route. It jerked as it stopped. Erect, lit in acorn and peony, a robot fronted us, juggling a tray, a warrior armoured with wasted walnuts. The contents smacked our clothes before we could react; flung, flailing to the mirror, soundless, hollow.

"Government Robots aren't authorised to wander," I said fiercely. "Let us go, now!"

Its metal veneer paused: nonetheless, pursued by a want I neither saw nor understood, it meddled the keys and the lift parachuted. We crouched for the second time that morning, paralysed. Fighting was in vain: steel clamped cries: we meshed into clay figurines; crushed, broken.

The air was alive with invisible blackness, gulps penetrating the ceasefire, shaft juddering and stumbling underground. In a subterranean lair, the Robot compelled our knees to the clandestine dark, and we groped for light. It jetted to the lift and ballooned upstairs.

Lamps chinked in the corridor. Amalgamated offices stood, fitted with metal codebreakers. Cut-glass panes exposed jackets sleeping in chairs, whiteboards scrawled with equations and ruptured pipes plop plop plopping, inviting entry.

Ogling the system, Pearl shuffled, a rat scampering after the Piped Piper. Her gloves dialled, punching code after code without success.

"Stop!"

"No." Her bones set. "It's about that thief; I *told* you they'd come after us. Know the enemy, that's what Mum always says."

"No, Pearl!"

She encrypted the phrase: M-a-g-m-a.

A voice buzzed: *You have entered the right password. Authorising your entrance.*

Not knowing how her gears solved this enigma as it had playset wires in her infancy, I twisted the knob — it budded, a clover's felt petals. Brandy bottles ripened on the desk, half-opened with a seal. The label read: *Medicinal.* Snorts bubbled in the chamber.

"I'm Dr Dracula," Pearl said, marking a moustache, pretending to solve tacked papers.

The dim view boasted a lawn and bricked cement. A giant, stocked computer replaced a fireplace, ashes whispering in the debris. Its switch was snapped off. Coffin-like cubicles met our gaze, nailed, so cold our warm blood became reptilian. We expected Snow White to rise and metamorphose our abduction to a fable. Was this our igloo, where we would reside until ages hence?

Shadows skulked the glasses and a raven-furred tabby mewed at my ankles. Pearl's "oh" of adoration converted to repulsion when it modelled its *other half.* One part exhaled, but its parallel fleece was etched with wires. When it next wailed, copper teeth stained it, clones of Pearl's old braces.

"Is it dead?" Pearl said quietly.

Déjà vu soaked my brain.

"It was," I said hauntingly. "A long time ago. That was Magnus' pet cat."

Heeding Dad's caution of fact over feeling, I knew my foe had goaded it to chase me in the garden of my home, a decade ago. He had apologised, hanging his floppy head, claiming it had been a game. The scar could've turned septic if Dad hadn't immunised me at birth. He and Mum had hoarded credits until they could afford a robust, perfect baby.

One day Magnus had tramped into school, not even harassing Aero about his dated sandals, ruined as he'd dashed for the unreliable shuttlebus. Rumours swirled his dad had blundered and knocked into the cat, and it had died on his son's birthday.

"Did he create this?" Pearl was wide-eyed.

"It's not a *creation*," I breathed. "It's a... recovery... it was hit by a car, right there... it's patched up, good as new."

A low voice wondered: "Did we do enough to treat him?"

It was Bo.

"We'll never know," Professor Stone told her. "'Tis been a trying day. Excuse me; I must attend to my office."

Feet stamped the pasture.

Pearl's elbow impaled mine as we jumped.

"Did you film the kitty?" she said, teeth rattling.

"Saved to the microchip," was the buoyant response. "We need to leave."

Flashy lights shone from Pearl as she snapped the office, springing into me as we careered forwards. The door clicked behind us, betraying no trace. There was no way the Doctor would welcome a camera presence here.

The resonant chamber rose and fell with their voices, edging closer and closer. We had minutes.

"We can't climb a metal mountain." Pearl sounded as though she were in tears. "They're going to find us."

I gauged my bag. "We've gotten this far."

Scanning the surroundings, my foot wrenched mechanisms from the tube. Pearl sliced them to tatters with her nails, and my eyelids hammered shut as I cast them to rope.

"Ivy." Pearl bit her fingernails as Stone conversed with his colleague above. "Now."

Thud.

I fused the rope with beams at the top, flinching as the mark hit, teetered, connected. The force of the blow shut down electricity. Arms tangled as we scrambled for a grip. Quaking, I fastened the belt into our waists, feeling for grips in the tunnel. Our bodies lifted, combined the weight of one hundred ice creams, and coiled around the other. Feet first, we scampered noiselessly uphill, breathing into the shallow space. Thank goodness I'd only eaten granola.

Ow! Heads cracked the platform – we'd arrived at the peak.

"Hey." Pearl's panting expression. "Two heads are better than one."

Mirth tore silence.

Manoeuvring hips to wheel ourselves onto wood, the luminosity seared our retinas, arguments sounding in our ears, essences of mocha and fried meat smoking. We scoured grimed cloth, catching our breaths, the wrecked funnel incriminating evidence.

With a sidelong search, I tidied the scraps of metal and dust, snipped the last of the rope so it disappeared down the chute, and taped the lift door with Pearl's handy stationery. On it I scrawled: *Not in use.* Pearl contributed a skull sign to indicate peril.

Dr Stone's voice was presently inches from us.

We compressed our bodies to a side corridor, holding our breaths. Sentences filtered from the centre of the floor.

"— could have an army of refugees soon," he was saying. "Britain could be overwhelmed. If they sneak in without treatment, the nation could be infected."

"That's why we need a Doctor," his colleague joked.

"Very droll, Andrew, very droll," he said generously. "Meeting at twelve?"

He swore as he spotted the notice. "Lift is blocked. I'll have to use your room." He summoned a couple of Robots. "Clean this up. I want it usable by midday, understand?"

We could not see them, but we heard them recite: "Absolutely, Professor Stone. Assisting you now."

Their breakage of the shaft echoed.

Pearl shot me a glance. "Are they all evil?"

"Don't know. They're not human so they can malfunction: or perhaps they have a consciousness, a python quiescent in their software. Perhaps it's a matter of time before they snap."

Pearl wrinkled, greying.

"Listen," I said commandingly, gripping her shoulders. "Don't tell Dad anything, or we could face jail." I bent my mid finger. "Never – return – to – his – offices. We have no idea what's waiting to be unleashed down there – or *who*. Swear."

Adventure kernelled in her almond eyes. She swore on Dad's history book, on Magnus' life, and the kitten in Dr Stone's gothic office.

She cantered to the café, and the identity of the saboteur struck: Magnus.

Chapter Two: The Time Travellers

The door squeaked as I slid in, nine pairs of eyes fixed on me. Stood at the round, wooden, chipped table, Nadia's rich woodsy hair framed her rickety chin, rimmed mouth wide. Her agate pupils swept mine, wine dress adorned inelegantly. To her left, Magnus' Alice blue gaze X-rayed me, resembling the fluids in his father's office. They were blank, for a hair's breadth crumpling unfathomably, square jaw taut in a paroxysm. To her right, Aero and Cessie bristled, red-and-yellow vipers, tongues forking the air. I darted my stare.

"Ivy," my mentor said croakily, "it's eight a.m. exactly. You made the task."

My chest sucked oxygen from the windowsill. My legs moved to the timbered table, disregarding the stifled box feel of an autumn morning. The billboard updated with a piece on spinal conditions in pets, authored by Bo Marsh.

"You will be divided into three teams of three. Ivy, join Ms Belle and Aero. Magnus, you are teamed with Aurora and Bo, and Mars will unite with Alexandrina and Fire," Nadia said.

The room sizzled with unvoiced rage at my pairing with my first friends, and Magnus with his – well, we were unsure of their relationship status. One had followed the other since middle school. Ears peeled to absorb the assignments.

"One, with unique transportation, you must use the online navigational clue to find your first task. It involves driving to a wormhole and retrieving moon matter for comparison with the modern galaxy, within the time limit."

'Aaaahs' sounded.

"Two, you must locate treasured, depleted materials via the clue. At the location, you engineer a break-in, minding the alarms and booby-traps. Two of you will steal the clothes and the remaining member will await as the getaway. These items will prove vital to the challenge ahead

– or behind you." Amusement arose. "Finally, before the sand timer dries, you must enter virtual nature, battling key elements, scaling tall trees, ducking predators and deciphering the riddle. Solving it will salvage the key that unlocks endgame, whizzing you to my office. The losers will be drenched in chemical liquid and have to figure out the way back. Is that clear?"

Murmurs issued.

While teams bustled together, I revved the internal chip, sending my friends the file of Professor Stone's office, a note on who sent the robot, and whether I'd experienced two attempted assassinations this October.

Instantaneously, Aero buzzed an email:

The Doctor is not involved. He was guiding me in the gardens, and he didn't order any Robot.

Aero, I fired, *he put you in an awful position. He was completely unsympathetic.*

He retorted: *It was my own fault.*

Cessie interjected: *Dr Stone is a good guy. Someone ambushed you, and the stuff in his office is creepy, but I've always said science was creepy. Calm down – I'm sure there's another explanation.*

Cessie, I typed, *it doesn't give me the creeps, it gives me the heebie-jeebies.*

"The three triads," Nadia Ludwig commanded. "Set off." She upturned the timer.

Cessie threw one jet boot to Aero, indicating we gain a head start launching from the ledge.

"Take my hand?" she said tentatively, balancing the other jet.

The roof of my mouth roasted. "O...K."

Succeeding Aero, who cried he'd never done this before, our gloves interwove, and in a fleeting moment we powered off the sill, gliding with the engine in Cessie's footwear, clinging for dear life. Towers emerged from below, leafing my vision, spired flags painted in primary colours. There was no terror, only flight as we wheeled the skies; airless, cloudy.

"Ivy, press the brakes!"

The grass that had taunted me in Stone's tunnelled office was vaguely seen, drifting like weeds, before the realisation: we were about to crack our pates.

Two inches smaller, the steering was in reach. The hefty button stung my pinkie, and I jerked it; we were a whisper from the ground and landed with a dramatic *bump*.

"This is the third bloody time I've nearly died," I said, but Cessie only hiccupped from the impact.

I spotted Aero lounging by the garage, whistling at my chained motorcycle, crafted with spare hands in the scorching mirage of June. It was untested thus far. He unleashed compartments in the weighty moonstone bike to reveal extra cushioned seats.

Cessie clambered aboard, but a remote device halted me. It twitched, crimson, crushed under a powerful shoe. I pocketed it and saddled myself on the driver's seat, helmet screwed on. Pushing the gears, we zigzagged the race roads, steering lampposts, dogs and old folk, Cessie interpreting the initial clue in her mind. Aero watched our backs, sniping that Mars' group lagged.

The roads rose in and out of view, my arms lolling as they adapted to the controls. Magnus, Aurora and Bo were seen flying in his car in the clouds, incensing me. Bo's ear-splitting moans cut the air as she clutched the upholstery. Diving a little lower, Magnus smirked from his throne overhead:

"Hello, Ivy." He gestured meditatively. "Not figured out the clue yet? Have fun tailing me."

In a rush they vanished in the mist, swear words mixing unpleasantly with my spit.

"What a loser," Aero said dismissively, seeing my bared teeth.

"We'll be the duds soon, if we don't solve that clue," I said fiercely.

"You're letting him get to you," Cessie said coolly. "I'm trying my best."

"Read the clue; I'm a bit preoccupied at the moment," I hissed.

"*Day of the crescent moon and walking the footprints of power is on the horizon*," she intoned. She ruminated: "It can't be the Wolves corp. – that's too obvious." Her fingers twisted. "Power... a place of power... the moon... ministers... Westminster!" She clapped gleefully.

"What are you babbling about?" I said.

"That's the answer," she decoded slowly. "Mum used to visit for hours on end. It's Halfmoon Street, Westminster, London. Drive there and we can still beat Magnus."

It was the magic phrase. I adjusted the dial, speeding well beyond legal limits, chocolate strands blowing my face, muscles constricting, drumming the handlebars as we approached the credible street.

"I'm the brains, you two're the brawn, so look for that damn wormhole," Cessie said.

We puckered at the shimmering particles, time seeming to freeze, skyline iridescent, classifying the bulge in space in awe. Not large, it allowed enough room to squeeze in, piece by piece. But would it rip our flesh, melting our skin?

"We'll have to zoom through at the highest speed," Aero estimated. "'Tis the only way to break the barrier alive."

"You're gazing at time," I said mystically. "The present no longer exists."

"Great, we don't have to pay our rent," Aero said.

Cessie's giggle chimed like Tinkerbell, rippling with the effects of the hole.

I frowned at my friends – this was no laughing matter (literally). "We'll have to push the machine through, one bit at a time."

"Imagine Magnus shoving his car through that," he said. "And he'll have to leave his quiff behind."

Our giggles mollified teeming terror. We loomed before the wormhole, advancing, gnawing a crater in our tongues, and sped until we fell onto cheese-sized rocks on the moon. We were chilled, winded and unscathed.

I dug the cement with my shoe, smothered in gloom, sweeping the fibres. They thudded like asteroids, gigantic. Cessie's lids fluttered, groping the horizon for signs of the wormhole closing, spectral and mute. Meanwhile, Aero scoured the moon for samples, digging, sweat pinking his forehead, deftly seizing up the most vital fragments. It may have been the moon, but he appeared shivery and it occurred he stored the material in the same trouser the refugee had donned. I shivered. My mouth opened in confrontation when Cessie shrieked, spearing the sand with rock.

Imprinted immortally were the letters: M-A-G-N-U-S W-A-S H-E-R-E. She swore.

"His mother's a politician... how could I be so slow!"

"He left that message for us." My fists clenched to steady my breathing. "Bastard."

"Ivy!" Cessie's cry echoed oddly in space. "Time – it's sealing!"

We mounted the vehicle, gripping the steering with sticky hands, embalmed with the moon's crust, almost skidding down, down, down into an infinite abyss. Aero grasped my fingers, Cessie the controls and we swerved flying ash to missile through the envelope.

Returned to real time, the motion sickened us and we rode to our tube in Nadia's room: missing as we aimed our grains. They slipped and dropped below.

Cessie half-leapt from the machine with the slivers, misjudging the distance and dangling at the boot, screaming. Her palms were so sweaty and caked they defied her will to survive, deprived of her jets: however, our powerful grip pulled her. She cupped her residues in the tube.

"I – am – never – doing – that – again," she said, greening as we heaved the bike downwards: it could levitate, but for minutes at a time.

"You'll have to," Aero said unkindly. "It's the second mission now."

She marched the dirt.

We clued into Task Two, which yielded: *I am the key to your second mission. Choose wrongly and you may freeze, overheat or find yourself in jail. Choose wisely... I am one of the last of my kind.*

Even with three heads the answer was not forthcoming. Nonetheless, it turned out we didn't have to hang in suspense for too long.

We were drumming our knuckles on the dial, still perplexed by our moon trip, when we eavesdropped the Design and Technology intern, Mars, debating the enigma. Spike-headed Alexandrina and near-silent Fire collaborated, seeming to possess the geography. Cessie put a finger to her lips, and we steered the motorcycle behind a town wall.

"Quaint shops... my cousin works in retail, and I'm pretty certain the only boutiques are in Camden Street. We were slower than Magnus and Ivy's teams to the moon, but I doubt either specialise in clothing."

"Hey!" I whispered.

"Let's go," Fire said austerely. They climbed inside Mars' cheap, self-made mini; flightless, tortoise slow.

Three hearts thudded as we faced each other.

"Ivy, know how to ride to Camden?" Aero asked.

"I do," Cessie said firmly, and directed me until the lanes whittled to the cobbled passages of Camden Street, ruefully realising the motorbike would run faster than the competition.

We nearly trampled crowds of raucous buyers. Aero was on hand with alerts as to when someone was about to be killed. We disappeared to the striped, fancy, glamorous shop, diamond-shaped, calligraphic sign spelling: Closed. If it was padlocked, we'd have to smash in.

Cessie's breaths caught at the brainstorming, and she watched the neutral spectrum of paint, at war with herself.

"We can't ruin it," she said sadly. "Please, Ivy."

"We aren't going to destroy it," I said cunningly. "We're going to *hack* it."

The tools in my microchip droned and in settings, it necessitated the password pin. Consuming a lungful of air, I considered what type of password a vintage shop owner would set. One they would believe impermeable to an intruder, beyond knowledge in our resource-drained ecosphere. It hit – it had to be fashion.

But in twenty-three centuries of history, which would resonant? Displayed were plaid dresses belted on mannequins, rose and emerald scarves waving. My brain tried: m-i-n-i-s-k-i-r-t. Hardly anyone'd heard of this, but then, hardly anyone was the best friend of a history nut, whose parents were gifting a clothes-laden inheritance. It unbolted. We observed in wonder as the curled handle hummed.

"What did you type?" Aero asked thinly.

I lifted my brows. "If you have to ask, you'll never know."

"Ah, Ivy, Mars and his posse have arrived. We took too long with the password." Cessie wailed as the beaten-up Nissan arrived, paint flaking, the interns buzzing frantically.

"Aero," I said suddenly, "wait on the bike, and encrypt their minds to disorient them. Make them doubt the shop is the right location. While you brainwash them Cess and I will figure out the alarm system. See you in fifteen."

We slunk inside the shop as our competitors' victorious faces grew flummoxed, trailing exhibited fabric: beaded, glittered and fluttering like rainbows.

Cessie's knuckles broke the glass guarding the alarms and she began disabling accustomed buttons.

My feet shuttled forwards, carefully placing one in front of the other, wrenching pleated skirts, high-waist denim, velvety wool, silk camisoles, dated blazers and vivid platform heels. Tripping under the mass, I didn't see a trapdoor unleash in the fan, only feeling chemical fluids hail.

Acid was seconds from my convex nose when I dived into a black-suited dummy, sending us clattering down. Claws full of materials, I watched Mars' group bump into each other outside, heading into the pub, convinced their destiny lay in beer and rum.

"Ivy," Cessie said, as she twiddled the system. "Opt for multi-purpose, multi-habitual guises; we may need these." She huffed. "I suppose I'll be the clown sewing these together."

Clawing armfuls of items, Cessie's gasp didn't register at first. Squinting, Magnus, Bo and Aurora arose at the roadside, eerie as the three witches on the heath.

"Shit." Cessie hopped as she realised she hadn't paralysed a button, resulting in red beams skimming me.

My midsection did a matrix to dodge the blow, while Aero distracted Magnus.

"What's wrong?" he said spitefully. "Mummy and Daddy couldn't buy the clue to this task? We got your note, by the way… pity you wasted pointless seconds when you could've been chasing us here."

Magnus' thumb was on the handle.

I acted quickly. The eight-inch heel was hurled before he'd second-guessed the ploy and glass showered as it had this morning.

"What's wrong?" My tone was sugary as I toyed with time, squeezing in the jagged gap. Splinters poked my scalp. "Don't like the taste of your own medicine?"

29

He entered the boutique as alarms blared, higher-pitched than ambulances, or crows squawking as they spied worms, or vultures scenting rotting flesh; or Pearl when she had been born in the purpled shock of the delivery room.

I flung the material at Cessie, who fitted her pointed shoes onto the engine, slightly above my trainers, whereas Aero shrugged apologetically at Bo and Aurora. We gripped his arms and swept him into the haze of customers.

The third task was no brainteaser, but a straight scroll of instructions, which the motorcycle rumbled towards as an owl arrowing for brown mice.

Aero consulted Nadia's commands.

"We need to find a transport hole," he said, fatigued. "Says it will transport us to Task Three."

Driving in rings, after an eon the glowing lure of the vacuum appeared beside a tube station, swirling in stripes like a hypnotised mirror, gleaming and depthless.

"I'm not sure about this," Cessie whimpered.

"What would Caesar say?" Aero demanded.

"I came, I saw, I conquered," she said steadily.

"Ivy." Aero raised his eyebrows. "Power the bike."

It did look awfully like a Trojan horse, or an enemy's plant.

Swallowing caution, I drove inside the void, quiet breaths overwhelmed by Cessie's whines, Aero's heartbeats and the particles bubbling: growing, growing until we were encased, soaring in a world of Nadia's making. We buckled on the honed wood of an apparent GP practice. It was certainly a nightmare-of-sorts.

Half anticipating a dragon firing us to our deaths, the clack of Nadia's footwear was startling. Sheepishly, we dignified ourselves, forfeiting our clothes and realising with chagrin the other teams were here. Triumphantly, I noted they'd far less clothing, Fire was tipsy and Magnus was sponging glue from his eyelashes.

Professor Ludwig coughed for attention. "Your third mission is the most perilous of all. You'll be strapped to a locked chair and I will insert a red chip, shipping you to a cyber-maze. Inside you combat thorny plants to retrieve the winning rose, tackle an assault course, outwit 3D

30

beasts for the key-card to the next stage, and clash with foes. The final cards are masked in the gnarled twigs. Does everyone understand?"

"Are there any rules?" Magnus drawled.

"Just one." Nadia paused. "Not a soul shall be slain."

Cessie and Fire gulped.

Aero 'volunteered' me to be manacled first, and the red programme alit in my cranium.

"Relax," Nadia said, as the blood pressure reading ratchetted. "Or I won't enter you in the game."

"Sorry." Images of the lifeless thief rose. However, so did Dad's soothing grin and Pearl's astronaut ambitions. They were flames that kindled valour.

Parallel streaks shot in a reverie, the wooden room transmuting to cyberspace, rosettes attached to two-metre hedges, cubes dividing opponents, a digital clock counting down. At six my heart squeezed, at three no thoughts sprung and at one my simulated body flexed like a cheetah's.

Zero.

Thwack.

I was shoved aside by Aurora's dash for the vast bush, coal-tinted tufts wafting.

She leaned her tall spine to pick a rose, jasmine at the stem and carmine at the axis. She stuttered backwards as it spiked her bone – she'd chosen a placebo. Virtual blood splattered the outlines, geared as athletes' launching posts.

Tremoring, I profited from the diversion and inspected the hedge. Hundreds of roses nestled, blonde, sunlit pink and jade. One was golden, hidden in the middle, where Alexandrina, Cessie and Bo hacked at plants. Something drew me up short. This was not reality – there were no rules.

I stepped onto a square, which swelled five inches, and picked up a handful of lines, ripping the design. It caught competitors' toes like a rolled rug. They thundered like nine pins, dominoes in a private game. A laugh echoed – mine.

I used taller shoulders to catapult myself to the core, sniping the offending rose with a line and carving a square. From it arms and legs wedged in and I abandoned the lines in the wall to spike the succeeding adversary. There was no breathlessness: my lungs resembled a ghost's.

Frontwards, the threads of an assault course wound, with papered climbing frames, nets sheathing the grid, marble clubs in place of a chandelier and monkey bars at the head.

Wasting no more time, I propelled myself in the network of webs, entangled, wriggling towards the exit.

A foot crunched on mine. I was met with Cessie's sparkling beam, cheering me on, unwinding a net from a right ankle – her safe passage had been assured by one of her co-players attaining the rose.

We stumbled out, faced with a stream of sand, grainy and waist-high. We'd to swing across with the thick ropes, but sinking seemed inevitable. Cessie beseeched me to go ahead. Alexandrina, Fire, Magnus, Aurora and Bo entered the realm.

"What's with the clubs?" Magnus said slowly.

"You're meant to hit yourself in the face with them," Cessie said sweetly. "It would be a drastic improvement."

"To look like your mother?" Magnus threw back his head. "Isn't she on her fiftieth surgery?"

Leaving Cessie snarling, I pounced on the ropes headfirst, bounding at such haste my hands fell, sending me plummeting to the predatory sand. Neck-deep, chokes ensued, limbs warring against a gold tide; drowning. Sand reached my nostrils and the granite diced my thumb. It split in slow motion, flesh fizzling in earth.

Appropriating one of the clubs, Cessie brushed the sand to the side, hauling me onto the monkey bars. We were about to throw ourselves to the next dimension, Aero tailing us, when Cessie threw each of us a club.

"The next room is beasts," she said warningly. "We need weapons."

We were transported to leafy lands, where live-motion alligators swam, scaled fish were armed with spears, lions prowled their territory and a rhinoceros snorted in the corner, the key card to the final phase in its jaws.

A leaping lion, matted fur magnificent, obstructed our path, emitting a thundering roar as it tackled Cessie's throat. Aero and I brought our clubs down, brandishing them towards the rest of the pack, and they vanished in a fog.

"We have to defeat all of them before we get to the card," Cessie said she gathered herself. "A few isn't enough."

"Ivy!"

Aero pushed me aside as a fish shot its spear towards us, hitting the wall with a *thunk*. Ceaseless blades fired across the air.

I wrenched a spear from the wall and Cessie and I grimly executed them all. Their glassy gaze leaked into the lines, their blood dissolving, and they were gone.

I had an idea. As alligators fenced us like sharks, I yelled to the others to sit on their rubbery, ridged backs, airlifting us to the rhinoceros. Magnus and Bo had the same light bulb moment, smoothly instructing a gator over.

We rode in a cantering dance towards the rhinoceros, whose horns butted us so we overturned, heaping in the cranny.

"We deserved that," Aero said firmly. Bo was the lone person who nodded. The labyrinth had animalised us.

The rhinoceros struck, sending me flying towards the card.

"Stop it," Aero said in a panic. "We've got minutes."

Cessie fired a spear and for a moment I thought it would make contact with the creature, but it struck the fruits, crunching in the Rhino's tombs. I keyed the card, and five of us were thrust into the ultimate piece of the puzzle.

Magnus and I were nominated by our teams to attempt the huge oak trees, where numbered cards dangled from topmost branches. A timer ticked, a cuckoo in a birdhouse.

Feet first, the twigs broke off around me, but my fanatic scrambles ignored this.

At ground level a sticky flytrap appeared, enmeshing Cessie to Aero and him to Bo. The more they wrestled, the faster they stuck.

I almost gave up mid-point, the breadth of the oak overpowering me, sticks pounding downwards, slashing holes in my bodysuit, battering the necks of the trapped flies below.

But the reward of time travel, sliding in and out of reach, set me ablaze.

I ran up the tree, not risking a look backwards, hearing the thuds of Magnus embedding shoe after shoe in the holes.

I was nimble but seven inches shorter, and lacked my enemy's strides, who was millimetres from card three. A strategy formed when all seemed hopeless.

"Was that your remote outside headquarters?" I said congenially. "Interesting device... one would almost think it was *planted* in a robot. It's funny how one kidnapped me earlier, before this contest. Your work?"

He hesitated, a tenth of a second from the card. I snuck further up the tree, adjacent from my own card. We were tooth-and-nail, head-to-head.

"I didn't touch the Robot," he said bitterly. "I'm not threatened by a defenceless cry-baby."

It was a shame he didn't notice me soundlessly cut his stems.

"When everyone finds out what you are, you and your father are done for," I said politely.

"At least we have a reputation to lose," he said savagely.

"So you admit — ?"

"I admit nothing," he said coldly. "Step aside, Ivory, I've got a prize to claim."

It was too late.

I toppled the branches around him and he tumbled to the bottom, glued to our co-workers. The clock tick-tocked. Snatching the opening, the three passes were in my grip, and I tossed two in Aero and Cessie's direction.

They made a dash for the remaining cards. I didn't have time to see who won, as the twigs blasted me into a cyclone, spitting me into Professor Ludwig's office. Seconds later Aero and Cessie steamed into the room, glancing at the time.

There was a drawn-out pause. No one breathed.

Nadia showed us the wrist face.

It was static on 00:00:04.

"Does that mean — ?" Cessie said unsteadily.

"Hats off to you three." Nadia hardly smiled. Nonetheless, her grimace arched, deepening her crinkles. "You've made the time zone: therefore you are members of the Time Travellers' Unit."

The 'intern' badge was exalted to a bronze membership.

"There's no trick or twist to this?" Aero said, cooling off.

"It isn't Halloween yet, Mr Smith," our mentor said kindly.

He buried his face in his sodden T-shirt.

The conquest hadn't yet sunk in. I was like a wooden puppet, operated by forces higher up, scripted with their dialogue, robed in their wardrobe.

I had not asked for this challenge, but it was true, space adventures were made of dreams, the occasion to rewrite timelines, meet a cast from the past.

Nevertheless, seeds curdled in my gut. Foreboding told me there must be another reason. Mum's mantra was never to trust a free lunch, especially if someone else ordered it.

The door erupted. The six losing members plodded in, saturated in taupe chemicals, square-jawed, vicious-faced and radiating fury.

"The sextuplets have arrived for lesson one," Nadia said tranquilly. "High-fliers in this organisation have to be the fastest, bravest and most skilful. Our very own Dr Stone hatched these trials around Darwin's survival of the fittest." She held up a finger. "Yet I put a lot of stock in second chances, so another slot may be filled in future."

Drones, as the hum of midges, purred in response. They didn't seem thrilled.

"This isn't a holiday," Magnus said tartly. "You better not disappoint my father."

"We know it's a job," Aero spat.

"Then do what you're paid to do," he fired.

Bo was solitary in her congratulations. She twiddled her paw-printed collar.

"You can prepare at my house, if you like," she said.

Aero and Cessie agreed at once.

"It would be lovely," Nadia added, "if the losing six would assist."

Mars, Alexandrina and Fire submitted.

"OK." Aurora blinked. "It may be us next time."

"Alright," Magnus said colloquially.

"Ivy?" Bo said silkily. "Are you coming, too?"

My breath halted, trainers shuffling. "What preparations?"

"As a fifth-time competitor, I know what I'm doing." Her bob skimmed her cheeks.

My ribs stirred, and I said: "Yes."

Chapter Three: The House of Marsh

I hung in a crook, imitating the tentacles of a widow spider. Bo conversed with Aero about the thief's demise, Magnus kneaded his glass-cut knuckles, and Cessie engaged the newly arrived Professor Goodwin.

A swish of ruler-straight hairs announced pink-cheeked Aurora.

"Hi," she said, wigwagging. "Sorry about earlier. All's fair in war, huh?"

"Don't worry about it." It were as though I orated through gritted teeth.

She watched me glare at her boyfriend-of-sorts. "Oh, he's just envious."

She called him over.

Magnus approached, turfed mane flying in his eyes, and shrugged. "If you hadn't noticed, a lot of lives rest on this trip."

Aurora's trimmed, shaded hair blurred her expression. "Don't panic the poor thing before she's gotten started."

My shoulder blade made an irritated spasm. "I never panic."

"Everyone's afraid of something," Magnus said amicably. "Even time travellers."

My maxilla motioned furiously, however was interrupted by Professor Goo   dwin, Cessie's old history Professor, proposing we tramp to Bo's house now.

Cessie strode between Magnus and myself. "Come on, Ivy," she said pleasantly. "We've got a holiday to plan."

In a misfit mob, we advanced until Bo stopped on a windy, chimney-thatched street, pushing a splintered and centuries' old gate. She rapped on a medieval, tacked sign, knitted and handmade with lavender teacups, embroidering the emblem: "House of Marsh". Crimson oils ornamented the margins, and the design lifted to unveil an antique spyhole. The circular, scoped instrument poked out, tracing the intestines of the disturbers. The rusty magnifier was clogged by mushroom locks, skidding like a key through the chinks.

"Alright," a gravelly voice said, "you may enter."

She twisted it back, and the lock snapped, conceding access.

Inside, the brass corridors were ascended by rows of stairs, a mechanically winged chair attached to the wall. Magnus stretched to travel on it.

"We'll trek the staircases." Goose pimples sprung on Bo.

"This isn't your place?" Aero said timidly.

"My Grandmother's," she said civilly. "Don't make a racket; she's a hundred and three."

The stairwell steered to a garret, where we crowded the mammoth computer on velvet poplar seats. Bo's Grandmother reclined on a settee, armed with chunks of raisin loaf, teapot steaming hotter than fire.

"As my sulky granddaughter didn't introduce me, I'll do the honours," she said impishly. Her face and the tray were alike; one caked with wrinkles, the other crumbs. "Non-relatives can address me as Grandmother Marsh, since I'm all and sundry's Grandma now."

Bo flapped her middle parting.

"Well," Professor Goodwin refereed. "Why don't we watch the files Dr Stone sent?"

The lecture commenced with a Star Wars-esque opening, broadcasting the tour in space as an unmissable opportunity.

Aero said what everyone felt: "Get on with it."

The clip mutated to Professor Stone contemplating a frame on his counter. "Right," he said commandingly, "you are about to glimpse your first time zone. A wormhole has become available - an irreplaceable voyage to the Dinosaur Age." He loosened his bow tie. "Beware the risks. The last voyager didn't make it out alive."

"The dinosaur age?" The colour sapped from Cessie. "We'll die."

On the other side of the coin, a grin painted Aero.

Bo paused the clip.

"Play it," I said curtly. "I want to see how that guy died."

The screen displayed a giant pie, sliced into millions of years.

"In an earlier epoch, what was once Pangea split into separate landmasses; forming the world we have today."

"What we have left of it." Aero was muffled.

"One of these was the Cretaceous Age, the last era of the dinosaurs," the voiceover continued. "Sixty-six million years ago, mosasaurs, ammonites, ray-fins, snakes, tiny mammals, tyrannosaurs, plant-eaters, birds, beetles and triceratops creatures walked the earth. Your job is to possess the valuable herbs and flowering plants that bloomed in this period, harnessing medicine to combat the superbug deaths. Fail and thousands expire. Succeed, and the trade of your wildest daydreams is yours, as well as curing dozens of souls."

The link cut to a shot of a pouched, hairless nomad shearing leaves on the cusp of a forest, T-shirt logoed with the "Wolves" aphorism.

He tossed his bald scalp in triumph as he stole fresh berries, walnuts and barks, starting too late to see the twenty-foot monster grasp him in its tire-textured arm, hollowed teeth champing as if on wires. The berries descended and were eaten by a furry creature. The man did not scream – that would have been less unsettling – but greyed, and became the T-Rex's dinner. The shot seemed abridged.

No one spoke for several seconds.

"My father," Magnus elucidated, "thought it superfluous to show his ex-peer chewed and digested."

"Of course he did," Aero said furiously. "They didn't lift a limb to save him. Is that what's happening here – we're being thrown into this arena, and left to do-or-die?"

"You know the risks." Magnus straightened, buckles colonising the chair. "I knew you didn't have the guts to go through with it."

"I've got a gut, but I've also got a brain, and it doesn't like what it sees," my friend bit back.

"The lion with no courage," he said pensively. "Pull out while you still can."

"And have you take my place?" Aero said disgustedly.

Cessie placed an arm on his chair. "It doesn't matter. We'll be OK. We'll follow instructions; we'll be in a pack. That guy was alone."

They swivelled to see how I was consuming the news.

"I'm still going," I said bleakly. "I don't think there's much choice."

"That's the spirit," Magnus said loftily. "Just think, if you're eaten, everyone will remember your name."

"If I'm eaten," it came out swiftly, "I hope you're next on the menu."

Aero chortled, but Cessie was insipid.

"You're looking for items of value," Bo said tiredly. "Don't fuss over details. Grab anything and everything."

"A bit like the Design team on Black Friday," Mars spoke.

We sniggered.

Cessie thumbed the rickety shelves, swarming with literature such as "Robotics: Land of the Future", "Amsterdam: When bicycles marched the streets", "Beatrice Marsh: My Spy Memoirs" and "Superbugs: How We Killed Our Future Selves". Passages were bent in this creased, jaundiced volume.

Bo's Grandmother proffered a basket of white wine.

"For the nerves," she told the three of us. "Mellowed for forty years. More invaluable than those plants."

There was a jangle as Bo swept the bag away. "They don't need that," she said crossly. "They need *this*."

She slammed a bound, boxed tome on plants, cotyledons crimping the cover, charcoaled in saffron and lime. She slid it out of its uniform, brushing the illustrated, crayoned notes printed inside.

"My ancestors' work," Old Marsh said proudly. "One of the last printed books from the twenty-first century."

Aero appropriated it immediately, sequoias, water herbs, oval capsules and pollinating bees flashing as he tousled the folio.

One speculated why Bo hadn't been sent, with her wealth of resources, practice and insight. But it wasn't the business of interns to probe further. We had the book – it was adequate.

Mars propped his elbows on Cessie's armrest. "I could lend you some materials. For the Regency Ball we cut a lot of cloth. Reckon it might be of use where you're going."

Cessie lit up instantly: "Thanks, yeah, brilliant."

Returning three-quarters of an hour later with wrapped garments, Mars summoned Alexandrina and Fire, who invited Cessie to sew diligently, until the brightness acceded to navy dusk.

At a prompt from Aurora, Magnus waylaid me to discuss mechanics.

"You know what an engine is?" he said courteously.

"We dismantled them for three years in the same workshop," I answered.

He regarded me. "You know they used copper wear to build the machine, twenty years ago? Well, it's about to jack in, but don't let that alarm you." It was clear he would tamper with the device if he could.

"Your car looks older than that," I said cynically, "and it's still running."

"Always look on the sunny side, don't you?" He addressed his Doc Martens. "So... it's vital you punch in the right digits, or you could be stuck in outer space or a foreign era forever. Now that would be a tragedy."

"Why hasn't it been renovated in two decades?" I said.

"We can't afford the money or the power," he said tightly. "Do you know how much it needs to work? It isn't easy to source in an earlier time, so be warned, if you crash."

"Like with the Robots?" I gnashed my teeth. "One blunder or button and they malfunction, right?"

Cessie and Aero scowled at me.

Magnus paused, grimace trembling on speech; yet shook his head. "Exactly," he said.

His false smile roused the sense I were falling, falling from the machine and into orbit, where I would rotate like a planet for infinity.

In the corner Bo unwound her decades' old telescope, onto which she'd added improvements to her kin's previous models.

"I use this to perceive the movements of the planets and stars," she said, stepping aside to let him test it.

Magnus and I paused as Aero examined the sky at a deliberate angle, yelping occasionally when he gauged Pluto or the Red Planet.

After a while, his ridge crumpled before the glass, and he zoomed in. I zeroed in on his view with my microchip, crestfallen to see the shredded ozone layer, meteors in flames more potent than Cupid's bow, the sun sinking on the horizon, debris disembodied. It was dizzying, like watching a fair wheel revolve before a throng.

Inwardly, the quandary rung as to whether the oxygen belts would work, and if we could pass the emptiness alive.

No one but Magnus and I were listening to their low-key interchange. I discerned the woodlouse grating the bannister, endeavouring to be inconspicuous.

"How long have we got?" Aero said faintly; only faeries could've interpreted the query.

"Impossible to say," Bo murmured.

The telescope sagged between them for ten heartbeats.

"Are we all going to die?" he said, miming the inquiry.

"I don't know," she said, "but I fear the work we do – will not be enough."

My gaze scorched the floor. Pearl sought a cosmonaut career, but would there be a planet to launch from in ten, twenty years' time? Time glided like grains of clay, immaterial, unknown. Doomsday prowled behind the raisins in Grandmother Marsh's dough.

"Do you see what my father's up against?" Magnus said in an undertone. "Why he'd risk all those lives?"

I shook my shoulders. "It may save everyone else, but we'll have to die for it."

"What about the honour?" he said evenly.

"I don't fancy being a sacrificial lamb, not even for your father's experiments," I retorted.

We were disturbed by Grandmother Marsh offering tea from her hotpot. More to get away from me than thirst, Magnus accepted a thistle-strewn cup. He spat it into the china an instant later.

"Soy milk!" he said aversely. "I should have known."

The big computer droned with a video message. We gathered, regarding the figure of Dr Stone, fronting us urgently.

"Some news," he said in strained octanes. "The wormhole's closing quicker than we thought. A misjudgement in the Astronomy department." His knuckles cracked. "Ivy Moss, Aero Smith and Cessie Belle will have to report for take-off immediately."

An undercurrent of alarm seeped into the group. Cartwheels pricked my insides.

"Coming?" Aero said to his two friends.

"Cessie?" I said.

"I suppose so." She was white-faced.

Excitement disintegrated like a visualisation.

"Just a second," Grandmother Marsh said, unclicking her bag to divulge a conical, quaint, almond-tinted thermos. "For the historian."

Cessie clasped it. "What for?"

"The journey," Old Marsh said, surprised. "It's conserved cocoa for centuries."

"Why didn't they choose someone experienced?" I said unthinkingly. "We aren't going to make it out of there alive."

"They tried that," Magnus sniped. "He died. Tactics evolve."

"We're not tactics, we're people," I said.

"And plenty more'll die if you don't head to Wolves now," he said.

The manipulation was tiring, but the three of us roamed to the bus stop outside, uncommunicative. Our inbox flooded with directives from our mentor, but we snubbed them.

Aero buried himself in the book to pass the ride, Cessie sewed and I mentally calculated how to operate a time machine.

What had Nadia told us in the lecture last spring? Vague snippets of the plug I'd doodled on Paint was the forefront of my knowledge from that lesson. I'd sat at the back, always, the racket from Magnus' row deafening – how apt his actions had come back to haunt us.

So long as we obeyed the manual, we should survive. My father had been one of the ones who'd drawn it up, twenty years ago. It'd happened in the very same library he was confined to now. He'd been paid a pittance, 'rewarded' with credit and acclaim.

"Flattery doesn't pay the bills," Mum said when the story was recycled.

Even then, I'd itched to govern the gears and vacate this icy civilisation. It was never in my thoughts to heal the sick: escape had stretched like a bridge over a snowy cliff. The idea was suffocating, soul-stealing.

Our mentor stood by the caged silver building, clad in a diamante scarf and jewelled rings, struggling under the bulk of the 500-page guidebook.

"Ah," she said introductorily. "You three, follow me."

Cessie motioned to Aero, and we squeaked across the clean surface, the latter stopping to bid farewell to his mother. She patted his black coils. Pearl was no longer present: there would be no goodbye.

"And you two, be careful," Lydia said to Cessie and I.

We promised, one of us wondering if Pearl would recall her own oath.

Aero was pushed aside as Mr and Mrs Belle sprinted in, the former silver-haired; his wife teased with platinum rinse. They were airy, ethereal, and spun to their corkscrew daughter.

"It's too dangerous," her mother said firmly.

"If Stone had given you more time, it might be different," her father joined in.

"I'll be fine," Cessie said, in a way as inflexible as they were. "There's nothing you can say."

"The killed traveller was a colleague of mine." Cessie's mother was ruby red, as though she had a cold.

"You could be next," Mr Belle said gravely.

"Someone has to go," Cessie said thinly. "Everyone is someone's child."

She wriggled out of their grip. "Let's go," she said to us.

"Are you sure?" Aero stated. "Last chance to change your mind."

She was watery, and could simply nod.

"When will we see our daughter again?" Mrs Belle asked Nadia.

"When she retrieves enough condiments for a return trip," she replied dispassionately.

"I've already lost a husband to this organisation," Lydia said sharply. "I'd better not lose a son."

"We've a communicator in the machine," Nadia said assuredly. "We didn't have access to the technology last time. What happened last time was unfortunate. Your daughter will be one of the first to set foot there in twenty years."

"I'll be in the history books," Cessie said, recovering her merriment. "It'll be worth it."

She kissed them and trailed us to the end of the corridor. Beyond the barrier lay our pitch of the dice, our Queen of Hearts. Nadia coded a password and it swung to admit us. Beneath the textile waited the depths of a burrowed shoot, oxygen belts draped at the orifice. Nadia detached the hooks, and handed over three upper-body suits, weighted with metal, a survival tank no larger than a tiger-fish bowl, and straps to secure ourselves. The suits were clearly intended for a Yeti.

"One at a time," Nadia said. "Smallest first."

I peeped down with a nauseating feeling.

Paralleling the lift shaft from earlier, which seemed a faraway time, it was like a series of nightshades. I was suspended, oxygen belt chained to cabled wires, wiring downwards at the rate of electricity. There was no difference between opening or closing my lids; I merely plummeted like a boulder.

Ouch! My crescent socks whacked into khaki hiker's boots, leather-skinned and abrasive.

"Move – out – of – the – way!"

My best friend Cessie nearly took my neck off – I dived onto a platform, making out tubular wagons in the murk.

"Take – your – own – advice!" Aero careered in the air and almost trod Cessie, who kangarooed to land by me.

"Space boots," she said mistily. "Featured on the cover of *Astro Vogue* September 2218."

"Why're we in a tube station, again?" Aero said breathlessly.

"Didn't you pick up the clue?" Our mentor tutted wryly.

"We were a bit busy," Aero reacted sulkily.

Nadia prised the gridlocked slides open. Lights engulfed the station. "It's not in use," she informed us. "Hasn't been in —"

"— twenty years," I said.

Cessie removed dirt from her boots: "You're scary when you do that."

"Your carriage awaits," Dr Ludwig said, and she could've been the Fairy Godmother.

A three-legged race band, we entered the beaten-in, leaking carriage: fitted with a board of controls, an inactive monitor, a steering pulley and a few seats. Cessie covered the middle seat in her tartan pattern, trialling the hot drinks machine, and filling the flask with frothy hot chocolate. Aero was adjacent to the triangular window, where deepness loomed. Sheathed in plastic, he lowered the hardback onto the tottery bench. Nadia gestured to the anterior seat – where the captain sat.

Quaking, I forced myself onto the high seat, within reach of the shimmering buttons. One read "Catapult", another "Emergency", another "Eagle", and another "Exeunt".

"Don't be alarmed," Nadia said serenely. "You've seen the diagram a thousand times."

She could second that. The sirens already sounded in my imagination. The catapult button was itching to be pressed, if it wasn't illegal. Pleasure seemed to be unlawful in this establishment. Even as death loitered in the café, the hospitals and our own timelines, it was difficult not to feel the buzz.

The mentor read my expression. "Many have driven themselves to distraction to trade places with you, but few've succeeded," she said. "To qualify as Intermediary Travellers – three in a million manage this feat – you face grave danger. Lethal predators rule the landscape, and you'll fall to the bottom of the food chain."

We were beady as we consumed the counsel.

"I'll have to impart some wisdom," she said, crunching a stray apple. "One, hide the machine. Two, *never* travel at night. Three, I will intermittently be in contact with you via the Video Link, but we can't continually spare the power. We have Robots to run, cafeterias to light, hospitals to cater for. You can reach each other via microchip, but not as far ahead as the twenty-third century."

Nadia mustered her stamina. "Ivy, you must correctly wire the contraption, stamp the 'Eagle' button and steer the controls. A skilled engineer should be up to the task. Cessie, a historian's role is to punch in the digits that will fire you to the exact age and location gifted by the wormhole. Your comrade Aero must monitor outer space for signs of imminent meteors, planets and obstacles. I remind you that patients will succumb to the pathogen resistance if you fail." She binned the fruit core. "One more thing. We're strict about the numbers down here as the machine can't take much weight. So no plus-ones." She eyed Cessie's slight appearance. "Perhaps that's just as well. I'm too old for such adventures."

"Did you ever go?" I said frankly.

46

"Just once," she said, and a flitting smile dissolved her years. "But never again. Farewell, Ivy, Aero and Cessie. It seems a twinkle away when you were undergraduates."

Her advice still whistling, she vanished.

I perched on the front booth, Cessie nursing the thermos on her plaid seat: Aero sealing the glass-panelled, sheltered window.

"I wonder," he mused, "could we get plants in there?"

Cessie unscrewed it. "Maybe." A frown emerged. "Say I get the numeracy wrong; blast us into inner space?"

"Then we'll have great exploits," I said laxly.

Aero poked the flask. "It looks decent. But the Marshes might have something to say if we ruin it."

"Weird Bo's never been," I voiced. "People say she was already a late-comer, and this was her fifth failure."

"'Tis the pressure," Aero said solicitously. "You can have all the knowledge in the world, and not like to compete. If I were in Magnus' team I'd try to fail, too."

We smirked.

"You heard Nadia," Aero said. "There'll be a second chance."

"And a third, and a hundredth," Cessie said meanly.

The name embossed on the machine jarred me: *The Mary Anning*. The weeds and grains of the beach rushed my veins, and my father's yarn ghosted. I'd been eight, and my parents had shuttled me to our holiday home before Pearl's birth. They said they'd needed a little more time. The engraved limpets, shiny pearls and whorled seashells had sunk my bucket when Dad had relayed a tale that had stuck, like cream.

"There was a little girl just like you," he'd narrated, "in a different century. Mary Anning. She spawned from a family of fossil-hunters. Sadly, when she expressed her data and findings, others would take credit for her work, as she was a woman in the wrong time. Locals branded her a drunk. When she fell ill, her discoveries were forgotten. That's why I'm telling you."

"Why did she get sick?" I'd asked.

"Because there are some things even very clever scientists can't cure," he'd said.

Aero disordered my reverie. "Ivy, we have to go now. From the mini-scope, the wormhole seals in fifteen."

I squatted to examine the intricate wires. They were lavender, crimson and periwinkle: almost toys to be inserted at will. Shearing one from the wall, my finger was electrocuted. Familiar with the tremoring impression, I inspected the welt. If it ached, it meant the person was conscious enough to function. That's what Mum said, and she'd tasted toxic mushrooms, irrefutable herbs, and contracted viruses abroad. She rarely came back.

"To be robotised here?" She'd said on one occasion. "No bloody way."

"Are you OK?" Aero and Cessie unified.

"Sure." Cursing, I prised rubber gloves from the shelf, having spotted them, and tore a colourful wire from the unit. Red and blue made purple; red on its own would disconnect.

I mixed green with violet and a spark banged across the room. Cessie and Aero bobbed to avoid injury.

"I've changed my mind," Aero said heatedly. "I'd rather have Magnus."

"He isn't that bad," Cessie chimed.

"He's repulsive," I said incredulously.

My fingers darted one layer over the next, crossing lines experimentally. A pump was wedged, squeezing palls of verve, about to give up the ghost. It beat like a muscle, thudding tentatively from one breath to the next. The wires clustered like sweets, ophidians crisscrossing in my grip. The burden to act was a skull before a death, a flaccid sword. If only seconds could be bartered instead of credits.

Inspiration struck and I nudged two stimuluses, fusing carnation yellow and fuchsia. They sparkled, comelier than fireworks. The cords betrayed no rip, ridge or stain. It wasn't taxing to tailor one to the other with surveyance of the manual, which modelled an intersected circuit, prescribed in complex lines. Following orders had never been a strong suit of mine, but lives were at stake. Spirit fluxed and my index intertwined the dots, currents waving in the latex. Hope overpowered anguish as the Controls gleamed, one by one, as if Christmas candles in firs, and the super-computer received me.

"Hello, adventurer," it said luminously. "Vocalise the Captain's name into the microphone."

Hesitant before the android, the name "Ivy Moss" was compelled into the screen.

"Commander," the computer continued, "select one of the settings."

"The buttons," Cessie said quickly.

Aero jammed the "Eagle" option. The machine gunned, preparing for airlift.

"Where would you like to travel today?" the voice said.

Cessie thought for a split second. She typed: **Earth, 66.8 million years ago, Hell's Creek Formation, North America, midday**.

The computer considered the information: "Permission granted."

"Does this mean — ?" Aero said haltingly.

Cessie's thermos was bumped as we bopped in triumph.

"We're heading to the dinosaur age!" I said triumphantly.

The steers stood in front and I thrust them, horizontal, sending the tube hurtling down the tunnel. The crackling was stifled by our whoops. It seemed to race faster and faster until Cessie yelled to disconnect the carriage from the others.

How did you divide such a bulky instrument?

On Aero's shoulders I drooped from the window, equipped with a magnet-sized cable. As we sped down the passage, I knifed the oxidised chains, and was halfway through when we touched the end.

"Quick!" Aero said into my oxygen belt. "Harder."

Collecting strength, I hacked the bundle of wires, sawing into steel, until it gave a great groan and flew backwards into the tunnel. We had moments.

I leapt from Aero's collarbone and found myself in the Captain's seat, thumped the steering forwards and issued a titanic heave. The compartment rose up, up, up until the passage was no longer visible, and we were drunk in the blackness.

The bodysuits radiated with potent particles as we powered to space, round window illuminating hunks of rock, ubiquitous stars and the rotund solar system. The Earth was a bluish fenland below, a speck as the illusory Milky Way flew us to extinct lands, sightseers of the cosmos.

Chapter Four: Hell's Creek

The wagon rattled in space, condensation sullying Aero's outlook, harmonising with the aureoles around orbs, before wavering and plunging in wobbly motions.

Black acceded to aqua and we swivelled, Cessie slopping her cocoa. We free fell onto stony terrain forested by trees, uncannily remote, plush and fruitful. After a *whack* it was immobile.

Aero demystified the glass and we clambered to peer at ficus woods; glittering with magnolia shoots, sassafras and bristly laurels. Drips leaked the machine: we were besieged by running, shallow seas, lapping turtles and salamanders: preyed on by winged, leathery pterosaurs, pelican-like and transient as film.

"If we don't move this," Aero said unsteadily, "the water will interfere with the electrics."

"But it's so lovely," Cessie said, thorny nose pressed on the sill. "I don't want to go."

"You heard Magnus," our friend said, forcing the barricaded exit. "'Tis a job."

"Forgotten this?" Cessie said smugly, flaunting cotton outfits. "You won't survive the Cretaceous clime in an oxygen suit."

Blushing, Aero retreated to change while I swapped the blistering suit for the white attire, grinning as a sun hat was wedged over my chestnut ponytail.

"Accounting for birds, there're no predators," Aero observed. "We should go, before they scent fresh meat."

The communicator silent as a corpse and patters gradually drowning the machine, we ventured outdoors, ankle-deep in water, and were bathed in a sultry sauna of sunshine.

The mountainous landscape was peculiarly flat and unsheltered, dense rock cemented and cutting our canvas wear, a kaleidoscope of reefs beautifying the chalk.

We debated where to transfer the machine.

"We'll bury it," Cessie said baldly. "They used to hide bodies. Daddy —"

"We get it," Aero said gruffly. "Ivy —the bottom, I'll shift the front, and Cessie the centre."

A corpus of arms, we tackled the fifty-ton car, breaking every few minutes, soreness swelling, sturdier than heavy-weights, enduring the wails of the engine. The rising carbon dioxide wore us out, but Aero posited we would get used to it.

"I inhaled more carbon monoxide from Mum's boiler," he said acidly. "You know what you signed up for."

"Actually, we didn't," I said red-facedly, pushing with a wheeze. "We were thrown to the wolves."

Cessie looked over her shoulders. "She's right; we'd no idea what we were walking into."

We halted in the soiled underbrush, which birthed new buds. Cessie and I were ready to tip it in the mud, but Aero exclaimed:

"We don't want to bury it – we want to *conceal* it. Start hoeing."

Wielding one of his trainers, he forked the ground and a miniature crater was created. Cessie staggered with her end, scraps of metal clunking her toe. Without further ado Aero and I dumped it sidelong, and Cessie showered ginkgoes over the mechanism until it was camouflaged. My scientist friend lined it with lavender clovers to dissuade explorers.

Aero and Cessie relaxed, but I nagged:

"We should begin hunting useful plants. Lives depend on us." I visualised hangers hinging on a terrace, one push cluttering them like skeletons.

They grumbled, realising opposition was in vain.

For a spell we scuffed the undergrowth, snakes weaving vividly as piano keys, coldblooded teeth nipping translucent socks (premeditated as a form of bandage.) Tall, stark monkey-puzzles stretched like arms, pencilled in moss; dwarfing the cinnamon species, scrubbing pinecones and florets dipped in carmine and almond. Aero waited by the copious thirty-five-metre araucaria, eyeballing jaundiced bark.

"Ivy, Cess, one of us will have to clamber up there," he said.

"All I see are pines," Cessie said bewilderedly.

"He wants edible seeds and the medicinal wood," I said learnedly – after all, how frequently had he bored on about them?

"Top marks," he said humourlessly. "Taking a leaf from Nadia's manual, I reckon the lightest should do it."

The prehistoric branches jangled supplely, startlingly brittle. A branch snapped and was gulped by a monstrous hole, evidencing this advice.

Seeing me pause expectantly, Cessie coolly remarked: "What're you waiting for? You're the shortest, so you weigh the least."

"It's almost forty feet," I said, equally as icily. "I'll be killed."

"The funeral will be spectacular," Aero said. "We'll erect a statue in your name. Magnus can sculpt your old nickname: P-o-i-s-o-n I-v-y."

"Go to hell," I said waspishly.

"I'm in it." My friend extended his arms. "Welcome to Hell's Creek."

I scaled the evergreens, knobbly-kneed, and printed a small sole in a wasted knob. Powerful but ancient even in this time, it could snap any second. Cessie supplied a muddied rod.

Hiking leisurely, it was pleasurable to discern bee droves, birds flailing, hispine beetles habituating the crevices. I whittled new place-holds as I mounted; bile rising at the breadth and peak. Soil from the stick embedded my palm, messier than a child's handprint, but serenity glazed the air.

Aaaah! The greased hand slipped, almost scalping me as hairs trapped prickly needles.

"Hold fast!" Aero shouted. "You can't give up now!"

Bones ached to surrender to gruesome death, strands sacrificed to the pit. Cushioning my body in hardwood, I gripped a half-cut branch, swinging above, ferreting onto the tough pillow. One dirtied nail cleaned the rod, grasp recovered. Cessie breathed in relief.

The branch shook from side to side, imparting restful music. Half-ripped, it was the penultimate, and seeds tempted like bonbons.

"Brilliant," Aero cheered. "You're a mountaineer."

Pride swum finer than a robin's velvet pelt. I picked three-centimetre, almond-sized kernels, storing them in Cessie's combat. They were nutty, harbouring the aroma of winter, bracing for the mammoth task. Dozens amassed by the time of Cessie's screech.

Far below an armoured, seven-foot, six-ton dinosaur hammered the bush with its broad, flat skull. Leaden antlers shredded Cessie's sleeves and she buckled into Aero.

"It's alright," he said blissfully, "it's an ankylosaur. She's after foliage."

"She's going to kill us," she shrieked.

On all fours, it skulked nearer, worming its silvery, clubbed tail. Its sinuses flared and it reared into the tree, scattering several branches. Its beak browsed pods and shoots. Aero was misty as he saved the feats on his microchip.

"Ivy," he called suddenly. "Tap the tree – the resin is useful."

"I'm busy." The tone was bitterly sarcastic. "Being bludgeoned!"

"Do it," he said. "We need it badly."

Sighing, I appropriated the stick, tapping the firs. Slimy liquid oozed. Thinking hard, I used a sock, seeping minerals inside, and tied it with a hairband.

"You need more," Aero said urgently. "The Burns Unit's dying. I've mixed every plant and nothing works."

Cessie whined: "I don't care what's a herbivore and what's not. Let's clear out."

Andy – Aero's pet name – retreated to vaunt files of leaf-shaped choppers, feasting fruits. The rest bite was all required to incise the bark, organs pounding, and tip substances. The ceasefire spanned a moth's life cycle, and we were soon assailed by bumps.

Andy's stout, plated physique was ridged with bones ringing its neck. Grunts escaped the snout. It was akin to swords on a giant tortoise; mad, bad and perilous.

It sliced Cessie's elbow as it charged, ensnared by the present of edible fodder. It was as though the great-bellied beast hadn't eaten in millennia.

Its horns swung headfirst, seeds pelting my friends' heads, and fractured the evergreens.

"Oh no." I was horror struck.

The bark split midway, the crack roving upwards. It was worth cupping healers in the sock, forfeiting the prize of freedom.

The skyscraper dithered, branches breaking one by one: they could've been my mum when she won Monopoly, disarming bamboozled players.

My eyelids bolted.

Similar to riding foot-jets, it wasn't petrifying to skate south, snowing further and further to the ground. Perhaps they would find me putrid in the dirt, primed with medicines and seeds, contorted in an infinite slumber.

Boom.

A crash drove me to a parcel of sticks, multitudes framing the underwood, punching the T-shirt; russet-leaved bracken blinding daylight, assembled as an open-air hideaway, width spanning miles. Bracelets of mesh netted me in dirt, a dragonfly in a web. My crinkly, silt-tinted waves melded with organic browns, greens and yellows. Citrusy perfume wafted and fearfully my eyelashes flickered. In my clasp were luminous ivory petals, taut on a timbre tablet. Radiance illumined the whorls, and a cry ricocheted. Around, glossy, bulb-shaped eggs nestled in the mud and the penny dropped.

This was not death or the ground. It was a huge mud home occupied by juvenile dinosaurs. Mire covered my clothes, my face. It was as though I was the baby, retaining the magnolia as one would a rattle.

A split moment later the central egg rolled, howling issuing from inside. A lungful of air washed over. The egg petered, silent, and fractured into fifty pieces.

A down of feathers fluffed its bony peony skull, fluffed tail rotating. Meagre legs kicked in the silence, gummy beak familiarising with sounds. It was a diminutive monster, born in the haze and heat of a forgotten afternoon.

Rumbles groused my gut. The bloodied creature gifted its eggshell, gooey as the slime in Nadia's office, oval as Pearl's face, lucent as Magnus' teeth. Inhuman, gluttonous fists brought the sustenance to my lips, and the chomp of skin penetrated the habitat.

My satiated belly swelled, rounder than an egg, gurgling guiltily. Thoughts of what friends would say came and fell, transient as snowflakes, but I borrowed in my igloo, in the land time bypassed.

Ranks of eggs incubated, not your usual Easter variety.

My downy friend squawked, twittering, a wingless bird, and an instinct awoke.

Dreamlessly I saved the inimitable, rare nest home on Microchip video, editing myself out. The striking dino-bird, in its crimson and auburn inks, was more spectacular than autumnal leaves. I hadn't entered a dying realm but a place incarnate, an exhibit of fireworks.

A three-metre silhouette cast the midday beam in shadows.

My heart ptt-ptted, robust as a steam train, and the air diffused as a sparkler when its final flame slices the night, populated with my yawps.

Plumed in emerald and cobalt like a jay feather, the infant's relations towered the saplings, marked crests imbedded in scrawny trunks; meaty thighs poised to strike. Analogous to a five-hundred-pound overgrown chicken, its crown considered me, raising its bowed claws, elongated tail swishing like an iguana or a rattle snake before it lashes.

One could not blame its fumes at a visitor, grotty with its baby's broken shell; perched in a robbed crib, glugging an alien tongue.

Its curved snout sung back, and I hoped for a reprieve, when a circle of ostrich-like brothers and sisters lunged from the gloom. It was judge, jury and executioner.

I sprinted from the muddied cot, staggering on shoestrings, the baby nipping my heels while its parents careened their ballerina necks to hunt me.

Holding the magnolia amulet, I darted in a bob of trees, but human feet couldn't outrun archaic athletes, and one belted its tufted limb across my cheek. A cut welled in a jagged streak. I nursed the bleeding gash but it was futile. An arm bashed me into a tree, and the calling family enclosed like Caesar's senate.

A flag of milk-white fabric streamed, and a dark golden coronet stormed the scene, flesh and bone, not rubber pincers, rippling the cloth cyclically. Monster and human were mesmerised by the flares. The wave transformed upstream, and the dinosaurs cantered in a stupor: leaving my principal torturers, Mum and Dad, to secrete foul odours down me.

"What happened?" Cessie said as I dared look upwards, into the ochre stare of my best friend.

"Ran – afoul – of – crazed – birds." I wiped the trickle from my cheek. "I could ask you the same question."

Cessie was jumbled in bracken, petals and nuts; thin jersey removed, bare in her beige T-shirt, where a slash disordered the cotton.

"Andy charged us." She shook herself disbelievingly. "Aero and I – we didn't hear you fall, so we were searching. The beast hackled its horns and chased us. I just escaped. We heard you scream, and Aero diverted Andy by speaking its language —"

"Typical," I said, cringing from the animals.

"Yes, so I found you, and the only thing I could think of was to take this off." She gestured the article. "I thought of bulls and you know the rest."

"Ah," I said apprehensively, "we're not out of the woods yet." This had the rare stroke of being factual as well as symbolic.

"They're *transfixed* by you," my friend mulled. "What did you do?"

The parents inflated their speckled quills, black gaze firing with fury. One claw spiked my shoulder into the tree as they prodded me, again and again.

"Parachuted in a giant nest," I said. "Mr and Mrs weren't there. There was a huddle of warming eggs and one burst. The baby gifted its shell to eat. I was starving. After I videoed it, they returned, took one look at me and called their relatives. I bolted but they're super-fast."

The talons dug in excruciatingly.

Cessie reeled the cloth and they eyed its progress, sweltering in a bed of fur. When she lobbed it, Frisbee-style, they crashed in the brushwood, trees caving in their wake, until only a flutter of hairs lingered.

I breathed out. "T-thanks."

"'S'OK," she said warmly. "You got the loot, didn't you?"

"In the socks in the combat." I patted the bulge to certify it was there. "It was worth it."

An immense roar thudded, deep in the forest. We whipped round.

Frontwards as if a zombie, Aero's honeyed complexion bore violet grazes, knees hurtling to avoid the advance of flinty horns, endeavouring to propel his top in its antlers. We didn't need his holler to run, and scurried further into the green space, torn in the hinds by the hail of its stampedes.

"Dead-end," Aero said hollowly.

We reached a cul-de-sac of mudstone, piled on top of one another in minuscule cliffs.

"We have to climb it," I said bluntly as the trucked lizard bulked into view.

"Ivy," Aero said warily, "I am glad you're alive."

"There'll be time for a reunion later." Cessie towed my sleeve.

We pounded the rocks, stones soaring in our flurry, the turquoise sky roasting our rears, skidding from roof to roof, jumping and diving to the top. Cessie's trainer snagged the bladed fangs of the fiend —

"Take it off." My foot pressed her curls. "Get rid of the shoe —"

Cessie unbuckled the fancy ties, collarbones juddering under my plimsoll, but they were fastened with sweat, soil and sap. Snot dripped with her sniffs.

"I always said your parents would be the death of you," Aero said, by now at the summit, urging her to rip the laces.

Cessie and I tore the shoe, me one-armed to retain my grip and the apricot soles took the bellied creature with it, thundering on the rocks. I heaved our bodies onto the top, and we descended, weeping.

We rasped on the myrtle mounds, mute, boiling.

"Water," Aero said out of the blue. "We need water."

"Trail the mud." I was subdued, nails implanting the desert.

They followed my track, falling into each other: puce and liverish. The dirt escorted us to whirling pools, lapping currents some feet downhill; garlanded by aquatic pads, which Aero labelled *pistia*.

Bending forwards, my comrades played the clip of the nest, and the name of my pursuers was at last uttered:

"Anzu wyliei," Aero said, whistling. "What did the plume look like up close?"

"Like a rainbow duster," I recanted, memories scrambling with the terror of the episode. "If they hadn't been trying to rip me limb from limb, they'd have been exquisite."

"You saw an egg hatch," Aero said smilingly. "I wish I'd fallen into the nest."

"You should've done your own dirty work," I said acidly.

He took that onboard.

"The *Anzu* name originates from ancient Sumer mythology," Cessie said. "Means feathered demon."

"Or the turkey from hell," Aero said wittily.

"You can say that again." I nodded vigorously.

"'Tis like a bird," he said melodically. "That proves the dino-bird link."

My fair-haired friend sighed. "Goodwin's always boring on about dinosaurs and birds and archaeology records, all the boring units I didn't revise in uni."

"Stone almost forced you to repeat," Aero said lowly. "It was Goodwin who stepped in, vouched for you in all other areas."

"Stupid Stone took the course," Cessie said, and I couldn't tell if it was tears from the rock climb or the recollection that welled. She swabbed them with her T-shirt. "I wasn't even a science student. He balled me out in front of the whole seminar —"

"*Cessie Belle, did you even take notes on the Cretaceous epoch?*" Aero parroted their customary ritual.

"*No, sir, I thought it was ancient history,*" Cessie recited the infamous words.

"You were bottom of the class for a term," I remembered wonderingly.

"He showed the lower levels my third class paper," she said, tearful. "For a horrible semester he hinted I'd have to repeat."

"You got a good pass," I said reassuringly.

"It should've been a first." She sounded vengeful. "That was Stone's fault."

"He was in lecture mode," Aero said thoughtfully, "he's an alright bloke."

"He's not a robot," I said irately. "He's perfectly in control of himself."

"It was my fault." Cessie traversed her arms, the waves cooling her rogued texture.

"And that son of his," I said bitingly, "strutting around like King of the Lecture Room, drowning out Nadia…"

"Don't," Cess said evenly. She wavered in the blaze overhead. "Mag – Magnus spoke to his dad about me. Persuaded him to let me continue the course. He was really sweet. If it hadn't been for him I wouldn't be interning now —"

"—or nearly speared," Aero interposed, watching the play of sentiments in our faces.

However, I wouldn't be deterred. "He ambushed Pearl and I yesterday."

"That again," she said resignedly. "For the fourth time, there's no proof."

Her discourse smarted.

"He's rotten like his father; always has been," I shrieked. "It's pathetic you defend him."

"What's pathetic," she capered backwards, bumping the sediments behind, "is your eighteen-year grudge against a peer who made childish blunders."

Too preoccupied to notice her shoeless foot wobble on the rock face, I ploughed on, scarlet. "He's a bully who bought his way into Wolves," I said righteously. "Why do you always *close ranks*?"

"Because that's what friends do," she spat. "You'd know if you knew how to make any."

It ruptured between us like a whip severing a quarry.

"We're here for the water." Aero raised his hands tactfully. "If we could…"

We paid no more attention to him than the beetle under the stone.

"What has he got over you?" I said shrilly. "What're you covering up?"

Jolting as if electrocuted, my best friend misstepped, lethargic in her heatstroke, sock ensnaring the sandstone as a nail in a frame. Her spine arched, arms outspread, and a *squelch* announced the halt in her descent.

Aero rushed to the cliff edge, whereas I was rapt, rooted to the slab of earth. The quarrel droned in my ears… I was sure I'd been inches from the truth, to why she'd forgiven his misdeeds and meanders over the years…

"Cessie!" Aero said wildly. "Swim!"

The surfs gurgled in swamped gyration, spitting seaweed and crab fish.

Finally, my trainers hobbled to the brink, half-afraid to look, scrabbling at the gritted pebbles. Red oozed like the blood sluicing my planes.

At first, only foams dribbled the shore, sweeping tiny ammonites, corals and clay. In the suspense we thumped our hands on the sandy shale. Suds dipped the surface and what appeared to be blonde seaweed trailed: a striped sock was regurgitated.

My index held my jawline.

Pistachio-sized pupils rose in the river, blank as a netted tuna fish, before they revived, and she was waist-deep but alive.

"It must be freezing," Aero said fretfully.

She jerked her straw tresses. "No." She gulped salt water. "Tropical — it's hot."

"We thought you'd drowned," I said madly.

"Don't be silly." She snorted soapy bubbles. She pointed to the seething underworld. "You have to see what's down there. It's a magical palace – I wasn't drowning – I was *diving*."

"I'll save my worry next time," Aero said resentfully, positioning himself to abseil from the rocks. "Get out the way!"

He somersaulted and was subsumed in a bellow of squelches.

They explored underwater grottoes before beseeching me to join.

I scrutinised the swirling hues of cotton pink, cyan and lilac, and vacillated. "I don't know about this. I've never dived."

"You'll catch on." Cessie jiggled encouragingly. "One small step…"

I scrolled my damp trousers, flung my sun hat and sprung on my heels.

Everything was blue-black as my eyes clammed shut and my being flipped into the lake. It rippled, broiling, and I was aerial on the tip of the creamed green surfs.

Cessie towed me under and I held my snuffles; my microchip transitioned to an imperceptible diver's mask.

"Look," she mimed, dispersing the sea.

As though summoned, sea slugs vied for saltwater mussels, rounded as inked oysters, filmed on our chips. Octopuses unwound their tentacles to nourish seaweed, gaping mouths blowing suds. Even they had a reptilian feel; raw and tough as workers' gloves, coated crimson. A heavy mantle of skin streamlined past, disorienting, clad in a neck that would've made swans cry; four metres of flabby, murky sinews, asymmetrical form unsettling. Its small, jagged teeth scalped scallops.

"A plesiosaur," Aero said in wonder. "Brute of the seas."

"Just as long as it doesn't prey on humans," I said, disenchanted.

"Don't startle it and you'll be fine," he said, eyes flashing with tape. "How would you fancy being a gorilla in a zoo? This is its zone. Stone says we have to respect that."

"Oh, if Stone says," I said querulously.

Cessie's mystic grin disappeared, and I didn't say any more. It didn't seem right, after my best friend had nearly tumbled to a watery fate.

In our heatedness, we failed to spy the craggy vertebrae of an alligator. Its jungle skin was vast and hanging in primordial glory. The wide jaw fissured to divulge latex-painted, gluey molars, cutting a beeline for us.

Aero flapped feebly, reddening as it prepared to swig us down, and Cessie motioned to us to swim.

"I can't," I said anxiously. "I never could, you know that."

"You'll have to learn," she mouthed. "Or we'll be eaten."

Cheered by that nugget of advice, my muscles motorised frantically. However, the sea monster was yards behind, immense tongue solid as frozen jelly; Medusa-eyed, muscular.

My hands formed a pyramid shape as I contorted and twisted past peachy squids, sword-featured cuttlefish and twirl-shelled nautiluses, glugging water like a shark. I hadn't swum before but my self powered swifter than a speedboat, Aero and Cessie afloat.

Rays lit the navy waters, glittering like New Year lanterns, radiating stings. The ocular music crooked the alligator's path, and it lumbered towards it: tremulous and astray.

We circuited the living lochs, Aero and Cessie abetting my last lap as we bounded to arid sand. Aero stored the videos in the microchip database – of course he'd rendered the gator the star of the chronicle, sea life animating the screen.

"I'm famished," Aero and Cessie said mutually.

They were sallow.

Unsteadily, I hoarded wood, slashes of rubber, bands and granite to fashion a utensil, and the latter two fished uneasily. We champed angelfish and squid for tea.

Aero ignited hunks of the magnolia block and Cessie collected water in her cleansed thermos, which we purified on the bonfire. I chewed stray nut seeds, sharing the stack. We faced the dimming melon light, sandbank bolstering our swollen backs, magenta winkles radiant in dew. Cessie chalked me in the Anzu nest, bole-coloured knots clipped with twigs, new-born waddling from its shell, and a nightmare posse of Anzus shocking me from the nest.

"We should visit Wolves tomorrow," Aero said resolutely.

"Do you think... Dr Stone will see I'm aware of natural history now?" Cessie asked sadly.

"They might assume it was all Aero, him being a scientist," I said morosely. "I suppose they'll think I did the time machine, the tools and the storage. They might think you recorded the proof."

Cessie's belly button bronzed in the sun. "I don't want to go back," she said. "I think... I'm tougher here, without the naysayers. Dinosaurs don't mind if you're filthy rich."

But the idea of returning bloomed like a parasite in a mollusc, evolving to a pearl, and reality seemed sweeter than the reef city flourishing ahead.

"We have to go back," I echoed Aero. "The hospital's counting on us. Pearl —"

"Sorry," Cessie said, softer than silk. "I forgot."

Aero hooted: "Mum will be going spare."

Cessie's white incisors were flecked with berries. "I'll prove them wrong, Mum and Dad. They won't have any qualms if they see the reels."

"I don't know where my mum is." I watched a shamrock turtle totter to land.

"Maybe she's found a cure," Aero said hopefully.

The turtle interred progeny in the gold granules.

"In thirty years of looking?" My answer was tinged with regret.

Cessie squeezed me. "Not on her own. But with our herbs it might heal them."

"You hope too much," I said.

"You don't hope enough," Cessie said.

The truth of her statement curved like the prismatic blaze.

Hours passed. We were as soporific as the sleepers in the sea, dusk acquiescing to alabaster cloudland.

Chapter Five: Lab Rats

The murkiness had a butterfly moment, converting to the irises and teals of Earth. A three, we clenched the controls board, flying into steel, two-sided buttons and steering brakes. My thumb fixed on the handbrake and we rode into the tunnels at the rapidity of bats, slugging to a stop. A deafening shudder preceded the hush.

Aero examined the carriage sill. "No Nadia?"

"We gave no word we were arriving," I said, gathering breath.

"We'll surprise them," Cessie said in a wheel of smiles. "It doesn't matter about an absolute cure – this'll help."

We picked through the platform and wires, inserting our suits, riding to the artificial lights. Spinning in our path, a plate-laden robot requested our IDs. We were scanned instantly, approved as employees and directed to the labs. We hovered awkwardly, waiting to present our plunder. It wasn't one of those scenes on TV when streets of parties hail your return. The lit corridor swum in and out of vantage point as my fatigued eyelids closed.

Aero raised a bruised fist to knock when murmurs flew from the doorway:

"I can handle it."

Bo's muffled protest.

"You fuss and dither under minor pressure," Stone snapped. "Younger and better colleagues are doing the job now."

We mottled.

"Wormholes to the dinosaur age hardly ever crop up." She was strained. "You swore to Gran this time would be different. You said I was next."

Professor Stone switched the microscopic slides, his back to a diagram of a stick insect's anatomy. "There are times in life when we must make way for new blood."

"Ten years at the Unit and I've never even travelled five years back." A sob stuck her retort.

"You would've done," he said, looking down his nose at her severely, "had you succeeded."

"The selection's outdated," she said sulkily. "It only tests reactions and brawn. I could diagnose the landscape and commune with animals."

Dr Stone tapped the spindly leg of the insect. "Reflexes are the difference between life and death. You're still a foolish girl. I've seen things that would send you scurrying to resignation. I've seen friends die."

"That was a different time." Bo had recovered her reflective tone. "That wouldn't happen in a group."

"We're trialling them, but they're completely inexperienced," he said. "Yet they won fair and square. We had to give them the opportunity. You understand. I'm not sure they could cope with someone they don't know particularly well."

"They'd get to know me along the way," she said.

"Sorry, Bo, there's always next year." He wrinkled his hooked nose.

His subordinate's posture slumped.

Aero pushed the agape door and they leapt, scattering slides. The lime glass gleamed, bearing the image of our worn visages.

"What in the blazes are you three doing here?" he said hostilely. "I made it clear not to return unless necessary."

Aero swilled the leaf-ridden thermos, I held the magnolia chunks tighter and Cessie reran the microchip film.

"Don't concern yourselves with his mood." Bo's tawny bob screened her tears. "What've you got?"

Aero was the double of a flamingo. His pinkie rinsed the herbs in the sink, bathing the dirt and cautiously bottling liquid. Images of oozing silt and scraped hands rose like the brewing smoke from Bo's cauldron.

"We – we retrieved Araucaria resin," he stammered. "I-Ivy found magnolia bark – it's a long story – and Cessie discovered incredible reef life."

Perhaps it was the luminosity: but wistfulness smothered in Bo's eyes.

She confiscated the mixture at once, pouring it into the stewing pot.

"Perfect," she said to the levitating vapours. "With the electrics, burns and shocks are surprisingly common. Robots from two hundred homes have reported casualties."

Aero trundled to scrutinise the cure. Bo passed him a lollipop-sized stick, though twice the breadth, and they stirred until pine odours clouded them.

"Ivy," Dr Stone said kindly, watching me hang from the action, "what's that you have there?"

A sugar lump stifled my speech. "M-magnolia." I displayed the wood. "I've got bits of bark, oils and leaves."

His glasses scrunched pensively as he took me in. "The honokiol has been proven to reduce damage from pathogens. A good find."

"Tested by rats." I could not see Bo; only hear her over the palls of mist, whisking the fluid.

Dr Stone readjusted his spectacles apologetically. "Bo's held back by her fixation on animal welfare. How could I send an employee who couldn't eat the tundra?"

"I could've survived." The volume rose like the fog. "Besides, it's only for a few days."

"My wife runs an airtight health and safety scheme, as you're aware," Dr Stone uttered. "You wouldn't slip through the net."

The fish latticed yesterday, bloodied and listless, lingered unpleasantly.

"Nadia believes in second chances," Bo persisted. "I don't have to be the speediest to be of help."

"Further to that, you are alarmingly prone to mishaps," he raged.

Bo's barn owl strands swathed her nape as she hung her head, the potion bubbling merrily. Stone strode over and yanked the stirrer from Aero with a thirst in his goggles, and black residue lathered from the smoke.

"If the solution's mixed correctly, it'll restore millions."

The phrase darkened my psyche. *Restore...* it was an abnormal way of saying it.

"How do you know it will work?" posited Aero, ghoulish in the steam.

"I don't," he said chillingly. "I have an experiment up my sleeve. Human guinea pigs – volunteers, refugees, the poor – will trial it for a fee."

Nausea tingled my abs.

"But you don't know what the effects will be," Bo said. "Some of the oils and saps are really strong."

Fervour flitted from the foggy worktop.

"I'll infect them first," he said hazily. "That way we can gauge if the fluids work: there's no pre-empting the results."

"You can't do that," Aero said darkly.

"There's no such thing as a free pay cheque, Mr Smith," Stone said steadily. "As with rats, sometimes you must tinker with the unknown to do great things."

The concept of queues of gullible, strait-laced, destitute volunteers was repulsive, a reptile's black tongue as it chomps the fruit fly. What sort of institution was I contracted to, and what horrors enlightened Dr Stone's laboratory?

I cleared my splutter. "Sir, that wouldn't be right. Using human bodies as speculative *toys*. The press will scandalise us for exploitation."

"We can't use human beings," Cessie chipped in with a quaver.

Dr Stone's specs travelled down his nasal bridge. "I want the whole world to know so as to snare as many volunteers as possible." He polished sheen from his frames. "What is necessary isn't always easy. As you climb this organisation, that will dawn on you."

"They wouldn't actually die, would they?" Aero said anxiously.

"Merely get sick and well again, with the marvels of our medicine."

The fumes detonated in a storm of cinders and mauve liquid spurted like a blue whale.

"Excuse me," Dr Stone said, creasing his sleeves. He swirled the potion until it thickened, oily smoke distilling, lucidity sieving the spots. "Science is a complex field I don't expect a historian or engineer to grasp. Aero here understands, don't you, young man?"

Aero was fixed on the multihued dots on his leader's bow tie. "If they consent, I can't see how we'll stop them." He ducked from our sight, redness permeating his twists of hair.

Dr Stone clunked his muscled shoulder blades. "That's the spirit. Someone has to be the bull in the arena, so to speak. Our Lab department are people, too. Would you rather they forfeited their wellbeing before their vital work's evident?"

I imagined factories and factories of Santa's little elves, concocting bottle after bottle, sending them down the chute, labelled "Mary" or "Sam" or "Jane" or "Henry".

Bo reacted in alarm as a concentration of solution burnt her thumb.

"We have to cool this down," Aero said sagely, as she pranced on tiptoes to rectify the swelling under the "Burns" tap. "Good job we got that resin."

He didn't add I'd scarcely avoided the Grim Reaper to obtain the fluids. How many credits was one disobedient employee worth anyway?

"I suggest you pay a visit to the Media department to upload your videos and provide a feature for Ms Thorn's rag," Stone said severely. "My scientists require peace and quiet."

The inference we were hindering them, like clogged drains, flowed in my arteries.

We zigzagged to the exit as Stone recalled Cess.

"Ms Belle," he said mildly, "submit my ad for the volunteers in the paper."

She was on the hilltop of tears; nonetheless, a mechanical nod sealed the pact.

The metallic lamps were ready to snap from the cords above but swung, chandelier-like, the remaining thread of skin after an accident.

The journalist department was a secreted, diamond-pointed, drab-coloured affair, deserted except for the buzz of devices glowing with the latest story and the lean physique of Aurora, picture-perfect strands swishing.

She pirouetted three feet when she spotted us loitering sheepishly.

"Were you notified?" Cessie frowned.

Aurora cast her hands around. "Clearly not." Her arched brows were ironic. "Aren't you supposed to be walking with dinosaurs or something?"

"Surprise!" Cessie said breathily. "We contrived to transfer our findings to the research lab."

"Dr Stone sent us to convey our files and be interviewed," I added quickly.

Robots rustled from the chintz curtains, scattering the beige rope. Cessie and I were lowered into high, iron, rounded seats, Aurora's temple red as the tape rolled.

"Stop blinking so much," she said to me in irritation.

A robot made to Velcro my hands to the furniture.

"That won't be necessary," Aurora said beatifically. She stamped an olive chip on its shoulder, and it rocketed from the set-up with its companion.

"Knackered design?" Cessie quizzed.

"Old models." Aurora displayed her teeth. "Due for upgrade this Halloween."

We worked and answered queries companionably for a period, when Cessie addressed the querulous matter of Stone's advert.

Aurora was silent for two minutes. "And who's the intended audience?"

"Everyday people," I said sunnily. "Convicts, the poor – those with nothing to lose. Stone wishes them to test the blend of our herbs with existing remedies."

"And if I don't write up the ad?" Aurora said.

"You'll likely be fired," Cessie said with a flair of theatrics. "I'd sooner camp in the Cretaceous than receive another sermon from Dr Bowtie."

"Readers may be disturbed by the exploitative angle of the piece," Aurora said in her singsong voice. "We could lose a lot of customers and the online market's already competitive. I'm paid by the story and influx of comments."

"This would court trolls and controversy," I said, "so I guarantee a response."

Aurora's veins were bluish. "I'll run the ad," she agreed.

Cessie lit up.

"On two conditions. One: I do this anonymously. Two: You recommend me to step in if any of you're injured."

Our souls sunk. It whiffed of a bargain, not a victory.

"In the Cretaceous?" I clarified.

"I want to be a Time Traveller's Understudy," she said, with a lively jiggle. "Grant me that chance and I'll save your careers."

"We'll do it," Cessie said in a rush as fleeting as the files, before I could rebel.

The lamps diminished before dazing in a starburst of lights. Aurora's mouth line stitched into a smirk. "Send Stone a memo." A filed nail, tipped with glitter, dug into the pew.

"You'd better do it," Cessie gabbled.

Inhaling deeply, I accessed the Note app, and mentally typed: D-e-a-r D-o-c-t-o-r S-t-o-n-e. I-n e-x-c-h-a-n-g-e f-o-r p-e-n-n-i-n-g t-h-e a-d, M-s T-h-o-r-n d-e-s-i-r-e-s t-o b-e o-u-r u-n-d-e-r-s-t-u-d-y i-n t-h-e e-v-e-n-t o-f i-n-j-u-r-y. S-e-n-d y-o-u-r a-p-p-r-o-v-a-l **A-S-A-P**.

I paused, Aurora puffing like a blowfish, and moved the request to my "send" folder. It infiltrated cyberspace, waving and jolting my brain. The sensation of linked minds, thought policing, hung. What if Stone hacked my memories; encountered me and my sister in his office, snooping and suspicious?

A reply pinged instants later.

I'-l-l g-r-a-n-t h-e-r w-i-s-h. B-u-t t-r-y v-e-r-y h-a-r-d n-o-t t-o p-r-o-v-o-k-e t-h-o-s-e d-i-n-o-s-a-u-r-s. I'-m c-o-u-n-t-i-n-g o-n m-y f-i-r-s-t c-a-n-d-i-d-a-t-e-s f-o-r t-h-e j-o-b.

I was wrenched to the present with Aurora's petition for the response.

I conceded defeat and she clicked the PC, writing: O-p-p-o-r-t-u-n-i-t-y o-f a l-i-f-e-t-i-m-e. O-u-r t-i-m-e t-r-a-v-e-l-l-e-r-s f-o-u-n-d a b-u-r-n r-e-m-e-d-y. T-h-e L-a-b-s d-e-s-i-r-e t-o t-e-s-t o-n w-i-l-l-i-n-g v-o-l-u-n-t-e-e-r-s. W-e g-i-f-t 1-0-0-0-0 c-r-e-d-i-t-s. I-f y-o-u —w-o-u-l-d n-o-t m-i-n-d —i-n-f-e-c-t-i-o-n a-n-d f-i-r-s-t-h-a-n-d r-e-s-t-o-r-a-t-i-o-n, s-i-g-n u-p a-t R-e-c-e-p-t-i-o-n. C-o-u-r-t-e-s-y o-f t-h-e R-e-s-e-a-r-c-h D-e-p-a-r-t-m-e-n-t, W-o-l-v-e-s.

Cessie emblazoned it with the wolf emblem and well-quoted motto, and the ad was considered by Head of Media for publication.

We abandoned her to await the head's decision, tampering the footage, riven as it was with glitches due to the time difference. Transparency was twenty-third century law.

We picked over the scrubbed carpet to present archives for Dad's storage.

"I-v-y!" Pearl's cry drew me up short, and her pimpled arms were around my neck. She was watery.

"Hello," I said stiffly, unclasping her chimp cling.

"Dad and I thought you'd been eaten," she said excitedly.

"I'm positive I said no such thing," Dad said mildly.

"He watched all the tapes of the dead guy," Pearl said relentlessly. "The T-Rex slaying in slow-mo."

"Is she serious, Dad?" I said.

"Until you've been a parent, you can't understand," he said plainly.

"You missed us, then?" Cessie grinned.

"Like mould in the walls," Dad said sarcastically, loading his giant library computer. "The goods, please. Museum revenue is shockingly low at the moment."

"We weren't nearly eaten," Cessie said, somewhat untruthfully.

"If you omit the armed Andy who toppled the tree and gang of bloodthirsty birds who almost pecked me to death," I vocalised breezily.

Dad blustered: "Mrs Ludwig assured me you'd be perfectly safe."

"She didn't even contact us via the Communicator," Cessie said, with a mewed expression.

"It's new technology; takes a while to connect," Dad said perceptively, as clips of the Anzu stick hut projected in Pearl's glassy pupils.

"Please don't tell Mum and Dad about the nearly eaten fiasco," Cessie said brazenly. "They'll make me live under the Belle roof again."

A snort sounded at the recollection of Cessie catnapping her parents' self-styled jet-boots, for a one a.m. jaunt across the skies for Aero's astronomy portfolio.

In her second year of uni, despite only studying in the city, Cessie had finally left her folks high and dry and paid a great portion of the deposit on our rented quarters.

"I won't tell anyone important enough to harangue your mum and dad," Dad said with a twinkle. "You staged some fantastic escapades when young."

"Ivy was no saint," Cessie said, and she sparkled with knowledge of my misdeeds. "Remember the All Hallows' Day when you snuck a mechanical pumpkin on Magnus' ledge?"

"He screamed so loudly the whole street woke up," I said delightedly. " 'There's a talking vegetable in my room!' "

"He deserved it," Pearl interrupted, a witness to our enmity during school. "He and his cronies cornered Aero, mocking him 'cause his mum couldn't afford immunity."

Cessie shrank from the reminiscence of the taunts.

Dad equivocally greyed. "Now, he was a young boy who didn't understand credits don't grow on trees for café workers."

"He didn't get why Lydia wouldn't save her son from those ghastly cases you get in the hospital," Cessie chimed in.

"He humiliated him in a crowd of his classmates," Pearl said matter-of-factly. "Magnus warranted the scare."

"Who made you the authority?" Cessie argued plaintively. She checked the glass, seeing Mr and Mrs Belle, and her curls whipped out.

"It'll repair itself," Dad counselled. "Relationships are elastic – they evolve like treatments in the lab."

"Devolve, more like," Pearl said as she curled on the crocheted, fleeced armchair, scribbling a canny likeness of the Anzu. She embellished my frozen fear on being encircled and shoved into the trees. "Mum returned," she said colloquially.

"You didn't say!" I said accusingly.

"She's outside," my sister said, scrutinising the tail brush of burgundy feathers on her design.

"And no, she didn't find it," Dad said smilingly, anticipating my query. "Go, put her mind at rest."

I rested by the *Historie* book for a while before determinedly curving the knob. In the theatre of workers bartering ideas, students departing and café visitors slurping cookie milkshakes, Mum clutched a plastic bag, apart. Her mocha-toned, shoulder-length 'do was unwashed, cornflower blouse loose, shorts bulging, tennis pumps half-raised.

I cleared my throat again. "Mum," I said.

She moved as though she heard but couldn't see me. I repeated it, shrill, and pity for the Anzu materialised.

"Ivy." Mum was sharp-eyed. "You're back."

"When did your flight come in?" I said.

"Night before last," she drawled, gulping a cardboard- contained espresso. "Brazilian Immigration objected to my poking around. Mrs Stone had to send a letter to gain permission. I brought mint herbs, but can't disclose too much." Her satchel changed hands. "Did you get anything?"

Her hawk lashes studied me. There was so much I longed to say, but couldn't quite parcel it into words.

"M-magnolia oils, bark and whorls," I admitted eventually. "Sap from a monkey puzzle tree. I climbed the evergreens to obtain it."

"All those years of riding balconies paid off," Mum said semi-sternly. "It was an adventure?"

I couldn't believe this enquiry, but picturing Cessie's stricken plea, decided not to pickle my experiences with excessive drama.

"We shot the reefs," I said instead. "Turtles came ashore, and there were winged beasts overhead."

"My daughter went underwater?" Mum said.

"It's not what I'd have chosen," I said honestly.

"None of us would have chosen this," Mum said. "But there's something it's imperative you find."

She led me to a barren waiting room, touching my earth- brown waves. "Hell's Creek's a wasteland," she started feverishly. "What do you find in a deteriorating, muggy habitat?"

"I don't see…"

"The volcano," she said gravely. "The core of the lava harvests pennies of priceless gems. The funding and ore would enrich the infirmary."

"You want me to mine the volcano?" I said dazedly.

"That's precisely what I want you to do," Mum said blazingly.

From the disorder, Mrs. Belle's argument drifted.

"Nine-thousand credits, interest, plus the rent they owe since they've been away?"

"Preposterous." Mr Belle see-sawed on the balls of his military heels. "They're on a special mission that'll more than pay for itself. This is blind robbery."

73

"I'm sorry," a supercilious sound bugged my ear buds. With a jolt I realised it was an automaton speaking. "The debts amount to £12,000 credits. If you lack the means to pay, press 1. If you would like to issue a payment, press 2. If you would like to speak to our independent financial advisors, press 3. If you would prefer the tenants were evicted from their flat, press 4."

Mrs Belle powered her microchip. "We'll cover the debts." She jammed the "2" route.

The transaction was processed in a drill of electronics.

I rushed forwards. "You didn't have to," I said hastily. "Sir, madam, we'll pay our own at the tail of our qualifications."

"That could take months, or years," the Belles said tactlessly. "We can't allow our daughter to be bullied by creditors."

"Cessie already blew her savings putting them off," I said in horror. "Take it back."

But Mr Belle acted as if I were invisible, starting afresh with the robot. "I have other business here," he said curtly. "A situation has occurred. I wish to probe the ancestry documentations."

Cessie was flummoxed. "What're you bleating about?"

"Not to worry, dear, it's all paid off." Her mother batted her away. "Run along with young Ivy."

Cessie arranged herself in step with me when a patter of footsteps silenced the lobby.

Aero arrived on the pinned floorboards, coils haphazard, jade glue sandwiching his knuckles together. Bo was behind, 4D goggles pinching her cerise skin, lab coat besieging her form.

"Ladies and gentlemen," she began, evocative of a ribbon being knifed. "The lab department has breakthrough news."

"She *is* the lab department," Cessie festered sourly.

"Shh," I muttered.

"Two thousand potions and fifty herbs later, we have the wound infection remedy bottled for trial," Bo said, hopping on the steps.

"A thousand deaths could be prevented," Aero said as murmurs broke out at the notion of a trial. "Read tomorrow's ads in the *Robot Express*, if you would like to be one of our fortunate volunteers."

Gobsmacked, ripples of applause and dissent rumbled from the addressees. I neither cheered nor booed.

"What do they think we are, lab rats?" a wizened, electric-caned woman said.

"Mad, the lot of 'em," her partner crowed. "Straight from school and treating lives like lemon drops."

"I think it's wonderful," a reedy-toned chemist said. "Our treatments have been stale for twenty years."

"Sign me up," someone with a Victorian pram called from the cafeteria. "The payment will be astronomical."

Opportunity of a lifetime bounced.

Aero signalled to us to come over. Cessie sucked bitter pears, but ascended with me on the hardwood.

"I can't believe you did it," I said gawkily. "You've done a lot for the hospital."

"It's our trade," he said coyly. "We did what we were told."

Bo was flushed. "There was an elderly man in bed six. Couldn't make head nor tail of Robot technology, and blew himself up. If the ointment works he'll be discharged within the month."

"Fantastic," Cessie said forcedly, and I was reminded of dentures clacking when their gummed owners weren't around.

"One last thing," Bo said falteringly. "Grandma always told me: *those who battle the faunae risk their vengeance.*"

I wandered the halls as commotion splintered; until a small, furry grasp roofed my lips, and a squeal hooted as I ended up in a derelict corridor.

Pearl's coin-flecked eyes arose as anxiety flicked to fury.

"What was that all about?" I said sharply.

"Keep your voice down!" My sister was as wide as a UFO.

"I thought I'd been kidnapped again!" I said, but dropped my volume.

"I had to if I didn't want to be noticed," she said timidly. Bags enlarged her eyes more markedly than air sacs.

I gripped her shoulders. "Has something else happened?"

It'd been reckless to abandon Pearl to Magnus' crab-like scheming, Dr Stone's machinations and Mrs. Stone's stringent reforms.

"I didn't tell you before because you warned me not to interfere," she said woozily, pinafore sullied with sugar and jam.

"Free scones again?" I said, in a kinder manner.

"Cornish raspberry." She revivified at the retention.

"So what went on between seeing me and those sugary treats?" I asked.

"I was passing your apartments to fetch my science exercise when… breathing arose from the vents. I'd a hunch it was coming from the top floor. Everyone in your block works – they have to. I let myself in and it was apparently empty. But I heard it again – it might be the Halloween spirit, but somehow I thought it was a vampire or a creature."

"Was it another rat?" I said fervently, cursing myself. What if it'd been a burglar? With the penalties for theft being so high, they wouldn't have hesitated to silence the twelve-year-old.

"The noise was from Cessie's bedroom. The strangest thing… Evangeline was snoring on the lounger."

"Robots don't snore," I said, more relieved than vexed. "She was charging, as computers do."

"No," she said adamantly, "not like a computer. PCs don't dream or mumble about the sea, sins or rebirth. It was as if she – it – were obsessed and she kept saying something awful happened…"

"She's no more alive than a suit of armour," I said.

Pearl's face was parallel to a hare in a lorry's path, or chickens when the red fox unlatches the coop.

"Are you deaf? She was dreaming… no, she was remembering things… she has a *past*. Have you ever heard of that?" The sentence broke as faintly as a B-string on a guitar.

"It'll be a new programme or game of Cessie's," I said, unthreading the line in my pockets. "Probably needs a new battery."

"Like the machines that shoved us down a shaft?" She was fuming.

"Forget about it," I said dispassionately, holding her shoulders once more. "Things are getting darker and darker round here. Pearl, it isn't safe. You mustn't meddle in things beyond you."

"What's that supposed to mean?" she snapped, a ball on a string, and it was as though I was looking into shutters.

"*I* don't understand, P," I said. "I don't want to get involved. You saw Cessie earlier. I've a job to do. Let it go."

"You never listen." She flounced off before I could emit another syllable.

My hands massaged the migraine in my skull. Pearl was stumbling upon some weird stuff, and my exertions to prevent her junior Sherlock Holmes act were failing. The outlook was bleak, mule as they nosedive an avalanched mountain, rocks ruining their fall.

My microchip bleeped and I thwacked the wall with my hefty boots. It was Nadia.

Aero has stoppered the remedy for a Halloween trial, she notified. *Return to the tube station immediately. This time you are tasked with purchasing berberine, an ingredient that'll revolutionise the antibacterial resistance.*

Access the communicator when you parachute and myself and my colleagues will be wired up with further instructions.

The errands wisped like rainbow pegs, cloth landing on pebbles below, taking me with it; an item to be used and thrown away, a robot whose parts no longer shimmered with electricity.

Chapter Six: Rite of Passage

The bare poplars sprung everywhere, spindly and knobbed as if lovers' carvings in stalks.

"Are you alright, Ivy?" Cessie shattered my speeding thoughts. "You're green as a gooseberry."

I revived myself. "I-I'm fine. These trees look thinner. How're we going to trace the berberine?"

Now was hardly the moment to propose the volcano stunt. Speech bubbles of Evangeline, copper crossed, snoozing from the iron passages, haunted me.

"We'll scour the locale tree by tree," Aero said resolutely.

"Do you remember where we buried the machine? When we've found the berberine, we'll have to contact Nadia," Cessie reminded us.

"**X** marks the spot," I said. "It's in the middle of the early woodland."

"We're looking for the barberry plant." Cessie consulted the weighty dome of the Marsh's records. "A conifer between three and sixteen feet. Leaves – thorny — pink and red like autumnal leaves. The flowers form in yellow or orange."

The loveliness of the image spellbound us before we mounted, trainers squelching soil, no longer parquet. We meandered, misplacing optimism, drumming every millimetre of foliage, when a nut-brown rodent scurried across my cords. Raven whiskers consumed its furred, ratty base; short muzzle the colour of felt pen, nascent casing speckled with nickel. Bo's caution chorused — we weren't to tamper with wildlife.

"Cimolomys." Aero was awestruck. "I've only seen them in textbooks."

Its mitt muzzled the rainforest, noshing hard-boiled, shiny fruits as it drilled holes in my socks, phlegm dripping from its incisors.

Cessie pointed out of the blue, ringlets sprightly in the ubiquitous maze of striped bark, scrabbling the rugged verdure; mirroring Dad's needle-in-a-haystack hunt when Pearl had toddled off one afternoon.

"What are you doing, lunatic?" Aero shouted.

"Lunatic, am I?" she said, imbedding her pinkie in soil and petals.

Aero retreated to facilitate her work, saying aside to me: "She's done some hare-brained things, but this has got to be the looniest."

"Shut up," I shushed, "she found something."

The cimolomys wasn't eating any old seed, but the produce of barbaris vulgaris – in layperson's English — the berberine-rich plant. The pine vegetation was effortlessly lost in an assortment of similar growths — yet the rose and ginger leaves were distinct, the angiosperms a potent sunglow.

"I recognise the yellow from the design department," Cessie said hot-bloodedly. "You might not regard this as important, but we needed the dyes for a costume, and there were no more yellows; not even diluted. The crown had to be cream." She was melancholy.

I fingered one of her wilting plaits. "So why else do we need the famous berberine other than dyeing wool?"

Aero stomped the ground. "It's a chemical component sourced from the stem and bark – a possible tool against staphylococcus aureus – the MRSA infection. It's antibiotic – even anti-ageing. We can mix it in the lab with an inhibitor, destroying bacterium. It's not just a plant; it's a life-saver." The shadows under his lashes were yellowed like the flowers, and he hadn't appeared so longing since he saw the Lab City toy in year five. Cessie and I'd pooled our cattle banks as a Christmas offering.

I guzzled. "I'm sure it's wonderful... but I haven't got to climb it, have I?"

"Ah." Aero's fingers vibrated as they indicated spasms in the axis of the fifteen-foot tower.

A mountainous hive of bees suckled the sepals and I couldn't believe we hadn't taken note of the livid tempo, deafening now our chatter had died. Their colony enveloped the waxen wings of the magnificent queen bee, millions of years ago, restored to her throne of piping workers.

"There must be another tree." Cessie was shaken, swabbing grunge from her corduroy trousers. "Another ingredient — I bet there's lots of invaluable vegetation."

This time Aero swallowed. "No. It has to be this one. We don't know when we'll see another – this is a declining world. 'Tis why they're all droning round. Nadia specified it – it's essential."

"Our errand couldn't be for the prettiest flower," I said acerbically. "It had to be the bee-populated nest egg."

"You know all about nests now," Cessie cheeped. "We'll let the expert handle it."

"I'm not the expert!" I jerked a thumb at Aero. "*He* is – he speaks plant gobbledegook."

"Aero," Cessie said heartlessly, "you have such rapport with the animals – this should be a treat for you."

I squashed my snickers.

"I would," Aero said slowly. "Only – I wouldn't deprive the historian or the engineer the chance to source what we've all been waiting for. What we've been waiting *twenty years for*. Be my guest."

"I'd sooner be on a plane to 23," Cessie said harshly.

"Well, we haven't got a plane, we've got a time machine, so if you go — we all go," Aero said dogmatically.

I glanced from friend to friend in deliberation. It sounded bizarre, but if only Pearl were here; she always knew what to do... her lissom pluck could procure the berberine.

The boughs rustled in the bitter gust, and I shunted our heads together.

"You're not going to like this," I opened fretfully, "but we should create a human ladder, and the person at the pinnacle ought to gather samples."

If Aero was astonished, it didn't show. "I'll take the bottom. Who wants the top?"

"I'll do it," Cessie said mildly. "But only if you collect the first blossoms below. Pass me some twigs."

Before she could revoke her word, we bundled sticks towards her, caterpillar-coloured beetles skipping off crossly. Aero went rigid as we steeled ourselves, Cessie making a visor for her face with scrunched cotton; me crouching to frog onto Aero's shoulders. It was a Russian roulette scenario, but with empty hands we weren't allowed home (if we still had our overpriced town flat). I picked dried berries with enthusiasm that suggested the bounty was summer strawberries, popping some in my jaws and the rest in Aero's unzipped pouch. They were lemony, with a mint essence drowsing my wits. Some of the barbaris' structure was prickly, scraping me, but I managed to acquire the new creations in abundance.

The bees were restful originally; milked on sugar, napping in the shrubs; but when Cess began pummelling the roots, in duos they lowered their pinions: buzzes melodic as hailstones, awakening as long-dead spirits. However, no rest is eternal, and in an insomniac jazz they nipped Cessie's onyx earrings, first stroking the pinked space, then entangling her beached plaits, stinging her.

"Ouch!" She teetered on my collar plates, the human-made stepladder wobbling. Strips of bark dusted Aero's locks, and he winced in unison with her as copse dizzied him.

"Tap the bark," Aero said desperately as the blare accelerated and bees swarmed, pinching our ears, our naked arms and cheeks; pink amplifying our features.

Cessie hacked fanatically at the honeyed leaves while Aero pontificated about the crisis of drug resistance, wincing at the stings from minute pests. My clamp sagged as minutes ticked, Cessie wobbling on top. A runaway bee settled in my waves, and I started as though I'd been stunned with three thousand volts.

"Get off!" I swatted; the bee apparently didn't speak English, as it utilised me as a stepping stone to pollinate a strawberry leaf, lapping the drip from the insides.

The hisses became a horde as bees emerged from their inertia, and circled us in fascination. I gathered sepals, breathing in the clean, alluring scent, a handful stowed away.

"Tap the centre of the bark," Aero said fluently, "— last task."

Cessie gaped as the cloud of buzzes focused on our cotton, frenzied by the jasmine perfume, and she cut into the sapling, sandy oozes flowing in a mini dust ball. A bee perched on my lobe, considering whether it was worth the puncture. The mixture landed in Cessie's agape thermos in the pasture — Aero stamped it shut before our little friends could swill the tonic.

"You did really well," Aero said painfully, lips sore with wounds. "We'll get down now."

The hordes were driven mad by the release of fluids, goring the wood.

Six surrounded Cessie and she tripped on my slippery, sweaty T-shirt, falling fifteen feet to the beetle-populated mound. With a *wallop* she lay still.

Gawking frantically, Aero and I toppled. I managed to piggyback into a multitude of needles, Aero moderating the blow with his camper's rucksack. We convalesced as Cessie remained motionless.

"We got everything?" Aero whispered, although the forest was noiseless.

"Never mind." I stood up, grooming twigs from my khaki shorts. A pulse throbbed in Cessie's splotched neck. Aero persisted in combing the earth, pilfering leaves.

My friend was warm… was that a hushed sigh, very unalike the final rasps of the crook? Not medically equipped, annoyance flooded at my other friend's ineptitude. What was he playing at, playing treasure hunt when she was in this state?

"Move out of the way." Aero was harsh. Cessie's circlets tickled my skin.

At my evacuation, he pressed the slimed herbs to her marks. The breathing became more laboured. At first she grew redder, but clearness leeched the painful blots and she spluttered, kernelled irises arousing. Berries dropped from my pouch, but I was too dumbfounded to act.

Aero pasteurised the fruits, wringing them into Cessie's mandible. She imbibed the juice, sitting up.

"The b-berberine," she choked.

"We got everything." Aero constricted the flask; not a bead leaked. "You might want a respite."

"No." Bewildered, her gangly legs exerted upwards, and the cimolomys scooted past, fruits daubing it like mauve wine. "W-we need to tell Nadia and Dr Stone."

"My interior compass isn't the best," Aero said warningly, as I veiled my distress. It was a Mansion of Horrors, an ersatz trip of dreams; an illusionary reward. "I know Ivy said the machine's earlier on, but we walked further than intended. I couldn't see another barberry, else we wouldn't have…"

"I know," Cessie said hastily. "I'm glad we retrieved it. Ivy climbed the araucaria and escaped a nest, you diverted Andy – it was my turn."

"You've already done plenty," I said liberally. "You don't have to risk your neck to prove a point."

"I'm not," she huffed. "We got it; stop being a Debbie Downer."

I tramped after Aero in the woods, flexing stones in my path, pockets weighed with hundreds of berries and wads of leaves.

"Let go," I said firmly, as the ratty mammal intertwined my laces, snuffling the muck. "I never did like my shoes licked."

Cessie purpled at this.

The cimolomys jumped on the soil, rupturing it, and my canvas was hauled with it. Its carved snout signalled the split where the glossy canopy was entrenched with the name: *The Mary Anning*. An incised fossil was printed in the zinc.

"Genius," Aero said to the scurrying animal, which capered into the forest without further ado. "Little fellow must've tracked us."

My lone concern was the louse poo garnishing my flaps. Aero gutted the upper layering until the entrance was visible. We climbed inside as though invited to a badger's tea party, and it was rather illuminating to venture underground. The buttons beeped on sensing my touch and I plugged two wires in, as Pearl had keyed her electric dot-to-dot, wasting priceless power. The contraption stuttered to ignite signals epochs away, but the Supercomputer eventually succumbed. Nadia's lustrous up-do, pinned with wire, soon emerged, and her cinnamon-tinged face was pinched.

"That was a complex move," she saluted me as an ice-breaker, and irritation substituted gratitude at hearing her. "We've been busy conserving the burn ointment from prying hands. A homeless woman forced entry to the storage room, but the robots intercepted her."

"Wonderful," I said, and it was a shame insincerity didn't translate.

"The berberine?" came the unmistakable inquisition of Dr Stone.

"We found the barberry tree; quite rare, so we decided to try it even with the beehive," Aero said, with an apologetic twinge at our mentor.

"And?" Stone persevered.

"We got it," Aero said buoyantly, ignoring Cessie's resentful huff. "Buckets of the stuff. Are there any stores of methoxydnocarpin left?"

"Bottles as unspoiled as brandy," Stone said exultantly. "We'll meld it with the antibiotic. The only effective chemical we've got against microcystiaeruginosa. You've samples of the dried berries? I savoured some in my youth, and there's no zest equal to it."

"We've got everything, even though we were almost stung to death," Aero said for his friends' benefit. "Would it be untimely to revisit?"

"You can't," he said simply, facial hair oppressing his square profile.

"What?" Aero's jaw was hanging.

Cessie's shoes pulsated the metal.

Dr Stone stepped aside to allow Dr Goodwin into the picture; a jittery, fidgeting, gingham-jacketed gentleman who frowned gently.

"Hello, you three," he said, friendlier than his co-worker. "Permit me to make a request."

Aero peeked from his sooty lashes. "Does it involve near/almost certain death?"

The professor wavered. "Our trackers identified a gang of sphaerotholus dinosaurs, and Stone and I have a wager."

"I've always believed this particular breed isn't developed enough for warring and copulating rites," Dr Stone talked over him. "There's limited evidence in MRIs they could perform such multifaceted acts. Geoffrey's a soft chap, and thinks fossil scars contradict my thesis. If you three could observe the group, our Natural History Unit would be most grateful."

They blinked over their dual spectacles, the screen blitzing every so often.

"Cessie?" Aero said politely, seeing her disinclination. "Up for it?"

Cessie's muddy tangles withered. "Suppose so."

"Ms Moss?" Dr Stone said zealously. "You won't see anything of this nature again."

But did it merit its exclusivity, jeopardy and warfare?

Lips nibbled bloodier than a canine's kill, concurrence flared: "OK: I'll do it."

My companions thumped my cervical back. "All set for some fun?"

A grunt was all it warranted.

The monitor crackled, and if rock bottom can sink further than an anchor, that was the reality as Magnus, Aurora, Alexandrina, Fire, Mars and Bo emerged in the controls room. Cessie appeared to be tasting grapefruit.

"They couldn't wait to see live footage of the site," Dr Stone was muffled, "so they resolved on the powers of Skype."

They nursed teddy bear mugs of marshmallow-topped, spiced hot chocolate, and Cessie now resembled slits. The shrubbery crunched in my purse.

"Good holiday?" Magnus said pleasurably, as his associates glared at him.

"I've had better," Cessie said, but there was a quivery element in the phrase.

"We're on duty," Aero said strongly.

"We don't need you to police the galaxy," Magnus retorted sourly.

If Aero could've packaged a Jack-a-Box in Magnus' mail, it would've clouted him. Instead he assumed a blasé air, so his rage had cooled over the years, leaving arctic friction.

"Ivy, being your usual chatty self," Magnus continued, pleased at his work. "Machine hasn't popped its clogs so far?"

If only he could.

"There's plenty of voltage left," I lied. "Runs like clockwork."

His scowl was the only way we were aligned.

"Like a model train set?" he said gloatingly. "Ideal for you."

Magnus didn't adhere to the normal rules but his own twisted stack of jokers, slapped down when you least expected, and interpreting him was like checkmate, or the paperback that doesn't adjust to the shelf.

A crescent of conflict ate Cessie's loyalties. "It was down to Ivy we got here. Aero and I were as dense as dummies."

"First among equals," Magnus said archly. "Right, Dad?"

His father clapped his shoulder pads. "You'll get your chance. But Ivy was first."

"It's a pity we couldn't switch places when the bees got you," Aurora said charmingly, slanting towards her sort-of boyfriend.

"Next time we'll be sure to get in harm's way," Cessie said sweetly.

Aurora tinkled as though it were in jest. "Well, you'd better, as we're all dying to see it! The readers adored your stories – my inbox was buzzing, get it?"

"Ha-ha," Aero said drily. "Let's budge this machine, shall we?"

A trio, we lugged the several-tonne steel, olive button flaming. Dutifully, our co-workers egged us on, and it was like a Roman gladiator contest when the throng's hounding you to death. Retribution for baited bears seemed certain, honed with Bo's counsel.

Muscles hackled, we toured the milieu, defenceless, microchips shooting every second, every sneeze, every squabble.

"You're getting closer," Dr Stone said, as excitedly as crickets in the weeds.

The drive to be *further* was magnetic.

"W-o-w," Aero said as spherical dome caps, crowned with corals, flitted from the branched beech shrubbery; proud bodies broadening as they ferried nearer, stooping compliantly.

"Herbivore, omnivore or carnivore?" I asked.

"Herbivore," he said, as its convex form lowered and nudged his elbow. He probed its emerald, coarse crust — it was a couple of inches his superior. Its wart-ridden orb was thick with reindeer rapiers, and abrasions distinguished it. Aero snapped as fanatically as a photographer's assistant.

A hunched mob of six of the sphaerotholus genus occupied the mid woodland, tufted and mahogany-capped. Cessie tinted their jewel-green, sprawled frames in her sketchpad. Awareness dawned on their domes as they gauged our presence: in diversion I hurled seeds and trivial berries, which they snaffled in one swallow.

"Only fragments of skulls pervade the fossil record," Goodwin garbled, chafing his sleeves. "This is the first live film."

"Come now, Goodwin," Stone clanged, "even grasshoppers have a will to live."

My eyes snagged Magnus', and we all knew what he was thinking: *it has more zest than me.*

"How large are they?" Stone's son said to sidetrack scrutiny.

"Six feet," I enlightened him. "Your size."

Aero hid his smirk.

"They seem moderate," Magnus said, as Bo's meditation alerted me she'd appropriated the Note app.

"I've never seen that shape, in all my years analysing Lab samples," Bo said viscerally. "What do they *feel* like?"

"Sugar card," Aero conveyed. "There're bumps all over it."

"How do you know the texture of paper?" his co-scientist said curiously. "That was outlawed a century ago."

He sampled fallen hairs for later accounts; its acorn globe convulsed. "My dad was a researcher. He brought a cardboard lot of them one night, destined for the trash. I solicited him for them. I made origami planes for show-and-tell. The teacher recycled them, and I never touched such raw textile again."

"Is he retired?" Bo said raptly. "There isn't another Smith on our payroll —"

"He's dead," Aero said impassively. "Killed in an experiment ten years ago."

She started; her almond cocoa went skyways. "Oh, I-I'm sorry."

Aero's back to the screen, he clicked a photo of the patched dinosaur. "Don't be. He made his choice."

His preceding argument refrained: *You know what you signed up for.*

No one at the Unit had ever bothered to wonder why Aero survived on his mother's meagre wage most of his life. Perhaps they assumed his father didn't care.

Cessie was garnet-rimmed. "It's not her business what happened to his dad. If that gets out, workers will treat him differently."

"Bo isn't a gossip," I said fiercely.

"In an elite workforce, hearsay moulds like a rash," she argued. "The rest of that lot won't keep their mouths shut."

Rather like her.

A *smack* left us reeling.

Snarling, the chief sphaerotholus pummelled its bowed neck into an ill-fated, chestnut-coated subordinate. Its mangled hip bent like a fawn at the end of a hunter's gun, and squawks pitched from its beak.

"A challenger," Aero said discomposedly. "The dead nomad recorded their ritual sounds, and when they rise higher, it signals a usurper. Some of the crew want to overthrow the old head."

"But they're *plant-eaters*." Cessie was emphatic. "They don't *kill*, do they?"

"Excellent imagery," Dr Goodwin interrupted. "Can you shoot the reactions of the others?"

The chief looped its neck around the juvenile, ramming it into the laurels. Avian reptiles chortled in the clouds. The other dinosaurs withdrew cagily, none intervening to save the struck unfortunate. The smacks and rhythms of enamel and muscle were ear-splitting: Cessie's earring blew out at the force.

"Aero," she said, ambling beneath their boxing ring, blonde masses matted with myrtle. "We have to referee!"

"*We're not to interfere with nature*," he said assuredly. "*You can't reason with animals.*"

"We can teach them," she said, Bambi-eyed. "We have to try!"

"Let it run its course," was Dr Stone's input. "Dinosaurs that size aren't capable of real dam—"

"Aaaah!"

The ungainly dragon tail thwacked Cessie and I like a released cable.

The impact spat us at the paws of the young sphaerotholus, who bulldozed us aside. We shimmied from the knuckle of its foe, which rapped its ribs. Aero sprung behind the sunlit shrubs, at the rear of the Chief, who bellowed; a noise reminiscent of a cheese grater.

The tomato-headed boss struck his weight at the smaller rival, sending a *splat* looping around the miniature forests, and a *slop* alerted us to the junior's retaliation, paces of movement lobbing from the laurels. Aero compressed himself against the front of the shrubbery to more closely tape the war, in line with our decrees.

"Watch out!" Cessie cried as the tomato head staunched an exploded vessel, hefty arms twirling like a fairground ride.

Aero was dashed into a divan of magnolias, warped stems soiled. The two beasts were now braying, anyone in their way an obstacle to their feud; an object to be subjugated. He seemed bemused but unscathed. We'd come to monitor them as if they were circus freaks, and now they'd budged us as if we were crimson-lipped Russian dolls, to be strewn: willows propagating their pips.

The chief was bolstered by his defeat, running forwards as though limbless, targeting the lower ribs of the juvenile, whose bones splintered. Half-covert in earth, Aero averted his overcast argil irises, which filled with shock.

"Most unusual," Dr Goodwin muttered, mystified. "We're aware they fought, but on such a lethal scale..."

"I concede you were right, old friend," a lethargic Dr Stone said, wringing his associate's hand. "Four hundred credits to you."

"Excellent; I'll buy the cyber reality app to re-enact battles for my classes." The history professor was mollified.

We'd seen enough revived warfare, but our superiors were deaf to our antipathy.

The juvenile thumped, wounded, at Aero's sandals, a growl of anguish weeping from its organ. Unhesitant, my scientist comrade snipped herbs and rotting moss from a stone, where proof of the lesion dribbled like vampire juice.

"Aero: it might lash out," I said prudently.

As a groove pulsed in his brow, he doctored the fallen champion, the cucumber chest leeching out sludge and infection; the scarlet cranium sloped so we could see its crow eyes, tender and static.

Aero cleaved cloth from his backside, welding it to the dinosaur's injuries with vials from a cinnamon branch, taciturn. The mini sphaerotholus gulped the dioxide-heavy air as it was treated, wrath sifting to gratitude. He'd been powerless to heal the thief in his mother's cafeteria: however he'd spared the existence of this disinclined herd member, in the bowels of another era.

"Will the cinnamon halt contagion?" Cessie inquired.

"Hope so." Aero spat a mouthful of fibre onto the mat of lichen.

"I don't mean to alarm, but the Big Guy's returned!" I cautioned.

We reeled backwards as the domed rival surfaced, dried cuts brutalising it, cavernous snorts slinking nearer and nearer: slumped hunchback unbent, so its six-foot frame seemed incessant. It forked a mitt in the misty pollution, on the brink of whipping us.

This time it was Cessie who shrouded her forehead with unsown yarn, and none of us had the breath to squeal. The thrash almost hooked our membranes, when a three-horned interloper entered the fray.

The triceratops, frilled like a lace handkerchief, stomped its four hoofed feet, rhinoceros mass papered with bite blotches. Its pate alone was vaster than the chief, its silvery patina blistering under the rays, coarsened as dry cardboard. Its series of teeth plucked cycads and their oval harvest, squat goat's middle nose-diving to the crimson dome.

The sphaerotholus walloped its caved chest at the triceratops' horned eye, and the blinded animal sprawled into the prairies. Nobody dared respire as its trotters plodded into our combats, sending us tunnelling into the tropical undergrowth. We were at the furious heart of the hostility and the chief traipsed headlong, intending to finish us off...

From nowhere, the restored junior sphaerotholus bounded on its skinned soles, flooring its master; as rapid as poison darts, as steely as the heavyweight herbivore. Aero couldn't observe as his tape rolled, but Cessie and I watched eagerly as the adolescent strew white flowers over its ex-vanquisher, snorting in conquest.

The neutral relations fenced the young one, licking its injured ribs; garnishing it with sleek, leathery plants as the new major. The older chief resounded with roars and took off into the lowlands. Frail with victory, the juvenile exhaled alongside broad cinnamon trunks, where the triceratops dozed like a mossy boulder.

"Implausible such primitive beings could enact such rites," Dr Stone spoke into the microphone. "What say you, Goodwin?"

"How did the junior regain its strength?" Goodwin said bemusedly. "It looked on the cusp of death."

Not a word was confessed about Aero's act of mercy. Yet Bo's eyes constricted at the sap trickling down Aero's wrist.

"It'll live?" she said, quieter than a moth on a stone.

"Its ribs will repair." He hid his marred sleeve.

Perhaps it was the hitches in the monitor, but her gawp transfigured like a cottoned caterpillar when it seasons to a swallowtail butterfly.

Chapter Seven: Minefield

Nadia's husky inflection was primed with directives: "The tapes are impeccable for our natural history band. As it's dimming, it's advisable to set up a Camp Base near the time travel chute. Unsupported in an inhabited, precarious land —" The three of us shuddered, "— you require somewhere to occupy the night." The monitor fuzzed. "You've days left. May Neptune glimmer over you."

After a crackle she deserted us to the indigo-oiled gloom and we slogged in the plains, chary of fiends. I identified and serrated populous strips and cypresses, cutting grapevines. I styled hooks and sturdy poles from the broadest trees, and cast a clay flap and stone roof. Cessie constructed a pillow-smooth cover from nestles of angiosperms, careful not to startle wasps and hispine beetles. Aero pored over the site, gauging marauders. His muscular radial nerves sustained a fire by the silver machine, humming as we toiled.

I stood in the mangled guts of a thinly skinned carnivore, jaw misshapen in a last shriek; figure ragged with chomp marks.

"Aero!" I heralded him for analysis.

"Hmm?" He threw bark into the blaze, smoke saturating the landscape. "Any hardwood will do, you don't need me to dissect every tree..."

"It's a dead body," I said eerily.

Aero rambled over to the discovery.

"It could be years old," he said dubiously.

"No." My toe exposed the other side, fresh blood fetid, elastic case newly torn.

"You're right." He grimaced. "Did you see another animal?"

"Do you think I'd still be alive if I had?" I said mordantly.

"Good point." His grin was asymmetrical as he snapped an image of the quarry.

"What slew it?" Cessie said warily.

"A larger animal, that's for sure," Aero speculated. "Didn't mind swallowing chunks of meat. It wasn't a clash – it was an assassination."

"*It* could be hiding," Cessie said, curls spewing riotously.

My eyes rolled. "It's the Cretaceous, not a playground."

"She's right," Aero insisted. "It'll be back for the vestiges of its kill. If it's a choice between that –" he indicated the putrid remains, "— and us, I think I know who'd be on the menu."

I sharpened the nude cypress, uneasy. "How much larger?"

He stoked the flames with lumber. "I didn't bring my measuring string," he said at last, knobs showing when he craned his neck. "The faster we erect a refuge, the better."

"A cabin in the woods," Cessie said abstractedly. "Let's get stuck in."

It took an hour to mould our ersatz hovel of mud sticks and flora; Aero and I steadying the makeshift poles, Cessie bricking an exit with gluey matter. Aero confirmed only herbivores roamed the magnolias, yet disquiet crossed his boyish features. The snap of bark, glimmer of moss and cover of ferns were a pauper's distraction from the skeleton, half-gnawed to the bone.

Aero had studied many similar sights and Cessie had spent her life analysing the deceased, however this was novel for me. Fixing things was unequal to the stench of a grave, intestines discarded. No spanner could reanimate a corpse.

"The grass is greener, in a sense," Aero said ironically.

"How?" Cessie and I demanded, pained.

"It should be satiated for a while," he said assuredly. "These creatures consume more than us, but much less habitually. If it killed a meat-eater, it'll be full."

"It could've been a scavenger," Cessie pointed out. "If there's anything that stuck from those lessons, it's that."

"True," Aero said, "but the savaged remains seem suspect."

"I suppose we're not much better," I hiccupped. "W-we ate those three-layer feta beef burgers on your birthday." Condiments had dripped like entrails.

"Strictly speaking, we didn't make the kill," he said, shame-faced.

"Consumers drive the butchery," I snapped.

"You sound like Bo," he said finally.

"You can't be definite that she's a vegan," I said reasonably.

"Oh, I'm sure," he said secretively.

Cessie twirled her dark gold threads. "Is that how she stays so thin?" We fell about laughing.

"So, you've tried the paleo, the three-day fast and the flexitarian diet, and this is your new line of attack?" Aero was well-used to Cessie's labours.

"Works for Bo," she said snippily.

It was convoluted to comprehend my best friend as spiteful over an elder, less than immaculate colleague. Covertly, Aero's eyeball messaged alike thoughts: *Was this the bona fide motive for her acid attitude?*

We rose to inspect our primeval hub, welcome as a snow home in earthly tints, and cramped with rocks. Cessie let herself in while Aero and I observed the level terrains, blue dipping to a shivery horizon, acorn streaked with cranberry. 'Indoors', Aero rubbed surplus coppice to heat the natural abode, flinching as sparks sizzled. Cessie roasted a broth of nuts and fruit, and fish from the bounteous lakes. My dexterous digits fiddled with slippery bark, shaping bowls, leaving Aero and Cessie daunted.

"The kid who couldn't play electric cello," she said lightly, "assembling wooden crockery like witchcraft."

The screen burped, smoggy diamonds activating to present solitary Pearl in the Controls Chamber. Toffee wisps were tucked behind her elfin piercings, and she sucked a crazy straw of rhubarb milkshake.

"Pearl," I said thunderously, "who gave you access? Why aren't you asleep?"

She swivelled in the armchair, spectral pupils uttering what she wouldn't say. "You sound like Pa."

"You shouldn't be in here," I said inhospitably.

"Are you coming home soon?" she bleated. "Everything's bleak at the hospital — people are succumbing in the street – the burns medicine isn't enough. S-soon —" she burped on the mixture, "— there'll be more robots than people."

A freeze crept round the mock dwelling.

When the others weren't looking, I placed a raggedy nail to my lips, lest she mention Evangeline.

"Did Wolves issue a broadcast?" Aero asked cordially, and annoyance cultivated.

"Mmm-hmm," Pearl said groggily, headband splatting the cup. "Mrs Stone foretold a mass superbug. People are bartering housemates for androids." She leant conspiratorially. "That's why fees are so high."

I puckered an eyebrow. I didn't savour the idea of Pearl poking her beak in government secrets.

"Did Ms Stone pass on any additional information?" Aero asked assiduously.

Pearl made a scissor action with her bunches. "Refugees are converging on the borders, but Magnus' mother's quarantining them. She claims they'll pass on illnesses, and intoxicate the island." Her oval parting skewed towards the monitor. "Ivy... I don't know what they'll do if you three don't come back soon."

We were silent as we processed this data.

"We can't do anything," I said tiredly. "We're nothing but pawns."

Pearl's Snow White headband receded. "You're special there. They'll do whatever you say to extract what they want."

"We don't have long left here," I said smoothly. "One last mission."

"You always say that," Pearl said glumly.

My thumb switched the communicator off.

"Did you hear?" Aero said irritably. "The infirmary's not treating people – it's locking them up, shipping them away, to be somebody else's problem."

A ghastly vision of parcels shunted into peeling vans for an alternative destination spread across my neurons.

"They're nervous," Cessie said silkily. "Besides, we can't help them here. They aren't burn victims – they're carrying dangerous bacteria – we could be wiped out."

"But in a detention centre?" Aero was aghast. "It's inhumane."

Cessie started at this, but hung her varnished scalp.

Conviction galvanised me in currents, and I knew I had to mine the volcano's reserves. The inciting measure was one of Cessie's dog-eared texts: *Persuasion*.

Meteors and comets were downcast in an infinite puddle of night, bringing the stakes into the spiked limelight.

"Cessie, Aero," I addressed my friends, "there's something we've got to do."

"We know what we have to do," Aero said, irked. "Forage for more remedies, tape some more species and collect anything useful."

His rehearsed scroll was an irritant.

"This is distinct," I said stridently. "It's a fiery land, right? Rich in valuable matter. Well, Mum told me to plumb the volcano – she said it was crucial."

They didn't need to articulate their dissent for me to understand. Cessie's palate squared at the pitch.

Aero kindled the counterfeit hearth, and took an eon to react. "Have you developed cabin fever?"

"I'm not ill," I said snappily. "I'm the only sane member of our crew."

"It's too hazardous," Cessie mimicked. "Why weren't we notified beforehand?"

"It was Mum," I whispered, in case the monitor was still on. "I don't know if it's official commands. I think it's worth it."

"We're barely hanging on as it is," Cessie said, and it was like the jingle of doorbells.

Something advanced outside the camp, ravaging the vegetation.

"See!" she said agitatedly. "It's a carnivore at our door!"

"Been reading the three little pigs again?" I derided.

"Not your natural history book, that's for sure," Aero said mockingly. "Carnivores don't eat plants."

"It could be a supplement before they get to the real meat – us!" Cessie said frenziedly.

"The real issue," I said loudly. "Is the volcano —"

"I've told you, I'm not taking part in that stunt," Aero said, a ram with horns.

"We have to." I ironed the folds in my vest.

There was a raucous belch outdoors, succeeded by stasis, only the weirs rushing our lobes.

"I'm going regardless," I stated, packing a rucksack of vitals.

"How ignorant are you?" Aero bickered. "You're sleepwalking into a death trap."

"I'm wide awake," I said sullenly. "And the only one doing the job."

Cessie corded her nightdress, neon-wheat eyes unreachable. "Don't go. Not at midnight."

A chord twanged my resolve, but I discounted it, nails scrabbling at the acidic buffer, slitting a hollow and fumbling into nightfall.

A half-arc orbited the firmaments, stars slanted like rubble, curving the ethers, a fallen utopia. I marvelled at how such quixotic asteroids could liquidise the Earth. Clunks behind informed me my contenders had straggled me, the Milky Way rolling as if magicians on pocket broomsticks. It mesmerised them for the instant I needed to wrest my ankle from the rainy quagmire. My coco tangles barricaded me from their calls.

"Ivy, it's storming out there!" Cessie bawled as torrents infested in gales, toddler cyclones opposing my gaits.

Filth attached to my laces; nevertheless my soles strode on, ignoring the winds that blasted me backwards, the menacing clouds ready to blow, the masticating in the savannahs. All that mattered was the volcano, and the stores that would fund all ills.

"I don't care!" I said pitilessly. "You can postpone this for as long as you like, but it has to be done at some point."

"There'll be other means!" Aero shouted. "Don't be a fool."

It was the match that flared me. "Shut up, you coward! You may be too scared, but some of us have an operation to complete!"

"For robots' sake, you're going to get blown up!" I'd never heard him so livid.

"Isn't it your bedtime?" I taunted. "Run along."

Silt and chalky deposits nettled my half-nude forelegs, and the blueness demolished me. The marathon kept my ribs thumping, my tenacity; the orchid lustre in my cheeks.

Overlarge eye sockets shone in the precipitation, and dread washed my gut.

Amber pupils appraised mine, its night vision searing as a lizard egg draggled in its beakless hole, ostrich contour two hundred pounds denser than mine. Despite this it was lean and hollowed, hairy torso as drooped as a sloth, bipedal movements swifter than chattering human feet.

Running seemed futile; I rustled in my backpack and produced a selection of berries and herbs, leftover undercooked seafood and minted nuts. Aero's game replayed in my mind. This was no herbivore... the proof was in its gums. It didn't look as lofty as the predatory images I'd seen online, however there was no way to be certain.

It hooked the crop, guzzling throatily, and its scales appeared satisfied. It may have been an omnivore, but were my supplies sufficient to discount me as a small mammal in a scavenging, dog-eats-dogs civilisation?

It enunciated fowl songs, but they were indecipherable. It didn't strike me as an assassin; yet could Aero have been mistaken about a giant scrounger? Its femur was more than half my height, hairy and basked in taupe feathers.

It trilled again, but I shook my head: *I can't understand.*

Woodlice wormed in its beaky bill and a wiry forelimb popped my rucksack, sending the contents afield. Its three toes sprinted for the spoils, and its goose neck sank to ravish the crustaceans and roots.

At my approach, trumpet-like abuse barked. I had to ransom my assets to canter into rainwater, a belt of lightning zapping a ferret-like animal to cinders. More efficient not to think, not to breathe, as tornadoes fired the plates and sink holes barely eluded my combats, shivers marinating my top.

Sopping, a wrung sponge, I passaged out of the jungles and reached an eddying brook, marching onto toasted driftwood to deliver me to the crags. The tempest showed no signs of abetting, gustoes milking the night and shrinking my shoulder blades. My minute lifeboat tipped over the crests, half-sunken, but ultimately bashing against the rocks.

Bleeding, I careered out of it, snivelling in exhaustion. Prickles scorched my canvas; latex melted as if it were powder.

If it'd been dread before, it was cataclysm now.

I'd buckled at the base of the volcano.

Mantles of noxious gases secreted from the zenith of an aflame pyramid: infernos vied with thunderstorms for the most terrifying claps and in a crescendo, greasy asphalt bled out.

The stench was akin to thawing nickels or a mill set alight. The tectonic paves poached, on the verge of implosion. Toxic *pops* resounded like unloaded tins, the lightning overlain as gunpowder barrels. It was unfeasible to measure the minutes I had before it condensed me to smithereens, but the fire was the lone way forward. I didn't need Aero to infer the magma was immobile, crystallised until the blowout.

No scientist but an engineer, I mutated to a miner, scything shells at the foot. Inebriated by the plutonic trails, I mined the mineral belt, speedily invoking Nadia's module on metals and quartzes, two autumns past.

I smelted the pieces with teeming lava, rainfall impairing my cursing efforts. The organic wells lathered in lavish raven tar, singeing my knuckles at magnifying degrees. My hands clattered with shale stone – the iron, magnesium and potassium would feed our tan straw land, diversifying wastelands. Silver, copper and uranium abounded my pouches, yet the locale mounted with firestorms even as I irately hewed liquor and slick gemstones.

Opals and agates slipped from my germy palms, wolfed by the molten springs – diamonds fried in front of me; liquefied as if greased with acid. Jeopardy wasn't a word: it was the scorch in your throat, the tremors in your thighs, the Scotch mist blustering your lashes so you couldn't see, only feel the potted ornaments weighing your khakis.

Glittery bauxite jewelled inside a battered capsule, six-sided, featherweight; insulating the fever – it would survive the ravages of time treks. Aero said the element would convert to aluminium, more fuel for the robots. I targeted the greenstone belts, following the reek of nickel, emaciated crystals disintegrating – its resistance would thrive in our balmy, electronic world.

My inbox flooded with trash mail, no worried contacts retrieving me. The sense of betrayal curdled more ferociously than the fires, as pictorials of Aero and Cessie's panic rose. Why'd Mum mailed me to peril, a minefield?

The *core*.

What did you find if you rambled along greenstone, in the heart of a volcano? What would cause Mum's desperation?

Gold. All the credits ore could buy.

The veins hosting the dissolved metal were sheathed in a sauna, heightening with each tick as if Hydra's emergent vipers. Respiring, I fought the steep of lava, waves missing the glows by blind luck, capsizing in the feat of seeking an opening to the cavern.

My sole was sandstones away from barbecuing in blistering beacons. How awful to martyr myself in fiery exploits, masquerading as the heroine...

The tip of my fabric was ablaze, and queasily I shook my soles off. They combusted a millisecond later. My pouches inflated with pressure, and the trinkets bordering me chipped off one after the other, alike bats bulleting while predators napped.

I scurried onto a lodge, shale dinning as portions flew underneath, fastening my trouser. I could've panicked, but that would've instigated the sequence to my downfall.

I had a final shoot of verve, stronger than the burns.

My legs lunged for the cave, hitched on sandstone. An almighty tear saw half my combats plunge into a cooking soup of molten slush, softening in the carton.

I compacted my shoulder into the cleft, utilising my kneecap to demolish the wall. Rocks surged downwards, missing my scalp by centimetres. When the flume was over I shovelled droplets from my eyes and took refuge.

Gilt trickles drifted from the ceiling – gold was descending in liquid spirit, smudging my cupped hands, soaking what remained of my trouser pockets. I pointed sheer sediment towards the ground, mining it, the sheen of marvellous gems mine.

The hospital would be affluent beyond its imagination... what did it matter if fire engulfed the entrance, one shield of rock my sole guard? It was taxing when the enemy wasn't a person or swine but a state, a weathered phenomenon, soulless...

Pouches slobbering with alloyed metals, reserves and gunk, my shade on the wall crouched further inside the hollow, croaking as the smoke soberly, blearily infiltrated.

Not the embers but the smog... that was the old wives' fable. My bronchi felt airless; vents as nailed as coffins, abdomen keeled; skin defaced by coal.

I was acquiescent to death when the gravel split open. I recoiled from the shine glazing the level — were these more flames; or was this death, wingless, earthly?

Bash. Fire and rock diffused as moisture doused the grotto, ginger dewdrops marring my hairs. I squinted in the aisle, where a six-foot, mahogany-haired male with baby blue irises paused.

I tremored, delving further into the cavern, and we rattled into the hollow space, cheeks blotted; his locks blistering like beeswax.

An eternity passed before he spoke: "Ivy, don't be like that… we're friends."

"*Friends.*" I scuttled to the enflamed axis, raking my charred hair. "I – know – you – set – that – robot – on me."

The jagged rocks were beginning to burn.

He scowled. "I don't know w-what you're raving about."

"Liar."

"Says the person who broke into my dad's office?" I wasn't sure, but mischievousness lurked behind ire.

I jabbed my thumb: "After your metal mongrel threw me there."

One knee intersected the other as he rested, a gash in the denim. My cough stuttered as I thought of my own pair. Who was looking after my scooter?

He enumerated each syllable as if I were slow. "I warned you. I – I can't say any more. I had to —" He mirrored me, wringing his mane. "He's – getting worse —"

Aero's words – "*ignorant… fool*" ricocheted, and I dissected his features for a ruse.

"Prove it."

A flame dunked his side fringe; he snuffed it out.

"If you want to perish here, that's cool with me," he said serenely. I wondered what it would take to fragment his geniality.

"Who sent you?" I said brusquely.

"Hmm, let me see." He studied the bulwarks in maddening meditation. "Aurora's wrangled a place as Cess's understudy, and I'm yours."

I looked round sarcastically. "Did Cessie or Aero have a face-lift, or am I going blind?"

"Nadia activated the emergency flight button," he said starkly. "Aero got singed, so my father ordered Aurora, Alexandrina, Fire and I to aid you and Cessie."

My diaphragm flipped. "Aero – he's not — ?"

"He'll live," he said grimly. "Thanks to the burns ointment. Cessie told me about your tree-climbing – is that how you sheltered up here?"

His flattery didn't move me. "You'll be amazed what you can do in a life-or-death."

"True." His gangly leg criss-crossed again. "Believe me, I wasn't thrilled about this."

"Where's Cessie?" My mandate was grated.

"Manufacturing our escape," he said glibly.

"Why was I ambushed?" I demanded. "Who reprogrammed the bots?"

Shale unbolted from the earthen ceiling, uranium-streaked blades plopping our toes. I wasn't sure who squealed first – undoubtedly him.

"We'll chinwag later." His ruddy nose whitened as he ogled the rubble. "My chance of qualifying's nil if you die here."

"Charming," I said – it distorted to a glower.

What'd divided us from the volcano's exhausts caved in, the intensity as hypnotic as harp strings.

My checkmate was verbalised before I sensed my jaw unglue: "Tell me w-what's between you and Cessie. Or I won't c-come with you." I doubled up as whooping overwhelmed me. The cavern was about to bake us alive.

Magnus flexed his hand: he sought a pact. "It's not what you think. He *is* losing his grip."

He wouldn't elaborate further; it hit me he'd not been angry earlier – he'd been perturbed.

Sweltering, I shook on the contract. In single file we screwed ourselves past the blasting cranny, frisking to the blenching rim. I didn't know if the armistice would thaw as hurriedly as the loot, but dying was more dreadful.

Underneath, Cessie hunted shavings of wood, assembling a bridge over the red-hot creek, searing molten branding her collar. Aurora,

Alexandrina and Fire towed sacks of valuables, helmeted and brandishing mallets.

The spurts were so fiery we withdrew, appraising the expanse.

"For the love of robots," Magnus said hollowly.

More co-operatively, I added: "Can we jump?"

Cessie leached her rags with ciphers of water: "No." It was subdued; I strained to decrypt the rebuff.

"Look, Joan of Arc," Aurora said portentously. "Jump now or you'll burn." She leapt herself to elude the scalping bath.

It was as if somebody'd sopped petrol over the island: the poisonous vapours were that forceful.

"Ladies first," Magnus quipped.

"I'd rather die," I said.

He furnished water bottles for my budding fist. "For your safekeeping."

I didn't feel indebted as he abseiled down the sifting ravine, counting to two hundred, his footfalls sounding on the stones, until the murk roofed him entirely.

A pulse later, Aurora's order drifted: "Ivy – now!"

Cartwheels of soot steamed my textiles as I climbed below, beholding the aviators camouflaging the thunderclouds. When I was halfway down I sprung, unbreathing, into the murky quilt, the cigarette odours emanating.

In a scuffle, my tatty cloth was caught by the only real friend I had left here. My mouth unbolted to thank her when the atoms torched her bouffe. The particles rose slowly: one friend had been charred and the other was being killed in front of me.

Sharply, I grabbed the granite-crusted mallets from Alexandrina's stunned tenure and pruned the poor, blackened portions of bumblebee blonde. The bristles were adrift as though conscious, and consequently were digested by the bloodshot sea. Above, the cliff where Magnus and I'd waited erupted, and severed lumps grilled.

"Let's head for land," Aurora said composedly. "Alexandrina and Fire, secure the log. Magnus, we'll use the twigs as sails, and Ivy and Cessie keep together."

Nobody spoke as the vessel evacuated the puking slough: the blizzard had ceased, lucidity drenching the skies.

"We'll go back soon," I said restfully. "The burns unit will know what to do."

It was irresistible, the feeling that somebody higher-ranking could relieve our cargo, direct our ensuing steps and amass our plunder.

"I'm f-fine," she said unnervingly.

We shipped to the verge, bounding mildly over the waterway until we were ashore, blundering over the logs and kneeling in the warm grains.

"What happened to Aero?" I queried, as soon as I could speak without bile.

Cessie's new shaggy do smoked in the clear evening; she sniffed what had once been lemony cologne. "We couldn't see you below. We mined what we could find, but Aero suggested you'd gone for the middle of the volcano." She hiccoughed. "I thought even you wouldn't be that mad, but we were ascending when a fireball lit his sleeves. He took it off but it was too late. He nearly fell into the lava lake. I assisted him back to camp, and Nadia —"

"She knows the next bit," Magnus said politely, handing her water for her shrivelling strands. He carefully sidestepped my moping manner: was the truth going to come to candlelight, or had I been hoodwinked?

At Aurora's urging we rambled towards a fresher, less detonative ocean. Alexandrina and Fire executed the usual rituals: cleansing water and trawling fish. I thought Magnus had forsaken our deal, but as the sunset illumined the strangled heaths, Cessie's eyelashes swept mine.

"How did you get Ivy to follow you?" she said inquisitively.

"Sure about this?" Magnus muttered.

"Positive," I sniped.

"What's this about?" Alexandrina and Fire recited through a wedge of salamander.

"It was a last resort," Magnus said, almost to himself. "The walls were caving in, the core was about to blast. I'm sorry, Cess."

"Sorry?" she said testily. "What are you on about? I'm glad we're all safe."

"Famous last words," he said grimly. "I said… I'd relay the story of Evangeline."

Cessie's pallor was bloodless: "You can't."

"There's no other option." Magnus didn't look at her. "She's been suspicious for a while."

"We swore," she said croakily.

"We were children," he said. "I don't want to lie any more."

Cessie quavered like a Jack-in-the-box. "I won't tell you – I'll *show* you."

My lifeless email imparted a memory inscribed: *Lyme Regis, 2206.*

Skittishly, I clicked on my first friend's darkest memoir.

Chapter Eight: Impressions

My brain downloaded the memory, the toasting of fruit and fish unnerving, my co-workers chilling themselves by the streams. The surroundings were as distilled as glassed potions.

The date loiters, as vague and faded as a passé visual, baked brown grains littering the patchwork below, where effervescent whitecaps immerse sandcastles, as erect as medieval manors.

The vertical cliff stairs kink round trusses of sward, fifty feet high. The turquoises and teals of the coast boast a starry palate, alighting my zebra print cardigan, moist with perspiration. My candyfloss slip-ons are flaccid as I skim Lyme Regis' bookshop of rocks.

I cannot see Cessie, I am Cessie, euphoric as I tap-dance the margins, a fine-haired, suited middle-aged man grappling a satchel of water-colours, teddies and porcelain dolls.

"Cessie, watch your step." My father sounds cross.

Titters detonate from my throat, and I turn to the boy on my left.

"Bet you can't tightrope the edge," I goad.

The brown-haired companion eyes the powdery rock face. "Only if you do it first." His chin is rigid with the challenge, and I see no mercy in the pastel blue.

"Magnus, you always cheat!" I say, tossing my ringlets.

"I'm watching you two," my father breaks in angrily. "One more step…"

The itch to win is alcoholic, for I footstep towards the brink, irresolute. My parent's presently plum-coloured as he waves my bag.

Almost there. I stray the threshold of gravelly mounts and the grass tickling my flip-flops, and execute a Nutcracker pointe, smirking at Magnus…

"Your turn," I say wickedly.

Magnus jars at the writ. "It looks awfully steep —"

"You're afraid," I say victoriously. "Scaredy-cat."

"I'm not afraid of anything," Magnus says wobblingly.

"You won't see fresh air for the next decade if you don't get back right now!" Apollo Belle orders.

I quirk my brows. "What're you waiting for? He can't ground you."

Magnus hops on a precarious boulder, dislodging it from the pebbles. He steps onto the next one as though in a video game, and I am spurring him on; we are invincible...

"Hey, Cess," Magnus says, shiny-faced. "Fancy a game of see-saw?"

He stamps on the daisies and I jump on the opposite side, sniggering, and we play for ten minutes on the tape. Even Mr Belle has given up, retiming his Apple watch.

"Humpty Dumpty sat on the wall. Humpty Dumpty had a great fall," I sing.

"All the King's Horses and All the King's Men," Magnus joins in.

"...couldn't put Humpty together again!"

Elated to have reiterated the rhyme, I lean forward too far to laugh, and Magnus ebbs from the penultimate rock. The footstep discharges the final, ugliest shard of cliff.

I wished I could roar, but I was mute.

My squirrel gaze is mirrored in Magnus' as I hang fleetingly before toppling, squashing the stems, daisies disseminated. There is a microsecond when Magnus caterwauls and then I am over the pier, a china figurine about to detach in a hundred pieces...

"Cessie! Cessie!" The plea is lost in the vultures circling the precipices.

I felt her thoughts... *would they scavenge my flesh?*

As I jet downhill, Magnus' howling stops and feet thunder on the rocks, calling a different name. There is no slow-motion special effects as surfs thrash my forelegs, abdomen, neckline: until only sunny clumps glimpse over the top, embroiled with seaweed.

It is difficult to calculate how long I am under before I float like a cork in a jar, transiently relieved from a watery grave. A dart of iron drifts laterally and a tin figure bears down, and I am swimming my arms, help! Help me please!

The trundling servant is blinking coldly down the crags, fine-tuning its faulty button.

"I'm sorry," it says mechanically. "You will perish in three minutes. It has been charming serving you."

"No – you exist to help!" I scream as the robot accelerates out of sight, and I'm not buoyed now. I'm overpowered, swamped in a tankful of saltwater…

The man arrives from nowhere, bare-footed, hairy, rolled-up shirt crinkly. Eels tack the zebra pattern as I'm airlifted, semi-conscious, to land, wet with blanched corals and grit.

I am saved but something is wrong – it is like looking into a gorge. His sagging jowls are all I can see as my lungs are resuscitated, and light impales the realm.

I vomit a lungful of weeds and brine, and someone is alerting the emergency services, the red-and-white van we crayoned in school…

"If Magnus hadn't been so quick-thinking," Dr Stone says, "I don't know if she'd have made it."

Remotely, I hear my parents' commotion.

"It was his reckless game that landed her in this position," my mother is arguing. "Why you couldn't keep a leash on your son…"

"It's a good job he was here," Dr. Stone says sombrely. "Magnus says your girl was the initiator. She's a sprightly kid… it would've happened anyway."

"I couldn't stop her." Apollo is dismayed. "It's my fault…"

"It's that bloody robot." My mother saunters in her azure heels, jabbing the professor in the chest. "Your model. Completely unethical; it would've left her to die…"

"It contravened the most basic principles." Dr Stone is bemused. "Amazing how premeditated the rejection was, I've never seen –"

Mrs Belle cut into his glee. "You would've eaten your words if that had been Magnus. The modern designs aren't safe."

"So we regress history; undo our innovative work?" Stone says markedly. "If I just fiddle the settings -"

"First the bike, now this," Apollo says gravely. "Your robots answer no code of ethics. They couldn't do the most primal thing – spare my daughter's life."

"Purely logistics." Stone harnesses his spectacles. "It refused to destroy itself..."

Mrs Belle ploughs the champagne sand. "If you fail to design a robot that values life, we'll tell everyone what occurred on the beach. The scandal will ruin you."

The adults clearly think I am insentient, but my heart is strumming. The blare of the ambulance grows like cactuses in a desert, and I make myself completely still.

Dr Stone measures their threat. "Alright," he says guardedly. "However, know the consequences are unforeseen. If anyone finds out, Wolves will squander its profits."

"The worst has already happened," Apollo Belle says bleakly.

"Do it," my mother asserts.

My legs were hoisted, as though winched from a black creek, and the excerpt became sightless, static.

It was as though I'd ransacked her private journal, the rabbit-eared one she'd had when she was six, that I'd scrawled over to prove I could join up my signature. She hadn't disowned me then, but this was now; the harsh, windswept present. I forwarded the link to Cessie, for her custody, always.

"What happened afterwards?" I said to my teary friend.

"Magnus." Her snuffles evolved to sobs. "Tell her?"

"First... she has to swear not to tell anyone, even Pearl," Aurora said, who was palpably familiar with the tale.

There had to be another portion of the story, for no true calamity had befallen the memory; she had survived...

I swore.

"My father interpreted the Belles somewhat loosely," Magnus said tightly, and if he was mortified by the scene I'd witnessed, no hint of it was borne in his leonine face.

"So he fixed it?" I said lightly. "Is that so catastrophic?"

"It wasn't a renewal, it was a creation," Magnus answered. "Nothing like this had been made in human history."

"Without *her* I don't know if he'd have had the idea," Cessie sniffled. "Evangeline was no robot. Originally, she was a twenty-two-year-old succumbing to an unbeatable injury during the worst period of the infirmary. Professor Stone couldn't save her, so he offered the route... he altered her."

"What are you —?" I started to say.

"In the sinews of chemical, iron and consciousness, my father undertook his greatest experiment. He saved Eva's life when all seemed hopeless. She became an android, but one able to think, moralise and empathise. She'd been the first," Magnus concluded.

"The first Human-Bot experiment," I breathed.

"Mum and Dad *never* intended it to go that far," Cessie alleged to the appalled stares of Alexandrina and Fire. "They merely wanted a programme of sorts, equipped with ethics. Never to mechanise a vulnerable patient or create an advanced race."

"There's something else you have to know," Magnus said ruefully.

"Don't tell her that." Cessie was freaked. "We can't ask her to hide that from Aero."

"You wanted the unabridged truth," Magnus said faintly. "So here it is. My father was successful, but not without casualties. During the operation, Aero's father was electrocuted. Dad recorded it as an experiment fatality in Cotton – your dad's archives. Aero's mother didn't want him to know."

The waterways journeyed past, frost enveloping the group.

"How could she keep this from him?" I said incredulously. "How could *you*?"

Cessie writhed from the accusation.

"Better that he didn't know," she said, and her tears dried like the barren lands. "Better he didn't have to carry that around with him. You've seen how his mother had to raise him. He'd suffered enough."

There was a sphere-like burn in my tonsils. "I won't tell him. But one day, he must find out."

The three conspirators nodded.

"And Evangeline?" I mumbled. "Did she live with you straightaway?"

"Her new existence began in a laboratory," Cessie whispered. "Dr Stone tested her reactions, memories, emotions, cyborg brain. She was amnesiac – her remembrance blotted out forever. Stone said that if we reminded her, her new body wouldn't cope and she would burn up."

"Her awareness is absent?" I checked.

"She feels; she was my guardian in childhood, but her origins are foreign to her. She's been in our charge since I was eleven," Cessie confessed.

The knowledge went unabsorbed in this hellish wilderness. I ached to postpone when it would sledgehammer my thoughts, arise in guilt every time I saw Aero, disturb me every time I saw what was left of the woman; and blemish me every time I had to deceive Pearl.

Had Dr. Stone been right to recreate the invalid, to synthesise skin with motors?

"Will she die?" I said, because it was too intense to pity the half-human.

"Oh, yes," Cessie told me. "But many, many years after a human form would've wasted." Her shorn haircut slouched on her lap: "It's a half-life, not truly human."

The plots were feeble, but the tides disintegrating what was once Pangaea, yielding to a ripe era.

"Don't tattletale in 23," Magnus said mutedly, and his softness was more threatening than his terrorisation.

"I gave my word," I grunted.

"Good, 'cause it's strictly classified. This Hell's Creek… far from the cameras… is the only confidential retreat."

"I'm sure you've a dozen stately homes you can scuttle into," I said aloofly. "After all, the standard rules don't apply to your lot."

"I'm not a breed of dog," he glowered.

"Yeah? Well, you act like it," I refuted.

"Listen to the pair of you!" Cessie interceded. "Even after everything, you can't put your issues aside —"

"My opinion's unchanged," I said ruthlessly.

"Likewise," Magnus concurred.

"Why don't we stopper the liquidised gems?" Aurora advocated timidly.

Cessie obeyed wordlessly, groping the mineral sacks, as milky as lactose, wisps fierier than a furnace — but nothing equalled her magenta cheekbones. Alexandrina and Fire, who performed as a duo, applied their fish hooks to narrow the fastenings, lobbing them over their backs, as the dwarfs had in the folk tale.

A sextet, we combed for the construed camp, Aurora boosting her footage of the backcloth, whereas her boyfriend (in theory) made sport of the brushwood. Myself – I twiddled my thumbs at the scandal now in my safe, where it would lie undisturbed until an unspecified date.

Aurora 'oohed' at a gaudy sunrise sapling; a pure, youthful maple, the thickets rebounding as Cessie's bouffe had before it was aflame: too opulent for twenty-third century regard.

She motioned precipitously, where sunflower flakes avalanched rotting bones, and a leather of goo textured the loam. Aurora still recorded in heed of the law. Remarkable how this body of frauds picked and chose which conditions to follow.

At first I believed the comet had trampled the terrain prematurely, elicited by our imposition, but slowly it dawned it was a footprint. A sandy, freshly printed heel was engraved, a clawed footmark dimpled over the moors; besprinkled in chalk, spanning fifty centimetres.

Cessie and I didn't require telepathy to infer the creator.

"The carnivore outside camp," we unionised.

Magnus dredged the marks for later testing with a twig. "Were you going to wait until before or after we were eaten to tell us that?"

"After," Cessie grinned.

"We all keep secrets," I trilled.

"It fed recently," Magnus deduced.

"The other one was a fresh kill, as well," Cessie said before I could pour scorn on him.

"The identity of the slaughterer?" Magnus questioned.

"Don't know," Cessie and I chimed.

"Tweedle-dum and Tweedle-dee don't exactly make great junior sleuths," he said despairingly.

"It's well-executed," Alexandrina and Fire offered their two cents.

"Question is… will it find us before we find camp?" Magnus ruminated.

A cube jammed my gullet. "I think Aero's correct… nothing could make such large rips… except —"

"What?" Cessie said in trepidation.

"This rings a bell," I said, levelling the lines in my forehead. "It's uncommon – but it can't be – only – nothing else leaves impressions like that."

"Tyrannosaurus-rex!" Cessie blustered.

The redwood flora convulsed, the ground drumming as if the volcano reignited; my throat weakened.

The monster who had slain our predecessor, with eyesight as penetrating as Professor Goodwin's glasses and a smell more primal than a hyena's.

We'd been tailed.

All we saw at first were storeys-high limbs, inked in russet, pewter and liquorice, flopping beside shamrock climbers, fiddly digits fronting us; whiskered veneer blanketing a plasticised sandwich of tissue. It was natural, then, to behold the marmalade markings scaling its claret binoculars, sharper than a sheep's, more ancient than ours.

We were not the only onlookers; it craned its cabled, s-shaded neckline, magnet jaw unwiring to unearth cabinets of rectangular, titanium tusks. We were fixed on the Medusa leer until its oesophagus issued hoarse, mellow noises, this tyrant of reptiles butting its beefed, double-chinned drumsticks.

"Survival of the fittest!" Magnus cawed. "Go on – run!"

One breath…

I took flight, scarcely discerning the clout of stems showering our track, eyebrows knifed by bee-sucked barbs, diminutive stags stampeding the glades…

Two breaths…

Our shapes interlinked; his hand could've been mine, my hair could've been Cessie's; we were confined in the wastelands, perspiring through our garments.

Three breaths…

"Ow!"

The yelp could've been anyone's as Herculean fists walloped the stones, blighting our sight: eleven tonnes of might, thrice our statures.

The rock fall clogged our escape. All I could think was why Aero didn't mention that ogres could be so intelligent, breathtakingly lethal.

We dislodged the stones with as much toughness as we could muster, headfirst in the disarray, and its venomous breath brazed our T-shirts: we wrinkled our nostrils.

"The shore!" Aurora cried. "Head for the shore!"

We didn't need telling twice – every traveller for themselves. A sickness congested my throat, and the opacity was so horrific I couldn't repel a squint back. A Bo-sized, huge skull (I observed at last), was bedded in mandarin fluff, chisel teeth like rubber knives.

I filmed its every move as if it were fiction, not happening to me. My dad had said that when terrible things ensue, you disengage, you stop feeling.

"What are you doing?" Magnus said feverishly as Fire unfurled layers upon layers of foul ray-fish bones, clicking his parched tongue.

"Something useful," he said stanchly.

He unrolled the picnic of sea dwellers, obscured in conifers, and his knotted planes were firm.

The T-Rex's minute forelimbs stretched and it handpicked the fleshiest meat, reedy structure counterbalancing its helicopter dimensions. Toothed digits clinched the meal into its entry, bloodied Barbie mouth unsatisfied.

"It's not enough," Magnus said, harassed. "It can chomp through five hundred pounds – shit —"

The troll grappled with Fire's pleated jacket, and giant and man wrestled for twelve throbs.

In the interlude he seemed to win, burrowing down its edgeless muscles, exclaiming at the steely ridges.

I knew it was hazardous to assume a monster cannot fetch another card from its itinerary, and none of the leftover five revolved from the finale.

It took an aeon for the giant to recover him as though he were a pygmy, and we hadn't been friends but he'd liberated me from the lava. It was a cruel deck that saw his still acned visage gored in nanoseconds.

"No!" Magnus said as the creature gagged, incapacitated.

A miniscule, zinc disc drooped in a salivated puddle, twenty times the lakes Pearl had danced in as a little girl. Discomposed, I shrouded it in tissue and unblinkingly slotted it into the deceased's knapsack. Apt that was all left... no corpse...

"I thought it was a legend – I mean, I didn't think it'd actually kill him." Cessie sounded revolted as her chopped hairs gusted with the brines.

"We should've been faster." Aurora exuded teardrops. "The beach – it isn't too late – Ivy, take the r-rucksack."

"Give it to me." Harshly, Magnus reached for the bag.

I chucked it at him, tongue-tied.

The brawny hind limbs, quelled by its latest supper, vivified and its uniform lamellas clucked, a carnivorous rooster. It eructed, acidic with the excretion of our co-worker.

We bolted; its short strides seemed deliberate, rapider than the tube despite hardly fluttering a ligament, demonic with focus, pitiful in its fiendishness. My video rolled throughout the ordeal.

The chalked overhangs swam in my bloody eyelashes, limestone itching my palms, Cessie at my heels, Alexandrina tearless, yet I intuited her woe.

We waddled backwards, not quite touching, violent tides moistening our shabby toes.

Our patroller couldn't be unheeded; those curiously mini clubs cart-wheeled like meatballs in a blender, stalling to sniff our beating innards, pumping lungs and succulent odours. A shingle rumpled under Magnus' Achilles': this was surely the end.

We couldn't edit this chapter of our lives – it squandered no seconds, hunching so its barred sultana underbelly, twice as long as he stood, angled to thresh us. The cane-like tail strapped us backwards like Ferris wheels; the canary island, grubby shale and plesiosaur sky skated in and out of view as we held onto the wizened skin.

It jettisoned its skull frenetically to scoop us into its lizard lips, as though we were All Hallows' sweets, and we hunkered inside its vermillion middle. Its machete molars, resembling the 'D' in a nursery alphabet, were dense and field-wide in expectation of its next supper.

"Aim for the burrow!" I said out of the blue.

I was balancing on one of its Pearl-sized legs as though firing down incessant towers, and weighing my chances of survival if I took off from several feet. I swallowed fluid. It was preferable to being devoured by a giant.

"I won't make it!" Cessie said in foreboding.

"You're an experienced diver, you'll be fine." My voice carried over its upholstery as my pupils tapered.

In a pod chain, we escalated like missiles, ululating as we became short-winded: paperweights falling into a leafed, granular otter warren.

Bass-quality peals rebounded from the beach – our huntsman was bloodthirsty and raving at our duplicity. I didn't need a T-Rex translator to classify a dire reprimand.

"We're dead meat," Magnus mewled. "He disposed of Fire as if he were a waste bin."

A spittle of granite drizzled from my stomach. We were as squished as the sardines we'd eaten.

"Would you rather cower on its backbone?" I said briskly. "We'll sit and wait it out." The long game sounded sanguine.

Magnus sighed. "This is all Aero's fault."

Cessie and I synchronised our divergence.

Aurora still retained his hand from when we'd flown. "It would've happened anyway. It's doubtless been tracking the original group for days."

"But he would've known what to do," Magnus disputed. "Being a dinosaur-whisperer."

"Shut up," Cessie and I said.

Yet we were all rendered dumb by the sudden *clunk* outside the sanctuary, and a wrenching *munch*.

From my sightline, nearest the hole, the Tyrannosaurus-rex could be seen uprooting celastrus trees, from which he procured a gingery dweller about as lengthy as a primary ruler. Cessie squalled at the same time as the mammal, cindered locks jacketing her eyes as its yellowed crowns squirmed, but too late. Those action-man limbs placed the ferret in its jaws and it met its end. Bloodied viscera plopped down the warren, sponging my sleeves.

The T-Rex was not finished yet. It poked around for the rest of the family, babied fuzz frozen with their last squeaks, mangled bones building a grave alongside me.

Its potent neck ebbed in sovereignty. It beat the plugged, woody material; however there was nothing animate to bite.

"We're next," Alexandrina whispered.

She was the packer beside me. I perceived her question before she voiced it.

"I couldn't look, when it took him," she said tremblingly. "I don't suppose... was it quick?"

"I don't think he felt anything," I said. "It was too mighty."

Teardrops mingled with sleep in her cornea. "The disc... that was really brave of you."

"No it wasn't," I said lowly.

The T-Rex was still sibilating out of bounds.

"It's hungry," Cessie said heavily. "We have to get beyond its reach."

Strawberry-blonde seeds bristled in the tides, where our tormentor prowled the sands.

Aurora clasped weeds, half-standing. "I'm going to do something awfully rash."

"What are you — ?" Magnus started, but by now she had hastened out of the asylum, liquid black filaments flouncing.

Before he could claim the ringside, I peered to where Aurora strutted beneath the three-tiered T-Rex, gesticulating seaweed.

I had the urge to guffaw, but stopped short after witnessing the drabness on my foe's facade. "What in Mars is she doing?"

Fire's parting reverberated: *Something useful.*

"She's got something up her sleeve," Magnus said knowingly.

"We need an ace," I garbled.

Cessie, her weakness remedied, sat next to me. "Pay attention."

The Tyrannosaurus-rex pumped its incarnadine biceps as Aurora enthralled it with words. In her alternative fist she had a clump of celastrus wood. Was she going to bludgeon her way out?

"Hey!" she said. The switch pulsing her hairline divulged the film. "If you wish to eat us – you'll have to hound us first!"

"What're you waiting for?" Magnus insisted. "GO!"

The four of us heaved our tender bodies from the secreted shack, one by one, so as to become imperceptible.

As we sidled under a titan thigh, Aurora tarried to taunt: "Don't let your dinner run away with you!"

I snatched her arm towards the forests, where the T-Rex plausibly couldn't squeeze in.

We limped past its forty-foot span, prickled by its maroon rawhide, not daring to oxygenate, unless we courted our downfalls.

It made a stab at situating us, but where we hobbled it was too gargantuan to distinguish us. Its alarm amplified when we jogged rings in between its legs as we used to play tag or the three-legged race, floundering from its banquet. We palpitated with its beastly tantrum.

I mounted a cinnamon bark but its marches plagued us; we were as inconsequential as the ginger rats: more alive to the menace. The trace of pine and meat in its retches was the first clue before it demolished the climbing frame. We kited off like pharaoh ants.

Cessie was grappling with Alexandrina. "There's another way!"

"It has to be like this," Alex said solemnly. "Fire's dead."

She somersaulted in the path of our persecutor. It clinched her barbed hairstyle and rainbow raincoat, whetting its carnivorous back teeth. The once intimidating woman was minuscule as she was maimed and galloped in its whisks. It regurgitated her velour bow and licked felt handbag as we screened our lashes.

The diversion was the occasion we needed to sail for the coppice... she couldn't be saved, but we could sprint further...

Due to my wheeziness, my arch bulged. I fortified my forehead with my rucksack on the clay storey. I forgot what breathing was... I mimed sleeping in the brackets... I played dead.

The Tyrannosaurus-rex measured my legitimacy, doughy cerebrum near mine. I was entombed in mire along with my friends, who likewise grew slacken, so smothered in bracken and filth the air clouded...

"Now!"

Cessie collared me and we scooted through cones and hedges, as though evading the Minotaur. None of us knew where the time machine was —

Its baton armpits levered the branches, and it was looking in, blood-soaked — we waited for the deathly strike.

It didn't come, for it'd punctured its immense temple on a durable, silvery, agleam object. Wedges of gumbo fell on us as we blockaded the time machine with bags, human strength and Alex's ex-tools. It barrelled the husk with its mitts, splintering it. Cessie bewailed in my ear-hole.

I dialled the controls with a final shoot of heroism. We were half-airborne.

"The engine's failing," Magnus said gaspingly. "I told you —

"Out of the way." I meddled the faltering electrics with a screwdriver, the creature's maws scratching at the glass, its countenance insatiable.

Aurora appropriated the switchboard, releasing the communicator's electrics to torpedo us higher, higher, higher. The carriage chugged upwards, reeking like lead. Sunlight transfigured to blackness.

"Nadia was way off about second chances," Magnus said, with a siphon of toxin. "Darwin had it right."

"We fled, at least," Cessie said.

Some of us.

I swabbed the acrylic. The T-Rex's handprint was purely an impression, no longer corporeal.

Chapter Nine: Catching the Worm

Mobile bats skewered my flocculent fishtail, hyaline skeletons aglow, engorged cobwebs murky as mould on the posters. A foursome, we bucked into split-grin, seeded pumpkins, skittering streamers and beaming Jack-o'-lanterns, and my adversary uttered the words that would condemn us.

"Two co-players are dead," he said formally. "If talk starts, we're finished. If we just – modulate what happened —"

"We've nothing to hide," I gobbed. "Those were accidents —"

"We've blood on our hands," he maintained. "We didn't lift a finger to save them."

"I did!" Cessie said uproariously. "I *begged* Alex."

"That was before," Magnus stressed the line. "We did nothing when they were taken."

Blinkered, I said: "It was too quick. It was four times our size —"

"We didn't try," he reiterated. "For that, we'll be disciplined."

"That isn't right," I said, gripping my blood-drenched wrapper. "It'll be madness if we're caged for this."

"The tapes," Aurora said forcefully. "We filmed throughout. They can't convict us on that evidence. I know, I'm a columnist."

Magnus' rufous hairline uncurled as he muttered: "No, that'll be our death sentence. Delete the tapes and nobody has to know."

"They'll see we had to save our skins," Aurora nodded vehemently. "They were goners and I think with the risk to our own lives —"

"That won't matter," Magnus said. "*Think*. We were a team, to win and lose together. If they find out we bolted at the first sign of disturbance, that'll be the end of our careers."

"When they inevitably find out the truth we'll be disqualified from service," I said, ruffling a web.

"Then make sure they don't," he said severely. "The operation will be frozen if you let the rabbit out of the hat."

Aurora yo-yoed as she reapplied her glitzy nail polish: "No one will know?"

"It'll be as if they hadn't died," he said.

I hoofed my plimsoll when I saw Cessie was heartened at the prospect. "I'm hiding enough. I won't safeguard your falsehoods any longer."

Cessie's lob boomeranged as she annexed me to a corner. "Alright, we won't dupe them. But we can downplay our involvement in the expiries."

"You're been studying history for too long," I said emptily.

As they falsified their accounts, Fire and Alexandrina didn't seem extinct, decocting in the T-Rex's liver. You couldn't die in an earlier ecosphere, could you?

Magnus zipped word to Nadia that we'd recurred. We bunched in the halls, awaiting her; framed, straitjacketed officials skirted past with stomach-turning squints.

"Why're you so afraid of what your father will say?" I asked him unexpectedly. "Won't he let us off the hook?"

"It's not weak to second-guess people," Magnus said with abating infuriation. "He's not unkind, only capricious. His judgements are a labyrinth, difficult to determine."

I thought of how he'd undermined Bo with punishing phrases, keeping her like a hamster on a rotator, endlessly eager for the muesli but finding it gallingly out of reach. With a father like that I could begin to see why Magnus was desperate to fudge the events. It'd been the first job of my outer-space internship and two stand-ins were deceased. Maybe I'd merited my ignominy.

Hail, like a rod, flogged the clacking barbican across the street, and the date struck – it was Halloween.

Plated Automata converged on us; their Detention badges overmastered me into the webbing, Cessie in strings, the final two already shackled. Despite our exertions, we couldn't swindle justice. I wordlessly blathered with Cess: *How'd they known?*

Their titanium tendons herded us, and I didn't feel I deserved a breakout. Magnus wormed between the irons, but uselessly; only a cyber-sword could liberate him.

"This is illegal!" he said, empurpled. "You tin heads may've forgotten, but my dad's in charge round here and my mum controls you things..."

They declaimed his rights upon arrest, but wouldn't partake in strife; I was reluctantly respectful, as it took an awful lot of restraint not to elbow him.

We tromped on the second corridor and shunted headlong into Aero's aubergine turtleneck, his shin bandaged to hide the scald sore. Shame plagued me like cockroaches: how long was the list of those I'd carelessly hurt?

He was visibly appalled: "Is it true? About Fire and Alex?"

Not one person resolved his query.

"We fell afoul of a – a T-Rex, and they were killed," I said openly. "They didn't stand a chance, or we would've – would've saved them."

"You left them in the clutches of that thing?" Aero said tacitly. "I know they pulled some stunts in their day, but that is something else."

"We didn't have a choice, Aero, you have to believe us," I vouched. "Once it's decided to eat you there's no reasoning with it."

"You just stood there while it dined on our colleagues," he ping-ponged back. "What's wrong, weren't they high-ranking enough for you?"

"You know I would never – status would have *no* effect," I chuffed.

"I don't know any more, Ivy," he said morosely. "Did the gig mean that much to you, that Fire and Alex could be damned?"

"Absurd!" I said as I was wrested, kicking and screaming, to the gaols under the pavestones.

Toffee beryl pieces shone in place of beacons and we found ourselves cowering in a dank, wee cell, the bars electrically watertight. Once our captivity had been fortified, the robots enunciated: "You have been found to be in breach of the Threat to Life Act and will be detained pending an inquiry. A Chair has been set up to determine what transpired. Is there a statement you aim to issue before our withdrawal?"

The satiny inhuman guard flashed at me, and Aurora jounced her pigtail. Magnus had been strong-armed into the booth next door, yet we shadowed his guidelines indisputably. Until we'd been enlightened, we'd have to hallmark the envelopes of our knowledge.

"Not 'til someone visits us to expound what's going on," I said tremulously.

As soon as they'd clattered away, Aurora realigned her crow hairs so they were collinear: "See, that wasn't too hard, was it? Keep up the righteous act you're so good at, and you'll spare our necks."

I wasn't sure I wanted to spare their necks – more like throttle them.

Cellmates, we poised our Achilles' heels on the craggy pew until we heard the habitual twang of our advisor. It appeared the androids had approved my wish.

Nadia's sylvan 'do was mussed; a magnetic clipboard was carted by her snakes-and-ladders belt and she wore a mercurial lour.

"You three," she said forbiddingly. "You've been interned as a consequence of the ends of Mr Jackson and Ms Jones. You'll not submit confirmation of your innocence at a trial, but an inquiry. Lives have been menaced and in some cases terminated. Do you appreciate the magnitude of the allegations?"

One by one, we curveted to our tiptoes.

"How did you know they were... gone?" I maundered.

Nadia repositioned her sheep print bandeau and I detected her unshapen cardigan was half-on. "Their CPUs had been expunged from the system. That only ensues when one's mortality is depleted."

"I recouped Fire's disc, Professor Ludwig, but he'd already lost the fight. If I could've done more, I would've," I said tremblingly.

"Is the disc in your custody?" my guru said tenuously.

"It's w-with Magnus," I said, making eye contact with my hemic socks.

"Ivy." Nadia deposited a squishy ligament through the bars so she could fasten my parka. "I was your lecturer for many terms. I know they gave you a rough ride. I regret turning my rather tubby nose away as they terrorised you. In all honesty, did you want them to survive?"

"All I know is I didn't want that," I imbibed.

"Ms Moss, when I was sponsored to become head of the engineering department a great deal of naysayers opposed my promotion," Nadia said delicately. "And one of those never came back from the Cretaceous. Like me, for you it was easier to sit back. After all, hadn't they deserved it, in their cruelty and apathy?"

123

The sopping sock glissaded off my anklebone. "I'm not sure what you're implying."

Nadia tsk-tsked and tackled Cessie: "Ms Belle, do you have any defence for your activities?"

"I dissuaded Alex from self-sacrifice, but she wouldn't listen. I clogged her, but she got free, and she waived to *it*. It was over in a wink," Cessie relented.

The clipboard scribed her testament, and Nadia's rutted facets awakened: "No judge in the land will believe she abdicated her existence for the sake of a nemesis. Ivy, is this truthful?"

"It's on my video," I said impassively.

"You *videoed* the event in question?" The magnetic board continued the transcript, so exhaustive it made acne seem as spotless as shampoo.

"The red light was on throughout," I related. "It wasn't my intention, but under the Freedom of Information Act —"

"Put that out of your pleats, Ms Moss – this was a life-or-death. That you had the *presence of mind* to film that'll confound the court."

Aurora pecked her neon lip-liner. "Professor Ludwig, I didn't tape anything and didn't see Alex die. Magnus told Fire not to attempt anything, but we'd no idea what he was arranging: he was a reticent individual. We would've done everything in our power had we been prepared. We were the understudies, for robots' sake. The frontrunners didn't issue any commands; they'd forsaken us to the clemency of a twenty-foot dinosaur."

"That's a misrepresentation," I said, flexing the bars. "If it's an inquest, why've we been enslaved?"

"You've lost minutes, while Mr Jackson and Ms Jones won't see autumn transfigure to wintertime, or any of the marvellous wormhole exploits," Nadia reproached. "Now, if your tantrum's finished, cease your endeavours to leave the coop."

She didn't need to exacerbate her vocals to cause me to take heed.

"Have you grilled Magnus?" Cessie said, poring over the lateral hammocks; rat-eaten quilts snuggled under military pillows.

"Scrupulously," Nadia said, more gently. "He's convinced Fire and Alex walked into their own kismets, and that he doesn't have any spools."

"Of course." I bopped in a circle. "That's it, then, we're guilty?"

"The innocent have nothing to dread," Nadia said, primping her earmuffs. "Goodbye Ivy, Cessie, Aurora. A machine will send refreshments soon."

"Oh, that's a comfort," I snarled as she left.

"Stop estranging our supporters," Aurora said, nuzzling her split ends in aggravation.

"Stop censoring the proof," I said back. "You're supposed to be a jour-na-list."

Aurora's oversized bow held the hairs so her veins tensed; they were slicker than a horsetail's. It didn't matter how much I preened, plaited and gelled my waves, they were never as comely. I conjectured who the jury would trust, and knew my name would be last on the list.

"I'm assisting you, Ivy, unbelievably enough," the newscaster said, however I was attentive to **Rule #1** – never rely on a reporter.

"You don't aid others unless it'll benefit you," I said as I tucked into the yoghurt and flaxseeds brought in, slugging the water as though I wouldn't eyewitness daybreak.

"Your venom consumes you in the end," Aurora said bitterly. "Didn't you learn anything from Jackson and Jones?"

"Only how-not-to-die," I said acerbically.

"Hey, stop it!" Cessie said, forking blackberries in crème fraiche. "If we divide, we'll be easier to conquer."

"This isn't *Lord of the Rings*," I said, as Aurora reserved the juiciest salad carton. "We'll be tried separately anyhow."

"Monkeys face the marshal," Aurora headlined. "That'd make a decent story, in retrospect."

"Excuse me," somebody disordered our chatter. "May I enter?"

"It's not our property," I said, working to eradicate my insolence – after all, we had a guest.

The pergola swerved to admit a woman with a murky, medium-length hairdo, pinched eye bags and grandmotherly pencil skirt. We held our peace as she cogitated our fates.

"You mustn't think this is an arrest," she said affably. "No, no, no, it is a provisional measure until the q-and-a session."

"We're here against our will," I said fiercely.

"Dear one, nobody wants to be quizzed and traumatised," she said fondly, though her lobes pricked up. "How else does one get to the bottom of enigmas?"

I cross-examined her. "Have we met?"

"In your most earnest dreams, I'm sure," she said pretentiously. "You may be familiar with me from broadcasts. I front the organisation. I run the Detention Centre, my husband's a Professor, and I'd pawn my mittens I'm so positive you're an acquaintance of —"

"Mrs Stone," I said, as I envisaged her pug features on online outlets and naperies.

"Magnus' mother," Cessie said slothfully.

"Guilty as charged," she said delightedly. "This is a wonderful social call, isn't it? Provided you cooperate, you've zilch to fear."

"Cooperate in what exactly?" Aurora sat up, dislodging the sardines.

"There'll be a hearing as an upshot of your friends' absences." She bent down to our eye levels: "Between the four of us, I'd rather hush-up this horrid business. But Fire and Alexandrina were fairly highborn, and their parents will bring a lawsuit to the table if we don't present a court martial. So sorry, but they allege we imperilled their children in a manner that contravened their human rights."

"When is the question-and-answer set for?" I said tartly.

"It'll all be over by sundown tomorrow," she said gaily, and the plucks in my chest felt irregular.

"What's the worst that can happen?" Cessie asked lucidly.

Mrs Stone behaved as if she were reading a brochure – that's likely what she'd spent her life doing. "The mildest sentence will be... one hundred days' strict labour with our detainees. The middling sentence will be...expulsion from Wolves. The harshest sentence will be... five to ten years' imprisonment, and an everlasting criminal record."

"Are we likely to be acquitted?" Cessie persisted.

"50/50," the official said, and without further ado, her kilt swanned to floors forbidden to us.

"Couldn't you use your influence?" Cessie implored Aurora.

"There's no point." Aurora dyed her tips with her smokiest palate. "The rubrics are her reason for living. She doesn't abide using personal contacts."

"She'd convict her son?" I said doubtingly.

"She'd do anything to preserve her detoxified skin," Aurora said snidely, and I had cause to reflect if this was why she'd never officially said he was her boyfriend. I used to think they relished the guessing game, but feasibly it was darker than that.

As nightfall prolapsed we squabbled over the two hammocks, Aurora marking her zone with a five-thousand-credit hairbrush and handbag, Cessie lolling in the second; me ambulating on the wolfish axle.

"We can share," my best friend said cheerfully.

"What, so you can inspire me to pervert my testimony?" I said, swiping a blanket and drowsing in the crepitating feculence. I kept one eye wide: "The truth will out, as they say."

Cessie utilised her earbuds to obscure the rebuke and while Aurora dozed, I'd a crafty sixth sense she was erasing her videotapes. As she feigned somnolence, I migrated to the hardware dam dissociating us from Magnus.

"If that's what your mother's like, it's no wonder you're the way you are," I heckled to the contiguous lock-up.

"And your parents are so thick I'm surprised you can see straight," he said brusquely.

"Ah, is diddums upset 'cause his mum didn't let him off?" I bickered.

"You're pathetic." Cessie was muffled under the duvet. "You spoke through a barrage just to say that."

"Be quiet, it'll be excellent practice for your double-dealing in court," I said snappishly.

Our neighbour shook a tin. "I've been sent a Scottish dog box of shortbread, so it turns out being me *does* have bonuses."

"You'll have to sell it to pay for a decent solicitor," I fumed.

It sounded like he'd loafed on his makeshift sheets. "Enjoy the crumbs."

Cessie clobbered the pumpkin nightlight so we could kip.

*

The court was orbicular, spinach-tinged samite enswathing the chairs, bistre slats tamping our backs, a school of bystanders parading in, armed machines installed at the avenues.

We the accused were front-facing, and at the manifestation of Magnus' parents as judges my tonsils squeezed, a baseball noosing them. Mr and Mrs Stone were shrouded in Georgian toupees, and the former thrummed his gavel in response to the gossiping emanating in pest droves, inaudible yet disquieting in its vastness.

Mrs Stone initiated the projector, which would keep minutes, and said soundly: "All rise to impart your versions."

My right patella was foremost; Cessie, Aurora and Magnus speedily aped my example.

"Ivy," Mrs Stone's vibrato was judiciously sympathetic, "can you springboard with your recap of the lead-up?"

"Fire and Alexandrina chose their lots and there was little we could do to foil them," I said, mindful of my waistband elasticising. "If you evaluate my live-motion, you'll figure out there's no need for a court case."

"Ms Moss," Magnus' mother said yawningly, "the parents of Jackson and Jones are braying for justice. You were with the daughter and son when they were taken – had it been your kin, wouldn't you besiege us for details?"

My heart pit-patted. "Except you haven't just necessitated answers, you've interned us and presented us with a press conference."

Dr Stone cocked his brow pitilessly: "Ms. Moss, did you enact every measure possible to impede this calamity? Once they'd made their supposed choices, were your efforts to help inadequate?" He allowed a breather for the onlookers to absorb this. "Or even non-existent?"

Cessie held up her hand. "Judge, may I say something?"

He exerted his gavel: "Granted."

Cessie expanded her arms to include the whole parish: "It was a hot-cooker state of affairs, obliging us to strategise on our feet."

"Yet you were cherry-picked for your clear-headedness and strength. Did this fail you in your associates' hours of need?"

"No, we did our best." Cessie eyed the room to gauge the temperature. "You act as if you've made up your minds prior to the evidence."

"We're not interested in your opinions at present," Judge Stone said drolly.

"Ms Belle, gag your ripostes," Mrs Stone enforced.

An automaton zipped towards her with a silencer and, an effigy, Cessie no longer had the power to object. As my workmate made an inexplicable 'mmm-hmm', a sight sent tics through me. In a starched pinafore, Pearl's shoulders cemented and she ogled the door handle, outwardly blind to her sister, metres from her.

"Before we examine those legendary tapes, I think we should hear from *all* the witnesses," Mrs Stone said equitably. "Aurora Thorn, you are invited to speak."

The writer bunged a strand behind her with a tie, and adjourned her statement for assiduous jiffies. "I corroborate Ivy's avowal that it was beyond our capacities to assist them. I, on the other hand, repudiate that there are any clips in my arsenal."

I suppressed my pique.

"Your rectitude extols you," Mrs Stone said, without the bat of an eyelid. "One further probe... had you any inklings in advance of the events?"

"A moment, o-or two," Aurora said tearlessly, and the magistrate clucked caringly. "But it was obvious they weren't going to make it whatever we did. I-I was a reinforcement – Ivy, Cessie and Aero should've drawn conclusions beforehand. As a reporter, I'd have picked up the signs. I don't feel they were cruel, but negligent."

A man who had to be Alex's dad and a woman with Fire's asymmetrical nose appeared vindicated by this.

"Was the line-up on the whole efficacious before the T-Rex's spanner-in-the-works?" Dr Stone wondered.

"We did well to clear up their initial ineptitude with the one-woman volcano stunt, yes," Aurora said. "Myself, Fire, Alex and Magnus were the driving force. Although Ivy retrieved minerals, she's no team player. Without back-up, there's no doubt she wouldn't have made it to 23."

The projector copied every word. Dr Stone archived the document and said: "Thank you, Ms Thorn, you have been most helpful. Take a seat."

As she bypassed my gape, Mrs Stone beckoned her son.

"Do you have proprietorship of any clips?" she said measuredly.

"I would never have filmed such a gruesome incident," Magnus said, knuckles blanching as he cambered the worktable. "You can rifle through every file from when I was a newborn, and you won't find it."

"Because he purged it!" I fusilladed.

"That's hearsay," Magnus said nastily. "I repeat, nothing like that exists."

"*You* won't exist soon if you don't start being more forthright," I ransomed.

"Extortion is not tolerated in the courtroom," Mrs Stone said, steelier than a yak.

"Please don't type that up," I said dispiritedly.

"Yet you and your father are so fond of records," Mrs Stone said giddily, and the throng chortled.

"You'll keep quiet if you know what's good for you," Magnus said in an aside.

"So will you," I reasoned.

Judge Stone leant towards his descendant: "Were you likewise lax with your squadron's wellbeing?"

"No, sir," Magnus said, in a style only prep boys could emulate. "I vocally discouraged Fire before I learned of his tactics – but he, you see, sir, he was dogmatic. I've known him since I was a boy. Even I didn't dream he would try to tackle it. We couldn't reach him and he was demolished. Moss picked up what was left – his disc."

The blethering had stopped; it was as though gerbils had ousted them.

But Dr Stone wasn't finished with his son: "Couldn't you have assisted in those final seconds?"

"No, it was too high up," he reasserted. "It would've been unreasonable – a death wish – for us at this point."

"Very well," his father said.

"Aurora, Alex and I were the ones invested in his welfare," he added. "Not to indict anyone, but Cessie and Ivy didn't inconvenience themselves as they were nemeses."

Cessie pelted the silencer: "That's not factual. I endeavoured to save Alex despite the deathtrap, but she was stronger."

"Bullshit," Magnus said. "You two didn't give a damn because of petty former altercations. Ivy here was *rooted to the spot* when the beast reached us, and if it hadn't been for my orders, none of them would've run. Her languid leadership was a liability."

"I'll have you know I had us all playing dead, and that's why you're regrettably breathing now," I said, and had my contender been a dartboard, I would've targeted the bullseye.

"Enough, I don't want to hear any more," Mrs Stone said twitchily, and her spouse milled his hammer.

"This isn't an impartial q-and-a, it's a stitch-up," Cessie said discourteously, thankful to have rid herself of the dummy.

"If naïve were a face, it'd be yours," Magnus hounded her.

Cessie sloshed her latte and didn't react.

"Men and women of the court, we have listened to the traumatic testaments, with conflicting statements, and now I ask that you retain composure as we showcase the videos," Mrs Stone said.

Alex's dad had a repulsed mien, and Fire's mum displayed her hankie, though she'd been dry-eyed throughout the proceedings.

Unstably, I tempered my stance and hooked myself to the projector; it siphoned my retentions like a parasite. I watched the unpolished recording of Fire's skirmish, ducking as he was scoffed, his CD freed for eternity. I cowered from my velocity in scooping it and Magnus' coldness afterwards. A chance dart at Pearl told me she'd curtained her view with her woolly coat, and Cessie also hadn't seen. I thought of her laughter with them weeks ago, and couldn't second-guess her mood. It'd been true that none bar Magnus had vetoed Fire's enterprise, and he hadn't so much capitulated as bungled his fish bait of the creature. How were we to know it would conclude so bloodily? Was I soulless enough to have cared exclusively for myself and my confederate? What had Fire been to me but one in a tango of tyrants?

Dr Stone zoomed in on Fire's fatality in the Tyrannosaurus' orifice: tranquillity washed over him and he was bitten to iotas, the monster's teeth as cardinal as gelatine.

"It's authentic, at least," the arbiter said. "Ms Moss, would you say you were static?"

"In shock, yes, but it wasn't in slow-mo like now," I said, sticking my head up finally. "The Tyrannosaurus-Rex wasn't going to free him, and when we realised what it'd done, we took his chip and scrambled to the seashore."

"That will be all for now," Dr Stone said with a stentorian deportment. "Projector, cut to Ms Jones' fatal showdown."

In this one it was indistinct if I'd dispensed warnings beforehand, but Cessie was shown grappling with the victim's designer gear, to no avail. This time I couldn't concentrate as Alexandrina, hitherto vivaciously selfish, gave herself up. As her father wept, I was aware that Pearl had for a second time affixed her eyelashes to the ingress. At the movement I saw my mother, glued to the smartboard, pokerfaced.

"You were too involved in shooting to inhibit Ms Jones' costly mistake," Dr Stone judged. "Had you joined in, she could've been overcome. I acknowledge you two weren't at ultimate fault for the perishes, but your slowness may've doomed the casualties. Did you exhibit disfavour to them?"

"Our enmity had no bearing on my actions," I said pleadingly. I'd strained to comfort Alexandrina, hadn't I? Somehow, I couldn't bear that detail to manifest in court. It was a reserved instance; afterwards I'd used her seizure to spare myself.

All of a sudden, Professor Goodwin coursed in, disporting a pearly, thrumming entity; Bo dogged him.

"D-Dr Stone," he said, "stop the hearing. I've diagnosed a wormhole."

Chapter Ten: Deus Ex Machina

The judge's fascia was murderous.

"Can I butt in?" Goodwin said lopsidedly.

Dr Stone acted deaf; accordingly his wife said: "You have five minutes."

Out of breath, he whistled: "My division have classified compounds from Elizabeth I's reign. The wormhole's unwrapped to the sixteenth-century and will plausibly be unavailable by New Year." He tautened his bow tie. "We cannot be sure."

Bo cleared her gorge. "The lab believes these're antiviral and may be the crucial antidote to the highway deaths. There's mounting ire on the streets, and society wants solutions."

"Scholars theorise this led to her longevity in a disease-ridden, unsanitary period," Goodwin recommenced. "She would've shot every twentieth man to spin out her supremacy. Inopportunely, it's unknown *where* that artefact is, so investigators are exigent."

"Be that as it may, Professor Goodwin," Mrs Stone simpered, "the panel cannot use that to *advantage* the young workers' cases."

"Spot on, Helen," Dr Stone said, with deceitful regret. He reframed his monocles. "*Someone* will be sent there for sure, whether or not Ivy and co. lose their livelihoods."

Momentarily, he assessed me as if he'd voyaged the excerpt of Pearl and I in his office – if he'd realised, why hadn't he rung the alarm? Would this be the advent of his retribution? Already I hungered for the next chapter, likely denied to me.

"Thank you for the interval," Mrs Stone said sublimely. "The panel must commune for the verdict now."

For a third of an hour wig heads schemed in a cordoned sector, and none of the scapegoats looked at each other. Would Wolves act to hang onto their coffers, or would verity prevail?

"All rise," the Stones said apathetically upon their reappearance. "The ruling will be read out now."

Pearl quailed, Mum stayed tight-lipped, Alex's dad craned forwards and Fire's mother rallied herself.

"We have voted unanimously to oust the four of you from the unit – permanently," Judge Stone briefed. "On the grounds that Ms Moss, Ms Belle, Ms Thorn and Mr Stone are unfit on a bodily and cerebral level, and failed as caretakers to the novel additions."

"Yes!" Alexandrina's father perforated his fins. "Justice." Leaving his side, Fire's mum departed with an appreciative 'thanks'.

My anterior was queasy as I lolloped impotently – Doctor Stone had been the one to direct them to their demises. Cessie rubbernecked her coffee as if construing tea leaves.

"Well," she said humourlessly, "we asked for that."

"We can appeal," Aurora said stormily. "Right, Magnus?"

"I – yeah, sure," he said, reminding me of a seal cub before the killer whale forays. "Mum and Dad will harken reason eventually."

"Codswallop," I decried. "We won't set foot here again."

Cessie bleated.

"If you hadn't shown those cassettes, we wouldn't be in this position," Magnus said.

"If it weren't for them, we'd be on a murder charge," I said cuttingly.

"My parents would *never* put me behind bars," he affirmed.

"Your dad loves those robots more than you," I said hurtfully. "He's content to give your career the kiss of death. Wake up."

We were chest-to-nose. Nadia's nonverbal pathos, mailed from the balcony, stopped me from earning myself another penalty. As a substitute for sparring, I browsed the court for exodus points, Cessie simulating. The public doors were the solitary outlet.

The brass doors surged open.

"What in the name of AI?" Professor Stone began.

Caramel-skinned, crinkly Aero straddled the doorway, Evangeline surprisingly in our midst.

"Why'd he fetch *her*?" Cessie said feverishly. "It's over now."

"Have you forgotten he doesn't know what she is?" I said aloofly. "Or is that something else you want to keep hidden?"

"Now!" Aero decreed.

Cessie's pet stimulated her buttons, boosting jack-o'-lanterns and manikin skeletons onto people's skulls. The spotlights went on and off as the sightseers carped; even Pearl had frozen in the aisles.

"Goodwin sent me a memo about Queen Elizabeth's secret," he said recklessly. "Run – we can make it to the Time Machine!"

Dr and Mrs Stone banged the gavel. "Anyone who exits will face severe punishments."

"Slipshod tortoises, were we?" Cessie said remorselessly, cupping my fibres. "Let's go."

Magnus tagged us as we gambolled along the gangways.

"Don't," he mimed.

"Fuck you," I mouthed as we loped over the podium, the projector uncoupling, government androids disbanding and escaper alarms cacophonous. Mars, who I hadn't noticed, bunged Elizabethan sartorial and accessories over our heads, and more unfriendly fingertips extended to hinder us as we neared liberty. I emptied the lukewarm latte on them – littering was a crime, after all.

Cessie shouldered the brass and the spooky hallway unwound on our course, robots gunning mucus at our backs. The cobwebs glued us to the spot pityingly, and we were renegades in flytraps, the machines whirring to restore us to our cubicles.

A spangled hand brought a fire extinguisher on the netting, and we were emancipated as punctually as we'd been bagged.

"This is your only opening," Nadia said as she harboured us from the robots' pepper spray. "Don't cock this one up."

"Nadia – I don't know what to say," I said thankfully.

"Don't talk, run," she said.

We legged it to the tail of the hall, where a succession of doors baffled us.

"Cessie, use your wits," I said, rubbing the stitch in my side.

"I haven't got any," she said, trying each doorknob in turn. "It's this one."

She drew me inside as Nadia yelled to us to hurry – we free-fell half in the oxygen suits, the belts pendulous. My waist, slighter since the Cretaceous, all but fell through. We disembarked as our harassers skydived and slunk to the tube. A peep back showed Mrs Stone stepping in nattily, carrycase in hand, victorious.

"The game's up," she said firmly. "Surrender without a struggle and we may – *may* overturn a spell inside."

"You're right," I said unconvincingly. "Cessie, let's hand ourselves in."

Self-assuredly, we outstripped her to the carriage as Aero fumbled with the bolt and savoured her petulance as we rendered it inaccessible. We earwigged her sending for the cavalry.

"A first-rate job," Aero toasted us. "We sure turned the tables on her."

"Don't you hate us... especially me?" I said.

"You nearly killed me with the volcano," Aero grinned. "But what're friends for?"

I cabled the monitors, skewwhiff after the dinosaur mishap, Mrs Stone's smites on the coach as troubling as the T-Rex.

"Come back here or it's a lifelong ban from Wolves!"

"She must be on something," I said inexorably. "We're already pariahs."

"If we impress with our steals from the 1500s, she might pardon you two," Aero said.

"I don't want to be pardoned," Cessie said snobbishly.

"Yes you do," Aero said forlornly.

Cessie ogled the watermarks left by the Tyrannosaurus: "Do you suppose... we're guilty?"

"In sentiment, not deeds," Aero said genially.

Cessie nuzzled in the chequered seat. "I used to Pritt-and-Glitter with Alex in Nursery."

"Until she tipped it over your head," Aero reminded her.

I felt this was discourteous.

"At any rate," I said tactfully, "we've got a time machine to restart."

"You're all business, no pleasure," Cessie said, trying to recap the numbers. "Ooh... shit... what was it again?"

"Goodwin didn't specify a date," Aero said. "We'll have to brick it through the arroyo."

"The 1580s are a good decade," the historian postulated. "For maximum booty, summertime would be prolific."

"We can't be confident that's what the professor identified," I said gingerly, "but it's worth a shot."

Keyboarding her dates, I lofted the carriage and we sailed in the solar system, paltry amid billions of planetoids, and my viscera softened: we were getting away.

"Ah, Ivy," Aero said splittingly, "this doesn't look right."

The machine went to-and-fro, volleying us, wilder than a ram, and fleetingly I thought we wouldn't make it – what was worse, an honourable debacle or home judgement?

The locomotive blew out and its ampule atomised: Cessie and Aero frisked to duck a mauling. I mowed the gearstick, howbeit we spun past Pluto, entering a lane with no more planets, stars the single light in the undying streaks, railroading to nowhere.

We brooded in the abysm until the engine strayed into an untainted greenness – we overrode rosebushes and were gridlocked.

"Is – is everyone OK?" I said circumspectly.

Cessie stood blearily, revelling in the time-spell. "Yes, of course," she said as though that were the least of her worries. "Ivy I – I've been here before."

"Nonsense," I said, ebbing as the wires electrocuted themselves. "You've had a knock. How could you've been here before?"

Aero cleared the condensation: "I don't see a castle. Cess, you must've made an error."

"I know when Elizabeth was alive, if the topography isn't textbook," she said grouchily.

The dashboard flared: *Ten minutes until the tube seals in a self-protective measure.*

The towlines were spritzing, the diesel indistinguishable from a bust appendix, the pomade exuding, the settees inverted.

"Damn." I nipped myself raw. "We have to get out."

"A paintjob or two will fix it," Aero said optimistically. "Let's not get our smocks in a twist."

"Shut up," I said crossly, leaving the floored spacecraft. "This is serious."

"It always is with you," he said to himself.

Prickles pranced on my tailbone as the welkin filled me with the spoors of chamomile, thyme and briars. Arboreal creepers, honeysuckle, woodbine and violets lined the hilltop.

"Oh, it's a storybook," Cessie lapped up the welkin.

The answer bobbled as if herbs on a water lily. *Bingo!* We were in Shakespeare's country hometown – the machine must've been addled by cross-instructions. Was he dead, alive... it was impossible to be definite. Apparently tuned into my brainwaves, Aero bit into the holed, acidic nucleus of a pippin' apple, referring to the Marsh hardcover.

"Shakespeare lives again!" he said portentously.

"It's not the foulest place to be stuck," she said, scooting around. "Let's change into our costumes."

Horror-struck, I felt the dilapidated gadget – we were well and truly entrapped in the sixteenth century. The aperture made a dying noise as I mooched inside, ribcage flaying, grapplers renewing the circuit; it bemoaned my stabs and was deathlike. I didn't dare touch the tank engine, disgorging as it was, in arrears.

"From pulling apart robots and working with innumerable tools, I recognise a catch-22 when I see one," Aero said behind me. No reaction sounded from me.

Cessie tarried over the apparel cubbyhole, squeezing into silky hoses, producing breeches, a tunic and doublet coat for Aero, and an angora chemise and uniform for me. It was bare, shapeless and discreet. The bodice boosted my breasts unpleasantly and Cessie put the outfit together with crotchets. For herself she produced a banded farthingale, looking like a float before it dissevers.

"Not a word," she said bullyingly. "I'm the altitude of chic in this."

"When's the baby due?" I said frivolously.

Cessie swatted me with a coif cap, which I hove over my tendrils.

"At least you don't look like a pauper," I said gloomily, towing on the yellow bib.

"*Moi*?" Cessie said in disbelief. "Never."

Aero, spying the fairy-story shrubbery, harrowed to accrue gold-hued tulips, mellowed strawberries, runner beans and peas. There was something of Jack in him before he bestrode the beanstalk, however no fictitious Hulk purloined payment.

A beard-clad Elizabethan half-watched us under the sunbeams: Cessie snapshotted him when he cockeyed his top. Having eluded confinement, it was as though we'd mislaid pennies and found pounds. We couldn't hypothesise what could go askew now.

Cessie and I steamrolled the apparatus until it sagged, naked, on the ant mounds. The bearded man proceeded towards us, the first Elizabethan we'd seen. For an unhinged minute we assessed he was here to assist us.

Cross-faced, he spewed: "What art thee doing?"

Backpedalling from the lianas, Aero levelled his crimps: "Pruning the plants, good fellow."

"Doth thee owneth the landeth?" he resounded, and Cessie retired from muscling our vehicle.

"Sir, 'tis a public lodging," Aero said speedily.

"Doest the knave dareth calleth me sir?" The Elizabethan reddened.

"Knave?" Aero said wonderingly.

"Fool!" Cessie said. "He hasn't the rank for a title."

Aero shrugged in surrender. "I didn't setteth out to offendeth thee."

"Thee deceiveth me." His middle-aged pork rumbled as if chicken pies incubated in his smock.

"Nay, we only meanteth to seeth the fairies," Cessie said baldly.

"Have you taken something?" Aero and I probed.

"Elizabethans believed certain plants had the properties to conjure fairies," Cessie educated haughtily.

"A likely defence!" The man rigidified his girdle. "Thee seeketh to maketh an clotpole of me."

"He looks as if he's had a stroke," Aero muttered, obscuring the vines in his overall.

"Art thee a sorcerer?" The Elizabethan grilled him.

"I am an honest sir," Aero entreated.

We hoped a reprieve would come, when...

"Countrymen, seize those folk!"

Pearl's Shakespearean dictionary wasn't needed to decipher that – yet we couldn't desert the time machine, if only to reassemble it. We stood in irresolution as Dr Stone's denigrations ensnared us in the topsoil, catatonic.

"Thee trimm'd the earth to poison thy neighbours!" the man indicted as his clique rocketed to apprehend us, Cessie caterwauling, a gerbil toyed by a Siamese cat.

"Petty sland'r!" Aero slighted him.

"Be quiet!" Cessie and I said as we rebounded into the motor.

"We art innocent, we art innocent," Cessie reiterated the fib.

"Quiet, shrimp!" A fish hook-nosed pensioner with peppery wisps said.

In a funeral motorcade, our rigs were lugged to the square, grimed nails nabbing firmer than tire tracks – from one trial to another. We were indicted on witchcraft and conspiracy charges. Which was more spine-tingling – 23 or this superstitious epoch?

The OAP claimed: "These cunning folk wouldst has't curs'd the whole district!"

"To be fair, it does look bad," Cessie whispered.

"We've hath caught the hags in their tracks," Beard said distastefully. He jabbed my cheek, sunken from the primordial episode. "Art thee unmarried?"

"Aye," I said.

Spittle sprung from him onto my apron. "Mine own fellow Rafe hath lost three children to the Black Death. Wast yond thee?"

"I didn't do it," I griped, as Cessie made a repulsed face.

Beard wasn't heeding my words, encircling us, consorting with his mob how "twast que'r" how we'd arisen, more or less occult. Aero sweated, knowing we should've been more judicious.

In synergy, our critics pronounced the charges against us:

"Fair wench, doth thee deny thy conjure of fairies wast malevolent?" the brackish lady said.

"I meanteth nay evil," Cessie said.

They focused on Aero: "And thee, thee prun'd h'rbs to finish us off and robeth our landeth."

"Ridiculous!" our friend spluttered.

140

Beard maltreated our mechanism because he couldn't yet hurt us: "Art thee the owneth'r of this malicious objecteth?"

"'Tis mineth, but t's harmless," I said thinly, wincing as he harmed it, very nearly wishing it were made of fairy dust and could whisk us away.

Salt-and-Pepper woman and Bluebeard convoked, prattles cutting us worse than the bees (who at least had a good reason), assenting we should be tested for revengeful witchery.

"By test," Aero said sheepishly, "what do they mean?"

"Ah, you don't need to know." Cessie unstrapped her choker, and tautness streamed into my blood vessels.

Aero ascertained the poolside as likelihoods putrefied my mind. The OAP and her cohort ruminated if we should be disrobed.

"Since those gents art already naked, we shalt not stripeth those folk," Beard decreed. Howbeit, he added: "If't be true thee floateth, we'll burneth thee at the stake."

My pleura dwindled as if I'd already been tried. It was drown or be deep-fried.

Cessie, 'the fair lass', was impounded to appraise her 'witch marks'. Hook-nose pricked her barely distinguishable freckles with a blunted widget, and as she squirmed it was as though I'd been pricked, Sleeping Beauty as she took to the spinner.

Even though the moles were clear, the bearded villager suggested: "Thy countenance thinkest a lot; thou art wise to the tests of the valorous village folk."

Cessie joggled.

"Confesseth, wench," a kindly squire, head-to-toe in black, besought her.

"I feareth wat'r," Cessie croaked, discoloured by the review.

"Owing to thee being a magician," Bluebeard said. His tolerance subsided: "Attacheth h'r to the wood!"

The civic paraphernalia mimicked a rangy solid pole, twofold planks steadying the width, more impressive than Bigfoot; itched with doodles. Cessie was harnessed into a chiselled (even now, I marvelled the design) wainscoted piebald rocker. Aero recurrently inculcated her to hold her wheezes, clamp her mouth and remain unflustered. It was well-meant but too common-sense for the victim, so I asked what we should do. He said: *standby.*

For when? For after she'd sunk or been parboiled? Of course, he hadn't been trusted with her erstwhile ordeal and couldn't commiserate with her consternation.

That was how we ended up standing back as, in a stupefying scene, the unblinking Cessie was depressed into the tarn, a wrung flannel.

"Witch, doth thee sinketh?" the salty lady cried as the rod dunked her deeper.

"Nay, enow!" I said, flimsy-kneed.

Cessie's ironed kirtle jetted upwards, but she was nowhere to be seen. How long could one breathe underwater; when did they shut down?

"We've did test the lass," the nervy squire said.

Beard complied, bringing forth our soused comrade-in-arms with cruel ease, and although she was frosted her thorax expelled air.

"The hag couldst feign innocence on h'r first tryeth," Beard said sagaciously. "Dunk h'r again, and we'll seeth if't be true the enchantress sinks."

The townsfolk geed.

The more sympathetic of her tormenters posited that they try the others now (hey!), but Hook-nose was unmoved. Seeing it was hopeless, Aero reissued the homeopathic mantra, and was commandeered to stem his charms.

As she was conducted once more to her watery catacomb I rootled at my bindings, pointlessly, and Cessie spritzed as she was fished out, a tadpole stapled.

"Thee've seen the lady is nay hag; releaseth h'r," the squire said.

"A third assessment may kill her," Aero said, sapped.

"I'm trying," I said.

"Try harder," he cautioned.

"Once m're, to beest absolutely sure," the aquiline-nosed woman said, greedily fathoming Cessie's waterlogged front and brindle gawp.

Hence it came to pass that she was thrice dipped, and on this occasion she was afloat, a paperweight as vindicated faces sponged up her cataclysm.

142

As they grouped to cast judgement, Aero spotted a vagrant kitten mewling by the lakeside, straggly pegs drawn out. A scheme took hold. Lower than a budgie, I crooned to the cat and it skittered over.

"This is early modern England," Aero whistled. "They'll be terrified of it."

"Sure this'll work?" I said.

"It's a gamble," he granted.

The tabby bulged its M-head as it pawed past, and we thought it would just walk among the folk but, gingerly, it loped on the pole. Satisfied with its vigour, it roller-skated and the residents squalled, abstracted from their chore of convicting Cessie.

"'Tis their familiar," a youngish woman announced, and we doubled up.

"Ah, a little help," Cessie nudged us.

As pandemonium supervened at the streetwise kitty, the bearded man watched over the dunking stool, where Cessie was midriff-deep and expressionless. The cat dribbled on the hirsute male's toes and he backtracked, narrowly shirking the lagoon. Aero usurped the wormwood-eaten bar and, coalescing with all our might, we tweaked Cessie, primrose reeds nosediving from her nostrils.

"It's – too – heavy," I said hopelessly, relinquishing my hold.

"Again," Aero said as Hook-nose deracinated him from the gizmo; Cessie was midcourse. The kitten tackled her cambric underclothes and Beak-nose freed Aero; immediately we upraised Cess until she slunk slantwise, pussyfooting to land.

The cat with nine lives, she unencumbered the moggy from the senior native's clasp, and we absconded into the baroque brightness.

The witch-finders were at our hindquarters as we floundered, stitches in our sides, onto a market boulevard, waylaid. Baste dribbled from a Santa smokestack; we routed on the fourth cottage as the kitten disported its fangs before Beard and Salt-and-Pepper.

"Nameth yourselves," the cottager said.

"Prithee alloweth us in, a mob has't accus'd us of being hags," Cessie, Aero and I said, the fiends to the three little pigs.

"Giveth me a moment," the cranky occupier said.

The Pepper Lady screamed blue murder as she was mildly mutilated, and we overhead an indoor spat.

"Will, the children art inside," a woman's tootle was made out.

"What if't be true Judy and Ham needeth a kind strang'r one day? Wouldst thee has't those folk did refuse?" the leaseholder said.

"T's too risky," his partner said sensibly.

"I haven't hadst excit'ment in ages," he goaded.

"Just this once," she said huffily, and Aero rejoiced.

Cess uninvolved the cat from the Salty Woman as the globular timber and hamper of bellflowers wagged and the postern uncapped.

The tenants had their backs to us, but bade us dry our sodden items near the inglenook.

"How didst this befall?" the man said.

"The townspeople nearly drown'd us as necromanc'rs," Aero explicated.

"Most wondrous," the man said. "Art thee new to Stratford-upon-Avon?"

"In a mann'r of speaking," I said.

As a wracked Cessie and Aero blow-dried themselves by a hearthstone that coruscated like balefires, I, fairly waterless, pried into the obsolete foyer mirror. My sorrel eye colour was shadowy, beehive jellied like fudge, the slack Venetian perimeter flattering my ego. We had no inkling whose ménage our asylum was: I quaked in the looking glass as the boarder was imaged there. His pigmentation was glassy even though it was as stalwart as buckskin, the exterior elfish and melodic; his follicles were greased back to accommodate his vaulted forehead. Vying with my plainclothes investigations, Cessie's cashew iris noted the ligneous board, strewn with parchment scrolls inked *Romeo and Juliet*, half-bitten by woodlice. Curiosities fanned, fast and thick... was he an admirer... was this published yet... it couldn't be.

Cessie pressured my toenail as I raked over the woman: she had downcast, watery eyes, a buttered bun, a hairline parted like a foxtrot of maggots, a hearty demeanour upturned with misgivings and a linen cap doffing her like flour. A coxcomb ruff cornered her and she was robed in an unflashy snowy gown... was she the abstruse spouse?

Yes, Cessie confirmed. We'd drummed on the domicile of William Shakespeare and the agrarian's daughter, Anne Hathaway.

The bard studied my valuation: "Thou art not a craz'd fan, art thee?"

With a semblance outclassing cherry cupcakes, I falsified: "Nay, nay, I've nev'r hath heard of thee."

Cessie fleered and Aero hid himself by the fireside so no one would catch his gibe.

"Oh." He looked rather put out.

"But I'm sure thou art fantastic," I enthused.

"Well, I maketh a living," Shakespeare grunted.

Fretful Anne twitched the drapery. "Will, we've did get bigg'r problems than thy fan club." Behind it, small glass pieces were roped together with lead, and she unsecured the latticework to lay bare the locals, who had brought adzes in retribution.

Bluebeard sported the axe-like, arched blade with its right-angled handle, and it was unclear whether they'd brought them to mallet us or the farmstead.

Anne Hathaway prised the window further: "What doth thee wanteth?"

Beak-nose stood to her fullest height: "The magicians and their pet."

"Shall thee spareth our cottage?" Anne said.

"Our quarrel is not with thee, Mrs Hathaway," Beaky said uprightly.

"Standeth aside and thee shall beest spar'd," Beard covenanted.

The goatee-clad dramatist swapped with his wife, arbitrating: "Those gents art acquaintances of ours, so their quarrels art our quarrels."

"What that gent hath said," Aero nodded excitedly.

As Shakespeare fathomed the townspeople his lenses were stern: "Fie! Putteth the pitchf'rks down!" The bearded man held his higher. "John, who is't did teach thee to feareth the unknown? Those gents art new neighbours — we ought to welcometh those folk. I seeth flesh and bone, liketh thee and me."

"Those gents did cast charms to appeareth human," John (we finally got his name) said, shirt straining against his paunch.

"What witchcraft hast been did cast in the village?" Shakespeare appealed for proof.

The frenzied pack talked over each other.

"One at a timeth," Shakespeare said.

We were taken aback when, bit by bit, the various ailments leaked out as though bifurcated on a genealogy diagram:

"The roots of disease forswear with those folk; I knoweth t in mine own bones."

"Joan wast a lively wench who is't hath fallen down dead."

"Agnes hasn't been able to farm since h'r armeth —"

"Mine own fusty ma hath passed lasteth wint'r; the lady wast fiteth as a fiddle."

"Evil things has't been done in Stratford."

"Those gents'll payeth f'r the fev'r yond, two springs ago, did steal mine own babe from the cradle."

The last complainant piped up: "Mine own hands art at each moment playing up."

"M'rtality is not the w'rk of spell-cast'rs," Shakespeare meted out his wisdom.

"Thee protecteth simple-mind'd murd'r'rs," John said.

"I wanteth not mine own neighbours to becometh killeth'rs," the playwright told him.

"Shagspere, think ov'r what hath happened to thy colleague Marlowe," the bearded gentlemen threatened blithely. "A dramatist's language endures, but his flesh doesn't."

"Wast yond a threat? I bethink the stage doth take m're guts than facing a lynch mob," Shakespeare crowed.

"We doth not dealeth in blood, but livestock," John said craftily.

Aero was quizzical but Cessie had understood.

Shakespeare turned to his spouse: "How many animals doth we keepeth h're?"

"Five pigs, three goats and two mules," Anne listed.

"Thee wanteth to robeth a did respect family?" Shakespeare called.

"Livestock 'r those gents'll roast on the pyre."

John's adze whammed the villa, upending the hellebores.

Chapter Eleven: The Kindness of Strangers

Beak-nose and her mutineers yammered the begonias, and Will and Anne debarked from their footrests as the lead cracked.

"I'm yet to seeth thy family coat of arms," John said. His razorblade whittled *Hags* so people could hound us. "Thou art nothing but a boil on this consistency."

Cessie leapt from the incinerator as a brick glided in.

"Bett'r a boil than a pig," the wordsmith quipped.

"Nay, antagonise not those folk," Cessie said.

John leaned forwards on his Achilles heels. "The taxman harks in London, Mr Shagspere — thee hoard food h're. Thee may has't did marry up, but this town hast a longeth mem'ry. Thy debts await as thee maketh thy f'rtune in London. We seeketh payment — our well is running dryeth, our marketeth rundown; the town ailing."

"Envy shall beest thy undoing. Am I not the same as thee?" Shakespeare asked.

"Thy wealth couldst floweth liketh a fountain through Avon," Beaky said.

"A giant's blood can only donate so many pints," Shakespeare sighed, and a heartbeat after: "What doth thee desire?"

A smile radiated on John like peanut butter. "Thy fattest brown goat."

Bounds were heard on the grandiose stairway: "Not Biscuit!"

"I'm s'rry, Judy, but I've nay choice," the child's father said.

The lank girl sparked as if a turnip, frizzling one of the *Sonnets* lines on the furnace.

"Not *Sonnet 2*," he quaffed.

"Thee has't too many, besides," Judy joshed.

Her mother commandeered the browned goat "Biscuit", who baahed at Mrs Hathaway; she haggled it in the courtyard.

"I'm sure thee can receiveth anoth'r," Aero said.

"Th're'll nev'r beest anoth'r liketh biscuit," the girl quibbled, clumping to her boudoir.

When Hathaway, re-entered her husband's crudely amended *Venus and Adonis* encased her palm. Seeing my heightened eyebrows, she said: "I bethought if't be true those gents hath broken down the doth'r, we couldst throweth this."

"Admirable tactics. Um, Mrs Hathaway, we has't to receiveth our machine backeth," I said.

"Not f'r the black art those gents accuse thee of?" Shakespeare checked.

"Nay, yond's our transp'rt," Cessie said truthfully. "Gramercy sir and madam, f'r sparing us!"

Mrs Hathaway hard-pressed the booth, taxing them to bring the source of the mayhem.

We could stay here, you know, Cessie thought. *We don't have to go back.*

It makes no difference if it's 23 or the sixteenth century, I remonstrated. *We'll always be hassled.*

Cess deflated.

Our senses were drawn to a brawl in the open air, the kind-hearted squire wrangling with the silvered punnet. In the five-second scuffle, Beard padlocked him into a throttlehold, before the time machine was eased through the hangings. I sucked in the zephyr as spittle relocated from the populace to the aide.

Shakespeare rounded on the rovers: "Shame on thee."

Grouses.

"Hence with thee, leeches!"

They sallied down the Roman roads, the squire weaselling away on the reverse route.

*

"Waketh up, waketh up," someone trumpeted in my earhole, and I trundled out of the spindly eiderdown, totalling how many spiders webbed on the rafters.

Aero's rictus sifted into my sightline and I overextended my armpits, tapping the cornfields of straw, bumpy and numberless.

"Welcometh to our new house, the barn," Cess grinned.

"We did sleep h're?" I said in sixteenth century diction, lest anyone was nosing round.

"Art thee sure thee didn't drowneth?" Cessie said.

It overflowed me – the sentencing, the getaway, the novel era, the mob, the drowning, the Shakespeares. Surely that last part wasn't genuine?

"Thee hath heard t h're first," Aero nodded on seeing sentience dawn.

"Guests, thy breakfast is on the table," Anne's singsong voice came.

"C'mon," Aero said.

We dallied before joining him in the clangour of saucepans, passé beams characterising the home; Hathaway ladling bread onto a crate, a fairy godmother.

We installed ourselves on a bench as stretched as a giraffe's neck, Shakespeare feasting at the head, his rapt offspring buttering rolls.

"Ham, offendeth not our guests with thy stareth," Anne said.

"Art those gents very much hags?" the ten-year-old said.

"Nay," his mother smiled.

"What's yond thing in the yard?" said a girl who closely resembled Hamnet.

"Susie, s'rve bread and milketh from the dairy," Anne shooed her.

Judy forked vegetables as she eyed us: "Thee hath lost me a goat."

"Judith, quieten down," Mrs Hathaway said, dispatching an errand to her child. The girl showed her father her tongue and stomped out, but not before she'd considered us as though we were firearm practice.

"All children loathe their parents," Shakespeare said. "Mind not h'r."

Anne served us rye dough with butter and a milk carafe as vast as her husband was tall. I rebuffed the home-brewed beer, but Cessie and Aero assented; the former having daydreamt savouring it and the latter becoming a scientific taster. His red button parped as he prepared to file his buds' reaction for the library shelves. On the thrush mat, the kitty licked buttermilk from a saucer with a supercilious air.

149

Yond's what I calleth cuisine past its sell-by-date, Aero e-messaged me.

At least we didn't receiveth a burning, I messaged back.

I've at each moment wond'r'd what yond wouldst feeleth liketh, Cessie caroused.

Wherefore has't we gone all Shakespearean? I emailed.

T's hath called getting into charact'r, she spieled.

Shakespeare weighed us up like Zeus with his scales, and I pondered whether greats sensed human hearts, their worth, how bona fide they were.

"Bid me," he said, deciding on an apple, "who is't art thee?"

Aero and I were tongue-tied.

"What shalt loosen their tongue? Those gents w're not so dainty in the square."

I deduced the scriptwriter was tickled.

"I am Hilda Morgan and mine own s'rvants art Miriam Marke and Francis Lucas," Cessie supplied our identities.

Am I Francis? That's news to me, Aero larked. I reformed my gaiety into an 'ahem'.

Shakespeare restructured his fare into a London atlas. "Thee'll settleth in. Thou art new to the town. 'Twas the way with me in London. Learn'd men hath called me an upstart crow."

Cessie smiled: "We're not staying – we're going to London, too."

"Ev'ry sir, mistress and dog — to London. Wh're the streets glitt'r with gold," he laughed. Thinking of the volcano, I thought all that glistened wasn't gold.

"Thou art from distant lands," Shakespeare stated. Conjecturing our agitation, he said: "Sayeth nay m're."

We stopped holding in our sacs.

Sociably, Mrs Hathaway dumped her bread and honey beside us. "Thou art duty-bound to earneth thy keepeth with housew'rk aft'r losing us our second-best goat."

The second-best sleep chamber, Cessie reasoned. *'T wast all a joketh.*

"'Tis fine, what doth thee wanteth us to doth?" my friend contracted.

"Not back-breaking labour, yond's f'r sure," Anne Hathaway contended. "But with Will coming and going from London, I couldst doth with an extra pair of gloves."

Shakespeare was voiceless, but his optics desiccated.

Cessie expressed no objection to grammar lessons with the children, photographing their hornbooks with the shaky twenty-four-letter alphabet, the klaxon binding them. "Doth thee knoweth thy lett'rs?" said the schoolmistress, unfazed by Judy's strop or the twins' callowness.

Restlessly I went with Aero to the aromatic patch; he clicked his microprocessor when he saw the odorous turf, perfumed with rosemary and thyme. Aero engaged the spade to neaten the rockery, coveting the hedgerows of basils that could revivify hundreds of persons. Even so, it was obvious the true inclination was not benevolence but curiosity, exhuming the parsleys and pioneering fresh properties. The reeks were blissfully uncorrupted.

"W'rry not, I've did get a job up mine own sleeve f'r thee," Hathaway said as the herbalist disentombed sweet-smelling nothings. Far from easing my disquiet, it made me more afraid.

We shambled to the poultry yard, me tape-recording as the bundles of machinery became palpable, Anne carting her dairy jug and outpouring it into an aged sandbag, which she put above an ironically witchy pail. She threw one end of a staff to me, and as we minced the cheeses the crucible was yellowish. I'd have to get used to a dairy maid's lot if the spaceship, piled and overlooked, stayed redundant. What were our jurors and workmates saying about us now; eternalising our disobedience in limericks and tall tales?

Anne hummed as she pressed, secretion riding down my frons as we jabbed the cheese. She harked back to her courtship and nuptials, musically saying: "Romance is milketh to the soul... 'tis sweet then curdles."

This'll be invaluable for Dad's references, I mused.

"Thee bethought only mine own husband couldst spineth a quaint phrase?" Shakespeare's partner-in-crime said. When I didn't feed an opinion, she added: "What is troubling thee? Thy mistress treats thee well?"

Vitriol evinced in my pharynx: "Oh, aye, the lady's v'ry kind." The insides of my pouches compressed to preclude my hysterics.

Mrs Hathaway mimicked my eye's course towards the outer-space baggage: "Thy cart, is't broken?"

"Beyond repaireth. I bethink not I'll ev'r returneth to mine own homeland," I emoted.

"Alloweth me has't a behold," she said, to my incredulity.

Vacating our shift, she inspected the crushed appliance with her rancher's knuckles, timeworn like a leather armlet. Leads started to sibilate at her pat, more treacherous than a historical farmer could grasp. "What hath happened to the instrument?"

"Th're wast a clash," I said, pleased I hadn't told falsehoods.

Hathaway arrogated her riggings to partially darn the impairment, but claimed that's all she could do, as: "I doth not und'rstand such an engine."

Googling an online early modern glossary, I said: "Gramercy f'r thy ex'rtion."

"Behold... th're is m're I can doth." Anne tripped away from the cheeses as they appeared level and alleviated my numbed forearms.

"What m're?" I said interestedly. Was Anne somehow in-the-know; had she been expecting us?

"I knoweth a handyman." Mrs Hathaway balked. "But that gent is wary of visiteth'rs, given his reputation."

A coolness formed like a package round my underskirt. "Wherefore... is that gent a criminal?" It was preposterous, asking Shakespeare's wife if she had felonious contacts.

"Oh nay, Ms Marke," she said. "The law-abiding art the ones to truly feareth, f'r those gents shall doth aught to avoideth breaking the law. That gent is a valorous knave, but cautious."

Anne directed me to her spouse, where Shakespeare and Cessie were denting the lumber with Judy, Ham and Susie's rude rhymes.

"Haply thee three shall followeth me to the stage," the Bard said with a soupçon of pride.

"Not yet — those gents're babies still," Anne dissented.

"We'll maketh a sir of thee yet, Ham," Shakespeare said to his son.

"I can seeth t in lamplights: Fath'r and Son presenteth: what wast yond playeth I hadst in mind?" He grazed his bounce.

"*Hamlet*," Mrs Hathaway said knowledgeably.

"Mine own greatest idea." It was as though he'd sidled into his braggart persona. "I meanteth to pen t, but the hourglass drains as apace as the children groweth." After stomaching this downhearted statement, I ached to tell him of the solar system and a tube that accomplished diverse places, different times.

As the children applied madder and woad to the textiles, Anne said: "Will, doth thee recall thy fusty cousin Cornelius?"

It may've been the oil lamp, but the scriptwriter greened. "'Twas a while ago, years hath lost to me anon. A cousin of mineth, labouring in a w'rkshop near the Thames, hath heard a rumour about Eliza. That gent hath grown up h're and I wast a family cousin."

He paused. "That gent's hath kept his headeth down ev'r since, and madeth me gage not to break with his secret. I wouldst rath'r teareth down mine own owneth walls than betray that gent. I'll bid thee this free of chargeth: the bright young sir anon shuns social-climbing in favour of po'r apprentice w'rk."

"A job's a job," Aero said heatedly.

Shakespeare lowered his scoped forepart: "Of course, thou art but a humble s'rvant. I meanteth nay offence. Bid me, Francis, what f'rtunes doth thee seeketh in London?"

"We require a vital objecteth in Bess' castle, and thy Cornelius might beest the key," Cessie said brashly.

"I'll giveth thee a did bite of counsel," Shakespeare said, suddenly grim. "Nev'r entrust all thy keys to one handeth. I traveleth from Stratford to London, seeth a new act'r, a new audience a day. Howev'r, I can holp thee writeth a lett'r, securing employment at Whitehall."

"Thee wouldst?" Cessie's inhalation induced neighs from Judy and Hamnet.

"Forsooth a fan," Ham said in his older sibling's ear.

Shakespeare and Cessie seated themselves at his flaked, topsy-turvy desk, rattlesnake friezes – surely Cornelius' – bedizening it. From a holder he passed her a prickly, stiff porcupine quill to pen the letter while he dictated 'recommendations' as our foregoing employer. If only he could 'recommend' us to Wolves. She transcribed:

Thy highness Queene Elizabeth,

I am a high-b'rn maid who is't hast s'rv'd esteem'd households enwheeling the Shakespeares, learn'd in the classics and diplomacy. I bringeth with me two s'rvants who is't can crisp, garden and cook. We has't been did train in tut'ring, gardening and cheese-making, f'r thy highness' sweet tooth. We art willing to w'rk longeth hours with a base wage f'r the honour of s'rving thee.

I heareth th're art vacancies in thy castle aft'r the t'rrible plagues. We cometh from faraway and art in pleasant health.

If't be true thou art int'rest'd in our s'rvices, prithee sendeth w'rd to this addresseth: The Boar's Head.

Yours Truly,

Mistress Hilda Morgan. Signature.

"The lady calleth t teaching," Judy said, impressed despite herself, "m're liketh t'rturing." Susie and Ham showcased corresponding smirks. A platform was unquestionably where they were headed.

"One lasteth thing bef're thee depart," Anne Hathaway said, feeling her bib. She exhibited twenty shillings and a handful of crowns.

"Nay, putteth not yourself out of pocket," I declined as Shakespeare sent the despatch on its way.

"Prithee," Hathaway spread her hands, "mine own cheeses art selling well; as art mine own husband's plays. F'rgive me, but thou art but a s'rvant, penniless and industrious."

Story of my life, Aero thought.

"This item sounds m're imp'rtant than mine own petty chinks," Shakespeare's spouse persevered.

"We knoweth not how to repay thee," Cessie said, welcoming the Elizabethan coinage. Could she bear to spend it, with its coppery picture of the fiery Queen?

"Then repay us not, f'r thy company is wage to the ears," the tragedian said.

"Beest careful in London… lots of vagrants about," Hamnet said scarily, whereas Shakespeare imparted his oxen-drawn cart, onto which he loaded the mending time machine.

In a pipedream, I cupped the bullock wagon with its prized four wheels, fuller at the back, the semicircle construction the bow on the donation, the linden seating nettling my backside as the Shakespeares saddled us into the bucking waggon.

"Is this safe?" I said, short-winded over the tidal winds.

"Quite safe," the scribe guaranteed.

"Father, keepeth t down," Judy said, as faces emerged in next-door's panes. Even Bluebeard and Salt-and-Pepper were taking Biscuit the Bribe to graze on the grasses, and telephoned their aggression with their lasers. "The neighbours art watching."

"The sir who is't w'rries what his fellows bethink is a sir to beest piti'd," her parent said.

"I'm not a sir," his oldest child pointed out.

"Thee receiveth the gist," Shakespeare said facetiously. "Hilda, Miriam, Francis; goose wonneth't tempteth thee?"

"Nay gramercy — we receiveth enow of yond at home," I lied, aghast.

As our patrons began to send us off, Aero got hot around his jerkin: "Hamnet – he dies within the year. Can't we do something?"

Cessie rested her blonde head on an arch. "Forget it. There's nothing we can do for the boy – his passing's fixed in the past. Bo says we shouldn't interfere with wildlife and, equally, we shouldn't revise history as we'd like it."

Aero rubbed his chin. "Dr Stone's mantra is that potential should never go to waste."

Cessie geared up the joysticks, stroking an ox. "We're not Dr Stone. We don't play with life and death."

"All the same, there's something I can do," Aero said, and hunted for an interval.

"What's this, knave?" the scribbler said, as Aero held up bunches of rosemary and thyme.

"F'r illnesses," Aero endorsed. "I heareth th're's been a most wondrous p'rcentage of plague round these parts. If't be true any of thee ev'r — needeth something to ease thy suff'ring, taketh this. T's not a remedy, but teen relief."

"Thee shouldst runneth an apothecary," the Shakepeares complimented. "Gram'rcy f'r thy kindness."

"'Tis nay kindness, sir," Aero said, hunching over the bulls, who giddied.

"Thou art from gentle stock, I can bid," Shakespeare said, signalling to the oxen, who pulled us onto the thoroughfare, our debts (somewhat) repaid.

Anne scurried to catch up with us: "Taketh this — mine own grandmoth'r's recipe," she said, and we accepted the warden tart.

"Seeth thee," I said.

"If 't be true thou art ev'r in dire straits, thee can at each moment writeth to us," Hathaway adduced.

"I wouldst but — I bethink we've both'r'd thee enow," I said ruefully.

We champed on the pear pastry as we transacted the reins in turns, exploring a Shakespeare navigator with wistful pangs for the dead poet who walked alive in his cottage.

The farm cart went to and fro with the cargo, and we dreaded its breakdown as we rode into the Cotswolds, the bleeding poppies sieving into our outlook and the leas on top of each other like watermelons. In comparison, the Chiltern Hills was so simple we mislaid our route and imploded over the ramps, Cess harnessing the bridles just before we would've fallen.

"The Valley of the River Stour," Aero said impressively; the hilly spring encompassed us, the turquoise canyon startling.

The oxen came to an unforeseen standstill, sloshing water in the meres, and Cessie screwed the reins tighter as they hydrated themselves. Sundown arose and we bathed with herbals, yodelling higher than our cabdrivers at the chilliness and dank, aqueous beings who snacked on our fibulas.

At my suggestion, we kipped in a rundown cowshed, hay mitigating the jaggedness, the lead bovine cramming his hooves beside our belongings. It fed on stubble involuntarily and we kept an eye on the access point, lest a raider crossed our paths. Aero perused the roadmap for our subsequent travels from Oxford to Buckinghamshire. Our diets at this juncture comprised of slices of pear pie, sugary and nugatory in our bellies. I squirrelled the last triangle for Pearl to try when we came home.

Twenty-four hours after, we hitchhiked on the nickering cattle to Marlow, inflowing the Thames Valley within its wonky floodgates and continuing to the Grand Union Canal. It was plain, watery and bricked, the doppelganger of the industrial isles in 23. With the tube in tow it was hit-and-miss whether we'd withstand our tumbril jaunt. I half nodded off as I drove, Cessie's nudges keeping me watchful, peckish and parched as I was. Under my supervision our chauffeurs snuffled on, fast-tracking onto the Thames Path with such brevity I was emphysematous.

Dreamily, I documented the Thames, disembodied heads besprinkled like origami on Tower Bridge in a grotesque 'No-Smoking'-style signal to pilfers. The colosseum-esque structures raised the butternut apartments from the downpours, and sailboats honked at us with their tickertapes – we'd been welcomed into the grubby merchant city.

At Aero's shout the oxen grew inert, shrugging off our mashed goods as we planked from our saddles to the brickwork beneath. A thirsty Aero limped to the terminus: The Boar's Head, Southwark, disreputable enough to facilitate our secrecy.

Externally the alehouse was toneless, a boar drawn on a rocking insignia: inside, burbles ruled under the crescent creaking beams, oils of bear-baiting, wild beasts and swordfights curtaining the lair. The balminess lent me a migraine as we were greeted by the innkeeper, the latest cash cows.

"Art lodgings available?" Aero said forthrightly.

"F'r the right price," the innkeeper bared his yellowish molars.

Aero joggled the coppers tantalisingly. "Nay price is outside our range."

"One oth'r thing," Cessie said blushingly. "Shall thee notify us if't be true thee taketh any lett'rs intend'd f'r Hilda Morgan, Miriam Marke and Francis Lucas?"

"T wouldst beest mine own pleasure," he said, and was salaried with our beams.

The spur-of-the-moment applauds and clanking of pints overawed our tête-à-tête, as the draughts contestants crowned their winner. A twentysomething with pyrite pupils and barred labials was showered in pints, and his name was read out as: Cornelius Smelting. Cessie and Aero widened like almonds.

"Who is't shall beest his next challeng'r?" the innkeeper dared.

"I shalt playeth thee," I said, and the victor's equals tooted.

"What? A mistress in a gambling house?"

Cornelius infolded his monies, noticing me before saying: "Thou art a w'rthy opponent, and I shall taketh thee on."

The innkeeper glared at us while spring-cleaning his tumbler, and the drinkers abandoned their ales, setting up the black-and-white boards, betters padding the tavern.

I was conducted onto an apatite stool and said colloquially: "Alloweth's changeth the rules."

"Nameth thy t'rms," the carpenter said, and if I hadn't been forewarned I'd never have guesstimated he was the guardian of secrecies.

"Answ'r an inquiry each timeth I winneth a pointeth," I said informally.

Cornelius premeditated behind his turret of gold-and-silver winnings. "Of what nature?"

"I shall anon attendeth Queene Elizabeth and am curious about h'r household. I heareth thou art the keepeth'r of secrets."

He lowered his tone: "Who is't toldeth thee yond?"

"'Twas William Shakespeare," I volunteered. "Will hath said thee w're an exemplary carpent'r."

"Is th're aught else thee gamble f'r?" he said.

"If 't be true I winneth, shall thee fixeth mine own vehicle? I cometh from faraway."

"And if't *I* winneth?" he said, furrowing his monobrow.

"Thee keepeth thy secrets and I shall doth thy w'rk f'r a week," I said.

A painful interim ensued.

"What sayeth thee?" Cessie said.

Cornelius folded his hands behind his skull: "I'm in valorous humour, so t's on."

158

If that's his good mood, I'd hate to catch him on another day, Aero processed to me.

What if you lose? Cessie thought.

I won't.

The licensee expounded the rubrics, placing a dozen chequers on each side: the objective was to loot the other player's pieces, and if one of our draughts made it to the opposing side, it would be made a 'king' and awarded superpowers.

"Wherefore a king, wherefore not a queene?" I asked.

"Nobody ev'r bethought of a queene," the tavern owner said. "Though we loveth kind Queene Bess."

"May the duel beginneth," the ruffians tolled.

Cornelius' Adam's apple cleared.

I had the lighter checkers, therefore operated with an oblique move, soon closing in on the darker squares via blockades, not ascendancy. The apprentice copied my moves until we were level, neither having notched an actual point.

I ranged towards a dark piece, meaning I got a leg-up twice, netting two of his counters. I abraded my hands with an exacting look: "Bid me what thee knoweth."

His army chirruped a dirge as he resigned to my mandate.

"Mine own moth'r's aristocratic connections did secure me a position in Elizabeth's Palace," the gamer said blankly.

Cessie group-messaged Aero and myself: *he knows the ins and outs of the castle.*

"T's strange such a proficient carpent'r toils in a w'rkshop," I said as I readapted my head cover.

The malt had thinned his rings by the time he reflected: "M're peculiar things has't hath happened."

One of his stockings slewed off his peacock breeches as he slashed my cubes, kinging one of his own.

"Damnable rogue!" Aero said in aggravation.

But then, he hadn't realised my inward workings were permanently strategizing, more reliable than a sundial. I monopolised *two* of his players.

"What doest this objecteth relateth to?" I searched over the drunken jeers.

Cornelius was lower than ravens when their spawn sickens. "1562. 'Twas weird. Elizabeth shouldst've been hath killed by smallpox. The lady hath sent Drake to purchaseth m're abroad in the '80s — a substance. The lady couldn't liveth f'rev'r, but the lady did want to pres'rve h'rself f'r as longeth as possible." He was on the tether of additional speech, but caught himself. "Playeth again, and I shall bewray m're... but art thee sure thee wanteth to knoweth?"

"Aye."

On his go he overcame three of my counters, halving my squares.

"Deadlock," the licensee aspirated.

While the drunkards cheeped, Cessie parcelled to me: *You can break him. Like feta cheese in an oven, he'll disintegrate under his burdens. Keep working.*

Don't let them put you off, Aero bolstered me.

Cessie kneaded her shorter split ends as the tie-break got underway, and I combatted towards a timely imperial placement.

Cornelius was forced to abdicate his reticence. "The agent Elizabeth hath used wast *monolaurin.* 'Twas scarily effective. The lady hast nev'r been so closeth to death again. I w'rk'd und'r Bess – the lady dislikes vuln'rability. But I knoweth not how the lady did mix the compound n'r wh're twas st'r'd. Yond's all I can bid thee."

Cessie translated straightaway: *He has no more to tell you.*

She adores her sweets, Aero participated. *'Tis a fatty acid. It kept her alive.*

"Nay medicine can maketh h'r imm'rtal, but it can maintaineth h'r longevity," the carpenter said.

Although it was an unclouded season, a wintery unrest arrived with the newest client.

"I liketh thee, Cornelius," I said, surmounting his residual chips in a landslide.

The ruckus died down, and the innkeeper chirped: "Champion!"

Chapter Twelve: The Secret Service

I'd come, seen and conquered, and toyed with my newest enquiry: "If 't be true we hath asked, wouldst thee help us searcheth h'r castle?"

Cornelius' army were so thunderous only he heard, rubbishing my pitch. "Breaketh into the castle? Thee wilt beest nimble-footed. The lady wouldst has't thy headeth on a spike."

I elected not to shotgun the loser. "I seeth. Cometh, Hilda, Francis."

In spite of himself, the novice clamoured after me: "I has't nev'r seen a s'rvant addresseth a mistress liketh yond."

I said: "I may beest a s'rvant, but I'm not a slave."

"At which hour shall thee wanteth me to s'rvice the device?" Cornelius said.

"At mine own convenience." I sashayed towards the kiosk, saying in an aside: "He'll be dying to find out why we want the monolaurin. He'll knock on our inn chamber within hours."

"What can I receiveth the champ?" The innkeeper sucked up.

"A double room, prithee," I said without reluctance.

He produced a puckered summons behind his whisky, Elizabeth's italic autograph signing it. "This arriv'd while thee w're playing. T hast the royal stampeth."

Cessie unfurled it across the stand, reading aloud:

"Thee has't been did invite f'r an int'rview at Whitehall Palace at four this noon. I shalt assesseth thy credentials, as I am an fusty mistress anon, as mine own assistants keepeth dying. Signed: Elizabeth I of England and Ireland."

"How doth we receiveth th're?" Aero put a dampener on affairs.

"T's one penny to crosseth the Thames," the innkeeper specified in East-end vernacular.

"Gramercy," we said, pushing past the Boar logo, Aero fingering a stale pence as we spurted towards the Thames.

"We need the East passage," Cessie said, uplifting her corked clogs to malinger on the water-stones, attracting the attention of a boatman jabbering: "Eastward-ho!"

The ferryman boated like a missile at our shouts, parking himself like Charon, conveyer of the departed.

"The coin?" he said voraciously, inviting us aboard the angling vessel.

"We're head'd f'r Whitehall," Aero said embarrassedly.

"Yond's grand. An appointment with the Queene?"

"Forsooth," the scientist said.

We rowed past the spiny drawbridge gate in the ligneous sail, bashed from side to side as London sleet bulleted down so we could scarcely see. Again, thieves' crania struck me, portraits on London Bridge. I experienced a potholed backflip at Cornelius' caveat. The storms led us to the ledge, and the oxidised incisors of the boatman bore into a scowl: "Whitehall Palace, ladies and gentleman."

"Thank thee," Cessie said speedily as we docked.

"I wouldn't p'rsonally wanteth to receiveth closeth to fusty Bess," the Charon figure pooh-poohed. "Those gents sayeth the lady reeks."

"Aye, well, we didn't asketh thy opinion," Cessie said rudely.

My responsiveness coasted as the riverbank palace rippled; several stories high, lengthwise a chessboard of bastions, Tudor turrets jetting out like endoskeletons. The watercourse paralleled the flinted panes like crystals inside the peripherally marbled chateau. Scrublands characterised it as if Aurora's prince had yet to run it through, a replica dollhouse of the manor Cessie had been desperate to outgrow.

The woman in question streamed smartly to the outsized embowed doorway, Aero rallying to rap it when it punched him rearwards. He quickened to his feet when one of Elizabeth's agents came forth.

A portly, ageing man with cheeks like soured toffees and tinsels of bleached hair was cuddling annals. "The new employees?" he verified.

"Aye," Aero and I landed on the one word we could recount.

"Names?" he said gravely.

Cessie said confidently: "I am Hilda Morgan, the lady is Miriam Marke and that gent is Francis Lucas."

"We're the new s'rvants of the loyal Queene," I said stutteringly.

162

Cessie mentalised a note: *Be very careful. He's William Cecil, genealogy expert and extremely watchful official.* Aero yellowed on receipt of the duplicate message.

The elderly statesman concerted his hooded eyelids. "Yond's comical, I recall not the Queene ev'r ent'rtaining the Morgans."

"We're from a retreat deep in the state. We wend not out much. Mine own fath'r doest not believeth in mingling, n'r publicising rec'rds." Cessie brought out our birth certificates in a flurry, and Aero laced his jerkin.

"F'rgive me, lief maiden, I am growing fusty'r." He nosed through the forgeries. "This looks to beest in 'rd'r. Thee seeketh an audience with H'r Highness Elizabeth, thee sayeth? Followeth me." Chuckles scooted down his Tolkien beard. "The lady'll beest in a valorous humor — a platt'r of marzipan treats wast bestow'd by the cook."

"Excellent, excellent," Cessie said, in a freaked flute of her customary airy-fairy lilt.

The bowed floorplan was classically architectural, fabricated aloft to dumbfound the onlooker. The ritzy corona alighted the mural of Henry VIII, walled by the reawakened Elizabeth of York, Henry VII, pious Jane Seymour and modish Prince Edward.

Cecil tolled into the reception hall: "Thee did request assistants, madam."

"Bringeth those folk in," summonsed a sepulchral idiolect.

There was no time for braked heartrates as the bricks and mortar were unbridled, and there lounged Elizabeth I in a roseate-gold throne. It floodlit her frazzled apricot meringues, tailored in a French knot, haggard forehead pockmarked and grooved, lipless organ an 'O' of cynicism. Hundreds of coconut pearls shimmered on her neckline, pinioned to a mule brooch: a diadem of carrot rubies abutted her mermaid fan. She seemed to have stridden, *Harry Potter*-style, from a miniature to relive her Virgin years. The infirm left elbow was syrupy with teatime sweets, accentuating the cosmetics – every bit as theatrical as Dr Goodwin had sworn. As she assuaged herself from the beanbags, the greying lead make-up toxified her ratty features, zircon lipstick garishly matching her jasper rouge. If the particles met daylight, would she liquefy, as an iced raspberry scone?

"Thy highness," we all curtsied.

"And what maketh thee bethink thee can liveth up to all those who is't cameth bef're?"

"I am from a high-ranking household; familiar with s'rving imp'rtant people," Cessie said fearfully.

Elizabeth moved her hips. "Wherefore art thee so shaken? Art thee who is't thee sayeth thou art, wench?"

Cessie's arches rear-ended with a straight-backed chair.

"Riseth bef're me, maid," Elizabeth said impassively.

"We're so s'rry about h'r," Aero said to deter the deer hunter from the spoor. "The lady hasn't hadst any breakfast."

"Is yond so?" Elizabeth disconnected a ruby ring. "Thee'll receiveth what the pigeons art did feed in this institution."

Cessie stooped again. "I'm s'rry, madam, I knoweth, madam, mine own n'rves quite did fail me. I nev'r bethought I wouldst receiveth to w'rk f'r one such as yourself."

Aero and I swapped an eye roll out of Elizabeth's sightline.

"Well, yond remains to beest seen," the monarch chawed. "Proveth thou art who is't thee sayeth thou art. Thee couldst beest an assassin."

Cessie recovered herself: "I am nay assassin, but a humble maiden. Nev'rtheless, I shall proveth myself."

How is she going to do that? Aero communed online.

The resolution came six microseconds after.

Cessie strode in the vicinity of a scabbard of arrows, a magpie as she selected a birch longbow as long as a cello is plum.

Is she going to let the Queen shoot her? I mind-linked with Aero.

It's a good a plan as any, he discoursed.

"Thee'll needeth thy wristwatch," Cessie said lucidly to the Queen.

Elizabeth's doll-sized timepiece, placed in a band, timed the antiquarian as twelve arrows axed the gift-wrapped archway in sixty seconds.

"Couldst I has't done yond if 't be true I w're not gentle?" Cessie spoke.

"Who is't did teach thee yond? Tis a sir's sp'rt."

"*Thee* liketh hunting," Cessie said bashfully.

"I'm a sov'reign — not thy usual feeble mistress," Elizabeth affirmed.

"Has't t not been lonely," Cessie said discreetly, "all those years pretending to beest weak'r than those thee reign'd ov'r?"

I worried she'd gone too far.

"Talketh not to me of loneliness." The Faerie Queene was resigned. "Thou art barely b'rn." The covering scrunched where the barb had scalped it.

"Shall thee employeth us?" Cessie requisitioned. "If't be true not, I shalt returneth to mine own fath'r, s'rvants too. I'm sure mine own lord wouldst beest amus'd to heareth of thy rejection." She warped her clogs and strutted towards the stoneware.

Elizabeth uncurled her festooned, veiny hand: "Waiteth."

Cessie dawdled under the panelled casing. Aero and I ruched our arms behind our apparel.

"Wh're doth thee cometh from?" the sovereign said. "Thee sayeth such unusual things."

"I might has't toldeth thee one day. Hadst thee employ'd us," Cessie bustled.

"Thou art on trial… but I'll taketh thee. Marry knoweth I needeth all the holp I receiveth," Elizabeth said, as dithering as a gentian in May.

"We knoweth not what to sayeth," we babbled.

"Talketh not, w'rk," the sovereign told us.

Hired, we playacted at housework, dusting and reordering in the expectation of ransacking Whitehall for the crucial compound. My scruples were dust, my virtues besmirched. What did it matter, when the sick were dying in their beds?

"Thee, knave," Elizabeth spooked Aero. "Thee hath said thee couldst garden. Cometh with me."

They disappeared to the gardens so he could validate his sixteenth century CV; Cessie played find-the-Easter-egg in her bedchamber and I snuck into the private library to rid it of 'germs'. Leathery spines bucketed down, titled under Shakespeare, astrology and navigation; there wasn't a single hidden niche, no pills or incantations.

There was a *tread* on the sheepskin.

I almost had a mishap on the stepladder as I encountered Merlin, or a lookalike. He had winking dolphin eyeglasses, metres of snowy wisps and peachy cells.

I screenshotted him to Cessie, who wired his bio: *Elizabeth's counsellor and astrologer. Early scientist; communed with angels and the supernatural. Loyal to Elizabeth, very astute but an imperialist.*

I fumbled for a pretext, but the old man raised a gaunt forefinger.

"Thee wonneth't findeth aught in the library."

"I wasn't looking — I wast dusting," I prevaricated.

"Forswear not to me," he said, and it was his equanimity that made him glacial. His sinuous cape became entangled in the hinges. "What is thy purpose? Wherefore has't thee cometh to the castle?"

I bit the bullet: "Behold, sir, I cometh h're on a special mission. Wh're I am from the sick art dying."

"The sick shouldst kicketh the bucket, in the natural 'rd'r," he said honourably.

"Those gents art dying of ingraft ailments. A source to combat yond — lies in Elizabeth's chamb'rs," I said. "Thou art a sir of the stars — if 't be true thee hadst mine own f'recast, wouldst thee doth nothing?"

"Mine own responsibility is to mine own Queene and h'r subjects — not a landeth with — with ingraft ladies and moores."

"I cometh from the same landeth as thee," I said unbendingly, "wh're men, ladies and diff'rent races art equal."

"How can such a thing beest possible?"

"I'm from the future," I said. "And if't be true thee holp not me, thy descendants shall kicketh the bucket out. The human raceth shall kicketh the bucket out. Thou art mine own only chance."

"Elizabeth wouldst has't thy headeth," John Dee presaged.

"Then on mine own owneth headeth shalt beest t, f'r I shall not stand ho until I has't yond ingredient."

"I knoweth nothing of this — this witchcraft," Dee said.

"Thee consulteth with occultists," I said, infuriated.

"With the blessing of mine own most gentle Queene El-"

"— Elizabeth doesn't needeth t anym're." My timbre broke. "I knoweth hist'ry — the lady liveth to a mellow age. Holp me holp those with plenty of years to liveth. If't be true thee can extracteth yourself

166

from thy ambitions of dominion and wealth — doth one valorous thing bef're thy taper blows out."

"How dareth thee!"

"I speaketh only the troth, sir."

"What doth I receiveth if't be true I assisteth thee?" he said gluttonously.

"Thee receiveth the privilege of f'recasting Elizabeth's longeth life and regaining thy status at court. I've seen thy lasteth years. Thou art ruin'd and penniless und'r the next monarch – I can changeth yond."

Dee propped himself on the table as if it were his personal rattan: "To speaketh of the next monarch is treason."

"Thou art an intelligent sir, John, and th're art some things m're imp'rtant than treason 'r laws. The whole of humanity – f'r one mistress who doesn't needeth t. Bethink about t."

Aeons passed between us.

"What doth thee wanteth me to doth?"

"I needeth to searcheth the castle, at which hour t's quiet," I said.

"Thee can't did bid me breaketh into mine own owneth mistress' chamb'rs," John said, confiscating the tufts from the joints.

"Thy w'rds, not mineth," I said steadfastly.

"At dusk the church bells ringeth and the city gates locket," Dee said. "Anyone hath caught out faces prosecution."

"Ah," I said, "but thee couldst useth one of thy keys to alloweth us into the palace?"

"Thee'll rest're mine own honour?" he said eagerly. "I wonneth't passeth in disarray?"

"I can't gage aught."

"How many p'rish if't be true I inf'rm mine own mistress?" the forecaster said.

"Millions, haply billions," I said, wild-eyed. "The w'rld anon – I cullionly in the future — is v'ry large."

"I'll doth t," he agreed. "But knoweth this, ma'am – trait'rs visage the scaffold, mine own fath'r witness'd those laws being drawn up. If't be true thou art hath caught, I shalt absolve myself of censure and thee shall meeteth thy endeth, Ms Marke."

I directed *The Taming of the Shrew* at him: "How doth I knoweth thee'll keepeth thy w'rd?"

He tidied his magician's mouser: "Wherefore, wench, thee can seeth the future."

*

In our tapestried accommodation, parqueted with reeds and lavender, Aero, Dee and I flocked around Cornelius' hand-pencilled atlas of Whitehall's nooks and crannies.

Cornelius moaned with a drop of amenability: "I'm still not declaring I'll cometh 'long. I liketh mine own headeth as t is. Bef're the lady hath caught the plague mine own moth'r hath used to sayeth twas as healthy as wool."

"T'll beest a lot healthi'r if't be true thee taketh a few gouts of the monolaurin," I said optimistically.

"Dropeth t, Ivy — that gent's helping us, yond's enow," Aero said.

I pressed him: "We needeth a lookout and an extra pair of hands."

"First mine own headeth, anon mine own hands — what m're doth thee require?" Cornelius asked.

"Jokes art meanteth to beest comical," I said callously.

He recouped his poise. "Right, the most wondrous route is through the backdo'r and Dee shall alloweth us in. The guards usually catch but a wink — I cullionly patrol — the middle section, near the Queene's private bedroom. I knoweth not how thee bethink thee'll receiveth past those folk — the Queene h'rself is a sleeping beareth."

"A draught," the astrologer recommended. "I'll slipeth t in their evening ale."

Aero contributed an impression of abhorrence.

Cessie's memorandum came in (she was holed up in the fortress):

Elizabeth never sleeps alone. I've been entrusted with being the Lady in Waiting who sleeps in her quarters – she keeps a sword beside her at all times. She zoomed into the riches: *can you see anything that might be hiding the monolaurin?*

Aero, accessing the same material, jerked his kinks: *No.*

It's funny, Cessie e-messaged, *I have the strangest feeling it's in there, but I can't take the whole thing without it being noticed. We can't trample on history with no repercussions.*

"Art thee sure thee knoweth not wh're twas hath kept?" Aero faced Cornelius.

"I only ov'rheard a conv'rsation, and I wast sw'rn to secrecy by the sir in questioneth." He quivered. "That gent hath said I'd beest in the Tower if't be true I toldeth a soul."

"Who is't wast t?" I had the will to wonder.

"William Cecil," he said distressingly.

"The sir we bump'd into?" Aero said dubiously. "He knoweth?"

"Elizabeth, liketh h'r fath'r, hast at each moment did play courti'rs 'gainst each oth'r. Believeth me at which hour I sayeth I didn't knoweth," Dee said.

"But thee has't a senseth of the mistress. Wh're is the lady likely to encave such a thing?" Aero persisted.

"Has't anoth'r cracketh at yond jewelry boxeth," the astrologer said wisely. "Elizabeth is v'ry practical in h'r clothing, and h'r jewels art precious to h'r — from cater-cousins, from family."

The timer and encroaching sundown informed us it'd been hours since John Dee had taken his leave, and we'd have to mosey amongst bandits and London's deadliest convicts. Frighteningly, I figured out I'd be a convict if we botched tonight or the old man's spirit divested from him.

At eventide we couldn't see rowboats, so Cornelius, Aero and I heave-hoed a moored one, inches from the waters when a man shouted: "Thieves! Receiveth off mine own boat."

We freed it from its hawsers as the poorly-lit man shook his rubber at us, singing 'Row-row-row-your-boat' across the Thames.

"Yond wast too closeth f'r mine own liking," Cornelius remarked; Aero and I tittered.

My envoy (Cessie) revealed: *The guards are in a deep sleep. John Dee is waiting to let you in.* I updated her we were almost there as we reeled from the dinghy, unseeing.

I perforated a premediated configuration on the backway knocker.

Dee undid the locks; Whitehall was blind man's buff dark, and Aero began with the pantry, freely rooting for oranges, asparaguses, saffron, mace, parsnips and currants.

"Powdered it could treat cardiac plaques," the low-ranking researcher said.

"Don't hold back," I said satirically.

"Dr Stone said anything could be an organic tonic," he said earnestly.

"Don't bandy about that name," I sniped.

"You and the Pretorian guard go forward. I'll raid the kitchens."

I doubted the nobleness of his intentions – Aero had a master's in raiding kitchens.

"Pure jewel and pewter bowls," my associate whistled on the metallic crockery, nudging them into his sack as we stole away.

I stepped over the inebriated guards, their tankards clanking to the cobbles, the spiced wine a slick to dodge. Cornelius pointed me around them and through the opacity to the nub of Whitehall, Elizabeth's dusky boudoir.

"Thee stayeth h're as the lookout," I masterminded to Cornelius, whose goose pimples made him seem youthful.

"Cess, I'm here," I whispered as I felt around, toenails gouged by swan quills far below.

A rocker rattled… my pumps grew irregular.

"It's alright," Cessie susurrated back. "I couldn't see you – short-sighted, remember? Elizabeth's an insomniac – but she's dozed off. I coerced the other maids to slack off for one night."

"Where's her jewel box?" I stammered.

Cessie ineptly piloted me and my middle finger tugged the wood, pins and needles addling me. Ornaments, bracelets, crystals and rubies were moons in the blackness, a Heart of Diamonds' valuables. Carat candlesticks and goblets filled the hearth, alongside salt cellars, ewers and trenchers dusty with treasured condiment, worth more than the entirety of Wolves. It was mouth-watering, the inducement to nab the whole catalogue and leave, never return. If only we had an operative contrivance…

"Not that one Ivy; it was bequeathed by her best friend Robert Dudley."

Ghoulish, the way she orated... as if Queens had allies ...

"Any of these jewels may harbour smidgens of monolaurin," Cessie schooled. "Knowing Elizabeth, it'll be in something irreplaceable, not a bag of flour. Comb the wardrobe for minor articles – things thrifty Lizzie won't notice."

Was there a veiled sack with the substance we hankered after? I smuggled sapphire-embossed black and white cloth, timely and seamless for the Design Sector. A blouse and hooped farthingale made its way into the basket when gruff conversation sounded in the passageways.

"Cornelius, art thee still th're?" I called.

Silence on the other side – I was in the throes of panic. The sentinels must've awoken –

"Certes not in h'r bedchamb'r?" one man discussed.

"Th're's nay telling what these rats cameth to doth."

It was a menacing hide-and-seek, only a matter of time. I cloaked myself in Elizabeth's gable cowls so I couldn't be described.

Elizabeth stirred in the four-toned log bed, imported silk sashaying, bedcap failing to obscure the dwindling patches, the attrition in her toothless gums; a wasted form without her paints.

The guardsmen butted in.

In a front roll I ferreted under the grandiose bed just as the candelabrum swamped the chamber. It was like a salsa of dandelions.

"Fair maiden, what hast transpir'd in this chamb'r?" a guard said to Cess.

I rubbernecked Cessie attesting to her unsewn gown in the rocker. "'Twas burglars who is't invad'd Bess' space and tooketh robes and jewels," she feigned dramatically. "I wast on duty, but those gents w're too stout — I did dive in front of the queen, but those men did attack me."

The guardsman broached: "Those gents may beest in the cubiculo."

My entrails were like a PET scan when it's shattering news.

"We're sniffeth those folk out," claimed his sterner brother-in-arms.

Sniff?

An office of bloodhounds drivelled over the threshold, cornuted braces in their flabby vibrissae, scenting the stench, decoyed by my thudding nucleus. They scrammed faster.

"Those gents w're b-i-g, scary men," Cessie fabricated as they impelled her for niceties. "M're liketh polar bears, and those gents hadst clubs."

I skedaddled for the outlet, the elf-eared hangdogs woofing at my wrap, rescinding what would've been bone, scooting into the haziness. The alpha leapfrogged, treating my forearm like a sandwich and, drooling, it came at me again —

"Ow!" I cussed, revising Cornelius' floor plan. The hound hung in shame, pules ricocheting.

I curved a handle – *please be the right one* – and closed it.

Aero's words banished my abstraction: "I thought you'd been caught. Cornelius fled this way, but I said I was waiting for you, we'd agreed –"

"That coward," I said uncharitably.

"We need to keep the foxhounds out," Aero said urgently.

We blockaded the cubed, flaking lumber with skillets, twenty-ton pots, a brick oven and saucepans to postpone them and their controllers.

An opera of whines sounded and I jibed: "See, Aero, this is why I favour cats."

"It's not going to hold," he breathed as the door was beaten.

The scullery trumpeted open, encumbering the stacked paraphernalia, mutts scratching brass. Lamplights blinded us.

Shit.

Accruing the sweet potatoes, Aero lithered on the soaped marble and they disbanded. Recklessly, I beleaguered them like javelins at the flinty security – it felled them like bowling bowls. Hurdling up, Aero chucked ginger and flour at our aggressors:

"Consume cauliflow'r, thee pests!"

"Halt, thee cockroaches!" the uniforms said.

My friend slung the ragbag onto his muscly shoulders, and I congested the entryway with Snow White apples.

"Thee'll beest did boil alive at which hour we findeth thee!" claimed the tougher underling as Aero's crocks tinkled in the twilight, lined with musky mint, sage, cumin and coriander.

"Aero, we're quartered if we're collared," I said.

"I don't care if we're eaten by lions. These'll transform medical care," Aero said classically. He'd never cared about minor matters like judges, juries and executions.

Our attackers chased us to the shoreline – our yacht had departed with the quitter – we'd nowhere left to hide.

"Ivy, one of these."

Aero unmoored one of Elizabeth's beauties, a Madonna sail with *Queene Elizabeth* in calligraphic script.

Shrouded, he used the pole to ward off the custodians; their corneal rings broadened as he repelled them once more.

"If't be true we findeth out who is't thou art, thou art done f'r," the lead guard said.

Throughout our getaway currents jockeyed us as if from the South to the North Pole; we embedded our hands in the planks to ensure we didn't overturn. The flare of rocks whanged us onto shore, streaked but unharmed.

Outlaws twirled at each junction, but the capes lent us an anonymous indomitability – I supposed we were one of them now, executing heists, crosiers crossing the streets of brutes.

The landlord furiously authorised our advent – we'd bribe him heavily at sunrise. It wasn't noteworthy while we zizzed untracked in velour draperies.

Therefore it came to be that we bought his discretion with sovereign change, as we paid 2d for a loaf of bread at dawn. On receipt of this the innkeeper unloaded spiced grapefruit mead, on the house. He braced himself, dispensing a monologue in cockney dialect: "At which hour Cornelius wast threaten'd out of Elizabeth's employment, that gent hath lost his riches. Food is scarce and prices high. That gent hath lost colleagues to a riot this year." He wiped snot with a rag. "Things did get so lacking valor apprentices did plot to Robin Hood the affluent — and those gents end'd up on the gallows. The lad sw're yond month, nay m're plots, nay m're appealing to the virtue of Elizabeth — the lady wast h'r fath'r's daught'r in hair and spirit. Marketh this: bef're thee judgeth, first und'rstand people."

My bowels squirmed, even though I tusked.

"Beest not too hard on the lad. Beest grateful thee did escape with thy liveth." He back-flipped behind the kiosk: "By the way, Elizabeth expects thee at Whitehall. The lady's inspecting h'r house to uncov'r the robb'rs. Thee'll beest lucky not to beest skinn'd alive."

Our flea-bitten kneecaps telescoped.

We're in dead people's shoes, Aero emitted to me.

We gurgled our sorrows (me with fresh orange liquor) like cowboys and girls, when the saloon admitted an entertainer with a remex burgundy hat, chariot-motif tunic and maroon brocade. Shakespeare made to plonk himself on a bleacher when he processed our crimpled forms.

"W'rry not – th're's a planeth. Thee'll receiveth the elixir."

Chapter Thirteen: The Comedy of Errors:

"Beest not a blinking idiot," he said without sugariness. "All hast did not slip hence yet."

"How dist thee knoweth?" Aero said, lower lip distended.

"Mine own fusty cousin Cornelius wroteth to me, pleading f'r assistance," he said seriously. "T appears his courage did fail, but th're is at each moment anoth'r act in a playeth, at which hour the entrance garn'rs apples and pears."

"In plain English?" Aero said emptily.

I jostled him.

"Anne hath said I shouldst stage *The Two Gentlemen of Verona* for Elizabeth — in the chaos nay one'll noticeth thee ruffians running 'round," Shakespeare said. "But beest quick — and receiveth not hath caught. Mine own reputation's on the line. I wanteth not the same sticky endeth as Cornelius."

"Wh're didst the dram coward scamp'r off to?" I said unflappably.

"Cornelius hath asked me to passeth on – that gent did manage to fixeth the damageth," the comedy writer said. "That gent hast nay clue how to reconnect the wires and yond thee needeth a new calculat'r as the fusty one is broken."

"The numbers," Aero said. "The reprogramming can't happen without it. But what —?"

Shakespeare's pocket watch phosphoresced and I knew what I had to do.

"Thee'll help us? Pity thee didn't during the year eleven finals," Aero said.

"I begeth thy pardon?" The scriptwriter cocked his goat earring.

"That gent's hadst too much ale," I said loudly, glowering.

"But this ingredient," Shakespeare said intelligently, "t'll help thy fellows backeth home? T isn't f'r — ah — illicit purposes?"

"'Twill contribute to medicine fin'r than a Queene's," Aero said effortlessly.

Our patron spread his arms wide: "Dally not — wend, pleadeth thy innocence. A dropeth of Dutch courage?"

I didn't cave in, but Aero sapped his flagon of the honey-sweetened beverage. "Free booze always tastes better," he exempted himself.

Shakespeare nibbled our marinated wheat: "Thee mind not, doth thee? Busy day ahead."

"Consume thy heart out," I said, the squeaky joints blacking him out.

Aero and I casseroled by the throne room, determining when to dirty the doorstep.

I'm inside, Cessie telegrammed to us. *Rip the plaster off.*

"You first," Aero said humbly.

Tibia doddering like gelatine, I fast-tracked my clap-clops upon seeing the choleric queen. Crescendos seemed to echo as soon as she spoke.

"I has't hath brought thee h're the present day as th're is a cut-purse in mine own admist."

Shockwaves tidal-waved amongst the staff in the portico.

Elizabeth's pearls protruded: "Aye, lowlife knaves raid'd mine own kitchen, mine own draweth'rs, mine own robes."

Aero scuffled the textiles.

"Nev'r hast a monarch been so did humiliate. Stepeth f'rwards if't be true thee procur'd mine own silv'rware 'r knoweth who is't didst."

It was as though a ghoul volleyed through the hall.

"I couldst've been hath killed. If't be true I findeth out any of thee w're hath sent h're to assassinate me, the block shall beest the lasteth thing thee seeth!"

Cessie dipped her braids.

"Mistress Morgan wast given a fright on h'r first shift," Queen Elizabeth said. "Thee, Miriam, doth thee knoweth aught about the events of lasteth eve?"

"I knoweth nothing, madam," I obtruded my neckline firmly. "If't be true I didst I wouldst rat the impost'rs out betimes."

She carried on without sentiment: "Thee, garden'r, w're thee responsible?"

Aero's comeback flew from his arsenal. "Wherefore stealeth at which hour I has't such a gen'rous wage packet at the palace?"

Elizabeth flapped an eyelid at the audacity. "Yond doest not pardon thee. But I am not one to prosecute with nay evidence."

We soughed.

"Thee'll beest gazed closely, but art free to continueth thy duties f'r anon. If't be true I receiveth a whiff of scandal from any of thee, marketh mine own w'rds 'twill beest the lasteth act thee commit. I has't spies ev'rywh're."

William Cecil regarded us lugubriously; we swallowed as she excused us to slave away in the ménage.

I scrupulously mopped the woven carpet with lemony water; Aero conspired that he would first go into her bedchamber, before me, once the concert was underway. My backbone was as fine-tuned as a xylophone when Elizabeth proclaimed we'd ten minutes left. Aero laid out the dining kit for the nobles to feast with during Shakespeare's special performance.

Cessie issued an 'oh': the company of actors had arrived to set-up a green Verona venue.

"The second Earl of Essex," Cessie said, softer than a cheetah before it forays. A pixie-chinned courtier in tights and lambent slops, conflicting with his neutral doublet, sat alongside the Queen. "Executed in 1601."

"Quiet in the audit'rium," Cecil projected.

The performers in starry costumes of linen and jewelled make-up began. As the audience's heads perked up, Aero skulked out.

"Cease to persuade, my loving Proteus: home-keeping youth have ever homely wits. Were't not affection chains thy tender days," spoke an actor, and my attentiveness stonewashed for awhile.

I made out the Essex Earl's stubble unscrewing: "Lief Bess, who is't art thy new s'rvants? Thee entrust those folk with events already?" A surly sneer frolicked on his greasepaint.

In the blink of a cub's infancy, Cessie spooned hunks of swan and cherry cupcakes onto Elizabeth's cumbersome salver.

A second thespian spoke: "Wilt thou be gone? Sweet Valentine, adieu! Think on thy Proteus, when thou haply seest some rare noteworthy object in thy travel."

Something clunked. *The wind-up clock*. It was two custards away. So long as the craven carpenter had kept his end of *that* transaction, the dividend was within sight.

I wrested a foiled tray from a cook when the gentlefolk were occupied, stretching towards the clockwork tun, a regal pair of salts situated beside it. The cask discharged rosewater onto my maiden's wear, when:

"What art thee doing?" Robert Devereux rebounded.

The actors froze.

I genuflected, revolted with myself: "S'rving, sir, yond's all."

"Giveth me some of those Portugal eggs," he yapped, narrowing.

I spilt the eggs and fifty-year-old mead down his ermine poncho, and whilst he drafted in subordinates to clean, I carted the artefact towards me and hid it in the padded overall.

"I'll dealeth with these," I said, ridding the courtier of the yolk, as any good-natured maid should.

While I legged it towards the exit, Elizabeth complained: "Thee can't receiveth the staff these days."

"Tail h'r," the earl told two ladies in waiting.

At Shakespeare's conduction, the performers clamoured as stagy passages were voiced. My sternum seized up as if I had pneumonia.

Chests, knobs and drawers were in smithereens when I united with Aero.

"Any luck?" I said weakly. "The earl's onto us. Two of the maids are watching my every breath."

"Elizabeth?"

"Cessie's distracting her, but it won't take long for her to mash two and two together."

"What was the expression – as thick as two Armada planks?" Aero joshed.

"Save your stand-up for later," I said briskly. "We've got an antidote to find."

"Yes, ma'am," he said, extricating her ornamental pearl necklet. "What's that whiff?"

"Don't look at me," I said sensitively. "I'm not the one snaffling Portugal eggs or fruit tarts." It dawdled, the incident in ninth grade when Magnus had 'experimented' in culinary class, dyeing my chignon with yeast. Alexandrina and Fire had dubbed me 'Queen Victoria' all term – little and grey-waved.

"No, it's not you, it's the box." He flustered it. "There's another compartment – hang on —"

Zeal mounted in my bosom.

The play-hands made fanatical noises: Aero squirrelled inside, displacing plastic wallets of Elizabeth's foundation, gaudy lip-liner and polychromatic blusher.

"I didn't know you were a fan of venomous make-up," I hummed.

"Think, Ivy – why would Elizabeth want such a powerful element in her paints?" Aero hulled a plaster on his scraped brunet appendage, absent-minded.

The solution struck: "To mask the *real* ingredient," I said. "Monolaurin, pelted into coconut triturate, applied each morning."

"*Cessie* showed us this," Aero said. "How could I be so base?"

"But where in it did she put it?" I said distrustfully. "How can we know without a tester? If we nick it all, she'll know."

"We'll switch it with vinegar and egg paste from the tables," Aero said, tipping the case's contents into an urn.

Exploiting my newly acquired servant's skills, I neatened the boards so signs of our raid were eradicated, and refurbished the dorm using Cessie's former blueprints.

"Doth thee has't p'rmission to ent'r without the Queene?"

Entering like malevolent stepsisters, Elizabeth's ladies eyeballed us, as we were squatted. "W're thee looking f'r Bess' jewels?" a plump, black-robed woman challenged. "I am keepeth'r of h'r chests."

"Mary, ado not yourself. Evil shall beest out'd in the endeth. Behold at those folk, on all fours liketh animals — in their rightful lodging," her hoop-skirted workmate said.

"Quite right, Lady Stafford, those gents condemn themselves," Mary submitted.

"We w're tidying up. But we'll wend anon," Aero surrendered.

We re-joined, the players reaching completion.

"Forgive them what they have committed here/And let them be recall'd from their exile: They are reformed, civil, full of good/And fit for great employment."

Robert, Mary and Lady Stafford provided Frisbees of scowls.

Aero's brows focused as he mailed Cessie about the switch. Her deer eyes brightened a second after. Self-effacingly, we commandeered guests' dinner plates, Aero trickling egg, salt and vinegar into his arsenal.

Nonetheless, as in a Shakespeare comedy, certain schemes are made for storybooks.

In freeze-frame, Aero trolled, sozzled, healing shin making a *snap*. Our thievery (from last night and that afternoon) bespattered the lavish banquet, the wallets mooring beneath Elizabeth's clawed nose bridge.

"What is the meaning of this?" she warbled.

The performer faulted the line: "Please you, I'll tell you as we pass along, That you will wonder what hath fortuned."

The sovereign chunked her wine glass: "Stand ho the playeth!"

"Aero, Ivy, leave!" Cessie said.

I fled crossways onto the bar, the many-headed marchpane carving of the Spanish fleet shimmying, crème and sponge breaking off. Talons strained to bind my ankle; I sidestepped them like a rodent before a trap.

Aero hit the end of the playhouse, slanting when Cecil's ceremonial dowel barred me. The councillor's fox-fur sleeve seized mine, and I was motionless. Devereux bore a Polar-bear-that-fished-the-seal glim.

Elizabeth was up in arms, joggling Cessie's strings: "Didst thee participateth in this plot, wench?"

Cessie fought off Elizabeth's pinchers: "Nay, nay, I'm innocent!"

Scenting the distraction, I booted Cecil's rapier and zipped after Aero.

"The monolaurin?"

"Managed to keep hold of it," the biologist said languidly.

"What on earth?" John Dee materialised from the library.

"We've did get what we cameth f'r, but those gents're aft'r us," I garbled. "Thee has't to doth something."

Dee flexed the wooden flooring, where a trapdoor undid.

Thoughtlessly we lowered ourselves down: "Thanketh thee, sir."

"Wend, wend!" He stole into the reading room as lieutenants upended it.

"Where does it lead?" Aero said faintly.

"The backway, according to Cornelius' diagram," I said, more nobly than I felt.

In the endless lair we heard them tunnelling and Aero was slackening, reflexes poor with drink and injury...

"Ivy – I – I can't go on any longer," he hyperventilated.

"We – have – to," I said, crawling in the tarantula-infested ash, platform soles in our ears.

Guards roughed our tailbones onto the panelled smut. As we tussled for freedom the wallets were trodden, tincture amalgamating with soot.

Impure, valueless.

"Titles," they spat at us.

"Miriam Marke and Francis Lucas," I said contemptuously, since Aero appeared too aggrieved to defend himself.

"Then thee two shall h'reby beest taken to the Tower of London for treason and theft," they said cruelly.

They boxed us into handcuffs, and if it weren't stark, cold reality we might've twittered.

Were you netted? Cessie posted to me.

Aero's shinbone gave out. We're in cuffs, I self-confessed.

We were moved like labradors in a kennel to the amphitheatre, Cecil's double chin enclosing him like washing lines, Robert's gremlin stare trouncing us, the Queen's crown misaligned, Cessie the sole sympathiser in a drumbeat of hisses.

"To the prison, thy highness?" The more moderate jailer said.

"Swallow the key," Elizabeth answered, and the flatterers nickered.

"Despicable," an unknown spat at me on our way out.

It was a morbid hour, sailing upriver to the Tower of London, the hobnailed souls on the ramparts prophetic of our ends.

"Sorry about the leg," Aero slurred.

"Don't be silly; I should never have quarried the volcano."

It'd primed a sequence that'd terminated in my tormenters' demises. It'd not resolved the queasiness in my midriff – they'd plagued me so persistently that for years, all I saw was raw red. I didn't see blue either in their departure; purely a blankness, a 1920s cinema spool. The redness I used to feel mingled with the cloying heads; faceless, lifeless. The feudal citadel drew ever nearer, granular architecture topped with canister roofs, dissimilar to the muddy embankment with its insistent rowing. It was a version of the cut-outs Pearl glued into her collages, a three-dimensional cardboard compound.

From the bankside, featureless locals launched abuse.

Diffusely, I made out:

"What didst Elizabeth ev'r doth to thee?"

"We'll waiteth t out h're, until thy heads meeteth the axe!"

"Bethought those gents'd stealeth instead of earneth an honest living, didst those gents?"

"A harlot and a moor, robbing us blindeth!"

Aero scrooched, and my pleat lay in rats' tails as I was forced shakily onwards. It was a history tutorial like no other.

We barged under Traitor's Gate, more a pigpen than truly baleful; the tributary was like avocado nectar this side of the railing. We debarked.

The crusty, chalky battlements were fifteen feet width-wise and soared to ninety feet. Granite columned like headstones ate our soled toes as the warden unconfined the stairwell, prototype knights loaning a melancholy air.

The Warden produced newly minted parchment: "Elizabeth wishes the two of thee to suff'r a Spanish Inquisition without delayeth."

Spanish Inquisition?

Aero goggled me.

I started to regret my sympathy for him.

The detachable steps were uninvolved once we'd been poked up.

The regally dressed beefeater buffed his knuckles: "Bethink not of running again, girly."

"What did Cessie say about torture?" Aero said.

"She didn't," I said soberly.

"Now you know why I drink," Aero jibbed.

"How high's your pain threshold?" I tested.

"It wouldn't take much to break me," he baulked.

The beefeaters had a stronghold on my shoulder pads as I was balanced onto hard-backed seating along with Aero. The interrogation pod was hemmed, dank and odorous.

"Prepare to be cross-examined," Aero wisecracked.

Commissioners and a royal attorney graced our presence; the wardens malingered outside, nationalistic housecoats unreceptive, in soldier mode.

"W're thee hath sent to spy on our Queene?" they interrogated.

"Nay, sir, we w're cleaning," I said, tight-lipped.

"Mr Lucas, how doth thee answ'r the chargeth?"

"Not guilty," he said punctually.

Commissioner one struck the wood with his maul. "Thou art falsing, aren't thee, moor?"

Aero twiddled his thumbs. "Calleth not me moor," he rebuked.

He's trying to break you, I messaged him.

Commissioner two signalled to the wardens, who unconcealed twofold racks like cyclopean roly-polies, to spur revelations.

"Alloweth me impart a dram lesson. In an int'rrogation, the prison'r usually submits to his questioneth'rs, if't be true that gent wanteth to leaveth the Tower intact."

"Toucheth not that gent," I said.

"Break thee off, wanton lass," my torturers contradicted.

"Don't, Ivy, it's not worth it," Aero said unblinkingly.

I always wanted to be taller, I dispatched to him.

Don't, he airmailed.

Remotely, I mulled over whether Cessie had been believed. She'd previously been tortured, on the dunking stool.

Commissioner one reshuffled his papers. "On the aft'rnoon of Octob'r 25th 1595, wherefore didst thee stealeth from Queene Elizabeth's bedchamb'r?"

"I wasn't stealing, but polishing," I said. A disembodied calm diffused my arteries.

"W're thee responsible f'r the burglary on the night of Octob'r 24th 1595?" Commissioner two insisted.

When you were guilty, how did you deny the indictments laid before you?

Don't confess, Aero transmitted.

Never, I replied.

"Mr Lucas, how doth thee answ'r the questions putteth to Mistress Marke?"

"I eke deny all accusations," he expressed.

"Wouldst the rack loosen thy tongue?" Commisoner one thundered.

"Mine own tongue cannot beest loosen'd to admiteth falsehoods," Aero said placidly, though his frail knees rumbled beside mine.

"Wherefore didst thee wanteth to stealeth from H'r Majesty?" Commissioner two queried circumspectly.

"I didn't stealeth," Aero said, and I knew he justified it as recycling, as saving.

"We wanteth not to did hurt thee, but if't be true thee answ'r not the qu'ries thee f'rce our handeth," Commissioner one said brutishly.

"Thee can twisteth us into a hundr'd shapes, and we still wonneth't confesseth," Aero said mulishly.

The second lieutenant massaged his muscles: "Ms Marke, doth thee shareth his view?"

"I shall nev'r confesseth, as th're is nothing *to* confesseth!" I said spiritedly.

"V'ry well, madam," the first officer said facilely.

He beckoned the men outside.

Was the bracket going to snap my skeleton, relocate my limbs?

They won't rack us, Aero belled to me. *Not while they're in the dark.*

I admired his bravado, but confidentially felt that as a scientist he should be more troubled.

"Beefeat'rs, brace those folk in irons, dogs art those gents art," Commissioner two broached.

The wardens' beefy physiques stapled our protests.

Commissioner one had one last adage.

"Faileth to confesseth bef're the hourglass dries up and thee shall beest rack'd within an inch of thy liveth. If't be true thee still doth not yield, the iron maiden shall pricketh thee until thee bleedeth."

My temper quashed, I coursed into the lockup.

Aero whelped, strung in searing, rusty cuffs, growing slumped.

"Aero!" I said.

"Thou art next," the warden guaranteed.

"No – get off –"

Bodily, I was tacked by my scrawny wrists, vessels roiling as I draggled, seemingly limbless; a dummy to be strung from torture to torture until I broke.

"Enjoyeth thy stayeth, cut-purses."

As though squirted with corrosives, I readjusted my yokes, whinnying more passionately than the donkey who'd brayed on the circus ring when I was small. The guards beheld us as my parents had in the stands.

"Hang on," Aero said.

"Well – I don't think I've much choice," I said, more breathily than I ordinarily sounded.

"I don't know about you, but I'd rather not take a guilt trip to the iron maiden," Aero said wryly.

I lunged to relieve my itching underarms, before retaining that I was in bondage.

Beep, beep. Cessie's link shipped me to her neurons, her viewpoint as Elizabeth's cruel beak flipped.

"Well, maid, art thee in league with the heathens in the Tower?"

"I testifi'd yond I kneweth nothing. I am but a simple maiden, a virgin liketh thee who is't desires to findeth a husband at court. I knoweth not the petty dealings of cut-purses. F'rgive me, yond I hath brought such fellows to Whitehall," Cessie said shallowly. "'Twas mine own only sineth."

Elizabeth's opal bangle displayed raven, amethyst and pea colours as she flopped: "I wast young liketh thee, once. I twirl'd at masques, the belle of the ball. Th're wasn't a gentle in the landeth who is't didn't admireth me. I wanteth not to amerce thee, but thee pusheth mine own patience, liketh nails through a board. Thee hath left me nay choice but to imprison thy s'rvants."

"Alloweth those folk wend — those gents meanteth nay evil."

"I'm trying to holp thee, Hilda, one gentlewoman to anoth'r. I can findeth thee men, riches, antiques. F'rget thy companions, and thee can riseth at court."

"I've did love playing cards with thee, styling thy wig, flatt'ring diplomats, singing songs. But I'm not from h're, Elizabeth, and thou art being selfish," Cessie hiccupped. "I wanteth to seeth mine own cater-cousins and families."

"Then thee condemn yourself."

"I des'rve to beest condemn'd if't be true thee wonneth't lib'rate po'r Miriam and Francis."

"Statute is statute. Mine own council shall ruleth 'gainst those folk. I cannot bringeth sediment into public affairs."

"Thy fath'r ruin'd thy moth'r, ruin'd Europe," Cessie maintained. "Beest mod'rate, Bess, beest bett'r."

"Thee dareth speaketh 'gainst the dead king? A half-grown wench?" she said, riled.

The oubliette was infiltrated by our warders, who unknotted our bonds so robustly the clip cut off.

We salved our stinging armpits, prostrate. I would've taken five hundred Cretaceous hornets in place of that.

"We've been reprieved," Aero said weakly. "I – I knew it."

"Aero," I spluttered. "I – I don't think…"

It was too late.

My organs flapped as we were frogmarched to another, more repellent, seldom unavailable dorm. It had elbowroom for the whiteboard-sized, acrylic machinery, and the beefeater leered:

"The mistress first; the lady's in bett'r health."

They strapped me between the rollers.

"P'rhaps this'll maketh thee speaketh."

"Prithee, I've toldeth thee all I knoweth," I supplicated. I was not beyond begging, after all, like the vagrants convicted in Elizabeth's queendom.

"Well, thee'll has't to bethink hard'r, girly," the patrollers said.

The leaver enlivened – I was going to be racked with guilt, section by section. I'd never have opted for this penalty. It was madness, a twenty-third century person being exterminated in 1595, centuries before her birth.

The warden cranked it as secretion ran down my cheeks.

"Waiteth, I'll bid thee what I knoweth," Aero said, near tears. "Stand ho the rack and I'll bid what hath happened."

They shilly-shallied… they had their directives…

"Aero, sayeth not aught. We're sw'rn to secrecy. Ow." I wiggled from the scope of the rack, a dolly's climbing frame, barbarous.

"I has't to, Ivy, t's law. Safety above secrecy."

Once Aero was in Hippocratic mode, there was no reasoning with him.

"Good now, knave, starteth talking," the beefeater said.

Hammer.

The cubicle was occupied by Mr Shakespeare, or possibly the mechanism had unhinged me.

"By the w'rd of gentle Queene Elizabeth, releaseth this citizen from the rack. In returneth f'r a thousand sov'reigns, the lady hast sign'd their releaseth warrants. If't be true thee harmeth those folk anon, thee disobey thy rul'r."

The brigadiers were unimpressed, but acknowledged the certificate, Elizabeth's handwriting classily scrawled. "Thee spineth thy usual tall tales, Mr Shakespeare. In all mine own hist'ry of imprisoning trait'rs, I've nev'r seen a repeateth offendeth'r alloweth off so lightly."

Shakespeare held up a ringed finger. "On the condition yond those gents partake in a private recital f'r Bess, and art did banish aft'r this night."

"We can nev'r cometh backeth?" Aero said flatly.

"We wanteth not to," I said happily.

"Unshackle h'r," the warden directed.

I bowled onto the stinging cellar floor, reflexing to check everything was in order.

"Receiveth off the prop'rty, bef're I changeth mine own mind," the jailer said.

When we were out of their range, Shakespeare added: "Thee might bethink me a madman, but I've did get a playeth in w'rks – t's nev'r been seen. Wouldst thee doth me the favour of acting f'r Elizabeth?"

Aero swiped a dust ball from his nostrils: "Which playeth?"

"T's only a rough drafteth… thee belike wanteth not to. T's nay valorous, but I bethought I'd testeth t out. Hilda's a true cousin to thee two. The lady did beg me to charm Elizabeth — but I hadst to sayeth thee'd p'rf'rm. The lady wasn't joyous with the wage." He imitated her: "*What useth is chinks to me if't be true courti'rs breaketh mine own heart?*"

"The title?" I said crabbily, taken aback by the terms.

Shakespeare unsnarled his knotted hackles, staring pensively ahead: "Wherefore, *A Midsummer Night's Dream*. A comedy about romance and fairies. Behold, young ones: coequal Queenes desire ent'rtainment."

I couldn't make eye contact with Aero.

There was a magic in being acquitted, though, as in the production, the Earth finding equilibrium in a forfeit. I for one venerated my dignity more than my welfare. I'd never been a sprite, more a bad-tempered goblin with a jinxed aura.

In the lobby of Whitehall, Shakespeare familiarised us with the Chamberlain's Men, comprising Will Kempe, a puckish, beer-bellied fellow; Richard Burbage, a pointy-nosed, melancholy individual; and Richard Cowley. It was to be an enactment on pain of death.

The meet-and-greet finished, people were beginning to elect parts.

"Ivy, if we don't choose now, we'll get the starring roles," Aero said hysterically.

"I *want* a starring role," I perjured.

As the ensemble put their crania together, Shakespeare fisted for noiselessness: "The handsomest playeth'r shalt playeth the Queene of the Faeries. Aero, stepeth f'rward."

"Nay needeth f'r a costume, then," Aero took it on the chin, but Burbage made fun of him.

Hoping to go unnoticed, I slipped behind Kempe, however Shakespeare recalled me: "Halt, ruffian. I've the p'rfect role f'r thee." He timed a gap. "The naughty mechanical Bottom shouldst beest agreeable to thee."

I paced in disgust: "Not Bottom. I'll beest a laughing stock."

"All the bett'r f'r the audience," Shakespeare said, and marshalled a symphony of mirth amongst his troupe.

I distributed a frightful glare: "If it hadn't been for your cursed leg…"

"It could be worse," Aero consoled me.

"How?" I asked.

"Thou art an ass — nay acting requir'd," he summarised.

"Sayeth the Faerie Queene," I scored.

Shakespeare sshed us once more: "Beest quiet, the playeth's about to beginneth."

"But we knoweth not our lines," I argued.

"I'll bewray the w'rds on a placard behind the Queene."

"I'm not equipped for this," I whimpered.

"Woe betide thee if't be true thee blund'r mine own first recital of *A Midsummer Night's Dream*," Shakespeare said, so tersely I began to see why people spoke his name over six centuries later.

"The lady's female, sir, the lady can't holp t," Cowley said helpfully.

"Is this a comedy 'r a farce? Starteth anon," Elizabeth rounded us up.

The demand for entertainment grew frenzied. It dawned on me the Tower wasn't a bad life.

"I know what you're thinking – and you're not getting out of this," Aero said meanly. "We still need the monolaurin."

"But it was pulverised!" I whispered.

"You think Queen Bee won't have a stockpile?" Aero said.

"She won't renounce it."

"If we personate…"

"I'm not doing it."

Chapter Fourteen: The Huntswoman's Heart:

Legendary last words. We were shepherded behind a portable rail, as unembellished as dummies.

Aero was festooned in a tulip fan, plumose cloth and a lotus umbrella sarong more billowy than Marilyn Monroe's. "Peaseblossom" plonked heavily dyed hairpieces onto him and the acclimatisation was absolute.

"Thee w're a good-looking guy, but art a most wondrous mistress," I clowned, like Mother of the Bride.

"Can't waiteth to seeth yours," Aero said evilly.

"Mustardseed" converted me into the porky, debauched Bottom, abrasive pumps implanted on size seven toenails and gristly hairs greased onto my chin. Lastly, a fat-suit jerkin was buttoned until I could hardly breathe.

"So that's what you look like without make-up," Aero said unsupportively. "I always wondered."

As the rabble quietened, Elizabeth said cordially: "Faileth to ent'rtain this delightful crowd, and thee'll beest did sentence without trial."

The organist keyed his spinet: the hour of reckoning was upon us.

I was sightless, unmoved as the "Act One" players felt their way into their roles, as one would escape an opaque purse. The viewers reacted to the script and stage directions with hecklings and chants as I tried to uncouple my stupor.

"Act Two – yond's thee." A random and six conspirators bundled me into the limelight, all observations upon me.

We were acting a play within a play, and I was to impersonate a braggart hogging the characters, reaping boos from Robert and Mary and oranges from a farthingale maid.

A bump coagulating underneath the masculine façade, I overlooked this, puffing my breastbone as though a pigeon.

"And I may hide my face, let me play Thisby too," I said, in an infallible mockery of Devereux and the alternate satellites at court.

The ribaldry was washed away as if by shower cream. *Ha!*

My unnamed fellow fed lines to me and I returned them greedily. Shakespeare merged concern and glee as he winched the placard.

I strutted. "Let me play the lion too: I will roar, that I will do any man's heart good to hear me."

On glimpsing Devereux's mortification, we hustled offstage before long.

Will Kempe offered a thumbs-up: "'Twas a weak starteth, but thou art shaping up nicely."

I overcame the impulse to clout him as he faced the spotlight for Puck's entrance, while Aero and I prowled behind the shutter like children.

"Francis, t's thee." Cowley molested him to have a squabble with his "husband" Oberon, over the ownership of their servant.

"I will not part with him," Aero averred in squeaky chords.

He swanked off with his 'fairies', including a sullen Cowley. Oberon and Kempe's Puck then collaborated to settle the score with Titania.

"What didst I ev'r doth wrong?" Aero bewailed backstage.

Oberon commanded: "... drop the liquor of it in her eyes. The next thing... she... looks upon/Be it on lion, bear, or wolf... she shall pursue... with the soul of love."

"Thou art done f'r," I muffled to Aero, as the listeners oohed and aahed.

"Act III — Miriam, thee knoweth the drill," Kempe pushed me onwards, as I strangled a "Hey!"

Devereux adopted a faux uninterested air, abusing us cheaply in Elizabeth's sapphire-embellished lobe.

"If't be true thee aren't ent'rtaining enow, the lady'll has't all our heads," Kempe said supportively.

One forefinger bled as I dug it, haranguing the other characters, Lady Stafford mumbling that I wasn't convincing enough. Kempe entered (with any luck to save my skin) for his hoax, cuing my withdrawal.

"Thee'll loveth this," an actor promised.

His playmates roofed my oval hairline with a horsey ass's head, enormous enough to cover all but the nethermost quarter of me. He decked me in a florid tunic, twenty sizes too big.

"That's the best you've ever looked," Aero said.

"I'll see you in the Tower," I said viciously.

"Onstage," someone said.

"Quince" exclaimed at my bestiality: "O monstrous! O strange! We are haunted/fly, masters! Help!" He frisked off.

My eyelashes looked from side to side before Shakespeare made my lines available. "…this is to make an ass of me; to fright me, if they could. I will sing… they shall hear I am not afraid."

I *was* afraid. Cessie's eyes broadened as she assessed what I'd to do.

My lips subsided like a seahorse's, and I quavered: *"The ousel cock so black of hue… the wren with little quill."*

The velvety head fell off.

Kempe and Cowley tiptoed on, fumbling with the donkey headband, smiles becoming increasingly static. My fondness for Bottom mounted.

Elizabeth clammed under her sundae lacquer. "One m're mishap and I'll throweth hence the key!"

Robert, Earl of Essex chortled: Mary threw a Lady apple towards me.

Ouch! I reeled from the knockback.

At the backdoor Kempe laced a ruff round my neck so my donkey-self wouldn't detach, and they swapped with "Titania".

Aero ruffled his ringlets and put a gloved limb on his heart (his character had been enchanted to love me): "…gentle mortal, sing again: Mine ear is much enamour'd of thy note."

The audience socked their goblets in a tennis-ball fashion.

Shakespeare buoyed the board; Aero read aloud: "Thou art as wise as thou art beautiful."

I batted my lashes for the room's endorsement.

"Not so, neither: but if I had wit enough to get out of this wood, I have enough to serve mine own turn."

Freaked, Aero had me by my lapels in front of an astounded Cessie. "Out of this wood do not desire to go: Thou shalt remain here, whether thou wilt or no."

'She' successively coached her fairies to serve my every whim.

Cowley (Mustardseed) resembled the Grinch as he knelt before me: "Hail!"

The watchers had tears driving down their faces.

A lovelorn Aero said: "…wait upon him; lead him to my bower."

The insinuation scandalised the aristocrats as we vanished.

"Their m'rals art as loose as their fing'rs," Robert said.

Out of the audience's eye, Aero lamented: "Shakespeare hadst mine own charact'r right. Thee'd needeth a potion to maketh me falleth in loveth with thee."

I spanned my arms: "As if't be true I'd falleth in loveth with anoth'r species."

"Just so we're cleareth," Aero said, as if I wanted to be solaced.

Will Kempe seemed to be the pet of Whitehall; there was a great deal of acclaim when he admitted to Oberon the mischief he'd prompted. Cowley lugged me frontwards for the penultimate Act.

"Scratch my head, Peaseblossom," I said to the unpleasant-looking player, revelling in my authority.

"Sleep thou, and I will wind thee in my arms," Aero said.

We fabricated snores, our arms around each other. Devereux appeared mollified.

Oberon asked Puck to restore Titania's wits, and 'she' cried: "My Oberon!"

Aero embraced the actor. "What visions have I seen! Methought I was enamour'd of an ass."

Who're you calling an ass? I emailed Aero. *Well, if the head fits*, he gibed.

Oberon and Titania boogied, the latter holding fast to his better half due to his leg, having a banana-peel moment by dwindling into the rail as the triangles were resolved. Thankfully, the gentlefolk took it in good humour; their whims were as changeable as the Thames.

Puck's monologue versed the symphonic moral and the surrealism, more tortuous than the chains, ended.

There was an ovation; roses bloomed at the feet of the thespians and they stooped.

"Miriam, boweth!" Kempe notified.

Discounting the guffaws of Devereux and meddlesome Mary, I bobbed my kneecaps into a knitting ball.

Shakespeare dashed to Queen Elizabeth for the verdict, enabling Cessie to peg it through the blare to enfold me. "Tortured in the Tower, and this is still your worst fear!"

She fooled around with Aero's wig: "You were a gorgeous Titania! I was her in year four."

"How can you be two people at once?" Aero said vacantly.

"I was only a set pinecone, and still wet myself," I said.

"Valorous folk of the kingdom, I has't madeth up mine own mind," Elizabeth said, gaudier than a foghorn. "If't be true these playthings has't did fail to prithee me, those gents shall beest did hang, drawn and quart'r'd in the Tower."

"Don't hold back on our account," Aero said.

The upper-class theatregoers made no sound: we'd playacted not for a pretty penny, but our lives.

"Some of thee putteth on a po'r showeth, and mishandl'd the costumes I ad're," she said, her blackening irises falling on mine. "Howev'r, in lighteth of the whole, I has't hath decided to grant Miriam and Francis m'rcy." There were gasps. "I wast c'rtainly amused, if 't be true not did impress. Hark to this: thy futures doth not forswear on the stage."

"Gram'rcy, Elizabeth, we shall not f'rget this," Aero and I said, unable to believe it.

"Well done," Cessie said subtly.

"Thou art an upstanding mistress, Elizabeth, but those gents haven't did earn the honour," the Essex Earl said as the lute stopped.

"He'll wish for mercy one day," Cess said darkly.

"I am the Queene of this realm, knave, and presume not influenceth ov'r mine own decisions," the Queen said. "Enow blood has't been did split this year."

"Not the right kind," Devereux said.

Someone shifted out of the coven – it couldn't be — ?

I was sure I recognised his tar-milked cornea: "Cornelius, Cornelius!"

He'd disappeared.

Before I could dog him, Shakespeare rounded on us.

"Rubbish starteth, but thee two w're brilliant. Elizabeth sayeth thou art free to wend, but only aft'r thee wend to h'r."

"Anon?" Cessie made sure.

"Aye," the scriptwriter said, "in the bedchamb'r. The lady wanteth to findeth out what thee knoweth."

A queasiness upset my front.

This time Shakespeare addressed me directly: "I didn't cullionly to humiliate thee earli'r – I bethought thee'd beest grateful f'r the mask."

"Grammercy," I thanked him, warmed.

"H'r life is a theatre and we art the playeth'rs," Shakespeare said.

"Shouldn't I seeth Cornelius about the device?" I said.

Shakespeare glinted. "This is m're imp'rtant. Thee did achieve m're this eve than thee bethink. The way to h'r heart hast at each moment been plays, sonnets, songs, v'rse — language. Wend to h'r. This is thy lasteth chance."

"The lady'd has't hath killed us t t'd suit'd h'r," I said. "Wherefore shouldst we?"

"Bess is loneli'r than thy dizziest hallucinations couldst predicteth," Shakespeare told me. "Thee may beest surpris'd by what thee seeth in h'r."

"What the lady giveth up something so precious? Elizabeth wast stubb'rn as cattle at which hour I spake to h'r earli'r," Cessie said.

"People shift with the seasons; th're is nay one self, but thirty suits of armour behind which we encave." Shakespeare doffed his boater. "Fare thee well. I shall meeteth thee again, in ink."

"Grammercy... f'r peventing our deaths and all," we sung after him.

"Thee wonneth't f'rget me?" he said over his brocade.

"Remindeth'rs of thee shall liveth f'rev'r on stage," I said.

Shakespeare's aspects grew peaceful.

"Thee'll beest good now?"

"Oh, we shall," I said, lachrymose. "Someday."

With fright, we wrung Elizabeth's handle. Late evening showed, inky and leaden via the windowpanes.

"Ent'r."

We rested by the independent chimney corner, and at her word Cessie took off her carroty wig, the hairless scalp barer than a bikini.

"Wherefore didst thee breaketh into mine own chamb'rs?" the older woman said. "What w're thee aft'r?" Like a pipe smoker, her ribs coughed.

Aero unbent: "This moment's been coming. I bethink thee knoweth. I bethink thee've suspect'd from the moment we setteth foot in this castle."

"I wast did educate by the most wondrous scholars in Europe. Thee bethink I wouldn't noticeth trait'rs in mine own midst? Wherefore shouldst I giveth up mine own sick st'res to s'rvants?"

"Because t's the right thing to doth," I said.

"Who is't art thee?" Queen Bess said.

Cessie's lids flickered in the heat. "I am Cessie Belle and I am rich, but hundreds of years in the future. Francis is very much Aero, a scientist — liketh thy physicians the present day. Miriam is Ivy — the lady fixes things."

"Such peculiar fables thee utt'r. Art thee a dream?"

"I'm flesh and blood, and without thy goodwill, thy subjects shall becometh extinct. T'll beest the endeth of ev'rything," Cessie forecast.

The wax light fulminated out.

"Thee has't seen?" Elizabeth said sportingly.

"Oh, aye," Cessie said.

"Thee knoweth not what t is to reigneth as a mistress."

"I knoweth what t's liketh to ent'r a profession yond mocks ladies," I shared.

"The constant strain — I needeth yond potion," Elizabeth said petulantly. "Mine own people needeth me."

"Those gents needeth thee m're wh're I'm from. Without thee, the human raceth reaches a dead endeth," I predicted. "From the day thee almost succumb'd to smallpox, thee've taken yond mixture. Thee've did ingest enow to ensureth a longeth reigneth. T's timeth to giveth t up."

Elizabeth straightened; her moth-eaten visage washed out like the candle. "Giveth t up? And reside und'r brick and m'rtar?"

"I knoweth what happeneth to thee. Thee still has't timeth," Cessie said.

Elizabeth pivoted to me, seemingly expecting an honest answer. "Doest mine own legacy endureth?"

"Thou art commem'rat'd in art and books and song and schools," I said.

"Ev'ry m'rtal wishes to liveth f'rev'r. I hadst the pow'r to half maketh t so."

We remained unforthcoming for a few minutes, and she rinsed the ruby and diamond signet she continually wore, stamped with herself and Anne Boleyn's portraitures. She unhooked the gold adjoining her mother's face; it had a cloisonné sheen. An emergency stockpile was visible: goose-white, depthless and chalky.

"This isn't f'r selfish ends? 'Twill wend to those who is't needeth t?"

Our crowns behaved like Noddy.

"Then taketh t, taketh t," she said, and Aero came away powdery with the solution.

"Thanketh thee, Elizabeth. Our colleagues — those gents'll knoweth what thee didst," Cessie gabbled.

"Despite thy sh'rtcomings, thee w're a faithful maid," Bess said. "And thee, the most artful h'rbalist I've ev'r encount'r'd."

As we approached the knob with our satchel of goodies, she said out of the blue: "And thee, wench? Is't true thou art a carpent'r in thy univ'rse?"

"A mechanic," I revised her statement, knowing I still twirled on the axe edge.

"Stayeth did marry to the job, Ivy," she said openly. "I am the Virgin Queen, partn'r'd only to mine own subjects. Nay husband rules mine own sleep chamber."

"Thou art m're Anne than Henry," Cessie said.

"Mine own council knoweth me as mine own fath'r's daught'r. But mine own chamb'r knoweth I am a Boleyn," she said, as the knocker shut.

"Wow," Aero said. "She did an unselfish thing."

"I thought she'd come through," Cess said.

"Will it clear us, though?" I said, as we dogtrotted past Henry VIII's frieze.

"If this doesn't, I don't know what will," she bemoaned.

Arm-in-arm, ring-a-ring-a-roses twentysomethings, we skidded on the lawns. Elizabeth had reminded me of my identity as a mechanic. There was no apprentice waiting but *hey presto!* The beloved tube, prior to now so pulped, was a reinserted Lego. It was sheeny and pigmented with tangerine and arctic paints.

Indoors was a chicken-wire breadbasket titled *Mementoes*, no larger than a birdcage. Amongst forget-me-nots was a note in shaky, highly-spaced cursive: *S'rry I couldn't beest brave.*

My midriff inverted.

"Ivy, look."

Cessie, unforceful, coxswained me to the hanger, where portrait miniatures of Aero, her and I were crayoned. I positioned the portraiture on the sill, to be educed whenever I forgot my courage.

"Told ya you were the favourite," Cessie smirked.

"He stuck to that contract, at least," I said; it would've taken the iron maiden to move me to concede my gratification.

I set to work rewiring (no layperson's affair), tinkering with the 'on' switch and feeling the electrons bewitch the machine to life. It was my own baby power plant, transformative.

The carriage heaved us into motion, my heart lisping as we went up, up, up.

I sought the hole-in-the-wall of Whitehall, where Elizabeth thumbed through *The Faerie Queene*. A ephemeral sunbeam made her as halcyon as her naval painting. She interleaved the heirloom behind her feather pillow. No fortune-teller, I felt her wakefulness would cede to a bliss even cut-purses couldn't discompose.

*

No one noticed us as we went, snail-like, to Professor Goodwin's office. His designer eyewear sloped as he clocked our attendance.

"You three," the history lecturer stuttered. "What in the name of —?"

"Sir, we made it," Cessie said.

Aero set forth the lifesaver, and Goodwin paled.

"The monolaurin?" he said. "You worked it out? Clever kids – interns, I should say. That's spiffing – I mean – Stone will be so impressed."

Cessie bit her fuller lip. "Are we blacklisted?"

"Officially," her ex-teacher said, "but I may be able to call in a favour. Don't move a muscle."

One hundred and twenty seconds later (Aero tallied it), Dr Stone and his wife made their arrival, no longer in their judge's gowns.

Mrs Stone felt the dip in respect, for she said: "Don't think you're off the hook. It was rash and unreasonable for employees to take a wondrous possession and ditch justice."

"What's that?" her spouse said, fingering the cereals of monolaurin, dowdy and profuse.

"Until this eve – well, hundreds of years ago – this belonged to Her Royal Highness Queen Elizabeth," Aero said informatively, for I was foaming at the doctor's opportunistic conduct.

"You won't want that," I said sweetly. "Given we're traitors and all."

"*Traitors?*" Mrs Stone said in a careworn voice.

"Forgive her, she's just been freed from the Tower of London," Cessie said, helping me to a high-chair.

"Oi," I quibbled.

Do you want to be acquitted or not?

"The Tower?" Mrs Stone questioned. "What — ?"

Cessie related the story and Goodwin, straw-like, made copies of our fly-on-the-wall links: Dad's library would be bettered.

"She let you have it?" Dr Goodwin said. "Who swayed her?"

"We all did," Cess said. "Specifically Ivy. Her rectitude worked where force would've failed."

"Wonderful," Professor Stone said, taking stock of me.

"The charges against us?" I said arrogantly.

"Forgotten," he said, as his partner changed colour.

199

"What about Jackson and Jones' parents?" she said, clawing her tea. "We'll be ruined."

"A pay-out should shut them up," the educator said. "As many credits as we can spare."

"The sanatorium needs our taxes," Aero said through his backteeth.

"And you need a salary, so I suggest you accept my terms," Mr Stone said.

"My p-parents, t-they'll pay," Cessie said.

"Good girl," the Stones said, fulfilled. "Ivy, Aero, are you both willing to endure the programme?"

"If our past isn't held against us," I said, "I have no quarrel with that."

"I'm in," Aero said.

"Mr Smith, you're needed in the lab to make carbon copies of the monolaurin," Professor Stone said. "It isn't an artless undertaking. Bo will back you up."

"Me?" Aero said. "I'm a trainee, I couldn't —"

"You put your neck on the line and got the antivirals, so we are most grateful," Stone said. "Go on, boy. The hospital cannot afford further deferral."

"So when it benefits them, we're the scapegoats," I said as we took the stairs. "Yet in the afterglow of our findings, we're perfect again."

"They couldn't say anything else," Cess remarked. "Not after all we did. I'm going to see my parents about the payment. See ya."

One set of parents reimbursing the other's loss — it didn't seem rational. I was down as I looked in on my father, bunched in his study; he'd have appreciated Elizabeth's books.

"Ivy?" he said. "Is that you?"

"Hey, Dad," I said.

"Do you realise I'd no clue if you were dead, alive – you could've been in a cosmic graveyard for all I knew, what in the name of robots have you been doing —"

"I had to, we were going to be trialled," I said. I swung my stumpy legs onto the beanie. "I've got lots of sixteenth century bobbins."

We perused them as he kept me up to date about Mum's happenings abroad, how the ingredient could've prevented her plane ride.

"You know, Ivy," Dad said, who was in need of a shave, "one of these days, I fear you won't come back."

"That'll never occur," I said. "I'm too careful."

"That woman nearly had your head," my parent said. "I know it's great to live the nomadic lifestyle – your mother and I used to go all over. The perks of her job." He was misty-eyed. "But not off in the galaxy, where any barbarian could kill us."

"I'll be fine," I assured him. "I've got my friends."

"You're all twenty-one," Dad said. "What do you know really?"

"You got married when you were my age," I recapped.

"And look how that ended," Dad said discouragingly.

"What are you going on about?"

"Ivy!" Cessie's cartoon shaggy 'do was here before I could go further. "Mum and Dad assented to the settlement, but they have a favour to ask."

"What?" I said suspiciously.

"Don't look like that! The Stones say that if we complete one more mission, we'll qualify as Time travellers. My folks said we could go to early twentieth century London to trace their missing ancestral line. It's really important. Without it they won't be able to annex off Dad's effects in his will. The ancestor who disappeared – she could've descendants."

"Wait," I said, "who is this AWOL person?" Lately, Cessie seemed to have a lot of secrets.

"She was a suffragist," Cessie said intently. "One day, nobody ever heard from her again. Mum and Dad want to know what happened to her and if she has any relatives alive today – if anything happens to me, their belongings will be vacuumed up by the state."

"If this is another live-or-die situation —"

"Do you want to be like the carpenter, too scared to act for a good cause?" Cessie said. "Most people aren't affluent, they'd love to get their hands on my father's cash —"

"That would be a tragedy," I said frostily.

"Wouldn't you want your belongings to go to Pearl?" my best friend said. "I'm sorry most people are poor, but my parents worked their way up and they don't want their empire to be broken up or squandered."

"I haven't got anything to bequeath to Pearl," I said. "You know that."

"But it's their *will*, Ivy, not mine," Cess said, frizzy layers bedraggled. "I'd do it for you. Besides, I mind-linked with Aero and he said the hospital needs bags of blood – different types, and people aren't contributing. Patients are on their last legs. And in the 1910s, electrics was way more common, so picture what you could do, what Stone could do with the robots."

"I want nothing to do with those machines," I snuffled.

"Well, Aero and I are going," Cessie said. "You'll be the one left behind."

My gut felt as though it'd been nipped by condors.

"I'm going to see Aero," I said, stumping out.

The laboratory was fragranced with an alcoholic, fruity tang. Aero was in a lab coat, the length too long; Bo's hair was like a gerbil-chromed starfish as the reek swaddled her.

"Did you get Cess' email?" the junior scholar said. "We're going to the 20th-century! With the right pseudonym, I'll be able to see how they doctored people then and pick up some of their gear. The blood department are disconsolate."

Bo, conscious of the thin press of my gills, said: "You don't have to go. It's just, it'll be full of women's rights protesters and the suffragist archives were burned a hundred years ago, and we still don't have equal pay —"

"Can't you go?" I wondered.

"The monolaurin will need months to ferment," she said, "and the lab has to make duplicates so we don't run out. Your mother's searched high and low for this, but there's scarcely any. Stone – Stone doesn't think I'm ready to be sent yet." Her tenor pealed like driftwood, a wireless signal on a Eurostar.

"Who goes if I don't?" I said, careful not to sound too pitying.

"Aurora," she said. "She'd be celebrated if she went back in time and recaptured what it was to be a woman back then."

"When's take-off?" I said.

She accessed her zodiacal watch. "Half an hour."

"Why so soon?"

"You know the answer to that," Marsh said. "No transfusion operations can take place, and people are terrified to come forward. In this day and age, it's a cat-eat-cat world. For every match who agrees, there's five who don't. Are you ready?"

"As I'll ever be," I said.

*

The clusters of Neptune, Saturn and Pluto illumined through the mizzle, whiskey twilight whooshing us through the gateway to the past.

"You're livid with me," Cessie said, when three-quarters of an hour had passed with no prate.

The formerly Piccadilly tube disseminated us backwards, the dial like a weighing scale, flitting between numbers before determining on June, 1913.

"Don't fake the good-girl, I'm-here-for-the-patients act," I said. "You're here for yourself, as is a nasty habit of yours. You don't care about women's rights. The cargoes of inequality are for the great unwashed, right?"

"Get lost," she said. "I've spent years wising up on the sources. I knew who they were before you ate solids."

"That's not hard," I said, snowballing. "When I couldn't afford them half the time."

"I couldn't afford them all of the time, so you both did better than me," Aero chipped in.

From nowhere, we were in stitches as if in a cable sitcom.

Clonk.

As the groundswells overran us, the dresser barnstormed into the window, and screams cheeped inside.

Pearl.

Chapter Fifteen: Accidents

Pearl backfired towards the sliding doors, formatted like retail mirrors: her density was going to sling her into interstellar. Cessie and Aero were backed into their seats by gravitas; their attempts to claw Pearl were counterproductive.

"Aaaaaaaaaaaaaaaaaahhhh!"

As the right side of my sister leant towards Saturn, I discarded the controls and transacted a tug of war to retrieve her. I won't pretend it wasn't tough, defying Newton to save someone almost the same height as you, but panic had given me super-wings, and I rugby-tackled her towards me. Exclaiming, Cessie and Aero boarded up the whishing flap.

"You're bonkers!" I said into the junior Moss' fronds of ash-brown, swept across her ovate conformation.

"*You're* here," Pearl pointed out.

"I'm on a job," I bit back. "Wholly different."

"Ah, Ivy." Cessie pried the mouldy, cupcake drapes. "We're too far off to go back."

"Aero," I said high-handedly, "do you concur?"

"Cessie's correct," he said lukewarmly. "Pearl should stay."

"*One* day," I said, wagging my square ring finger. "*One* sightsee of 1913, and that's it."

"Oh, allow her a real tour," Aero said obdurately. "She's got that Christmas-time PowerPoint to prepare for."

"Imagine Blueberry's face when she sees the pics and tapes," Pearl daydreamed. "If I ever question that you're the finest, most reasonable sis around —"

"I'll know you've recovered from your fall," I said drily.

It took a microsecond before I marvelled: "How'd you get into a tamper-proof cupboard?"

"I'm a hacker," my sister said, with a darting look at Aero and Cessie. "It was easier than the times table."

I brooded over this. "Well, you're a spacewoman now."

Pearl's wakeful eyelids guttered.

After twenty-five minutes we pussyfooted into a shopaholic's utopia: there was the plaid Hamley's triangle, a barber's, a butcher's where rabbits and chickens hung, flaked; bonbon stalls, a dentist's with medieval instruments, and a fishmongers with squalid salmon. Straight out of Mary Poppins, gaslights proliferated and shoppers hurried to part with the week's wages, flying into clop-clopping omnibuses and Fords peacocking on daytrips.

"Saturday," Cessie said, as if it were a unique day of the week.

As pollution smoked the roads, Pearl crowd-bowled into an obsolescent sweetshop, scooping wine gums, gobstoppers and jelly babies.

"I'm eating samples!" she justified.

Tetchy, I spared a few bob for a Dairy Milk (a literal extravagance in my day and age), pink 'n' mix and bubble-gum. While I tasted grapes, Aero guzzled down a Toblerone and Cessie infixed a jaw-breaking aniseed ball in her gob.

She kowtowed beside an article article in a newsagent's:

SWEET JUSTICE by FRANK BURTON

East Londoner Flora Belle and her candy-cane posse did an extraordinary act last evening — they handed Herbert Asquith a jar of sweets. Inside were thousands of rolled-up signatures for a hearing about women's right to vote. Astounded, the Liberal prime minister responded: "Well, I prefer candy to dog whips", resulting in hilarity in the stands.

Idealist spinster Belle will seek any means to justice.

"Ivy, that's her," Cessie said, reviewing the black and white, freshly published likeness of a thirty-year-old campaigner with wasp coils.

"She isn't missing yet?" I quizzed.

"No, it's this summer — 1913 – vanished without a blot on a broadsheet," Cess said.

"Where in East London?" I wondered.

"Nadia couldn't trace it – the records died with the owners."

"Any clues?"

"I don't know," she frowned. "It's outlandish, the sweets. Why not – I dunno – egg ammos?"

"You said suffrag*ist*," I cued her.

"Absolutely… but I intuit there's more to it."

"It may've been someone else's id-"

"W-o-w!" Aero moved like a bolt.

A Ford black taxicab approximating a vampire hearse drilled towards us, its cycling wheels a pebble's throw from a hit-and-run on our clump.

You say you'd get out of the meat cleaver's path in time, but actually, you're toothless, and that was us as our hobble skirts and lampshade pullovers latched onto the rudders. Our satiny buskins snagged and tucked us onto the wheels.

"We're gonna go under," Cessie panicked.

A shoeshine having a break under a gaslamp scuttled like a paraglider into our region and barbered the silks, leaving us with shorter togs.

"Your lucky day," he whistled.

"A hit-and-miss," was all Cessie was capable of expressing.

"Who ran us down?" Aero spoke his annoyance.

"That would be me."

From the overpriced cab a beaky, saucer-eyed woman in a moleskin trench fleece stood over us.

"Sophia Duleep Singh," Cessie said in a trance.

"And you might be?" the Princess said, her flexuous knot tonally like a cygnet's.

"Cessie Belle," my friend said. "She's Ivy, he's Aero and she's Pearl."

"What fanciful names!" Sophia said, blushing. "Apologies for my maniac of a driver. Fancy a hitch hike?"

She's a member of the WSPU, Cessie mentioned. *That's one more rug up the ladder. We ought to tail her.*

Somewhat gauchely, we installed ourselves in the upholstered invention.

"I knew I shouldn't've let you come," I muttered to Pearl.

"Give over; you were nearly run over as well," she tsked.

Cess threw the newspaper snipping under Sophia's muffler, however she shook her sheeny skull at the snapshot.

"Where are you going?" she said, her accessory camouflaging her mortification.

"We don't really know," I acknowledged.

"If she's your family," she challenged, "why aren't you aware of where she resides?"

"Um," Cessie said with a sloped tongue.

"Break the cab," Aero caterwauled at the driver, in his most darkly cool tone.

"Why, am I about to smash someone else?" he asked.

"No," Aero said edgily, "a kid needs first aid."

"There's always somethin'."

In a terraced patch, a boy of ten or so vomited a Niagara of lifeblood. I was no expert; nevertheless, he seemed to have seconds to live.

"What's eating him?" Cessie said worryingly.

"We're about to find out," Aero said, departing the creation.

"Hero complex again," I said, rolling an eye.

"Jeez, Ivy, he's very ill," Cessie said in astonishment.

"You said we weren't to interfere," I retold her own words.

"Hamnet living could've altered Shakespeare's legacy," she said exactingly.

A hoop and racquet were laid down with the comatose boy when Aero secretly 4Ded him. "TB," he hollered. "Where's the closest emergency room?"

"I know," Sophia said, and slid instructions to the cabman.

"I know that kid," the chauffeur admitted. "'E's a lost cause, even his ma says… father's National Insurance don't cover 'im. Very sad and all, but it's the way it goes."

"Aero can save him," Cess said wrathfully.

I shuffled to and fro on the comfy seater as Aero carpeted the child in his jacket. "Contact with him isn't safe, specifically for Pearl and Aero. I might be OK, and *you'll* be fine, but we aren't insusceptible to these diseases. Even your system might not cope with such an old illness."

"And you said I was self-serving?" Cessie said disgustedly.

"Sorry," I said, "but I've Pearl to think about —"

"That's all you think about," my best friend retorted.

A muteness plagued us like smog.

"Sorry," she said to the two of us; meanwhile, Aero batched the boy into the passenger seat.

"Can you record germs?" Pearl said with interest.

"No," I shut down her cross-questioning.

"Hold on, that's my Fred!"

A porridge-coloured woman in coveralls approached us, as tangerine-haired as her boy.

"We found him in the street in a puddle of blood," Aero said, point-blank.

"He's been a bit – under the weather," 'Ma' said in a screechy voice. "But nuttin' like this. We thought it was the whooping cough. 'E was playing out for half an hour."

"He's got tuberculosis," Aero said.

The woman peered at him. "Ooo are you to be diagnosing my son?"

"A doctor," he said, even-tempered. "From overseas. I'm his only hope."

She blacked out beside the wet patch.

"A man of medicine, you say?" the Princess queried. "I've not heard of you."

"I'm a doctor, not a celebrity," Aero said, unbuckling his briefcase to reveal his honours.

"Not to worry," Sophia said, placated. "I know a sickbay round the bend."

Fred moaned as blood frothed his back teeth.

"You'll be okay," Aero said. "We're taking you to hospital."

He gave a splutter, and there was no more response. I couldn't gaze his way.

The compressed, flat-as-a-desert, low-spirited building faced us, and Fred was taken by trolley past catalogues of the scarred, the fevered and the haunted. Pearl's green apple cheeks became anaemic.

"It's alright, they're just sick," Cessie said guiltily.

"Will he pass away?" Pearl said.

"Don't know," she said, and I glimmered at her.

"We need to crack the fever," a doctor with a handlebar tash said.

"Allow me," Aero said, but the men curtailed him.

"No guests permitted any further."

"I can help him," he argued.

"We're the wizards round here, young man," Handlebar said.

"You need to earn your stripes," said another.

"I have," he said, signalling his overseas papers.

"Your credentials aren't useable in this nation," they said.

"We don't need your hocus-pocus from abroad," a secretary added.

Aero supplied an expletive.

After some time in the waiting room, Ma commented that the docs implemented wet cloths. "I'd better tell Flora – my boarder — why I'm astray," she said, helter-skelter.

"Surname?" Cessie induced her.

"Belle," the redhead said. "Why, what do that mean to the likes of you?"

"*The likes of?*" Cessie reiterated, unused to being spoken to that way.

I stubbed her showgirl footwear.

"You ain't a grass, are ya?" Ma said snottily.

"What're you drivelling about?" the history enthusiast said.

"Your mates aren't coppers, are they?"

"Why do you ask?"

The woman made strides as though on a catwalk, lowering her voice: "Miss Belle's always 'ad airs and graces above her post. Fell afoul of the law." She jerked her thumb. "*Women's lib*, of all things. When communities are starvin' in the streets."

Our faces grew quizzical.

"She's not militant," she said. "Nuttin' like that. She's a *suffragist*." A proud note slunk into her tenor. "She's from the Women's Tax watsit League. Got 'erself slung in 'Olloway for tax evasion. Gotta love British lawmakers – one 'alf of the population vote-less, and money's all they're uptight about."

Cessie was floored.

We must go to the house, she urged me.

Have you got a screw loose? She won't trust us if we just turn up.

209

We'll make out we're there because of the boy. We'll offer to tell her.

I don't like this. We've to get to know her. You heard what Goodwin said about figures of the past.

This isn't "A Christmas Carol."

We can infiltrate group meetings.

I cleared my oesophagus: "When was she freed?"

"Not long ago," 'Ma' said, low-key. "Back when Emily Davison was killed by Anmer, cops got worried. Prisoners, they go on 'unger strike, get so weak they 'ave to be released. It's a cat and mouse. She'll be arrested when she's well."

See, I wrote to Cessie, *we could be dodgy for all she knows.*

"She got a trade?" I said dialectally.

"Why you nosing if you ain't a snitch? You gonna get paid for ratting Flora out?"

"No!"

I disclosed a purse chock-full of farthings.

"We – just – it sounded so exciting," Cessie salvaged me.

"We're thinking of signing up to the NUWSS," I said, stabbing in the dark.

We are?

Keep quiet.

"She's a posh sort, but you wouldn't know," the woman said. "Works for that sweet company – watsit? In Bermondsey – Peek Freans."

"The biscuit factory," Cessie said dreamily, and across her neural complexes: *Got her.*

"It's a hospice, really," Aero said while Pearl checked out the privy. "He won't come out. It's caveman therapies – they think air's a tonic for TB." He sifted Ma as she finished our toffies.

"Wonder if Freud's said anything about emotional eating," Cess disdained.

"You two wouldn't know, but Mum was like that when I was little. Paranoid about me dying. I didn't undergo gene-editing. I'm defective. Mum's worst fear was that if I got ill, antibiotics wouldn't work. There were no state-of-the-art cures then. I'd have died if Mum hadn't been so watchful."

"I thought she was being mean when you weren't allowed to play in my garden," my candyfloss-haired friend said. "My folks of all people were the cleanest of the clean; they wondered what your mother was suggesting."

I abstained from rolling my marbles.

"Interpose with antibiotics," Cessie said overpoweringly. "You'll need to be licensed by the Stones – and to check with Goodwin if the boy has any historical significance."

"He doesn't," Aero said. "It's like Ivy says – he's one of the unwashed. His own mother wrote him off."

"Do you blame her?" I said. "It was the cancer of its day."

"They still had cancer, on top of that," Aero said brainily. "We've hundreds of unusable capsules – Cess is right. I must go back."

"Bring Pearl with you," Cessie said, to alleviate her conscience.

"Is she not back yet?" I said.

"She ain't in the privy," Ma said. "I've just relieved myself."

My breast rose like a puffin's.

I quested every bed, discounting the risk, calling for my sibling. Cessie might've been tracing an ancestor, but I'd a living relative to sustain. Pearl was nowhere.

"Sorry, Ivy," Aero said. "I'm going without her. Fred will die otherwise."

"Mum and Dad will rue the day I was born," I said.

"She must've heard us," Cess said. "She'll have gone off somewhere." I gawked at her. "We can't let a tween run around in a misogynistic past century." In the time machine, I telegrammed Nadia about Pearl's emergence and disappearance.

"Ms Moss, how could you lose sight of her? Did you not perform the appropriate checks before departing?"

"It was hectic," I said, quailing from the communicator. "How did she get in a locked wardrobe anyway?"

"How did monkeys write Shakespeare?" Nadia said. "Do you expect me to have the answer to everything? You should thank Uranus that you still have a career, young lady."

"I know… is this the last straw?"

"Second chances soon become third, so no," my mentor carolled. "But do better next time."

"What'll I do about Pearl?"

"That's your issue."

The line hung up.

"WHO STOLE MY RALEIGH?"

I hot-footed outdoors with Cessie as a man uttered swear words.

"BLOOMIN' KIDS!" He looked at us blazingly. "WAS IT YOU?"

"Pearl," we said.

"Who's that? Your accomplice?"

"My sister," I said.

"You owe me hundreds."

"We'll regain it," Cessie pledged; I pot-shot a filthy look.

We started a goose chase, asking shopkeepers if they'd seen anyone 'about this high, with Minnie Mouse buns.' A coiffeur claimed she'd permed Pearl afore.

"She paid?" I said amazedly.

"Coins are missing," Cessie said inconsolably.

"She can't be far," I said.

"*She's got a bike.*"

"Oh yeah," I said.

"You're getting old," Cessie said musingly. "If you were a pre-teen let loose in the twentieth century, where would you go?"

My boot clipped a flier of *Mr Spoon's Amusement Carnival*, coloured with raffish clowns, jugglers, freaks and water rides.

"The fair," Cessie said.

Vanity would've been a polite term for the fire-breathers, three-foot men, surreal-faced triplets, merry-go-rounds and Haunted Houses that met our faculties.

"I want to go on one of these," the historian said, and went aboard a show pony.

I found deformed glasses and Ferris wheels – no Pearl.

Giddy, I squinted through the English summer to see the fugitive on a tilting roller coaster, a grin plastered on. She detected me and shielded her eyelashes. I connected with the following line and dumped myself beside her. It was like being on the London eye, or a skateboard ramp; as long as you didn't glance down.

"One more time," she said. "Please."

My spleen squeezed, until I remembered being trademarked as a killjoy in year nine. "Once."

The belts were ineffectual and commodious; nonetheless, I endeavoured to savour the bird's-eye view, convincing myself it was one of those European railway tours. Hadn't I sworn to give Pearl a day she wouldn't forget?

We went around the swirly framework before flashing forwards to the parking spot; the spectacle tipped towards the tracks.

"Is it safe?" I respired.

"Safer than a schoolroom."

"Is it an additional feature?" I said when the wobbles started.

Cessie was a speck below on a carousel.

"The design's faulty," I said, orientating myself higher.

"Loosen up: it's FUN!"

The coaster issued a croak and began to tumble. Cessie was shouting something.

"We won't make it out alive," I said.

Pearl's floss leaked to the clown show below – where we were headed. Commuters began to drib popcorn on Pearl and I's napes. Crows circumnavigated us as though awaiting supper.

"You're an engineer," Pearl said screamingly.

The speed was dizzying.

I half-scrambled onto the choppy morphology, feeling as if pleasure-seekers were tracking my every twitch.

"What's the girl doing?"

"Madness; she should leave it to the professionals."

"For pity's sake, George, we haven't got time!"

The rail tracks were aslant, and there were *snaps* as I stripped the framework. I was re-setting each track, holding onto my horses as the hastening decelerated my headway.

"That's men's work," George said to my spine bone. "She'll never succeed."

"At least she's trying," his wife snarled.

"Ivy, that's enough, get back in," Pearl chided me as I triple-checked I'd set them just so.

I was going to collide with a cyclopean commercial sign and plunge into the mountainous pleasure park.

"GET BACK IN!" Cessie and Pearl said, blue in the face.

My left knee stole inside before I was bowdlerised to smidgeons.

"We still don't know if this'll work," George carped.

"She did her bloody best!" Pearl said, scarlet-faced and ashy.

The roller coaster cannoned forwards. We stood still before interchanging course, slewing to the ride's launch.

It terminated.

"Phew," said Pearl.

We jigged off, infighting like Cinderella's stepsisters.

"They're so thankless," Cessie said as George stalked past. "If it weren't for your intervention —"

"Let's not go there," I said, wincing.

"It isn't all rosy," Pearl said, sticking out her funny bone, which hung at a zig-zag curve. "Got wedged in the mayhem."

"To 23?" Cessie said.

"It'll be too much," I said, sickness fluttering in my gastric tract. How could I have gone along with it to please a schoolkid? "She'll have to go to theatre."

"It happens," Cessie said.

"Only 'cause we let it," I said remorsefully.

Handlebar settled on revamping the breakage with metal plates. With no Aero, there was no astral hardware to whizz her back anyway. I napped in the dowdy waiting room during the surgery.

"Missus?" a sharp voice said.

"Cessie informed me about your misfortune," Sophia said respectfully. "I might be able to help you out re: the Belle woman."

I snapped out of my lassitude that instant.

"Firstly, I want to know why you're looking for her," she said evasively.

"We'd – we'd quite like to join the suffragist union," I said.

"For what it's worth, I may know her well enough to put a word in and get you a job at the factory," she said, fluffing her hairdo. "I've graced many society parties with the owners."

"Flora," I said graspingly, "what's she like as a person?"

"Neurotic," Singh said. "Though I abhor casting her as a hysterical woman. The most effective way to merit her trust is piece by piece, not intrusively. If I were in your – charming – shoes, I'd fake a casual curiosity at work."

"Is it hard work?" I said.

"Well, do you know how to package creolas?"

"I do now," I said.

Sophia loaned a meccano toy to Fred and Pearl to pass their recovery stage. Pearl glared at the gendered marketing as she serviced a screwdriver. As the gramophone's "It's a Long Way to Tipperary" went round on a loop, the children accumulated a bloodshot, nickel-plated locomotive. Screws and bolts were freely disarranged.

"Are you any good at ping-pong?" Fred said.

"I'm ace," she swanked.

The curtain was tweaked; Aero had come with a white pill bottle, doing a double-take when he spied my sister.

"Don't gawp, get started," Pearl said, contorting herself into an upward position. She began yelling her lungs out, complaining that the instalments were faulty.

"Are you okay?" Aero said.

"It's a distraction, you dipstick," Cessie said. "If you don't give Fred the tablets now, that's it for him."

Aero released them as if they were lanterns into an elastic ampule of H20, and Cessie taught Ma how the antibiotics were to be taken over the next couple of weeks. It was just as well...

"What foreign treatments have you injected Fred with?" Handlebar demanded, while the rest of the Medicine Men made a boxing ring round Aero.

"He'd have died without this," Aero said as the sweat-beaded, weary child was brought back from the brim.

"If he has an allergic response to that *thing*, we're accountable," a crony said.

215

"It's all about your status, isn't it?" Aero said wilfully.

"Step aside," McTash said, and he shovelled an opium-laced syrup down the kid's tonsils before Cessie could push him aside.

Fred's fire-shaded hairs fell over his burning bones and he timed out. Prudently, Pearl fit the remainder of the poser silvers, and the docs forsook the sickroom.

"There's one other point of contention," Aero said, out of breath. "And you won't like it."

Behind the hangings, Magnus hypostatised, an Eiffel of beams scored into his phiz.

"Not you," I grumbled.

"'Fraid so," my oldest arch-rival said.

"Are you on crack?" I conflated at Aero.

"Smith had no choice in the matter," an apathetic Magnus said. "After your – ah – *blunder*, Nadia believed help was in order."

"Why you?" I growled. "Mars and Bo are worth fifty of you."

"We're old chums," he said agreeably. "Old hands."

Leaving me seething, he went on: "Pearl, what's with the sling?"

"*Don't pretend to care.*"

"Fractured it riding Mr Spoon's roller coaster," she said, shrew-eyed; the last time they'd interacted she'd pelleted him with a macadamia profiterole.

Aero seemed shifty, though I couldn't put my finger on why.

"Are we signing up with the suffragists?" Magnus ticketed me.

"*You* aren't," I said cold-bloodedly, with a scowl that outshone antifreeze.

Aero's collarbones decreased. "He'll have to. If he doesn't pass muster, our covers are blown."

"There's another get out of jail card," I said. "He can be sent to 23."

"Our boss referred him; he has to be our lackey," the researcher said.

"Grand, suffragist land!" My challenger prevailed.

"You wouldn't know an activist if they snowed you in," I said.

"Is that what they're doing?" he said without a falter. "Blimey, in the middle of July?"

After this patronising, vomit-inducing discourse, I snubbed him with professional diligence.

"I'm sure we can do with an extra pair of gloves," Cess said more understandingly, matchstick legs looping over the buffet.

Pearl watched enviously as Magnus bit into the ultimate liquorice. "How's your cat?" she said out of the blue.

The sweet became jammed in his Adam's apple. A Man of Medicine bashed him to his senses the way I'd craved to for a long, long spell.

Quieten down, I belled to Pearl. *I doubt he knows the pet's still alive.*

"Tabitha died years ago," he said rivetedly. "You were barely born when —"

"What is it Nadia sent you to do?" I broke in.

"Dad's upgrading the robots," he said, with a sidelong peek over his shoulder. "Professor Ludwig thought we could target the overhead cables and factories for materials. You in?"

"Just you and me?" I said.

"We are the engineers round here."

Cessie sized me up expectantly.

"I'll do it," I said heavily.

"It'll take a while for Sophia to reach Flora, so do it now," Cessie said. "Aero and I'll smuggle blood out."

"We will?" Aero said.

Cessie zapped him with a corrupt web-link.

"Blood trafficking?" Pearl said. "Need me to cause a disturbance?"

"You're out of action for now," I said stiffly. "Keep piecing the meccano."

"As a matter of fact, you are needed for something," Cessie said introspectively.

Pearl essayed her 'symptoms' to the captive consultants while Cessie and Aero did a raiders-of-the-lost-ark on the stocks.

"Blood, blood and more blood!" Aero said as they canted it into our spacecraft.

Magnus and I cantered down the tiered backstreets, Ford 'T' models zipping.

"No one else's coming through?" I said.

"Aurora and I flipped a sovereign," the mechanic said.

"Were you head or tails?"

"Tails."

"You certainly came with that between your legs."

"Tell me… are we pouncing on any rundown workhouse we see?"

"It depends," I said, overstressing the syllables. "Did Nadia hand you any tools?"

"Elephantine gardener's shearers," he said. "They're in the interplanetary thingy."

"Well? Get them."

He really made me wait for it before coming into focus with biodegradable bags. "If anybody asks, we'll say we were at the meat-house."

"Cess and I are suffragist sympathisers seeking shifts at a Bourbon sweatshop," I said. "Who're you?"

"Given I just got here, I haven't the foggiest idea," he said. After a lull: "A male ally?"

"Not bad."

"You're warming to me."

"As one warms to scarlet fever."

"I've an excellent notion," my enemy bleeped when we'd street-walked for the best part of thirty minutes.

"What?"

"Not exactly heartening, are you?"

"What's the plan?"

"There're creaky railways running throughout London," he said. "Guess what we find there?"

"Live-wire cables," I said criminally.

As we skimmed the motorways, he said: "Tell me… Pearl, did your parents do that intentionally?"

"Do what?"

"Have another child, knowing the rules?"

"She was an accident."

"Why weren't they jailed?"

"Mum globe-trotted and Dad became an archivist."

"I'd have loved another sibling."

But he didn't, not verily. It was somebody else to lose.

Chapter Sixteen: Predator and Prey

It wasn't faultlessly what Thomas the Tank Engine had glamorised when we barged into the vagabond terminal, Carillion-type leaves dangly on the fences.

Magnus focussed his shears on one. "I could cull you a floret?"

"No! It's nightshade."

He lowered it as if it were a hand grenade.

"How did you know that?" he said groggily. "T-there aren't many plants left in the UK. Hemlock, mainly."

"Mum," I said. "She's globe trotted looking for aromatics."

"Do you – er – ever miss her?"

"What's it to you?" I strapped my get-up tighter. "Let's get stuck in."

"Go on, then."

"How do we get at that?"

"It's the theme of your twenty-one years, reaching things – you should know."

"We weren't all born as a giraffe."

"Ivy, manners," he said, striking the palisade until it came undone. The fence sprung on the plasticine greensward. "Escalade."

"I'll be electrocuted," I stated.

"That would be a real waste," Magnus commiserated.

He marched on top of the banister, I on his shoulder blades, bonier than I'd assumed. The shearers cast me as a demented murderer. I said a ritual in my head and edged towards the lead. It crackled and broke in my fingernails, but no shock lurched through me. I truncated them with strains, teetering on my leg-up.

"More," he ordered.

Stretching farther, I inverted and dug my nails into his grimalkin mane. I well-nigh strangled Magnus as I made snipping motions towards the final power lines. Not a single electric jolt... it was infeasible.

219

Magnus leapfrogged off the fence and I toad-hopped down.

"It's insulated against cablings," I said, throwing the shearers back at him.

"It slipped my mind," he said impertinently.

"These'll slip in a minute…"

"Can we stop arguing for ten seconds?"

1… 3… 10.

"Can we bicker again?"

The warehouse we located was straight out of Roald Dahl, a yellow-washed, impenetrable skyscraper. The trillions of windows made me think a surfeit of little persons lived inside, like a lace-trailing wellington.

"Yes," Magnus said without a tremble. "We'll have to get in through the bracket."

"I did the last one," I said.

Remarkably for him, his smugness grew enfeebled. Nonetheless, with support onto the brick, he put his feet onto the ledge, whitening.

I splintered panels and donated them to him; he sited them on the thin bridge and inoculated a breath. He was halfway through, lizard pupil shut, when he peeked at the expanse. A stray panel almost took my toes off.

"I can't," he stage-whispered.

"You've got to," I said.

Another sock went forward. An additional panel clear-fell: I swooped to elude a pommelling.

Magnus dillydallied.

"A little further," I prepped.

He scooted onto the latter part of the bracket and fell stomach-wards, a turtle without its shell.

"It's OK," I said, "you won't fall."

It was me who'd get my eye taken out!

He marshalled himself and razed a window, resting fleetingly. Shards dropped onto my centre parting like snowflakes.

He stabilised himself into the manhole, drainpipes riddled with rips.

I heard frissons being made in the nailed-in deadbolt so I could ghost in.

"Now you know how Cessie felt," I said, hard-nosed.

"That was an accident," he snapped.

"So you say," I said, sloping at the retro automobiles. "What kind of upgrade is it?"

"Mind your own business," he said, snapping Polaroids of the goods.

I'd a niggling sense he knew I wouldn't obey orders if I found out.

We shoplifted rusty odometers, waist-high tyres, bone-hard titanium (I presumed it was to make the newbies hard-wearing) and stainless steel. They'd be unassailable. A prick of chilliness went through me.

"To the spa?" I surmised.

"No," he said, "to my father."

The bootie was pulverising our backs when Magnus drew me back.

"What're you doing?"

"Use your wits."

A star-badged policeman, complete with a bowler hat and truncheon, was fluting a few yards away.

"Under here."

Magnus and I sated the grazing with our loot while he scolded two wayward dog walkers before frogmarching across the patio.

"You're breakin' and enterin'," he reckoned.

I eyeballed him powerlessly, rattling my cells for an exegesis.

"I'll take your statements at the cop shop," he said, since we'd been too slow to conceive an explanation.

"Hold on," Magnus said, "I'll apprise you."

"Don't want to hear it," the cop said babyishly. "You 'ad your sticky paws on those Wolseley Motors, didn't ya?"

"I – I –"

"We were kissing," Magnus invented, as gravitational as relativity.

I contained myself so I didn't seem too horrified.

"A summer romance," the policeman chewed this over. "And there was no better date than a car warehouse?"

"The danger's what made it romantic," Magnus lied.

"A moment of madness," I said. "You see, we're married to other people. If the neighbours saw —"

"An illicit affair." He played with his bowler.

"It was our send-off meeting," Magnus dreamt up. "If you take us to the station, it'll leak out."

"We won't do it again," I crossed my heart.

He adjudicated.

"Just this once. If it happens again —"

"No, sir," Magnus said, at the same time as I said: "It won't, sir."

"Run along, lovebirds," the policeman said sunnily. "I've got my glass eye on ya."

When he'd gone to bombast teenagers about litter, we recaptured the bootee.

"Bloody hell – it's hefty," I said.

We quit the territory from the backway.

"This is a raid, not wedlock."

"Ha-ha."

Come quick, Cessie wrote to me. *We've got the blood – A, O and whatnot – that the hospital are missing.*

"Taxi," Magnus said, dashing into rush-hour traffic and hailing one.

I was later told my death glare was so intimidating geese migrated back to Canada.

*

"I propose that Ivy, Aero and I have a little homecoming," Magnus said, who appeared to be channelling Mr Burns.

"Why you two?" Aero said. "One man can bring the blood."

"Ivy and I will be reconstituting robots with my dad," Magnus said.

"And how does Ivy feel about this?" Aero said earsplittingly.

I was having second, third, four-hundredth thoughts. Pearl's instincts appeared to be along similar lines, for she looked scandalised.

I have to, I typed to my sibling, *or I won't be licenced.*

"I'll make sure Pearl's alright," Cessie said. "By then, Sophia might have news from Flora."

"That's settled, then," Aero said repentantly.

In a bumbling threesome, we revved up the contrivance and winged away.

"It's like old times, isn't it?" Magnus said as Aero did a 6D on the waterless, intemperate Venus, the harbour of volcanoes.

"There were no old times," Aero spat, "unless you count when you used to butt my head into puddles."

"It's a peerless planet, Venus," Magnus said, deaf to his reproach. "What I wouldn't give to live there…"

"Go on, I dare you," Aero said. "You'll bake before your girlfriend can move in."

"She's not my girlfriend."

Aero shot me a nonplussed look and I didn't twig it, either. Were they still denying it like they were thirteen?

Bo spurred a keyed-up Aero into a transfusion operation – his first.

"If I fuck this up, lives could be terminated," he said.

"That won't happen," Bo said. "You're too good."

"Good people slip up," he said.

Forsaking my stricken buddy, Magnus and I trod to the mechanics precinct. Dr Stone was handling a microscope, yet looked up at our tracks.

"Hello," he said forbiddingly. "The way you reset that roller-coaster was quite something."

I was aphasic.

"Where should we start?" Magnus said.

"*You* brought the supplies; you know what to do."

"'K."

There were cardboard, end-of-school-style boxes marked "Transmitters", "Detectors", "Ammunition" and "Interaction."

"Ammunition?" I said hauntingly.

"With the power of a machine gun, no realm will dare spark World War Five," Dr Stone said. "No more will we have to divorce ourselves and respectfully tread boundaries. We shall go where we like, take what we like. No other nation has access to AI like it. We destroyed ourselves in the forgoing battles."

Biliousness pecked my ribcage. "No. Not weapons of war."

"Self-defence isn't viciousness, young friend," the science professor said. "There are people who fought in wars before your father was born."

223

"We'll barely use them," Magnus guaranteed. "Just when endangered or on a high-risk prisoner."

"What!" I said.

"Say they had a bomb-belt and they were going to unleash it on your sister's school?" he said. "Would you chicken out then?"

"It's reserved for emergencies," Stone said compellingly. "We don't want to spill guts, believe me. When you've as many grey hairs as me, your naïveté will die."

"That Dutchman died because of extreme force," I said.

"He acted first," Senior Stone said with a gleam. "If you want to work in this organisation, you'll do it. And if your parents want to hang onto their careers, you won't have a problem."

My neck veins were rowing throbs.

"You're seeing shades," Magnus said. "If you're not a loon, lawbreaker or pyromaniac, you'll be fine."

"O...K," I said.

The sensors felt like icicles, enthralling circles sprucing it up: when I touched its slimy middle vocals sounded.

"W-what's that?" I asked.

"A gimmick," Senior Stone said. "We all relish a humanising touch."

I plugged it into Magnus' ginormous AI until there was a colony's worth. "How many are we fashioning?"

"These are high class," Young Stone said. "The price tag alone will sell on eBay."

"What if you could buy your best friend?" Stone said heartily. "It's psychology, it's exceptional. We'll prescribe robots that heal depression."

And so the dialogue went in, too.

"Who made the sounds?" I said inquisitively.

"You ask a shopping list of questions, Ms Moss," Middle-aged Stone said. "It's not worth asking about."

He sent for a wrought-up Mars to aid the recreation of the robots.

"Why're you getting him interlaced in this?" I said in a hiss.

"*I'm* not," Magnus said. "Dad said we need adept designers if these androids are to sell."

In a multi-fabric toga, Mars heralded us with: "What do you want me to do?"

"A paint job on these," Dr Stone said. "Start with the one Ms Moss is operating on."

Mars intermixed with me for the paintwork after I'd fructified the speedometers, and we were left with a slick, celadon, steel-blue artwork.

"Brand new," Professor Stone breathed as Mars fitted patches from another aeon, impressive to descry.

The doctor skewered in the "Machine Gun" option (I was too squeamish), meaning that one light-fingered mistake could eject it like a grenade. I inserted a "Deadlock" resistor.

"Stand clear," the older Stone said, Mad Professor coat fretting. "Permit me to place the concluding touches."

From a minty icebox he produced whoopee-cushion style hearts – concrete, live muscles.

"We can't," I remonstrated.

"Why not insert a conscience," Stone said without a flicker, "between the ticks of its odometer. What the human race has craved – a robot whose muscle sculls."

"Humanoids," Magnus said.

"Where did you find them?" I demanded.

"From unfortunates with incurable illnesses, of the highest moral character," the head scientist said. "Now they'll be honoured forever."

"Was there a consent form?" Magnus wanted to know.

"Why, my boy," said his father, "it was their dearest ambition."

After beading the Limited Edition Bots as though they were argil, we chanced upon a pasty Aero.

"One of the retirees had an allergic reaction to the transfusion," he said.

"Oh no!" I voiced.

"What's the matter, did you make a blunder?" Magnus said, grizzly crests wrinkly.

"It's common," the practitioner said uninhibitedly, "so shut it."

"Sorry," he said, and we made our way to *The Mary Anning*.

"Just so you're aware, what we made is strictly confidential," Magnus said as Aero disinfected himself.

"Deep down, you know how sick it is," I said. "That's why it has to be shrouded in secrets and lies."

"People will know," he said, "when they're ready."

"You and your father are the most patronising people on Earth, were you *aware* of that?"

A cleaner Aero sat by the sill.

"Did he die?" I said, skittish.

"Bo resuscitated him," Aero said. "I couldn't do it, after last time."

Magnus' brows wormed mysteriously at this.

"Funny she hasn't been authorised," I reflected once more.

"If we cause too many waves in the Old World, that'll alter the century," Aero said.

"I got Cessie's pigeon," Magnus slipped in. "Singh's got us jobs at Peek Freans."

"Why'd she contact *you*?" I said.

"Wanted to ensure we stuck together," he said.

"Aero too?"

"No," he said, "the hospice want more of his magic hands."

"I'm not supplying more drugs," Aero said.

"Oh, you won't be drugging them," Magnus informed him. "You'll be operating."

Aero turned another offbeat colour. "I won't do it."

"You will, Smith," he said gruffly. "If my father falls, the two of you go down like Coca-Cola cans."

"Whose side are you on?" I quizzed.

"That's obvious. My own."

We submitted to meeting Cess at Ma's house to integrate with her forerunner on *Gingerbread Street*. We weren't exactly a dream-some troika, me in particular feeling nauseous. Aero ditched us to see how Fred was getting on and tinker with old people's lungs.

The red-brick had shutter lancets, triple-glazed, and an American porch with fury-budded dahlias and pre-war poppies. This is not what hypnotised me: it was the eyeful of the resident wailing, soft-bodied in a muslin slip, filigree necklace reflecting the suede pumps, Poodle rollers in the curls.

226

"What's going on?" I said to Cessie, who was overcome on the lawn.

"Creditors are stealing Flora's chattel," my friend said.

A tulle armchair with lotuses stuck into the punctures was hoven out, together with a marital photo frame and sequinned heels captioned: *Anno 1890.*

"If I'm ineligible to vote, I'm exempt from taxes and all," Cessie's forebear stipulated.

"You might think so, sweetheart, but the law says different," a heavy said, passing her articles to his Chuckle Brother, who thrust it into his van.

"We've got to do something," Cessie said, floating onto the doorstep.

She tussled with a heavy for an unfashionable twinset of curtains and a silver-lined journal, and Flora locked the keyhole behind her.

"Ah, well," the debtors said, "we'll be back in August."

There was a *repine* on the macadam as the White Van men took off.

"Who the bloody hell are you lot?" Flora Belle said.

"Sophia mentioned us to you," I said agilely, for Cessie was rigid.

"About the trade?" the resistance pugilist said, in the mode a Siamese cat assumes with guests. Her latchkey performed a *jiggle.* "You'd better follow me."

At the greyish Peek Freans, a raven perched on a smokestack; indoors a square of windows overlooked an assembly line.

"He's a very considerate man," Flora said as we crossed the threshold. "Has the highest employee welfare and wages in the county."

The boss had scalped-back bald spots and puffy cheeks, and he stalked around in a pinstripe ensemble. It truly was an interview with a vampire.

"We 'ave very 'igh standards at this company," he said autocratically. "If you don't cut the mustard..."

"You'll cream us," Magnus punned.

"If you want the job, you'll 'ave to fold the biscuits perfectly in record time."

He set his stopwatch.

There was a frantic disco of shuffles as we parcelled custard creams and cocoa-filled sweeties, doubling the seal to render them watertight. Custards went floppy in my hands and ended up on the factory floor, Cessie kept licking the cream and Magnus did a dozen in a minute.

"You, boy," the boss said to the doctor's son. "Come with me to be a taste tester."

As if he'd ever felt the pinch, anyway! The rest of our crew fulfilled enough of the boss' criteria to be sweatshop ladies.

"This is such an honour," Cessie said, live-videoing me ramming on the fish-like hairnet.

I used unnecessary vehemence to force hers onto her twines.

"I've never been so... unsightly," the amateur historian said.

"It's employment, not a beauty contest," Flora faulted her. "We ought to be grateful, since higher paid careers are denied to even the wealthiest of us."

"Oh, quit gobbing on," a member of the workforce said. "You're lucky you still 'ave a job after your Commons stunt."

"My personal life doesn't concern you, June," Flora said caustically.

"It does when you're sending round bloomin' women's rights flyers," June said stealthily.

"You do?" Cessie said with flowering hazel eyes.

"Every week; the membership's 100,000 currently."

"We 'ave it good enough," June objected. "Why upset the scales further?"

Flora groped the garibaldi package but didn't counter her demurral. Cessie made chewing motions into its fig-like midpoint.

"Oi, stop snaffling the stock," her great x a scary amount Aunt said.

"I don't realise I'm doing it," Cessie claimed, not too convincingly.

"Don't they feed you at home?" Flora said, delicate as sugar.

"Why, do I look corpulent?" She did a hopscotch in her "Peek Freans" body armour.

Magnus revisited with a heaving plate of cocoa dainties. "Hungry?"

I didn't ingest a crumb, my intestines in parcels over what we'd done beforehand.

"I hear you're considering networking with the NUWSS... even you," Flora Belle said as Magnus categorised the luxuries.

"Hard though it is to believe, he's very active about women's rights," Cessie said.

"If you're certain," Flora said, as if she didn't think this very credible, "the NUWSS meets later."

Flora ushered us towards Millicent Garrett Fawcett's out-of-the-way city garret, where the letters: **National Union of Women's Suffrage Societies: Nonviolent and Reformist** were corroded.

"After they threw out the amendment bill and Emily was killed by Anmer, things got impassioned on both flanks," she said cautiously.

"Are you sure I'm welcome at suffragist HQ?" Magnus said as we made our ascent to an upper storey.

"We aren't exclusive-minded like the suffragettes," Flora said, a tad too smug. "I may be able to spare you a place, but it's crammed with activists."

Millicent, an academic in her sixties with a beehive, was sitting upright, her Fairy Godmother features matching her monotint pinafore. Amongst the nation of crowns was Sophia Duleep Singh with her haughty minks and sideward smirk.

"I don't think I've seen this band before," Millicent said, tugging up her stockings.

"They're endorsing the suffragist revolution," Singh said with conviction. "Flora thought the factory employees would be impeccable at attracting an alternative echelon into the programme."

"Is that so?" the sixty-something said, peering at us forebodingly. "Well, factory worker or friend, princess or pauper, all are welcome here."

The European-style support she braced brought to mind a bichon frise on an April day. "We espouse an ethos of pacifism, nobility and politics," she said, sonority rising.

The orchestra delivered an oratorio of claps.

"Do you acquiesce to our terms of non-violence?" Flora Belle said to us.

"We do," Cessie, Magnus and I spoke, as if we'd banded with a cult and were undertaking initiation.

"When do we clasp hands in a circle?" Magnus maffled.

"Splendid; we require you three to amass funds and propagandise the imminent rally," Millicent went on dryly.

This seemed to clack in Cessie's observance: "Hyde Park?"

"Fifty-thousand converge within days," Fawcett said thunderously. "Will you consort with us?"

"It would be our pleasure," I simpered.

"Ouch!" Cessie said, as the hinge twanged across her vertebrae.

Discontinuing our rendezvous, policemen – comprising the one with the baton who'd intercepted Magnus and I earlier – were hovering on the landing.

Twentieth century Belle's tresses were up-in-the-air as her spiritual sisters trussed her into a laundry crate, twice-used socks and heart-dotted panties leaking out. Cessie's exclaim had given us seconds to buffer her.

"This a women's thingamabob conference?" the gormless PC said.

Obediently, his brothers-in-arms straitened their triceps.

"A session's permissible under law," Fawcett said, steely-voiced, although her thumb made scrunches on her knitting ball.

"This ain't a meeting – it's an 'arbour for criminals," he said, introducing himself as PC Foster.

"There are only good folk present," Millicent said, and though she spoke meekly her intensity made the PC misstep.

"Where's Flora Belle?" he said contemptibly.

"We don't have a fig —"

"She's on your books," Foster said. "Give 'er up, or you'll be slung inside yourselves."

"We're new here," Cessie said with a pleading quality, "and we didn't see a Flora. We're housing a Maud, a Jane —"

The cop perceived Magnus and I at last.

"Romeo and Juliet?" he said, bumbling forwards. "Thought that was your parting reunion?"

"W-what?" Cess said, eyeing us.

"It was," Magnus said, without a teaspoon of jitteriness. "It was a concurrence – you see, um – we were fascinated by this suffragist stuff."

"Had a psychic moment, did ya?" PC Foster said lamely.

"He doesn't need to speak for me to hear him," I said as Cessie half-stifled titters.

"And you didn't stumble on Lady Belle?" he queried.

The pannier crepitated.

"What was that?" he said alertly.

He debossed his feet within distance of the laundry hideout. I sensed Flora's intake. The PC swished the bedding, below it, the sideboards; he untightened the runner and raked the hole-in-the-wall.

Nobody regarded the spot, and bulks eclipsed the basket.

"She must've made a run for it," Foster resolved. He brandished a card. "If any one o' you catch a glimpse of 'er, telephone these numerals."

"We shall," the protesters said.

The PC had a caesura by Magnus and I. "Be thankful adultery ain't a crime. If I was the lawmaker, I'd string you both up."

He made a *belabour* on the tiles as he and his men saw themselves out.

"I had no idea the modern-day star-crossed lovers were with me," Cessie said in a splutter, as her descendant did a 180° out of the laundry.

"Yuck," Flora said, unscrambling underwear from her knobbly elbow.

"It was Ivy's suggestion," Magnus said, not missing a beat. "Who wouldn't play act being my mistress?"

"Firstly, Prince Frog made up that fairy tale," I said. "Secondly, Foster clocked us beside the warehouse, so we had to wriggle out of it."

"Did you go to the lengths of kiss —" Cessie said in a murmur.

"No!" I said.

"Though she'd have liked to," Magnus subsidised.

"I must have tinnitus," my best friend said, funnelling Flora to a dignified position.

"It was self-preservation," I said, threatening her with the bolster. "Tell no one."

"I'll forever hold my peace," Cessie chortled.

"I thought you'd been released," I said, doing a U-turn on the conversation. "How come they're chasing you?"

"They're rats – ever-present," Lady Belle said.

"It's the Cat and Mouse statute," Cessie said, patently unable to contain herself. "You go on hunger strike 'til you're so weak you need treatment; then they re-arrest you."

My jawbone unhinged.

"Is that what you did?" I said to the striker.

I inspected her more thoroughly; she was peaky, and beneath her defining braids was a thinning clomp. But, then, Cessie was slight: I hadn't realised there was a reason.

"The most genius tactic yet," she said gleefully; you'd think she'd come from a Mad Hatter's tea party. "It isn't only suffrag*ettes* who can notch headlines. The women in Holloway dissuaded me, but I considered it to be nonaggressive. I'm only hurting myself, after all. *The Telegraph* dubbed me the Famine Lady. I know, as the librarian showed me. Gave me a strawberries-and-cream slice and all." She vibrated wistfulness.

"When did you become a factory worker?" Cessie was ducking what we all imagined; had she been force-fed?

"When I figured that if we were to get the vote, *all* women should have a hand in it."

"Is all going swimmingly?" Cess said; I knew she was dying to lay bare when their objective would flourish.

"Well, you've seen June," thirty-year-old Belle said. "Some listen, some don't. It's a game of patience."

"A cat and mouse," I summarised.

"I'm commissioning my sisters to handcraft a quilt banner for the cause," Garrett Fawcett said. "Who'll do it?"

"We will," most said.

"And you three?" Millicent lobbied.

"We'll be happy to," I succumbed.

Don't freak out; I'm emailing Mars about needlework techniques, though I know a fair bit myself, Cessie keyboarded.

Suffragist artilleries were rotary cutters, secateurs, colour threads and batting. We began to scissor tablecloths into obsessive sizes, furnished with safety pins and polyester. We sowed the seeds of the theme: green, white and red (**Give Women Rights**). We sewed orchid cypripediums on top, diatonic rocking horses nearby and afterwards, valentines. The 'Singer' sewing machine resembled the gramophones, except it was storybook black with gold swirls, the needlepoint fateful.

The parade quilt was enlarged to metres' long, bandied around so campaigners could embroider it with their surfaces. My wombat waves were filled with suffragist clippers, Cessie's ringlets were like a lioness' and Magnus was caricaturised with crackers, his puff the colourant of a coyote. Two women made an illustration of Lady Belle behind bars: on the other hand, in the lea sisters waited to liberate her.

We took great care when carving: *Debarring women from the vote is akin to enchaining them*. Afterwards, with her own fingers, Fawcett darned her signature and drifted it around.

My nub quaked on my go. It'd smudge me there for perpetuity.

I transcribed: I-v-y M-o-s-s with mistletoe mellowing like toadstools.

"Don't bypass these," Princess Sophia said, rattling a treasury and knolls of credenda.

"You do comprehend why we're involved in this, don't you?" the sixty-year-old said.

"After witnessing Plod, unquestionably," I put in.

"The NUWSS requires figureheads," Fawcett said. "This is a promotion more than a protest."

If this goes loopy, we could reverse the vote, Cessie transmitted.

I wouldn't even be an engineer if this collateral 23 was consummated.

Chapter Seventeen: War Before War

"I've high hopes for you," the topmost suffragist said, "which is why I'm placing you in a small team with the Princess, your workfellows and Flora. I trust you're ready to accept the dangers and our peaceful policies?"

"Will we be set upon for our pains?" I said.

"There's no telling," Fawcett said.

"Figureheads?" Magnus said when she failed to supply reassurance.

"Don't be a wuss," Cessie said. "Are you functioning for change, or not?"

"We know we win," he garbled in a whisper.

"That's not the point," she muttered. "For all we know, our disturbance could rework the Representation of the People Act." The quilt was browbeaten as she stood up. "Whatever we do to ease their determinations will be prised."

"She's right," I said. "Do something noble for a change."

"Get off your self-righteous pedestal, *for a change*," my co-engineer said to my dorsum.

Feigning going on a ciggie break, I keyed: *Nadia, I'm contacting you about an extension. Fawcett has charged us with allotting leaflets and backing up the Hyde Park Rally. May we dawdle?*

Stay as long as you have to, but beware, Nadia replied. *The past isn't a haven – you could be hurt or decimated there. Attempt to return in the New Year season.*

I gave my co-campaigners the thumbs-up.

"This is nuts, isn't it?" Cess said eagerly. "Being at the frontline of the NUWSS?"

"I'd sooner be a suffragette," I said.

"Me too," Magnus agreed. "I thought we'd be shelling museums and red-bricks, and massacring portraits. Instead we're do-gooding as usual."

A couple of citizens saw fit to sling bile at us when we flashed the fliers, but nobody had kicked our heads in yet, which I accepted as a positive step.

"Hyde Park Rally, 26th July," Magnus said, stronger-pitched than a foghorn.

"Relating to what?" an insect-eyed gentleman in a boa constrictor scarf said.

"Women's right to vote," he said.

"Pin your eyes back, son," he said, pitter-pattering the engineer in the chest. "I don't support arsonists and window-smashers, got it?"

"No forcefulness," Cess said hurriedly into his earhole, for Magnus' boxy shoulders were gnashing.

"We're suffragists," he said in his deepest pitch. "We partake only in peaceable caucuses."

"I'll think on it," Scarf man said in the least convincing fashion I've ever seen.

Next we intercepted a bevy of manual workers, and Cessie ferociously sponsored Hyde Park.

"Suffrag*ists*, you say?" said one, tobacco searing from her lip balm.

"We're aiming to ratify change in terms of the female sex's say in politics, equity of pay and free will."

"Attend if you aspire to be emancipated," I said offhandedly.

"You might get in the papers," Flora gave her two cents. "A century from now, folks might say, 'they had real courage'."

"We won't be mauled?" a woman in homely Rabbit denim said.

"There's no clause stating it won't occur," Magnus said, "but what do you value more... independence or dullness?"

"We'll go," they said, signing up as participants; I pictured cash cryptograms in their corneas.

"See," Magnus said, "it's as easy as ABC."

Forty-five minutes later we were singing merrily, having acquired fifty odd converts, and set our hearts on a pub. The Dragon and Slayer, with harlequin-glazed panes and tartan-patterned stools, was ill-omened in hindsight. Retrospection is a beautiful ideal.

"We could do with some male affiliates," Magnus said. He headhunted a Jacks-playing troop on that irascible borderline between mid-life crisis and retirement. "They'll do."

He airlifted '**Suffragists, Hyde Park 1913**' information into the men's laps, and they bonged down their pints with groggy miens.

"What you after?" they bayed.

"Cohorts," Magnus supplied.

"Of what?" a pirate-faced individual said.

His drinking buddies regained their balance, thickset arms gritted, more alcohol than earthly.

"The suffragists," he enlightened them. "We're hosting a rally to sponsor the vote for w——"

The kilt-tiled workbench was reversed and they hitched towards us. The malt in their odours fragranced the troposphere as their rheumy pig-eyes irrigated.

"I don't 'member an activist cracking open my bungalow when my nieces were starvin'," Pirate said. "Nor when me wife left me, or when Bertie's paymaster didn't wanna know any more."

His palm became a jumbo jet and cemented Magnus' proboscis. It bled incessantly.

"Hey!" Cessie rebelled.

Drunkards gridlocked her attempts to aid Magnus.

"Hold your fire," Flora ordered her. "Millie said no violence, and if we administer it it won't even be self-defence."

I made a lunge for the brochures but a fist outdid me, socking me onto the worktop.

It girded my windpipe; I was airless.

"What 'bout men's rights, you bitch?"

"Go to hell," I said, lobbing a recliner at him.

It was a tense moment as I waited for it to connect: then he wallowed in inertia. Before the bobbed souls who'd congregated, he barfed the drinks he'd downed. Shakes went all over my body.

The pub proprietor fetched me a duster and I pasteurised my throat, gummy where I'd been assaulted.

"A life ban," the businessman penalised the yobs.

I swivelled. Magnus was using tissues to stanch the pour, Cessie was in a stack with Flora and Singh had withdrawn, not a strand out of place.

"Suffragists, you say?" a voice said.

"Fighting peacefully for the vote," Cessie said tremulously.

Lethargically, pennies and names began to soak the collection box and sign-up sheet, unevenly marked in pencil. I didn't betray a reaction, however my lenses assumed a lustre.

"Thank you so much," the trainee historian said. "Every name tallies towards a greater advantage."

"That was a clean sweep," a high-strung Flora said. "You three are my fluky charms."

*

The lashes of a July thunderstorm shepherded rain in oodles when daybreak loomed.

At Ma's bricked residence, Flora Belle endorsed that we attend our finishing shift at Peek Freans. "It's a chance to snatch last-ditch members," she said, like an auctioneer.

"Suppose we're half-killed yet again?" Magnus hypothesised.

"He has a point," I said, rubbing my neckline; we were both cursorily bruised.

"Look upon it as a badge of honour," Flora said enthusiastically. "Everyone'll know you're suffragist soldiers."

"You said violence wasn't a suffragist policy," Magnus said dourly.

"You didn't mind that when you gave that gorilla what he had coming," Lady Belle said.

"Are we going to be struck off?" I said promptly. "I know we weren't supposed to —"

"It was self-defence; he deserved what he got," Flora said.

"We don't regularly – you know – hit people," Magnus said.

"Irregular times call for irregular acts," Cessie's predecessor quoted.

"Who said that?" Cessie said.

"I did," Flora informed her.

That was how I came to jam-pack the snood over my half-up wavy ducktail. The contour in the beaker was attenuated, and I side-tracked my goggle.

Our profession was a wee bit more rousing this time round: I was employing an embryonic 'robot' to squirt the cream into the custard (a thrill filled my arteries). As Cessie made carvings of the company logo, she had moderately more than her fair share of the wafers. They were very artistic, oven-brown and blubbery.

"Calories don't count in the twentieth century, right?" she said, with commendable pseudoscience.

"We'll shed the fat on the ride home," I delivered false promises.

Magnus came galloping to 'test' our tasters, and judged them to be 'tolerable'.

"All the same, this ration could use more zest," the 'expert' critiqued.

"Would you like to changeover?" I asked.

"You wouldn't last three microseconds in the kitchenette," Magnus said. "You haven't touched food since last Wednesday."

What was he, a birdwatcher? I arched myself away from him.

At noontime, when floods of flour and grease characterised us, Flora passed round enlistment sheets.

"The better fed they are, the more pliable they'll be," she distinguished.

The response was disheartening: some reacted in antipathy, others questioned whether it would mean the end of their wages, and a few fearless bees recruited themselves.

"Are you relaxed about being paid less than your male counterparts for the same hours and the same work?" Flora blared. "Are you content to have your husband decide your opinions while you throw together his lamb and sprouts?"

"There's nought wrong with ladylike manners," a newlywed said.

"If you don't believe in the vote, what are you doing working here?" Cessie blasted her.

"Boosting me 'usband's wage," the superior-boned woman said. "I imagine you're a spinster. Got no idea how to hook a 'usband."

"I'm not a spider," Cessie ridiculed.

"That's not the way to persuade people," Magnus muttered.

"We don't need your brainwashing here," a blue-rinse said. "We 'ave enough men boring on, telling us what to fink. We don't need you four."

"Didn't you ever dream of the ballot box, being able to have your say about the parties who determine your lifestyle?" I appealed to her.

"I daydreamt once, before I caught on that the suffragettes —"

"Suffragists," Magnus rectified.

"— are only gunning for the wealthy; they don't care for poor folk."

"That's not true," Flora said. "I've slaved for *hours* in Peek Freans —"

"And don't you bloomin' rave about it, as if you're better than the rest o' us," the dissident said.

"C'mon," I said to my 'suffragists'. "There's no sense chitchatting with them."

"*Hmm-hmm.*"

We were stock-still.

"June?" Flora said.

"You're serious 'bout doing something?" the scornful employee said. "We'll get the vote, if we unite?"

"We aren't the politicians," Flora said with a gentler nuance. "But we'll sweat biscuits, bleed in Magnus' case and weep 'til our lips are blue."

"Don't you see?" Cessie implored. "Sooner or later, they'll have to pay attention."

"We'll strike," an anonymous person said. "That'll have the big guns runnin' scared."

"What's this about striking?"

The boss jigged out of his microscopic office, even more hairless than when we'd freshly met. "If you desire a foothold on your only likelihood of a job, you'll reword that statement."

Anonymous unstuck her hands from the biscuit automaton, gingerly recovered her bag and promenaded to the exit.

"See ya," she said.

Her fellows studied each other, overwrought.

"Who else wants to make the largest mistake of their careers?" the boss said, his semblance like a catnip's.

"We do," I said; the slippery hairnet came away in my nails.

Cessie consequently quit.

"Flora?" the manager said belligerently. "What say you to this?"

"I'm a Lady," she said. "If it's between money and suffrage, I cherry-pick Millicent every time."

The gloves were off – technically as well as allegorically.

"Our taste tester?" The manager moved onto Magnus. "You a big girl like these workers 'ere?"

Magnus overturned the freebies.

The boss went a glittery traffic-light red.

"Stick your custard creams," Magnus said, and breezed out.

"No factory in the world will take you on, boy," the director warned.

"They'd have to beg," he said through his tongue.

"Everybody back to work," he said, spanking his knuckles as the chimney puffed. "A pay rise for all who finish the shift."

Notwithstanding the boss' threats and slothful as a queen bee after a prickle, women were filing towards the sign-up, pencilling their signatures in narrowly readable lettering.

"What?" the boss said.

"It's bin nice knowing you," an operative said. "But I quit."

"June?" he said. "You don't condone this?"

"Looks like you'll have to find new meat to work like race dogs," she said soullessly. "Ta for taking us on."

A hundred worker ants routed towards us, genial, concurrent with us. It was a sincere occasion of: **strike, and you're out**!

When we showed our faces at the sickroom, Fred was playing with the do-it-yourself steamer, a grapey pudding clotting on his bedside. Pearl was beside him with her bandage, pins fastening it.

"Did you come with offerings?" Pearl said, decreasing her decibels. "The buffet here's rank."

Magnus was soft-hearted enough to mortgage her wafers and bourbons, left over from his stint. The youngsters disseminated the biscuits between them.

"It doesn't taste as mildewed as I imagined," the younger Moss said, "given it's three hundred years old."

"Ha-ha," I said.

Aero made his presence known, clad in a surgeon's getup.

"Is this Halloween Part Two?" I said.

"It's no joke," Aero said. That was a revolution, for him. "I've tampered with more bodies than Frankenstein."

"Nobody died, right?" I made sure.

"Ivory, I'm insulted," Aero said. "What d'you take me for? The invalids are in safe hands."

Pearl grunted, considering the clumsy dressing on her fracture.

"Most patients," he edited.

"I'll forgive ya if you take me along to the picket," Pearl said.

"Not a chance," I said to her bargaining chip.

"But in history Blueberry and I are doing presentations on twentieth century Britannia, and my speciality is the suffragists," she said. "If it goes banana-shaped, it could be on my permanent record."

"Well…" I was wavering.

"Oh, go on, it won't do her any harm," Cessie said. "It's scholastic."

"We'll bring you," I caved in. "You'll be out of the action handing out *The Common Cause* to passers-by."

"Oh," she said huffily, before it sunk in. "Blueberry will be green!"

"Don't you mean blue?" I punch-lined; no one laughed.

While Flora and Cessie ran to get our dresses, I updated Aero on our 'stolen' Peek Freans recruits.

"I know Cess will say it isn't equivalent, but this suffragist stuff is like Bo," Aero said out of nowhere. "People call her a nutter: oh, we're flexitarians now, we've done enough to shrink our impact. She would've liked it, beholding a campaign in action."

I spliced the film on my lips: "Why's she outcast?"

"Never wins the assault courses, and Stone won't stretch to a try-out."

Cessie kitted me out in a bonnet, swishy skirt and suffragist sash: her, Pearl and I coordinated, except the second was a mini-me. I meliorated her toffee threads so it seemed as if she wore Minnie Mouse muffs.

Foot soldiers, we tailed the ex-factory assistants to the cool-blue band drums in the epicentre, where they were hoisting a dominating flag and each held a pole as though it were the Olympic torch.

"Courage calls to courage everywhere!" Millicent testified, just shy of Hyde Park, a deluxe grid of gravelly plantations.

"I could live here always," I said.

Rainbows were saved behind my lens.

"We the law-abiding suffragists request the vote," the speechmaker's minions pled.

"Ives, you have to see this!"

I no longer unheeded the tug; Arabian horses with unicorn hair and caravans shaped like chamois flatcar boots were racing into the metropolis like Godiva, complete with cummerbunds. Many incapacitated the trumpets with their marches: all modelled sunbeams and red, white and green.

Pearl, masquerading as a delivery girl, gave out newspapers, and we were so preoccupied by the speeches we failed to pinpoint the hoodlums horse-riding in. They were chaperoned by Pirate, his pub pals and, shockingly, the boss.

Cessie's pucker matured to a yelp: "Anti-suffrage factions."

"They'll spoil the demo," Aero stormed.

"We won't let them," I said frostily.

Thirty-five seconds lapsed before I caught onto the irony of my situation. The men began to fuse their might in a tug-of-war, founding a semi-circle like a half-moon.

Cessie made a dive for my arm: "Get out of the way!"

They rushed us in a to and fro more resentful than southern beaches; back, onwards, back, onwards. Their acceleration heightened with each enactment, the impetus potentially fatal.

Flower-girls' stalls went down as if a mudslide had beleaguered them, and their shrieks synchronised with the seagull poo sleeting overhead.

After a bone-cracking rush my skin cells were tender, like pickaxes had scarred them. My veins smarted as I tried to decipher who was suffragist and who hooligan; who was from my world and who theirs.

Cessie levered me uphill and we, alongside Aero, Flora and Magnus, became a stumbling block to the gang, who'd been about to bash old ladies.

The rioters invocated: "What about Emily Davison?"

"How many times do we have to tell these trolls? We're not even suffragettes," Magnus said.

"This is in her name," Sophia said, who I hadn't seen up to now.

At the sight of the immoderate Princess, the gushes intermitted.

"We owe you one," Aero thanked her. "For the hospital, too."

She winked. "The fever upswings before it melts. We *will* get the vote – by any means."

It was as though we were the ones lacking foreknowledge.

"Sophia's imprisoned for debt by Christmas," Cessie said as the feathery Princess took her leave. "Sad, really."

"The law wouldn't abide suffragettes, like some don't tolerate Bo in 23," Aero said. "If you ask me, that's the bones of why Stone won't —"

"Don't insinuate anything about my father," Magnus chastened. "He's twice what those heavies are."

The evening meetings went ahead as scheduled and no one referenced the free-for-all.

Pearl was a mix-and-match of eggy substances, tomatoes and mashed spuds when we reformed for the closing announcements.

"Children and their mummies and daddies showed their indebtedness," she said.

"They egged you?" Cessie said, neurons clicking like a typewriter as she made note of the mindboggling occurrence.

"Rough crowd," Aero said drolly.

"Be discreet, please, for the speeches," a matron-type woman said.

"Despite our pacifist parades, we've been treated like battle-axes," Millicent said feverishly. "Yet that did not daunt our predecessors —"

"Hurrah!" said the elder ladies.

"— and it won't daunt us!"

"That may not daunt you, but this will," dinged a mundane modulation.

PC Foster was unmasked, straight-backed with "Baldy" the Boss and Pirate-face.

"My informers 'ere figure you're sheltering a wanted woman. Flora Belle."

"Drat!" Cessie said.

"My, my, you're the spit of 'er," PC Plod said. "She your aunt or somefink?"

"We don't know where she is," the dissembler said with restraint.

"Never heard of her," Aero said.

Rush.

The most wholehearted of the anti-suffrage rioters swept Flora to the helm like dustpans.

"Well, if it ain't Lady Flora," Foster said. "Come with me. I 'ave the right to detain you as your provisional exoneration for ill health is at an end. You're up and about, so healthy enough for 'Olloway."

"Holloway," Cessie said deeply.

"Those squealers," Pearl said insensibly.

PC Foster paced towards her. "You see, for every cat and mouse, there's a mole."

At daylight, we adventured by horse-drawn omnibus to the scandalous women's custodial. It was a subnormal shape, similar to upside down ankles. We found an aperture in the 'Cold War' wall, harsher than an Iron Curtain or a Celtic fort.

"How do we know which cell's hers?" a jumpy Cessie said.

"The airing in here's a killer," we happened to hear her remark.

"Up there," Aero said logically, and he hazarded a clamber up an old English buckthorn. "Flora, it's me."

He'd pinpointed the Lady who'd 'vanished' all those suns ago.

"You won't be arrested: I fibbed that you lot hadn't harboured me, it was all my own doing."

"Was it a tough night?" Cessie enquired.

There was a feeble response.

"Make an incision in the wall for ventilation," Aero suggested.

"I'll be punished," she said, sapless.

"Hang on," Cessie said, "we'll hammer you out if we have to."

"How, by photosynthesis?" she scoffed. "I'm alright in here. It's my reserve home."

"What've they done to you?" Aero investigated.

244

"Same old," she said begrudgingly. "Wouldn't eat the wretched bubble and squeak again. They'll make me."

"We'll break you out before they can," Aero said.

There were crashes within the cell.

Shit.

"Talking to yourself again?" a wardress said.

"Her routine tricks," another said. "Come on, we've to oversee another force-feeding."

There was little we could do as they shipped her away.

The five of us slunk to the designated spot, which we knew from Cessie's historical satnav.

"No, I'm not a suffragette!" Flora defended herself.

"We don't see any difference," the wardresses said.

From my viewpoint, I made out Flora in an electric-style chair, trammelled to a non-consensual locus. The feeding duct impersonated the Bunsen burner Pearl had conveyed from chemistry, only crueller: a backward-looking, chariot-bronze gizmo.

"Crikey," Pearl uttered.

"Psst, Aero, is there a side-hole?" Cessie said.

He rechecked the walls but returned empty-handed.

"The only method is through the guards," he resolved.

"Let's take a sledgehammer to the wall," Cessie said, ironically presenting herself as more of a militant than mediator.

"If we do that, we'll alert them to our attendance and be in line for a mugshot," Magnus said. "Think twice."

"She's not your ancestor," Cessie slung-shot him.

"You've known her two minutes."

"What do you know, you jumped-up —"

Flora gave an abhorrent cry.

On tiptoes I accessed the flaw in the barrage: Flora's plaits retroceded back like vortices, an IV thrust into her sinuses. Cess' lunges were restrained by Aero and Magnus: it educed Alexandrina's exertions to martyr herself. It was inverted now.

Dairy decanted like the feed in Anne Hathaway's shed even as she beat her arms about: wardresses tweaked her nostrils and she coughed the nourishment down.

"Good girl," they said as she downturned onto her side, milk trailing like snot. "That wasn't so difficult, was it?"

They wetted her with wipes, but she did not tic.

"Mayhap one hour you'll forget this suffrage nonsense," the doctor said powerfully.

"You'll be dead first," she said, spittle bucketing aloft.

"They've enforced our hand," Cessie said, convulsing as Flora was taken back. "We have t-to act. Words won't do it."

"What d'you intend to do?" Magnus said, his eyebrow as tall as a trapeze ballerina.

"Prison-break," Cessie said. Her star mouth knotted as she graphed the mortar. "What they did – lit a spark. *Milk-bombs*."

Pearl's pinkness toned down.

"We'll have to use gunpowder," Aero said long-sufferingly.

"Consider ammo your debt after what you just did," Cessie said.

"If I hadn't, Flora would be serving a life sentence," he opined. "But... I'm sorry."

"This is where Pearl comes into play," I shrilled.

They trained themselves on me like shrimp receptors.

I twiddled my bonnet, where slack waves purled. "If she slips into the kitchens, we can use their unethical milk to create the bomb."

"There's no smoulders without ignition," Aero said.

"Fireworks," Magnus said. "They flog them in the birthday store. I saw it when I came with Einstein here."

"Hurry," I said. "Pearl will steal indoors in the meantime."

Cessie and I were the surveillance as Aero and Pearl, identically to brown mice, squeezed into a hollow a quarter of their bodyweights.

My skips on my toenails pissed off my partner, as the fob-watch ticked alongside it.

Ten rounds of the timer later, Magnus made himself known with a brown paper bag.

"You go in," he said through rattles. "I'm too long-legged."

There were guards at the interior; consequently I enfolded myself into an alcove, feeling as if I'd whirled into Wonderland and lost a third of my size.

Wardresses were nattering: I fled further down the strip, which was less of a rabbit-hole now.

"Poor lassie: I 'ope she sees we 'ad no choice," one said.

"You think she'd be glad, given dear Millicent spoke against the Boer War famine."

"These suffrage sisters – minds function in ways you and me can't abide."

"Quite right, Jean. Fancy a slice of genoa cake?"

"Or three."

As they absented themselves into the staffroom, I more effusively embodied my mammalian instincts by diving headfirst into the scullery.

"This is a berserk experiment," Aero said as Pearl fired up the cow's produce.

"Lighten up," my sister said, "it'll be the highest exam of your career."

"Got the gunpowder," I said, shifting it to Aero. "You know what to do."

The gases gravitated, so I put a bonnet to my molars and Pearl secured hers. Aero experienced the deadlier part of it but was well-accustomed, and abracadabra! We had our bomb, in its infancy juxtaposed with the ones that'd detonate the biosphere in a year.

Aero bagged the dynamite and we were mindful to shuffle as we preyed on where security were eating ham and pickle butties.

"Who the 'ell are you?" a pimply man said.

"Everything you loathe rolled into a meatball," Aero said.

He blitzed their purlieu.

The three of us backpedalled as it detonated on the benches and cord-phones.

The oxidiser peroxided the workstation with foetid smells, and whizzes blew out on the bulletin.

"It's motley," Pearl said as I began to lug her from the firecrackers (relatively minor shells that sounded like bedlam.)

"We can toast marshmallows another day," Aero said. "We've got to be quick."

We headed for the stairs, cursing about there being no elevators, and triple-checked each number.

"Which's the right one?" Aero said.

"I don't know, I don't know," I said.

"For hemlock's sake," Pearl said, "it's one of the booths with the buckthorn outlook."

Aero deepened his vocal chords: "'Ello, is Lady Belle there? We've to deliberate whether you're eligible for parole."

"But – I just got here," she responded. "Are you here for additional force-feedings?"

"Then it's your lucky day," Aero said.

"That one!" Pearl said, slating the second from left.

"Flora, it's us," I mumbled. "Is there a way for us to break in?"

"The window's human-proof," the suffragist said. "It won't – give –"

"This is the *twentieth century*," Aero said. "The cells must be insecure."

He and I made earth-shattering thrusts, the cogency out of this world.

"Ivy!" Pearl said.

Wardresses were knocking on cells, saying prisoners must evacuate. The door was in disintegrates.

"Who're you?" somebody asked Pearl bellicosely.

"I'm on work experience here," she said.

"I'd sooner swallow cod liver oil than that," a wardress said. "After 'em!"

Flora with us, we streamed nearby the emergency exit.

Fluctuated maces interdicted our getaway.

Chapter Eighteen: Frost and Flame

"No one's allowed that way!" a wardress said pompously, as bouncers utilised their truncheons to pow our noggins into the wallpaper.

"Except in case of a fire," Pearl said knowledgeably.

"The only fire was your work downstairs," the bouncer said.

From her pocket, Pearl withdrew a sparkler.

The bouncer's complexion was lighter than a ghoul's.

"Don't," he said, stuttering.

"Clear out," Pearl said through her dolphin-blue braces.

The bouncers backtracked towards the wardresses, whose bosoms began to heave up and down.

"Defy us again," they said, "and you'll all choke down the Sunday roast."

Even so, we discarded these guidelines and Pearl locked the emergency escape from the outside so gracefully I'd no idea how she pulled it off.

"Damn your rulebook," I said through the mist.

Puffed out, creasing, we'd nanoseconds to scuttle out before thirty outdoor guards made us regret that we existed.

They, too, were armed, clubs swinging under our noses.

"Steady," they said as we approached. "You don't want to do anyfink rash."

"The only thing rash is your face," Aero said.

The security's flinch gifted us the opportunity to scram through the nook.

"I knew we should've walled that up," a guard whinged.

"We ain't got the money, Joe," his chum said.

"Why brick it up?" I said as I cast a final look at Holloway, with its trimmed hedges and patchy floors. "You'd sooner expend money forcing tripe down prisoners' throats."

"I do make an award-winning trifle," a wardress said, distantly.

We went on a circuit to fetch Flora's holdall, taking to the backstreets to shake off our seekers. Ma was at the orthodox red-brick with her correspondingly redhead son, Fred, and was startled when we started collecting jumpers, skirts, a v-neck, Dorothy heels and photo frames.

"What's all this?" she said. "Flora, you ain't going, are ya?"

"She has to go into exile," Cessie said by way of apology, "after the prison break."

"Prison break?" the woman said uncertainly. "Flo, why couldn't you 'ave just seen it through, like you used to? Where's the sense in going on the run?"

"Have to," Flora said through an Ogdens Tab's rollup. "I'm not having tubes thrust down my tonsils anymore."

"They wouldn't really," Ma said, her flame-lit centre parting screwing.

"They already have," Flora confessed.

"You can't come back?" her host said.

"Never," the deserter said.

Fred did a marathon into the hallway: "You're not going! You're the best thing that happened to Ma and me."

Flora unbuttoned the blinds, where policemen were marching up and down.

"Take your medicine and be a good boy," she said unwearyingly. "And remember that no matter what any of the other children assert, girls are your equals."

"I know it already," the little boy said, his cap obscuring him. "Pearl beat me at the games."

"It was nice seeing you," Pearl said tearlessly. "I'm sure there'll be lots of other kids to overthrow you at cards."

"Not like you," the boy said, as Aero handed his mother a sheet instructing her when to feed him the antibiotics.

"Thanks for – you know," Ma said to Aero. "You won't let what those suits say about your hocus-pocus put you down, will ya?"

"It's already forgotten," Aero said.

"Well, Flora," Ma said, head hidden by her bunny-patterned smock. "Be good wherever you end up."

250

"If you ever need company, Millicent will be more than happy to invite you to a sit-in," Flora said.

"My nerves couldn't take it," Ma claimed; nonetheless, I felt she might give it a go.

Through the back door, our feet hustled on the trail of a minicab, where we surrendered pounds to be taken to the docks. There was a barn-like country house, anchors stretching to the limits of the saline and office erections chock-a-block with oblivious slaves.

"What about my friends, my activism?" Flora said as her luggage ran slackly amidst the seashells.

Cessie became frustrated. "You packed in the factory, your housemates can scarcely support themselves and there are 99,999 suffragists to carry on the fight."

"No one'll ever know how I was suppressed," she said.

"Other inmates will broadcast the truth," I told her.

Flora hooked. "What about you lot? I tell ya, I've never seen more incompetent biscuit-makers. You won't survive without me."

"We ought to confess," Cessie said to herself.

"Positive about this?" Magnus said. "It's the 1910s equivalent of a spoiler."

"Just this once," she said, with cracks in her voice box. She faced her forebear: "I – I'm from the twenty-third century."

"Those pinwheels have unsettled you," Flora said – and I couldn't fault her. Cess hadn't minced the announcement.

"No, it's the truth," she confirmed.

"Asquith said that about the vote," Flora said wretchedly. "An' that was no more touchable than sawdust."

Cessie's heartbeat was more fitful more than an addict's. She extirpated her microchip and documented her experiences to Flora.

"What, we're related?" the lady said. "And I vanish?"

She palmed her waistcoat.

"I'm not murdered, am I?"

"I don't believe so," Cessie said. "You go missing on this day, 1913, because you espouse a bogus identity. That's why it was a mystery, all these years."

"You're so brainy I have difficulty accepting we're kin."

251

"I'm not really," she said. "I don't know my plesiosaur from my tyrannosaur, my decimals from my multiplications."

"But you know something," Lady Belle said. "Is the suffrage efficacious?"

"Would I be standing here if it wasn't?" she said weepily. "1918 for womenfolk over thirty. 1928 on par with the Y chromosomes."

Flora didn't ricochet a murine any more but an Egyptian Mau whose litter's seldom half empty. We'd outfoxed the brainchild of her intimidators.

Plumped pigeons ducked as the hull of the steamboat was gazed upon, in addition to a flagstaff with the British tints and a stern wheel harsher than a mixer. Beyond the waterfront was a tumulus that outclassed the fierce purple of noontime.

"I suggest you rename yourself Ada Robbins," I devised.

"There're blocks great enough to master the Titanic beneath that do-gooding rind," she said.

"Too right," I said.

"Where'll you end up?" a softer Cess queried.

"I'll cross the Channel; make a life there," Flora said.

"Ah," Cessie said, "you won't experience the vote for a while."

"Never mind that," her ancestor said, "have this. Since you seem so weirdly gript."

It was an anthology of pictures – a time capsule of Lady Belle in the grounds of her parents' mansion, on a *Secret Garden* swing, at the theatre, with a brand new telephone and, finally, a vista of a man and woman feeding one another raspberries like film stars.

"What became of him?" Cessie said as she patted the paisley coverlet we'd knitted earlier – a supplementary gift.

"Oh, we fizzled out at springtime," she said with a wistful exhale. "He was my third."

"Er, Flora," Magnus interposed.

PC Foster had put his stamp on the scene along with extra officials, and was accruing statements from the ticket office.

"'ave you seen this lady? Sun-haired, scrawny?"

"Ah," the deskman said, scratching his armpits. "Don't fink so."

"Don't sell to 'er."

"Right you are."

"Forget the permit," Magnus said. "Hide in the boiler room."

That was the last we saw of the lady as she shimmied onto the boards and vanished.

"That's it," Cessie said, nutty vision watery. "We'll never see her again."

The steamboat set sail as PC Foster and co. shook fistfuls at us.

"Stop in the name of the law!" they said (as if that ever worked.)

I claimed Pearl's holey glove, half-flopping as if a clam's, and hared into innocents. At one point PC Foster got a fish hook into Pearl, but I batted him away with the duress of karate.

"Oi, rascals!" he breathed after us. "If I nick you, you'll be sorry you was born!"

"In here."

Cessie rounded us into the outer-space object before our close-ups could be frozen in 1900s documents.

"That's the second circumstance where we've been persecuted out of a time zone," a florid Cessie said.

"We're becoming more alike," Magnus said flatteringly, "with your hitting."

"Would you like a demonstration of my gifts?" I threatened.

"No wonder the excursions pay so well," Magnus said, "with the near-death situations."

"We won't see a penny," Aero said. "We're on probation."

"Well, we got what we craved," Cessie said, cradling the album. "This'll be a bombshell to Mum and Dad."

In Goodwin's province, we employed the super-PC to trace the Belle lineage under Flora's concocted nametag. A blowsy, flaky yew branched out: Ada Robbins had married a man in wartime France, who, creepily, was her body double.

"You've solved the stalemate," the history professor extoled us.

"Lucien Bellerose," Cessie said lowly.

"Belle," I repeated.

Goodwin analysed the clan tree. "You won't believe this, but they'd four children. From two of those, your cousins are derived."

"Cousins?" Cessie echoed.

"They live in Southern France," the professor said. "You won't be able to acquire a passport to visit them, but your parents *can* include them in the will."

"Who are they?" Cessie said bewilderingly.

"Camille, Henri, Clara and Jules," Goodwin replied.

"When did she pass over?" Cess said.

"For you," Goodwin said, sliding a caked letter her way.

"To be given on this exact date," Cessie read the front, bound with a bow. *"I've lived a pleasant life, run ragged by now grown-up children and romanced every day by a Frenchman. I used the opportunities available to women to become an airwoman, and I spent many rash, free years gracing the skies. Thank you for your intervention, and thank your friends. I am in my ninety-ninth year and my doctors believe I will enter another realm soon. Goodbye, and always act on your desires. Love, the true Flora Heather Belle."*

Cessie disclosed two colour-free snippets; one of a smiling flax-curled pilot posing beside an aircraft and garlanded with medals, and another of a silver-coiled lady bordered by caramel truffles and reflective wine.

"What about Fred?" Pearl said concernedly. "Did he recover from TB? Did he abandon poverty?"

Dr Goodwin used the touchpad to search for the boy's details. He didn't say a word for a few minutes.

"Sir?" Pearl said. "Couldn't you find out anything?"

"What is it?" I joined in.

"Young Fred conscripted himself in 1918," Goodwin said in a hollow tone. "He was tall and healthy, and lied about his age."

"He'd still have been a schoolboy," Pearl calculated.

"Yes," the professor said kindly. "And – you see – there's no simple way to tell you this – they never found a body. He was missing in action a month before armistice."

"He'd be long dead regardless," Magnus said, not too comfortingly.

Pearl was noiseless.

"We taught him to lie," I said restlessly.

"He'd have done it anyway," Aero said. "I realised how strongminded he was when I medicated him. Then he had a sturdy will

254

to live —" He didn't end the thought. I knew he was a trainee who hated when patients died.

"C'mon," Cessie said, and she clasped both mine and Pearl's arms. "We'll surprise Mum and Dad."

At the robot-operated reception, Mr and Mrs Belle subjected their daughter to roughly two hundred hugs.

"You did so well," her silver-hatted mother said.

"Old Stone had his neck screwed on when he chose our Cessie," Mr Belle said.

He embellished his will so his newly revealed relations would receive two percent of his net earnings each. ('We transgressed time and space for two percent?' Magnus nit-picked.)

In Dad's medieval library, I eye-witnessed him slumbering in the beanie.

"Dad —?" I said, and stopped.

I situated the autographed, authentic quilt in a see-through cartridge with the notice: *Real twentieth century suffragist memorabilia, partially hemmed by twenty-thirdcentury space-travellers.*

My CPU honked.

It's Nadia. I am over-planet-Pluto to announce that after your coups in 1913, you, Aero and Cessie have been dispensed permanence as astronauts. Your bonds are fixed for springtime, 2218.

*

THE PRESENTATION CEREMONY

Ovoid candleholders cased the panel icicles to seem sunshiny and steel-headed automatons were in alluring opposition. They melded with Aero's greyish eye tone and lightened his dahlia tuxedo, differentiating his ecru membrane. To his right, Cessie brought charm in a tinfoil playsuit and tinselled pashmina, her swirls now at shoulder level. As for me, I was in mechanic's dungarees, Ariel hair slides scrabbling my temple, three-inch suntanned wedges elongating me. Aero kept flipping his porous mittens from hand to hand.

"I'm opening the show," Cessie said, her knuckles clawing her kneecaps.

"Then you'll get it over with," I said, drumming wisdom into her.

"Earthlings," Mrs Stone said from her plinth, "it's been a testing selection, competition and expedition. Three heroic winners had a spoonful of time travel, more addictive than credits in the slums. Three cheers for our spaceman and spacewomen!"

During the pause, tepid praise was given.

"Celestine Belle, who some of you may recognise from the history department, made the shortlist after review of her thesis on ghosts," Mrs Stone said, as Cessie's spiky teeth made whirling motions. "She has her bean in the paranormal; nevertheless, she's no airhead. Welcome to the stage, Ms Belle."

There were intensifying applauds at this, predominantly from Magnus' mates.

"Sign here," Mrs Stone said, and she took up the teeny-weeny pen, signing the digital concordat.

With a frenetic titter, Cessie seamed with us on the lounger.

I had my own taste of sickness as I waited.

"Our second recruit bewitched the judges with her self-made motorbike – the grapevine has it that it flies in spite of its quantum," Magnus' mother said. "Intersect with me, Ivy Moss!"

I lost my footing in the stilts and Cessie, Aero and Bo were singular in not heckling.

"Trusted with time travel, yet she still can't walk," started up an unpleasant engineer on Magnus' table.

I could see Dad's stubbly self and Mum's grown-up Dora Explorer outline, but glances around revealed no Pearl. She'd given her word she wouldn't hover post-school.

"Sign on the dotted line," the host said concisely.

"We can't quit once we're contracted?" I clarified, as the engineering table took turns swigging spirits.

"We rarely do things halfway at Wolves, dearie," she said in her mirror-perfected parental pitch.

As though digitising in my own marrow, I inputted: I-M. The engineers were open-mouthed.

Mrs Stone assumed a florescence like precipitate canopies of falcons. "I knew you'd make the upstanding decision," she said. "The future's Wolves."

To swerve her gleaming eyes, I veered towards my closest friends, a little less wonky this time, especially when I swaggered past the mechanics.

"Last but not least, ameliorating his unassuming rearing, we have a contestant who reversed – that's right, *reversed* – a lecturer's paralysis. The platform is yours, Aero Smith!"

After his fifteen minutes of fame, the PowerPoint underscored *Cessie the Celestial, Ivy the Inventor and Aero the Astronomer* above our five-year-old passport photos. Squinting at my sixteen-year-old self, I couldn't comprehend how babyish we used to be.

"We can't reverse the contracts," Aero said.

Cessie's threaded, near colourless eyebrows grew crinkly.

"We can witness the Northern Lights, the Milky Way," I said. "I don't want to annul it."

The microphone began to emit words, so I shut up.

"For every lead artiste, there's a subsidiary, so a round of applause to Mars Ang, Bo Marsh, Aurora Snow and Magnus Stone," Helen said.

Mars and Bo were jointly reddening, Aurora wore a simper and her not-boyfriend was even smugger than usual.

"You should've gotten that contract, mate," the engineer at Magnus' populous table said as the latter re-joined him. "Not Poison Ivy and her dumb-as-death friends."

"That's how it swings," he said, with a gander downwards. "I'll get another shot."

"Least it isn't Friend of the Earth," the mechanic said. "Then we'd be poisoned by almond Sherries."

"Yeah," Magnus said floppily.

"A hiatus for the fallen," Helen Stone said.

Breaths were drawn as if from a wellspring.

Alexandrina's two-thousand-credit togs and Fire's bulging nose were brought into focus, alongside tributes from their best mates.

"The great live fast," one of my bullies toasted.

My gums were aching where I'd champed too vigorously.

"Forget it," Cessie said, her whorls on my drubbing neck. "He didn't mean that."

My expression became an unalloyed blank.

Was he spot on; was I unexciting, removed?

The hair slides gnawed my temple.

Boring is too kind a descriptive for that one, one of the engineers had once said. *She's out of it.*

Out of what? My mind, emotions, life altogether?

I wasn't sure; nevertheless the subtext was inescapable, suffocating.

During the after party Bo tap-tapped to our huddle.

"Don't sponge up what they said," she counselled. "He and his followers dubbed me Bo the Hermit. Of course, that's mostly stopped now – now Fire and Alex are dead."

"Rather a hermit than a slimy tattletale," I solaced her.

"Hey, every ceremony warrants gifts," Bo said, the tip of her snub snout suffused with red, as if its wearer suffered from the flu.

We were the recipients of vegan champagne in brown dusters, the top toning Cessie's foil.

"You didn't need to," I told her.

"It's been festering in Grandma's basement for yonks," she said. "Effects shouldn't go to waste."

"Between the two of us, I've had a generation's crate of drink already," Aero said.

"If we didn't get sloshed, we wouldn't work here," Bo said, and she romped off.

"Why'd she give us presents?" Cess said. "Does she believe we want for things?"

"*You* buy over-the-top gifts," I pointed out.

"For friends," she sputtered.

Aero made to say something, but cancelled the effort as Dr Stone mounted the podium.

His list of announcements seemed to span two centuries, and it was only when he grew maudlin that I perked up.

"I'd like to wish my son many happy returns in his twenty-second year of life. I'm sure you'll make admirable androids in the years ahead of you," he said.

Magnus' rabble gave him back-slaps, followed by Aurora's smooch.

I couldn't understand it... he'd said they weren't going out. Was it the mere formality that put them off transparency?

I didn't have to wait long to twig.

"May I let the fox out of the house?" the fatherly Stone said.

"Go on, then," Magnus approved.

"I'd like to invite my son and Ms Thorn to the stage," he said with staggering volume.

Aurora was in a tea-length georgette frock like the cartoon Belle's, a boa scarf interlaced like vipers, and Magnus was in black tie, his anomalous mane sanded.

"I'm elated to report that these two delightful people are affianced," his papa said.

"Mars hewed the ring from the diamonds and opals mined in the volcano," Aurora input, fluttery dress overwhelming.

The engagement ring they spent two lifetimes boasting over was like multifarious mirrors, minimalist yet candied.

"Only worth less than our amour," Magnus said, and they air-kissed before the patrons.

"It's a ploy so they can social-climb," I said with a cringe.

"No! It's true love," Cessie said.

I'd bitched indiscreetly; Magnus' friend appeared as if murder was too respectable for me.

Lydia's lichen pixie-bob bobbled swiftly into my eyeline: she didn't approach Aero but Mrs Stone, her overworked hands parched.

"I don't know how – I – the department informed me —"

"Very well," Helen said professionally. "It's alright, Lydia, you've done your best. Chaperone the parents to the annexe."

Aero's mum led Mum and Dad as if they were eyeless rodents away from the prying Toms.

"The revel's at an end," Mrs Stone said through the megawatt microphone. "All except the recruits must depart."

"Mum, what's up?" Magnus pressured her.

"It's nothing for you to burden yourself about," she said tidily. "Skip along with your – with Aurora while I have a word."

The auditorium emptied with as much brevity as it'd filled.

Mrs Stone was painfully pathos-ridden as she climbed over the sustainable seats and seized my crumped fingertips.

"Dearie, there's been a misadventure," she said.

My lungsful came in lurches.

"Your sister – Pearl, is it? – was taken ill en route to the crowning. They're doing all they can."

Levity snorted around me – two split-seconds later I realised *I'd* uttered the sound.

"What do you mean?" I said, incredulous. "She's fine – she'll be in the meadows. I suppose she was held up – the lower forms, they adore a snow fight –"

"Ivy," Mrs. Stone rolled on benignly, "Pearl is vitally unwell."

"Liar – you can't stand to see me do well," I screaked.

"Ivy." Cessie was juddering my shoulder blades. "We have to go."

Aero hadn't orated anything.

"You," I said tenuously, "what do you make of this?"

A shrill laugh entered my trachea.

Aero's facial muscles had become rigid. "I reckon... we ought to see Pearl now."

"See her, see her?" I said. "There's nothing to see – what've they done with her? Where've they taken her?"

"Ivy," Cessie said dolefully, "let's find out what's happening."

Impersonally, I weathered my oldest friend leading me into oblivion, from which I would never surface.

"Bo," I said, upon seeing her consorting with jacketed women and men. "Y-you've got the monolaurin, you can spare her, r-right?"

"It's still being manufactured," she said with barely a flutter.

"It has to be ready," I said, "it has to be."

Where was her insistence; why wasn't she dashing through the halls, pocketing everything in sight?

"They've thrown treatments at her to reduce the fever," Marsh said, and it was the first I heard of Pearl's suffering.

"Fevers are curable," I said, dry-lipped.

"I don't want to have to tell you this... speak to your mum and dad. Say your goodbyes."

It was a breadknife to my expectations, and I was doddery in the wedges.

"She isn't dying," I said imploringly. "Why's everybody written my sister off? She's thriving, she's just a child."

Bo's look was indefinable. "Ask your father. He hasn't been forthright."

"Can we come in?" Aero asked me.

"Yes."

Within, Mum's eye-bags would have made a panda look alert and Dad's forefinger grazed his thumb. Withering pansies ailed in a bud vase, Grecian with an interpretation of defender Hektor with Andromache and Astyanax, who overreached to touch his pa's toilet-brush helmet.

My parents did not stir at my arrival, occupied as they were with the cataleptic twelve-year-old, whose toffee braids hid the yellowed boniness of her heretofore rosewood cheeks.

"Bo said I should ask you about this," I said unswervingly, as the IV line transfused what Pearl's body could no more produce.

"Her heart's feeble," Mum said in her softest voice; the monitor's numbers dwindled.

Pearl was in a crevasse I could not strain towards, a brand of meteoroid who would crisp up like a pancake when she transgressed the mesosphere. She'd invariably been too sharp-witted for this dreary and rainbow-less culture.

Mum triggered Dad's exposes.

"We didn't say it because we didn't want to make it real," he said behind his Cadbury beard. I wished I had a bush to hide behind.

"You were immune to the petty viruses and grazes that may've killed some of your classmates," Dad said. "When we violated the rules and conceived a second child, we ran out of credits to immunise Pearl."

"I'm not following," I said. "Pearl didn't get mortally sick with chickenpox or flu. She was strong."

"*Is*," Dad said as the figures continued to deteriorate. "You see, Ivy, she had a weaker than usual immune system when she was born. We fed her a lot of sugar to make her robust. We figured if we could just keep her out of harm's way, we'd see her grow up."

"She grew lots over the past year," I said. "She is – was – going to be taller than me."

"You were the kindest sister," Dad said, "but I suppose this was always on the cards."

Aero twisted towards the pansies.

Was it unavoidable, though? There'd been nothing wrong with her, immune system be damned, when we'd hung out in 1913. I may not have known about her quandary, but I'd have known if she was sickly.

Something else must have shadowed her, led her to this untimely aftermath. There would be no rest until I'd found out what'd caused this corrosion.

"Pearl?" I said to my debilitated sibling, for everybody else was acting as if she was dead.

"Ivy," she said. Her lids remained casket-shut.

"Yes, it's me," I said. "We're all here to see you. There're flowers and chocolates – as if you're Elizabeth Taylor."

"It's like Tunisia in here," she said.

Snowfalls were rapping on the sill, condensation soaking in teardrops.

"Yes," I said, as chills goosebumped her hooked wrist.

"I'm s-so scared," she said out of her swelled lymph.

"It'll all be over soon," Cessie said, cloaking her snivels under a breezy disposition.

"Aero," Pearl said valiantly, "I made a m-mistake. It isn't your fault."

My friend's peaked eyelashes grew blacker.

"Your CPU," he said back. "Should I show them — ?"

"Yes," she said, gasping oxygen. "Ivy, is it snowing?"

"It's all white beyond the vase," I said. "There're snowflakes greater than gremlins."

Pearl's intakes sharpened. "It's going to be cold out there, under the mushrooms."

"There'll be no frost," I said. "You'll find somewhere steamy."

"Thank you."

The finishing flushes of paint on her skin tone were no more.

Her last inhalation, the blackout of her organs, is a rattle that I hear every day.

Much later, Bo said she died at four-thirty p.m., but for me all pulses were nullified, all meaning perplexed.

"Ivy, don't leave yet," Mum pleaded.

It was snowing still, and robins were nesting.

I had to regress the hours. Time travel.

Chapter Nineteen: Silver Bullets

The teetering wedges limped for my lifeline – the oxygen suits.

The space was unfilled when I plummeted myself downwards. The sag did not disturb me – if anything, the electrification assured me my chambers were pumping, that Ivy Moss lived.

The tube station, as lightless as a hedgehog's grassy, muddy lair, saluted me with lamplights. My index mismanaged the lock; three bashes later I'd prevailed. Once Pearl was restored, she'd be able to advise me how to undo it best. Like *I* was the younger sister.

The engine refused to kindle, so I appropriated a wrench and slugged it. It strangulated, cablings shelling like gunfire. Some self-defence must have endured, for I hopscotched away from ruination.

I grabbed red, purple, bliss-blue wires, steeling myself to fuse them together.

"There's no point."

I gripped the spanner lest automatons or employees had come to usher me away, consistent with how they were planning to bury Pearl if I didn't roadblock them.

The profile of Magnus Stone lumbered into view with his lion's pompadour, his razor blade blue palette dissecting my darkest brown ones.

"You," I started venomously. "You've been after me for five months."

"I've been trying to tip you off for five bleeding months."

"It *was* your sabotage," I said savagely.

"Forgive me. I simply wanted you to know... this isn't an organisation anyone should be part of."

"You didn't think I could decide for myself?"

"No, I convinced myself that you didn't know the full story, and you'd gain the alternative of backing out."

"I can't," I said; the wrench flew out of my grip. "I'm bound to Wolves."

"I've known you for eighteen years, so I knew you wouldn't trust me first hand. I decided to *show* you."

His Valentino shoes came nearer. "At least see how it took place. Aero says it's key."

My forehead was excruciating, as though knives were puncturing it – his argument was out of focus, untrustworthy.

"With the microchip?" I inspected.

His mane communed 'yes'.

"Why you?" I said, timbre failing. "Of all people, why you?"

"He – er – totalled it'd healthier if someone estranged went after you."

"You know what? You have to like someone in the first place to become estranged," I said, and my arrows didn't spear him; he chortled mockingly.

"Information empowers," he reflected. "Don't deny yourself one thing. You never drink, smoke cocoa, party, jape with others. Do a small thing, and everything'll be richer."

"Will Pearl come back?" I said. "Will you service this?"

"Look, maybe with my father we'll one day resurrect the fallen," Magnus said, instead of what I was longing to receive. "I truly believe he'll revolutionise Wolves."

"While he's tied up being Doctor Doolittle, people suffer," I growled.

"You don't even know how she – er —"

"I don't need to," I said. "I know enough about your family."

"My friends died too," he said, with a scowl that could impale chalk.

"Good," I snarled.

"You attended school with them, sat beside their table term after term – yet it's like you don't care."

"The person I cared about is on her way to the morgue," I said with a hiccup. "I didn't want them to be eaten, but Alex and Fire were wicked."

"Who're you to lecture them?" Magnus said, with a maul of his tresses.

"My school years were nightmarish due to them," I said. "I don't want to care."

Magnus buckled on the spanner and caught himself before he stumbled. "We all do things we regret, even Ms Perfect."

So he regretted it?

"I'm not perfect," I hissed, "but I'm a damn sight better than you. *Weeks* I spent assembling that steamer for Pearl, and you dashed it to fragments."

"It's disconcerting when you admire a subject and somebody else is better," he said.

"Why?" I fired up. "'Cause I was a girl?"

"No – because you were uncool," he said, wholesome hands mid-air. "It wasn't fair you could do stuff like that when everybody said you were – you know."

"So long as *everybody* thinks it, I must've deserved it," I yelled.

In the lull, I carried on, even though I wished I could stop being honest: "You've got everything you want, haven't you? Understudy, fiancé, Daddy's pet."

"If I could reverse it all, I would," he said.

I wasn't sure if he meant my sister or the torments.

I dented the switchboard: "There's really zilch to be done?"

His countenance was aggrieved, and I could virtually see the intestinal wrangle.

"No. I'm telling you first-hand you won't be safe if you don't evacuate Wolves."

I found Cessie sobbing and Aero facing the robins. The littlest went hop-skip around the park, which had enough rime to mould a frost fair.

"D'you mind going to Bo's place now?" Aero said, as Cessie's pupils disengaged from mine.

"Not 'til… excuse me?" I said.

Nurses had come to hijack Pearl's posthumous, whitish body.

"Will you… will you wrap her in this?" I asked.

I fished for the suffragist quilt I'd bushwhacked out of Dad's pageant.

"She'll catch her death down there."

Did I mean the morgue, or yonder? It was difficult to distinguish.

266

The nurses put it over her so I didn't have to witness her deadness any more; the girl who'd never again erase my aloneness, prick my conscience. It was the sweetest blanket, sewn with my own nails. I felt an exultant surge that I'd slogged over it, that I'd suffered for it.

"Even if she's gone there's a hereafter," Cessie said, and she gave my shivery upper arms a squeeze.

She couldn't know what it was to have a sibling; what it felt like when they left you.

"She's not here any more, even if there's a somewhere else."

"But she was," Cessie said, blinking away her distress. "Don't forget."

The four of us walked past the twisty houses, where families played virtual monopoly, shopped online, ate birthday cake. I was excluded from them, apart.

Grandmother Marsh, Bo, Cessie and Aero deserted the attic when I accepted Pearl's diaries.

A cotton-woolliness festered in me, an infection, so I did not identify their absence. They weren't my allies, they were shamefaced, like Magnus.

I paused over Pearl's microprocessor. Was it wrong to peek into them?

Conversely, the minutes seemed to be against me, had been from the moment Mrs Stone had given me the newsflash.

Expending maximum brainpower, I rifled the microchip for any stores in relation to Dr Stone. The initial clip was dated to the autumn, mysteriously the day Aero had been singed.

I leaped with a tremor:

"Aloe Vera and honey will do the trick," Granny Marsh's crackly voice says, prying into her stores for the ointment.

"I owe you one," Aero says as my pig-tailed, backpacked self drops by the garret.

"We might require something stronger," Bo says, her mouse-esque visage even more apprehensive than usual.

Her grandmother applies emulsified swabs to Aero's charred calf, where pinkish, angry membranes sizzle upon meeting the pads.

"A calendula," Bo says as an orangey bud emerges. "For the blister."

"Volcano?" I inquire from the doorway. "Is Ivy trapped in there?"

"Don't bother yourself; a team are freeing her as I speak," Aero said with a wince.

"Did ya rob any diamonds?" I say.

"I don't know," Aero says, "I didn't get very far."

I snigger. "Wish I'd been there."

"You're too young," Bo cautions me.

"I don't want to live here any more," I admit with a sigh.

"Why?" Aero says, blinkered.

"'Cause of the hauntings."

"Who's been scaring you?" Bo says.

"Cessie's slave," I quip.

"Pardon? Evangeline?" Aero says.

"She snores, you know. Dreams. Thinks. Feels guilty."

"Have you had too many jelly snakes?" Aero says, adapting it to a joke.

"I'm not high," I say with trace impatience. "That's no robot. It's a cyborg, or it feels, somehow."

"It'll be a new software design," Aero says, puckering. "Is this about what you and Ivy saw in Dr Stone's office? The science department's going through an experimental phase; what did you expect to find in a professor's lodging?"

"It's unnatural," I argue. "It didn't sound like remote-controlled emotions. It sounded... human."

"If you're serious, I can ask Stone about it."

"No. He can't figure out what we saw."

"If you say so," Aero says. "I'll investigate."

"You won't snitch to Ivy?"

Aero smiles: "Of course not."

Like a plug, I felt myself plunge out with a shiver and clicked on the subsequent Stone-specific memory. This one was after we'd retrieved the monolaurin:

"The species in Shakespeare's era were unimaginable," Aero promotes. "I've inserted masses into your tome."

"Ooh!" Bo leans to see the oodles of plants with every colour under the sky; red-pink treasures, aquamarine beauties and mephitic hemlock.

"Who retains books in this day and age?" I say as I drift in as if life is my oyster.

"Geeks like us," Bo says. "Come see."

She presents to 'me' the bitterest apple core, cubed up like a muscle, and peaches with centipedes nipping them.

"I don't know what to say," Bo says. "No one's ever brought me anything of this nature."

"You can show your gratitude by helping Aero and I hone in on Dr Dracula," I challenge.

"We can't. We'll sacrifice our livelihoods."

"He's mad as a moose," I say. "He might like your snooping."

"How about I take you on a joyride instead?" Aero offers. "Wherever we next visit, you can come, too."

"Yaaaaaaaaaaaaaaaaaaaaaay!"

The resultant video cut to Pearl begging Aero:

"Please. I'm sure something's down there. I'll be speedy."

"He's changed the code," Aero says. "He must already be suspicious that someone's been down there looking."

"I can crack any code," I assert.

"If you're not going to drop this, your best chance is when we're at the presentation ceremony. He'll be in there, gushing over Magnus."

"Ta, Aero."

With my deepest gulp yet, I transited into the ultimate extract regarding the professor:

I jab the lift buttons to land outside the underground office.

New code, new code... I rollick in my star-textured tights... what could it be? If I were bidding to deter strangers, what would I make my password?

269

The PIN pad fronts me, made of zinc and static.

H-e-a-l-t-h I-n-s-u-r-a-n-c-e.

He's that elephant-headed, I'm positive... the door lets me in.

The kitty's in its den, half-sleeping, half-charging.

There must be another tier...

I thump the floorboards in my tap-dance wear, however nothing gives. Like a five-year-old, I begin rapping the wall as if it is the gingerbread brick at school, and it doubles back, revealing an unseen passageway.

The way is bewilderingly dark, lightened only by torches that lie in fourteenth century wicks.

Ouch... something hard has made a dent in my knee. I appropriate a torch and shine it over the entity.

It is a malachite refrigerator... no, tens of them, sleeping there like graves.

I unlock one named: Daan Blazer.

A transcendental figure reflects my chocolate-brown with its half-living eyeballs, a deadened primrose.

A jolt electrifies me... it's the thief from the café, who Dr Stone pronounced dead.

"He's been smuggling patients from abroad," I say aloud. "The fortune he must make..."

The patient's ribs are so hollow a less observant person might mistake him for a dead man. These fridges are a graveyard of the animate dead.

I clutch my hairband, woozy. My forehead is beginning to split, burn up...

The torch clangs onto the parquet and I collapse.

The sequence in Stone's double laboratory didn't shock, in spite of the fact it was the answer I'd sought for months.

A compulsion, a feebleness, meant I couldn't hinder myself from rolling the conclusive file:

What is that noise? It may be snowdrops, or my own thumping temple, it is impossible to untangle. That was everlastingly my hamartia – I never knew when to stop penetrating.

Ivy's voice, as drifty as an apricot blossom, is with me, euphonious and weakly noticeable.

I'd better do it... I croak out my gratefulness.

Ivy doesn't know that you cannot think of death when you are dying; there is too much vertigo, you are too wraithlike.

I release a breath.

Ivy's Swiss brown eye-paint, curtained by black-as-carbon lashes, are the last couple to swivel towards mine.

The audiovisual was cut off.

I was liable. I'd masterminded with Dr Stone, built the book-house, the stepping stones to my own kismet.

Despite this, what my sister had done smouldered.

How dare she have died before I could?

"So now you know," Bo said, slippers muffling the flooring. "We killed your sister."

"No, you didn't," I said robotically. Each bone was aching to agree with her. "But you should've told me."

"Yes." The auburn cast in Bo's mousy knots opposed the stalactites and liquefaction on the mantelpiece. "My sole defence is that nobody was going to thwart her, hence I thought it was better that she came to us rather than Professor Stone."

My rage was focused, like a solar radar, on another man.

"In warning us Magnus torched her interest," I raved.

"Don't be so punishing towards him. He couldn't see into the future. None of us could."

He should have tried harder, then.

I burrowed into my forged-fur jacket as Grandmother Marsh laid down twee Cheshire cat flatware and an Earth mug of boiling almond tea. Bo milled two dozen maple syrup into the mixture: "For the shock."

"Will we ever know what your sister found?" Bo said, realising instinctively that her name would scald me like the teakettle.

I discovered a peculiar warmth in the co-worker who'd been so unreachable. "One day."

"Is it a comfort that she may've died anyway?" Bo lilted.

"I don't know," I said gruffly, "I just loathe being lied to."

She didn't ask if I would ever forgive her. I didn't have a solution to that.

"If you desire frankness," Grandmother Marsh said after thirty rounds of the screw-on time-reader, "you'll let us show you something."

"S-show me what?" I said, dismay souring in my liver.

"It's imperative that you find this out," the one-hundred-and-three-year-old said.

As I surveyed her age lines, all I could contemplate was how she could be alive when my sibling's train had been derailed before her thirteenth birthday.

"As you're wised up about, I'm an ex-spy," Old Marsh said. "And it's high time that you ascertain where your loyalties lie."

Truth, loyalty – all of that was pointless.

Bo unravelled a portrait of a coin-choked treasure chest to own up to a fountain-width tunnel that skittered lengthways along the pipes.

I was lowered into a seat like an alembic and hitched with a seatbelt.

"Where are you taking me?" I cried.

Were they in with Dr Stone?

"Why, my HQ," Granny Marsh said. "And unless you want to confront Professor Stone, you'll convoy with me."

The hurtle was the wildest ride of my twenty-one years, the hideout going forwards in shafts, as blind as an underground burrow.

Before I'd gathered my acumen, I was foot-deep in shingle, an immemorial sixth sense crushing me like the trolls of the sea.

In the rock pools, five-armed starfish and cohered shrimp were scavenged by bloodsuckers, and moon jellyfish clung to the seawaters like brains. The beach ballooned, an omelette; behind crept trees like Brussels sprouts.

"Where're we?" A wind-blown Bo tested me, rain entering her nostrils.

"Lyme Regis," I said wonderingly.

The sands seemed to spring up like the puzzle of Stonehenge as Dad edged into sight.

"We are the antibiotics to an eye infection, the dopamine to depression. We counteract Wolves," Grandmother Marsh said.

A stripy Venus, helter-skelter auger and snail-printed periwinkle shells were brought forth by the streams, and in the thalassic an oyster hosted numinous, silver-moon pearls.

"We're an undercover society recouping power from Stone and modulating his nuttiest experiments," the eldest Marsh said.

"I don't —" I said numbly.

"If we don't foil the doctor's plans, 23 will perish," Dad said. "Are you with us?"

The pendant was glaring at me, fifty colours under the tempestuous sol.

"I want him to fall," I said dazedly. "No matter the price."

He extracted a handshake from me:

"Welcome to Silver Bullets."

23 Bibliography

Sources for the Dinosaur segment:

1. Wikipedia.org for the sections on the: tyrannosaur rex, Denversaurus, Sphaerotholus, Ornithomimus, Acheroraptor, dakotararaptor, Edmontosaurus, Triceratops, Ankylosaurus genus, Anzu Wyliei and the Hell Creek formation.
2. sciencedirect.com: The Hell Creek formation and its contribution to the Cretaceous: Paleogene extinction: A short primer: abstract.
3. britannica.com/Hell Creek formation: Geology.
4. Kids encyclopaedia facts: Hell Creek formation facts.
5. livescience.com: Facts about the armoured lizard.
6. www.newdinosaurs.coom/ankylosaurs: About ankylosaurs.
7. www.activewild.com/ankylosaurs.
8. britannica.com/Ankylosaurus.
9. www.enchantedlearning.com/Edmontosaurus.
10. www.prehistoricwildlife.com.
11. scienceview.com/Edmontosaurus.
12. Newdinosaurs.com: Edmontosaurus.
13. www.nhm/edmontosaurus.
14. www.dinopit.com.
15. www.howstuffworks/edmontosaurus.
16. livescience.com/Triceratops facts.
17. Bbcnature/prehistoric life: Triceratops.
18. www.thoughtco.com/triceratops.
19. nationalgeographic.com/t-rex.
20. livescience.com/t-rex.
21. smithsonianmag.com/science/nature.
22. Quora – what was the T-Rex's habitat?
23. howstuffworks.com/dinosaurs/Denversaurus.
24. Quora.com: What can you tell me about Denversaurus?
25. www.rmdrc.com/denversaurus.
26. thefreedictionary.com/Denversaurus.
27. prehistoricbeastoftheweek: BlogSpot: Sphaerotholus.
28. prehistoricwildlife.com: Sphaerotholus.

29. prehistoricwildlife.com: Ornithomimus.
30. paleo-studies-tumblr.
31. thoughtco.com: Ornithomimus.
32. https://www.nhm.ac.uk/discover/dino-directory/ornithomimus.html.
33. britannica.com: Ornithomimus.
34. phys.org/news: Ornithomimus.
35. dinosaursinthewild.com/vicious micro predator: Acheroraptor.
36. prehistoricbeastoftheweek: BlogSpot: Acheroraptor.
37. Blog- everythingdinosaur.co.uk – new North American raptor described.
38. Quora.com: What can you tell me about Acheroraptor?
39. prehistoricwildlife.com: dakotararaptor.
40. nationalgeographic: "New chicken from Hell" dinosaur discovered.
41. Theguardian.com/science meet Dakotaraptor: the feathered dinosaur that was utterly lethal by Ellen Brait.
42. dinosaursinthewild.com: T-Rex hunted in packs article.
43. prehistoricbeastoftheweek: meat-eating dinosaur article.
44. Theguardian.com/science/"dinosaur dubbed 'chicken from hell' was armed and dangerous" by Ian Sample.
45. www.science20.com: Anzu.
46. wikipedia.org: Late Cretaceous North American fish.
47. wikipedia.org: Late Cretaceous North American mammals.
48. wikipedia.org: Reptiles of the Late Cretaceous North America.
49. Britannica.com: The Cretaceous period information.
50. Britannica.com: Paleoclimate.
51. Nationalgeographic/Science/prehistoric-world/Cretaceous period.
52. www.ucmp.berkeley.edu/mesozoic/Cretaceous period.
53. Wikipedia.org: Cretaceous.
54. Encyclopedia.com for their Cretaceous knowledge.
55. Enchantedlearning.com: Plants of the Cretaceous period.
56. New Phytologist Trust – Extract from "Fire on Earth" authored by Andrew C. Scott, David M. J. S. Bowman, William J. Bond, S22tephen J. Pyne, Martin E. Alexander.
57. Wikipedia.org: Cretaceous angiosperms.

58. https://sites.google.com/site/paleo-plant/geologic periods-by a-Phanerozoic/Mesozoic-era-cretaceous.
59. www.kids-dinosaurs.com.
60. www.dinosaurfact.net/Creta.php.
61. Study.com: Dinosaurs/Cretaceous period.
62. https://www.nhm.ac.uk/discover/when-did-dinosaurs-live.html.
63. Paleonerdish.wordpress.com: A Brief Introduction to the Hell Creek Formation.
64. Digfieldschool.org: Plants of the Hell Creek Formation.
65. Wikipedia.org: Plants of the Hell Creek Formation.
66. Kickassfacts.com: Late Cretaceous Montana.
67. Wikipedia.org: Ore.
68. Wikipedia.org: metals.
69. Wikipedia.org: Mary Anning.
70. Volcano.Oregonstate.edu/What are some good things volcanoes do?
71. https://pdfs.semanticscholar.org/c057/a5175c1a3e5aabac0e5eefd f5e28c85c4214.pdf "SEQUENCE STRATIGRAPHIC ANALYSIS OF THE FOX HILLS AND HELL CREEK FORMATIONS (MAASTRICHTIAN), EASTERN MONTANA AND ITS RELATIONSHIP TO DINOSAUR PALEONTOLOGY" by Jennifer Noël Flight.
72. www.universetoday.com: volcanoes.
73. www.madehow.com: Oxygen tank.
74. www.livestrong.com/natural antibiotics.
75. www.researchgate.net: Plant-derived antimicrobial compounds: alkaloids.
76. www.ncbi: Fruit used as a natural medicine.
77. Ncbi.nlm/medicinal properties of true cinnamon.
78. Naturalmedicinalherbs.net/Araucaria Araucana.
79. BBC documentary: *Walking with Dinosaurs*.
80. The OUP blog: Timeline of the dinosaurs.
81. Natural History Museum: Cretaceous period and what killed the dinosaurs? https://www.nhm.ac.uk/discover/dinosaur-extinction.html.

82. Livescience.com: Tyrannosaurus-Rex, Cretaceous period plants, climate and animals and K-PG extinction.
83. Prehistory.com: The Cretaceous period/Pangea and weather during this period.
84. BBC.co.uk: Natural history of the Earth: Cretaceous.
85. "Life on Early Cretaceous Earth" penned by Dr Jo Wright.

Sources for the Elizabethan episode:
1. Wikipedia.org: Elizabeth I of England.
2. Schmoop.com.
3. Williamshakespearefacts.com.
4. Pbs.org: The Sonnets.
5. Datesandevents.org.
6. Absoluteshakespeare.com.
7. Nosweatshakespeare.com.
8. Thoughtco.com.
9. Shakespearedocumented.folger.edu
10. The British Library website: "Crime and Punishment in Elizabethan England" by Liza Picard, "Exploration and Trade in Elizabethan England" by Liza Picard, "The Social Structure in Elizabethan England" by Liza Picard, "Cities in Elizabethan England" by Liza Picard, "Key Features of Renaissance Culture" by Andrew Dickson, "Shakespeare's Life" by Andrew Dickson, "Shakespeare's London" by Eric Rasmussen and Ian DeJong, "Shakespeare's Playhouses" by Eric Rasmussen and Ian DeJong, Shakespeare, Sexuality and the Sonnets by Aviva Dautch, "Depictions of Countryside in Shakespeare" by Eric Rasmussen and Ian DeJong, "Multiculturalism in Shakespeare's Plays" by Andrew Dickson, "The 'Woman's Part'" by Clare McManus, "Shakespeare's Textual Bodies" by Jennifer Edwards, "Shakespeare's Childhood and Education" by Simon Callow, "Shakespeare and Friendship" by Will Tosh, "Shakespeare's Italian Journeys" by Andrew Dickson, "Witchcraft in Shakespeare's England" by Carole Levin, "Shakespeare and Italy" by John Mullan.

11. webpages.uidaho.edu: Stephen Flores.
12. bbc.com: Life in Elizabethan England.
13. Localhistories.org: Life in 16th-Century England.
14. Museum of London - What was Life Like in Tudor England?
15. Shakespeare's Globe: Life in Shakespeare's Time.
16. 8th-grade-english-shakespeare-blogspot.com.
17. Prezi.com: Living Conditions + Diseases.
18. Prezi.com: Life in London During Shakespearean Times.
19. BBC Bitesize - Audience + Social Audiences.
20. Shakespeareresourcecenter: Elizabethan England.
21. Shakespeare-Gesellschaft: What about Shakespeare's Times?
22. rsc.org.uk: Shakespeare's Life and Times.
23. timetravel-britain.com: The Historic Pubs of London: Pearl Harris.
24. buildinghistory.org: Inns + Taverns of Old London: Henry C. Shelley: Chapter 1: Famous Southwark Inns and Chapter 2: Inns and Taverns East of St Paul's.
25. historic-uk.com.
26. hrp.org.uk: Prisoners of the Tower.
27. tudorhistory.org: The Tower of London.
28. englishmonarchs.co.uk: The Tower in the Tudor Era.
29. seetheworld.com: Tower of London.
30. cnet.com.
31. britainexpress.com.
32. rmg.co.uk.
33. wikipedia.org: Inventory of Elizabeth I of England.
34. beadinggem.com.
35. elizabethi.org.
36. teachinghistory100.org: The Phoenix Jewel.
37. elizabethfiles.com: Tudor Jewellery.
38. faculty.history.wisc.edu: Elizabeth I Exploration and Foreign Policy.
39. ndla.no.
40. elizabethan-era.org.uk: Elizabethan Dictionary.
41. elizabethanenglandlife.com: Elizabethan English Language and Words.

42.   barbweb.net: Shakespeare's Language.

43.   A Quick Guide to Reading Shakespeare: J.M. Pressley, SRC Editor.

44.   shakespeare'swords.com.

45.   readwritethink.org: Elizabethan Language Terms.

46.   elizabethan.org: Life in Elizabethan England.

47.   Prezi: Language in the Elizabethan Times.

48.   Study.com: Elizabethan Era Words.

49.   shanleyworld.com: Elizabethan English.

50.   Royal Palaces: The Homes of Queen Elizabeth I.

51.   rmg.co.uk: Queen Elizabeth I.

52.   Wikipedia: Palace of Placentia.

53.   Museum of London: Elizabethan age.

54.   tudortimes.co.uk: Placentia.

55.   elizabethan/org: Ladies of Honour.

56.   elizabethan-era.org.uk: Lady-In-Waiting.

57.   TheSpectatorArchive.co.uk: Queen Elizabeth's Maids of Honour.

58.   theelizabethfiles.com: Elizabeth's Ladies by Claire.

59.   Tracy Borman's article "Elizabeth's Women: The Hidden Story of the Virgin Queen".

60.   tudortimes.co.uk: Ladies in Waiting: Chapter 1: The Lady Attendant, Chapter 2: The Role, Chapter 3: Gaining a Place and Chapter 4: Serving a Queen Regnant.

61.   elizabethan.org: Masters & Servants: Terminology.

62.   The Life of a Servant in Elizabethan England: Prezi.com.

63.   elizabethaneraenglandlife.com: Servants, Grooms + Maids.

64.   journals.sagepub.com: Journal of Family History: Servants + the Household Unit in an Elizabethan English Community: Abstract.

65.   elizabethan-era.org.uk: Elizabethan Women: Upper Class.

66.   elizabethan.org: The City of London: Sourced from "Shakespeare", Anthony Burgess, 1978.

67.   Elizabethan Museum: London Streets in the Elizabethan Era.

68.   nosweatshakespeare: Facts About Shakespearean London.

69.   "Hard Travelling as an Elizabethan in England" by Steffi Porter: Adapted from Ian Mortimer's "The Time Traveller's Guide to Elizabethan England".

70. prezi.com: Transportation in Shakespearean Times.
71. english-heritage.org.uk: Story of England: Tudors: Networks.
72. prezi.com: Elizabethan Clothing.
73. misterpeebles.weebly.com: Clothing and Costumes of the Elizabethan Era.
74. walternelson.com: Elizabethan Dining: The English Table.
75. bbc.co.uk: Time in the Shakespearean era.
76. elizabethan.org: Numbers, measures, Dates + Clocks.
77. elizabethan-era.org.uk: Elizabethan Architecture.
78. booty.org.uk (information on Tudor temperatures).
79. futurelearn.com (Elizabeth I's diet).
80. https://www.geni.com/projects/The-Court-of-Elizabeth-l-Queen-of-England/24006.
81. https://www.historyextra.com/period/elizabethan/personal-politics-in-elizabeth-is-court/.
82. http://www.elizabethan-era.org.uk/john-dee.htm.
83. https://en.wikipedia.org/wiki/William_Cecil,_1st_Baron_Burghley.
84. https://www.theguardian.com/artanddesign/jonathanjonesblog/2013/feb/13/elizabeth-first-portrait-face-age-unhappiness.
85. https://en.wikipedia.org/wiki/File:Elizabeth_I_portrait,_Marcus_Gheeraerts_the_Younger_c.1595.jpg.
86. https://shakespeareandbeyond.folger.edu/2016/05/31/elizabethan-garden-plants-shakespeare/.
87. https://www.motherearthliving.com/mother-earth-living/shakespearean-garden.
88. https://www.theenglishgarden.co.uk/expert-advice/design-solutions/design_tudor_garden_style_1_3833392/.
89. https://bardgarden.blogspot.com/2014/03/elizabethan-gardens.html.
90. http://www.shakespearesengland.co.uk/2010/03/29/elizabethan-gardens-2/.
91. https://hyperallergic.com/365003/a-compendium-of-shakespeares-botanicals/.
92. http://www.elizabethan-era.org.uk/elizabethan-witchcraft-and-witches.htm.

93. https://www.bbc.com/bitesize/guides/zmjnb9q/revision/3.

94. https://www.bl.uk/shakespeare/articles/witchcraft-in-shakespeares-england.

95. https://www.ukessays.com/essays/history/witchcraft-elizabethan-era-6740.php.

96. https://sites.google.com/site/medievalwitchcraft/white-witches.

97. http://elizabethanmuseum.weebly.com/double-double-toil-and-trouble-witches-and-what-they-do.html.

98. http://thetudorenthusiast.weebly.com/my-tudor-blog/witchcraft-in-16th-17th-century-england.

99. https://www.historytoday.com/victoria-lamb/witchcraft-tudor-times.

100. http://www.foxearth.org.uk/SwimmingOfWitches.html.

101. https://www.mtholyoke.edu/courses/rschwart/hist257/saraelena/final/identification2.htmlhttps://listverse.com/2012/07/27/10-tests-for-guilt-used-at-the-salem-witch-trials/.

102. https://www.oliverburns.com/architecture/an-introduction-to-elizabethan-style/.

103. https://www.woodworkersinstitute.com/furniture-cabinetmaking/techniques/design-techniques/what-the-elizabethans-can-teach-us/.

104. http://www.furniturestyles.net/european/english/elizabethan.html.

105. https://www.nationaltrust.org.uk/lists/tudor-interior-design---building-and-houses.

106. https://homeguides.sfgate.com/decorate-elizabethan-era-77936.html.

107. https://homeguides.sfgate.com/decorate-elizabethan-era-77936.html.

108. https://www.bhg.com/gardening/design/styles/best-plants-for-cottage-gardens/?slideId=slide_f24a20c9-b879-437d-85f9-ab657e370a56#slide_f24a20c9-b879-437d-85f9-ab657e370a56.

109. https://www.britainexpress.com/architecture/elizabethan.htm.

110. http://www.shakespearesengland.co.uk/2010/03/17/the-elizabethan-house/.

111. http://www.historyisnowmagazine.com/blog/2018/7/1/life-in-william-shakespeares-town-16th-century-stratford-upon-avon#.W_QUL-j7TD4= 110. http://www.historyisnowmagazine.com/blog/2018/7/1/life-in-william-shakespeares-town-16th-century-stratford-upon-avon#.W_QUL-j7TD4.
112. http://www.william-shakespeare.info/william-shakespeare-biography-stratford.htm.
113. https://www.shakespeare.org.uk/explore-shakespeare/shakespedia/william-shakespeare/shakespeares-wife-and-marriage/.
114. http://www.localhistories.org/tudorfood.html.
115. Wikipedia.org (Shakespeare's children).
116. https://www.shakespeare.org.uk/explore-shakespeare/blogs/ten-facts-about-tudor-farming/.
117. http://www.elizabethan-era.org.uk/elizabethan-food-availability.htm.
118. https://www.star2.com/food/food-news/2016/04/23/shakespeare-in-love-with-food/.
119. https://prezi.com/jr_2epvydwww/elizabethan-era-country-life-and-city-life/.
120. http://www.localhistories.org/women.html.
121. http://www.compendia.co.uk/draughts.htm.
122. https://www.mastersofgames.com/rules/draughts-rules.htm.
123. http://dreamquestgames.com/rules-and-tips/how-to-play-draughts/.
124. http://www.draughts.org/how-to-play-draughts.html.
125. http://www.googlism.com/draughts.htm.
126. http://www.ubergames.co.uk/draughts-rules.htmlThe rules of draughts.
127. http://awesomejelly.com/this-is-how-you-can-beat-anyone-at-the-game-of-checkers.
128. https://www.nosweatshakespeare.com/blog/shakespeare-travelling-marathon-man/.
129. https://www.gonomad.com/5167-elizabethan-england-looking-back-time.

130. https://en.wikipedia.org/wiki/Shakespeare%27s_Way.
131. https://en.wikipedia.org/wiki/Cotswolds.
132. https://en.wikipedia.org/wiki/Chiltern_Hills.
133. https://en.wikipedia.org/wiki/River_Stour,_Warwickshire.
134. https://en.wikipedia.org/wiki/Marlow,_Buckinghamshire.
135. https://en.wikipedia.org/wiki/Grand_Union_Canal#/media/File:Grand_Union_Canal_(near_Westbourne_Park).jpg.
136. https://www.selfhacked.com/blog/monolaurin-benefits/.
137. file:///C:/Users/carol.ukwu/Downloads/old_london_bridge.pdf.
138. http://www.everycastle.com/Whitehall-Palace.html.
139. https://www.beadinggem.com/2013/05/the-virgin-queens-jewels.html.
140. https://en.wikipedia.org/wiki/John_Dee.
141. http://www.faena.com/aleph/articles/john-dee-elizabethan-magician-and-metaphysical-guide-to-an-empire/.
142. https://elizabethan-era-food.weebly.com/kitchen-equipment.html.
143. http://www.oldcook.com/en/medieval-vegetables.
144. http://www.thehistoryreader.com/ancient-and-medieval-history/the-queens-bed/.
145. http://www.elizabethi.org/contents/wardrobe/.
146. http://www.elizabethanenglandlife.com/the-elegance-in-every-elizabethan-england-food.html.
147. http://internetshakespeare.uvic.ca/Library/SLT/stage/costumes/stagecostumes.html.
148. http://shakespeare.mit.edu/two_gentlemen/full.html.
149. https://en.wikipedia.org/wiki/Richard_Burbage.
150. https://en.wikipedia.org/wiki/Richard_Cowley.
• 149. http://www.william-shakespeare.info/act1-script-text-midsummer-nights-150. dream.htm.
150. https://nationalhistoriccheesemakingcenter.org/history-of-cheese/.
151. https://en.wikipedia.org/wiki/Ox-wagon.
152. http://www.stgeorgenorth.org/yahoo_site_admin/assets/docs/MAAS_Costume_Standards_2nd_Ed.224113649.pdf.
153. http://www.fashionencyclopedia.com/fashion_costume_culture/European-Culture-16th-Century/Sixteenth-Century-Footwear.html.

154. https://www.google.com/search?q=what+did+the+elizabethan+th
rone+look+like&rlz=1C1GCEU_enGB820GB820&source=lnms
&tbm=isch&sa=X&ved=0ahUKEwjmuOff-
7DfAhU7VxUIHcoyDN0Q_AUIDigB&biw=1368&bih=802#im
grc=CcB-5utbmoYH-M.

155. http://www.elizabethancostume.net/periodfab.html.

156. https://en.wikipedia.org/wiki/Brocade.

157. https://mens-
fashion.lovetoknow.com/Men's_Fashion_During_the_Renaissanc
e.

158. http://www.elizabethan-era.org.uk/elizabethan-musicians.htm.

Sources for the Suffragist segment:

1. wikipedia.org.
2. history.ac.uk: Reviews in History: The Politics of Hospital
   Provision in Early Twentieth-Century Britain: Reviewer: Dr
   Martin Gorsky.
3. https://gohighbrow.com/20th-century-medicine/.
4. npg.org.uk.
5. healthcaredailyonline.com.
6. bbcbitesize: 20th-century Medicine.
7. Britishlibrary: 1900s Food.
8. bbc.co.uk: Medicine in the 20th-Century.
9. http://www.localhistories.org/20thengland.html.
10. Britain-magazine.com.
11. Wikipedia.org: 1913 in the United Kingdom.
12. Telegraph.co.uk: "History: Storm Clouds Seemed so Far Away
    in the Summer of 1913" by Harry Mount.
13. Timelines.ws.
14. 1900s.org.uk: Public Transport on Roads in the Early 1900s.
15. Prezi.com: Transportation (1900-1919).
16. In these early times cars – not often seen. Folk travelled by horse,
    train, or boat. Most freight was transported by train as the
    railroads connected the entire US. 4 major events in
    transportation occurred.

17. Localhistories.org.
18. Localhistories.org: Life for Women in the 20th-century.
19. Fet.uwe.ac.uk: (Houses) 1850-1914.
20. Wikipedia.org: Emmeline Pankhurst.
21. Historylearningsite.co.uk.
22. University of Kent: 'Women's Sunday': Hyde Park Rally 21/06/1908.
23. Theguardian.com: The Women's Blog: Join the Great Suffrage Pilgrimage: One hundred years ago, 50,000 suffragists marched to a rally in Hyde Park from all corners of England and Wales. Author: Kira Cochrane.
24. www.Wikipedia.org: Great Pilgrimage.
25. Historyextra.com: The 1913 March for Women's Suffrage.
26. Royalparks.org.uk: Speakers' Corner.
27. Wiltshire & Swindon History Centre: The Suffragist Pilgrimage: Their March, Our Rights.
28. Financial Times: The Women's March: How the Suffragettes Changed Britain.
29. 1900s.org.uk: Gas Lighting in Houses in the Early 1900s.
30. Wikipedia.org: Timeline of Lighting Technology.
31. Oldhouseonline.com: Classical Revival, 1910-1915.
32. 1900s.org.uk: Weekly Menu for the Working Classes in the Early 1900s.
33. Wikipedia.org.uk: Dame Millicent Garrett Fawcett GBE.
34. Wikipedia.org: The Second Industrial Revolution.
35. BBC.co.uk: Economy.
36. Herofiles.org: Great Britain.
37. 1900s.org.uk: Money in 20th-Century Britain.
38. Bclm.co.uk: Cost of Living in 1910.
39. www.mirror.co.uk: "Everywoman in 1910: No vote, poor pay, little help – Why the World Had to Change".
40. history.ac.uk: Reviews in History: The Politics of Hospital Provision in Early Twentieth-Century Britain: Reviewer: Dr Martin Gorsky.
41. Royalparks.org.uk: Speakers' Corner.

42. https://www.countrylife.co.uk/property/guides-advice/the-history-of-electric-lighting-16206.

43. https://www.myutilitygenius.co.uk/guide/geeks/history-of-electricity/.

44. https://www.objectlessons.org/houses-and-homes-20th-century-to-present/gas-light-edwardian-original/s60/a1056/.

45. https://www.1900s.org.uk/1900s-street-lighting.htm.

46. http://www.nationalgasmuseum.org.uk/gas-lighting/.

47. https://www.thespruce.com/the-gaslight-era-2175011.

48. http://www.intriguing-history.com/gas-lights-lamplighters/.

49. http://www.bbc.co.uk/schools/0/ww1/25308203.

50. https://londonist.com/london/best-of-london/in-photos-london-in-1910.

51. https://en.wikipedia.org/wiki/Peek_Freans.

52. https://en.wikipedia.org/wiki/Great_Pilgrimage.

53. https://www.mrsimms.hk/blogs/sweets-blog/127178563-britain-s-most-popular-sweets-1900s-and-1910s.

54. http://www.localhistories.org/sweets.html.

55. https://en.wikipedia.org/wiki/Hobble_skirt.

56. https://hslmcmaster.libguides.com/c.php?g=306775&p=2044436.

57. https://www.mayoclinic.org/diseases-conditions/tuberculosis/diagnosis-treatment/drc-20351256.

58. https://en.wikipedia.org/wiki/Sophia_Duleep_Singh.

59. https://www.tbfacts.org/surgery-tb-treatment/.

60. https://en.wikipedia.org/wiki/Phonograph.

61. https://en.wikipedia.org/wiki/Meccano.

62. https://www.tbfacts.org/tb-drugs/.

63. https://en.wikipedia.org/wiki/It%27s_a_Long_Way_to_Tipperary.

64. https://en.wikipedia.org/wiki/The_Wolseley_Sheep_Shearing_Machine_Company#/media/File:1899_Wolseley_3.5HP_Voiturette_Front.jpg.

65. https://www.nhs.uk/conditions/blood-transfusion/.

66. https://www.satra.com/bulletin/article.php?id=2043.

67. https://www.bl.uk/votes-for-women/articles/suffragists-and-suffragettes.
68. "Hearts and Minds" by Jane Robinson.
69. https://www.wikihow.com/Make-a-Quilt.
70. http://www2.fiskars.com/Ideas-and-How-Tos/Crafting-and-Sewing/Quilting/How-to-Quilt.
71. https://www.bbc.co.uk/news/world-42879161.
72. https://www.ftd.com/blog/design/green-flowers.
73. https://romanceuniversity.org/2013/12/12/tips-on-creating-conflict-in-your-novel-by-janice-hardy/.
74. https://spartacus-educational.com/Wpilgimage.htm.
75. https://www.historyextra.com/period/edwardian/cat-mouse-force-feeding-suffragettes-hunger-strike/.
76. https://www.historylearningsite.co.uk/the-role-of-british-women-in-the-twentieth-century/force-feeding-of-suffragettes/.
77. http://www.ploddinthesquaremile.co.uk/crime/the-suffragettes-and-the-milk-can-bomb/.
78. https://classroom.synonym.com/steamships-early-1900s-17582.html
79. https://www.britannica.com/technology/ship/History-of-ships.
80. https://ualrexhibits.org/steamboats/files/2015/09/Steamboat-identification-activity.pdf.
81. https://www.woodlandtrust.org.uk/visiting-woods/trees-woods-and-wildlife/british-trees/native-trees/yew/.
82. https://www.space.com/44-venus-second-planet-from-the-sun-brightest-planet-in-solar-system.html.
83. http://www.equine-world.co.uk/about_horses/arab_horse.asp.
84. http://www.vintageadbrowser.com/tobacco-ads-1900s.
85. Museum of London: suffragette/20th-century exhibition.

Sources for the end section:

1. https://www.healthline.com/health/how-to-tell-if-you-have-a-fever.
2. https://www.verywellhealth.com/burn-remedies-89945.

3. https://www.visitsealife.com/london/discover/sea-life-creatures/rockpools/.

4. https://www.whalefacts.org/shrimp-facts/.

5. https://www.dictionary.com/e/s/green-words/#olive.

6. https://www.everafterguide.net/flowers-in-season-in-july.html.

7. https://allabouteyes.com/best-eyes-animal-kingdom/.

8. https://stylecaster.com/home-decor-prints-and-patterns-glossary/#slide-13.

9. https://lists.wordreference.com/show/black-things.319/.

10. http://www.uksafari.com/seashells.htm.

11. https://pearls.com/pages/how-pearls-are-formed.